"GIVE IT UP, LASS

Branwen struggled to keep from losing what little courage she had left. "Can't you understand why I must avenge my parents' death?"

"Because you still want to be the son they never had! Well, damn it, lass, you're a woman . . . made for *this!*"

Branwen cried out, startled, as Wolf claimed her lips roughly. She meant to offer protest, but instead parted them to a heady invasion that would give no quarter.

Her senses swam in the frantic tide whipped up with each stroke of the hand that moved up and down the curves of her back. "This is how the fire that burns within ye should be put to use, milady," Wolf mumbled into the hollow of her throat. "*This* is what you were made so soft and gentle for."

Branwen closed her eyes, but lights of desire still flashed, blinding her to all but the sweet torment of his fingertips.

"Stay with me tonight and forget this vengeful madness, fair raven . . ."

* * *

LINDA WINDSOR

THE KNIGHT AND THE RAVEN

ZEBRA BOOKS
KENSINGTON PUBLISHING CORP.

The Raven, so they call her
With hair as black as sin
And bright eyes that bewitch the heart
'Ere time did first begin.

The hunter must be fierce and brave
And quick to spring the snare
For tho' the bird may thrash within
Her heart will not be there.

No trap of wire, no wall of stone
Will this wild Raven tame
She must be coaxed with love and trust
To test sweet passion's flame.

Chapter One

The air was damp and cold. Last night's freezing rain had slowed the progress of the entourage making its way through the mountain pass by encrusting the blanket of snow with ice. The banners fluttering in the brisk wind that swept through the wood and rock-shrouded walls to either side were bright and distinct against the winter landscape. The sign of the black raven perched on a golden scepter was familiar to the villages they had passed. Owen ap Caradoc had fought bravely from south to north beside his cousin, the acknowledged Prince of Wales, in the attempt to throw off the English yoke encroaching Briton lands. Few lords had the love and respect of the people as did Owen ap Caradoc.

Yet, as the people of the ancient land of *Cymru* watched the proud lord pass, there were no shouts of cheer, only silent respect. The revolt had failed, starved by Edward I's seizure of the grain from *Môn mam Cymru*, the Mother of Wales, known as the island of Anglesey. It was a cowardly means to bring a bold and proud people to its knees, when might alone failed. Sooner than see his people suffer, the Prince of Wales and his warriors surrendered at Conway and now were being summoned to do homage to the victor—ironically, the very act that had precipitated the rebellion at the start. It was

7

hard to imagine a Prince of Wales paying homage to any king, much less the English one!

Branwen ap Caradoc found herself watching her father's erect figure ahead of her with the same sense of gloom as the weather. It wasn't fair. It was humiliating enough to be forced to do this dread homage, but to forfeit the land that had been in the family for too many generations for the most astute bard to recount was unthinkable. The very idea made her want to fight and cry at the same time, which was characteristic of her volatile nature. If she were the son Owen had always wanted . . .

She'd be doing the same thing, she admitted morosely. She would starve herself but not her people. They depended upon her now . . . *her*, not Tâd, as she thought of her father in her native tongue. She was to be the sacrifice for peace, the bride to one of the very knights who rammed the choking defeat down the throat of *Cymru* itself. Her heir, and hence Owen's, would still rule the lands of their ancestors, even if his blood might be tainted with that of the English. It was the only way, her father had argued until she saw the logic of the decision.

Which was why the Caradoc entourage was a good week behind that of the prince. Branwen and her mother had taken refuge in one of the fortresses in the mountains of Snowdonia. To retrieve them had taken Owen the better part of a week. To convince his proud and stubborn daughter of the necessity of this arrangement had taken the rest of it.

Branwen licked her dry lips and pushed back the hood of her fur-lined cloak, as if in defiance of not only her fate, but also the dreary weather itself. She was unaware that her eyes reflected it with a blue-grey glittering frost capable of stinging the flesh of all who crossed it. Indeed, her cheeks already showed evidence of the winter's assault, colored scarlet rather than their natural rose hue. So did her lips, which had been the temptation of many a suitor.

They would have to make camp early tonight, she thought, undaunted by the clouds that threatened overhead. There was no noble household between that in which they'd spent the last night and Chester . . . unless one counted those of the marcher lords who had helped Edward in his conquest. She'd sooner freeze than ask hospitality of those traitors.

That vengeful thought had no more been affirmed with a gentle snort of disdain, when her father gave the order to set up camp for the night. Although Branwen could see no fresh water, she was certain there was some nearby. Lord Owen knew the hills as he knew those tapering down to his own seaside commote. If there was a pool, chances were it would be frozen over, which would afford some diversion.

Branwen loved skidding about on the ice, with or without the wooden runners she'd tied to her belt as an afterthought before leaving. It was a part of the child in her, which her maiden aunt Agnéis had sworn would never fade away, no matter how many household responsibilities her mother taught her. Besides, she was stiff from riding astride all day. Being cooped up in the mountains did not allow her the freedom of Traeth Caradoc, where she was at leisure to ride along the rocky seashore at ebbtide, into the wild wind and rain so common to it.

Although, as a rule, she never needed assistance in dismounting, her packing for the journey to Westminster demanded it. It wasn't easy to move about with all the clothes she possessed on her back, not to mention the vast assortment of necessities she carried in pouches and sheaths about her waist. Much as she cared for her servants, she dared not leave one item to the temptation of theft. It came to them as naturally as the thin drop of common blood that made them clansmen and, accordingly, afforded them a self-proclaimed God-given right to take what belonged to one's kinsfolk.

"We'll have the tents up in little time, Mam," Owen said to the tall, slender woman who, since their daughter's birth, he always referred to as "mother." "There'll be shelter and man enough to keep you warm, I promise."

Branwen clasped the flesh on the inside of her cheeks with her teeth to rein in a wicked grin at the familiarity that heightened her mother's pale coloring. "But until then, Mam," she offered, "would you have my cloak? I vow I do not need it."

With three shifts and surcoats, not to mention accessories and a hearty Welsh constitution, Branwen was adequately warm in the worst of weather, while her mother, it seemed more and more of late, became chilled at the slightest decrease in temperature. Both Branwen and Owen had pleaded with Lady Gwendolyn to remain in Snowdonia until it was safe to return to Traeth Caradoc, but the lady had insisted on attending her only child's wedding.

"Nay, daughter. I'll fare well enough to walk a bit to restore my blood's movement while the tents are being erected." Gwendolyn ap Caradoc was an older version of Branwen, but that her daughter had not inherited her chestnut hair and blue eyes. Branwen's oval face, high cheekbones, delicate nose, and well-placed eyes were those of her mother. However, the untamed raven tresses she kept, to Gwendolyn's dismay, cut short so that they curled in disarray at chin's length, were as undoubtedly her father's as her fiery temperament. The hue of their offspring's eyes was a constant source of bewilderment, sometimes blue as sapphire and other times shining bright as polished silver, depending on the mercurial humor of the girl.

They were blue now, tinged with excitement instead of the melancholy grey that had dominated them the last few days. Gwendolyn smiled indulgently. "And what mischief are you about? Off to try one of Aunt Agnéis's spells?"

"Here, here!" demanded an older woman, who was flexing her pointed shoes some distance from them as if to be certain that her feet would still work. "I'd not make fun of that which I don't understand, Gwen. The Black Sow might well be about on such a devilish journey as this. My bones have ached three nights straight. I tell you, it's an omen." She nudged Branwen. "I'll take that cloak for Caryn, if you've no present need of it. Poor girl's half froze and won't be fit to see to any, if she's not warmed soon."

"For the love of St. Dafydd, Agnéis," Owen grumbled at his maiden sister-in-law, " 'tis the rheumatism in your old bones and no omen! Now stop this nonsense before you spook my men. They've enough to worry them, without the sow nonsense."

"Besides, Aunt Agnéis," Branwen chimed in more gently, divesting herself of the furred cloak for the servant maid, "everyone knows 'tis bad luck to cross the raven." She'd see no one frozen at her expense, servant or nay. It was a gift from a broken betrothal anyway, should the pale, trembling waif find the strength to run off with it.

"*We* know, Branwen girl," her aunt replied lowly, "but there's them that don't. She'll be grateful for this," Agnéis added in a louder voice, as she hobbled on arthritic knees over to young Caryn and wrapped her beneath the cloak like a mother hen with her chick under its wing.

Besides being an absolute dear, her aunt was an end-

11

less source of information when it came to mother knowledge—that basic knowledge nature provided of the workings of things in the physical as well as the spiritual world. She'd learned it from her Irish grandmother, having indeed devoted her life to its study while the younger Gwendolyn had devoted her attentions to securing a good husband. Both women had succeeded quite well.

"Why don't you walk with me down to the lake after I unload my things by Mother's trunk?" Her belongings would be entirely too cumbersome on the ice—if there were sufficient ice—but they would be safe with her mother.

"Branwen, you'll ruin your slippers!"

"I've another pair beneath, Mam," Branwen argued stubbornly. "I feel I must have some exercise or I shall simply come undone!"

"You are your father's daughter!" Gwendolyn chided.

"And I've the answer to your quandary, *geneth*, but not till you're properly wed." While most of the family was fluent in English, the Welsh slipped through once in a while. Owen used *geneth* as a term of endearment rather than "girl," which rang harsh to his ears.

"Owen ap Caradoc, how say you such to a girl still of tender age!"

Owen laughed at his wife's indignation. "Ask any man and see if he'll not swear, the sweet warmth of your company has a settling effect on me, Gwen."

"I'm eighteen on the day set for my wedding, Mam, but considering my intended is an Englishman, I fear I should find no release with him, but emerge the bridal chamber more wrought and restless than ever!"

"He is a full knight and seventh son of Kent, daughter, well decorated on the battlefields of the Holy Lands."

"Seventh son, did you say?" Agnéis interrupted, her

12

usual distracted manner instantly alert. "Oh, that bodes good, child!"

Branwen squared her shoulders and tilted her chin in an all-too-familiar stance of rebellion. "That means, dear aunt, that he is penniless and in quest of *my* lands. Do you think that I know not the workings of this political madness? I may be a mere woman, but I am not without wit for such things."

Dismay settled on Gwendolyn's face, consternation on Owen's. Yet, beneath her father's disapproval lurked a spark of pride. Branwen swelled with it. Her fate was settled, but she did not have to make it easy for this *estron* knave, this alien who would become her husband.

"Aye, and had our infant son lived, things might have been different."

The sad wistfulness of her father's words crushed Branwen's brief rise of spirit. "Had you a son, Tâd, you'd have lost your lands altogether."

Spinning on her heel, Branwen paced off in the direction she'd seen the stewards take the horses. She hadn't meant to strike out at her father like that, but damn fate, she'd done her best to make up for not being a boy. She could ride and hunt with the best of men. Her hawks were well known in the four northern cantrefs, enough that Llewelyn ap Gruffydd himself had purchased one. It wasn't her fault that her mother took her over and insisted she learn to run the household and attend to the duties involved, while Dafydd ap Elwaid, her father's ward, had begun his training as a squire in the arts of weaponry.

While Dafydd learned to launch and fend off attacks from his fellow squires, Branwen had learned the art of repelling his more amorous assaults. Her tongue was sharp as a sword, according to the young swain to whom she'd been betrothed by the bishop, his uncle, and Lord Owen on her twelfth birthday. 'Twas only his knighting, done by Owen himself on the field of battle but a month before, that had postponed the wedding.

Then Llewelyn's defeat banished their future forever. While she didn't particularly like his clumsy kisses, Dafydd was a fine figure of a man and she did thrive on their verbal jousts. Marriage to such a man would at least have been comfortable and entertaining.

A sick feeling twisted in her stomach, not the first since the plans for her future had been changed. She had practically grown up with Dafydd in her father's house. What would she have in common with this English knight? She felt nothing but contempt for him and his kind. It had even occurred to her that she might not be able to love his offspring, should fate be cruel enough to inflict her with child, in spite of the precautions she'd take. Branwen's hand moved to the lump in her bodice, evidencing the presence of the smooth blue-green stone from Anglesey that was reputed to ward off pregnancy, should she not be able to dissuade her new husband from his husbandly privileges with the offer to turn her head while he sought his relief with another woman. God's breath, he could have anyone . . . anyone but her.

The thick wooded passage to the pond was hung heavy with ice, like crystal garlands dangling from the treetops. Were the sun out, Branwen had no doubt it would glisten like a fairy kingdom. Indeed, fairies might well live in such a pretty place anyway. Secluded glens and hollows were favorite haunts of the pixies.

The stewards had broken the ice along the bank of the pond for the horses to drink, making it plain at a glance that it was too thin for frolic. That plan dashed, Branwen turned away and started around the perimeter of the pond, picking her way carefully. It wasn't the stretch of wet sand she was prone to frequent for long periods of meditation away from the household—the traeth that was covered by water when the tide came in.

14

There had to be some way to unleash this building frustration at having no say in her life, she thought in annoyance. Owen ap Caradoc could be no more disappointed than she that she was not a boy.

Her appetite for learning was unseemly for a girl, the tutor hired for the squires had chastised as Branwen waved her hand frantically to divulge the answer to a particular question. A man would rather have a good meal put before him than have his wife quote Latin. The tutor tolerated her for a short while, until she outshone his male students. Then she'd been forced away to help her mother with needlepoint and the large tapestry that now hung in the great hall.

Or did it still? Branwen mused, stopping to inhale the cold mountain air. It was dry, accounting for the inflammation that had led to a nosebleed only that morning. The moist salt air at Traeth Caradoc would never abuse her so, unless the presence of those English laborers had driven it out to sea, as they'd driven off to the hills anyone on the estate who had escaped their enforced bondage. Even now, as she traveled to meet the new lord and master of her ancestral estate, the fortress that her great-grandfather had built was being doubled in size. Part of the establishment of an English line of authority, it was said.

Oppression was more like it, although Branwen had been intrigued by the reported changes. What more could the English need in a castle than the keep, with its great hall and adjoining offices, storerooms, armory, and the few outbuildings to sustain it within the bailey? To her notion it was an exercise in sinful waste of manpower and money, something this Edward I had in abundance, it seemed. Doubled the size, the report came, expanding to include the village as well within its walls!

Finding it hard to picture in her mind, Branwen

15

broke a brittle stick from a birch and, slinging aside the aprons of her heavy woolen surcoats, cut through the icy crust to draw the image out on the snow. She'd hardly made a circle for the keep when she heard a shout of alarm rise from across the pond. Straightening, she squinted in that direction to make out the nature of it, for something indeed was amiss. Mingled with the red and black colors of her father's men were royal blue and orange. The clash of metal rang in the winter silence with fierce shouting and screams of the women.

Mam! As she started back around the perimeter of the pond, Branwen's hand went beneath the folds of her surcoats in search of the tooled leather sheath containing her dining dagger. By now, no doubt, her mother and the women were enclosed in a protective circle of Caradoc's warriors, but her father's men had not come prepared for the full-scale battle that seemed to be in progress a good distance away. They'd been fitted for travel and armed against vagabonds and thieves, not heraldic knights and trained combatants.

Royal and orange. She plied the colors over and over in her mind as she hastily retraced her steps around the pond. They were not familiar. Or were they? she wondered, a recollection of the account given by a herdsman who had escaped the English-occupied Caradoc surfacing. Those were the colors of Ulric of Kent, newly assigned upon his return from the Holy Land.

Damn the man! Branwen swore, her ragged breath steaming in front of her as she fought the weight of her heavy garments and the rugged terrain. A would-be Knight Templar, he had been extolled to her by her father and well known on the field of tourney. God's breath, no!

The realization that she might well be running toward her death did not slow Branwen's gait. Better to die shoulder to shoulder with a stalwart Cymry at her side than to suffer humbling herself to a deceitful Englishman, for what was this if not betrayal of the commonest kind? By all that was holy, this could very well stir again the war that her marriage was to seal in peace, for her father would never hand her over to such a lying knave as this. Owen would sooner run her through with his own fierce blade than submit her to that.

Such were her outraged thoughts that Branwen never suspected the crevice in the rocky terrain that was camouflaged by the snow until the ground went out from underneath her. Her gasp as she seemed to be swallowed up in the cold earthly abyss was knocked from her when she struck the bottom—hard and ungiving rock. The snow grew blinding white with the pain that grazed the back of her head, flashing bright and then, just as quickly, growing numb with conquering darkness.

How long Branwen remained in the icy netherworld she had no idea. As she swam back to consciousness, she began to feel the bite of her hard snowy bed and the pain, just within the hairline above the nape of her neck, that threatened to burst the swelling there with each pumping thrust of her pulse. But for the latter, she might have thought herself dead and buried, for snow lay all around her except for one tunnel of light over her face. A thick root had kept the snowslide from smothering her, she realized, uncertain that it had done her favor.

One by one, she tested her limbs to find them numb but in working order. Upon rising, she discovered she had not fallen nearly as far as it had seemed. The crevice was only shoulder-deep. All she needed to do was find a small foothold and . . .

She blinked away the fog that muddled her thoughts, her previous urgency coming back with alarming clarity. *Mam! Tâd!* Without a foothold, the girl hoisted herself

17

up to the ledge and scrambled out of nature's annoying trap. Something was wrong, she thought, turning toward the pond. It was too silent. There shouldn't be silence after the successful repelling of a foe. There should be shouts of relief and cheer for the wounded . . . *unless Owen ap Caradoc's men had not been victorious.*

"Nooo!"

Branwen swore through chattering teeth as she started running recklessly forward again. It was just that the shock from her fall had deafened her. Her frostbitten ears would thaw the closer she drew to the encampment, and she'd hear Tâd praising his men for their bravery and skill while Mam and Aunt Agnéis tended the injured in gentler tones. Her skirts were frozen and stiff, hampering her progress as much as the rugged terrain around the perimeter of the pond.

Quiet. So quiet! It was almost frightening to hear her heart thundering from within and absolute stillness from without. The closer Branwen came to the encampment the slower her steps became, partly because she was winded and partly because she suddenly feared what awaited her. As she made her way over a gentle rise, a scene came into view that far exceeded her most nightmarish imagination.

The white snow was soaked scarlet, melted by the once-warm blood that spilled from the bodies scattered around the protected glen. No one moved or showed any other sign of life and, for a good while, neither did Branwen. God in heaven, this could not be! Across the littered ground, her gaze skimmed over the fallen black-and red-clad soldiers until it found the dark blue of a woman's cloak, much like the fox-lined one her mother had worn. Next to it was a man clad in a dark furred mantle.

Branwen's heart stilled within her chest, refusing breath or pulse to her chilled body. *Mam? Tâd?* The names kept echoing over and over in her mind until recognition finally sunk in. With it came a stinging blade that wedged in her throat and prodded her forward in stumbling steps of disbelief. With each one, she prayed her eyes deceived her. Yet her prayers ended with a wail of grief as she dropped to her knees between the bodies of her parents.

She cradled first her mother's head in her lap and then made room for her father's, oblivious to the blood that soaked her sleeves and skirts from their severed necks. The terror with which her mother had died was fixed on her stony features, as vivid as the fierce anger that distorted her father's equally frozen ones. A sob tore from her chest, yet the blade in her throat would not let it pass unencumbered. Another and another followed it, building up against the unyielding barrier until Branwen thought her breast would explode from the anguish forcing its way out in little strangled sounds.

Above her head a thrashing of wings beat the hush of the winter landscape and Branwen raised her blurred eyes, which had yet to spill a tear, to see her namesake light on a branch overhead. "Look you at this carnage, my liege!" Branwen railed bitterly at the bird many Britons considered to possess the spirit of King Arthur. "It smacks of the same foul treachery which led to your death. There is a Mordred among us and I avow, as I draw breath, he shall be punished!"

Gently laying aside the heads of her parents, as if trying to put them right to their lifeless bodies, Branwen climbed to her feet. Her nostrils flared with the rage that was rapidly suffusing her agony and grief as she began look around at the other bodies surrounding her, mostly women who, no doubt, had been saved for last.

Yet it was one that drew her attention. Unlike the others, it was stripped naked and spread-eagled on a rich fur-lined cloak. Caryn! Branwen thought, sickened by the sight of the servant girl's bloodied corpse. It took no imagination to know she had been raped. Whether that was before or after her assailants had slit her throat, it was impossible to tell. Then they had impaled her to the ground with their spears, like a melon in a tournament of skill.

Driven, Branwen started to withdraw the weapons. The plunging sounds they made as they came out and the gore left behind forced her to stop many times to retch, but she continued until she was able to wrap the dead girl in the borrowed cloak. The inane attempt to restore dignity was the least she could do. She'd been little use beforehand. Not that she could have made the difference, but at least she wouldn't be left alone.

Branwen wiped her forehead with the back of her sleeve. What would she do? There were better than a score to bury. And how could she leave her parents in such a common place? They deserved a funeral worthy of their station and a resting place in the hollowed stone vault of their ancestors.

But Caradoc and kin were miles away, she despaired, glancing around, utterly lost. There were none close but the Marcher lords . . . lords who like as not were hosting the very murderers who had committed this atrocity. Damn them all, she avowed silently. Damn them all to hell, where they were surely headed.

Wings beating in the treetop drew her gaze to the spot where the raven had been. Now there were a dozen or so of them, all restless and eager to partake of the waiting feast. She considered a crossbow lying at the hand of one of her father's men but dismissed the vengeful thought before it took root. *It was bad luck to cross a raven.*

They all couldn't be King Arthur, she reasoned, half-mad with shock that would not release her grief. But, with her luck, she'd kill the wrong one and be cursed forever. She kicked the bow angrily. As if she wasn't, she mused acidly. Why had she been spared?

Her eyes moved back to the cloak-wrapped figure in growing suspicion. Had they thought Caryn, cloaked in the rich robe, to be her? For the first time, Branwen noticed something else about the girl's attire. Over her head a cloth of gold filigree had been draped—the wedding veil Branwen was to wear in London. Her throat constricted again, nearly cutting off her wind, as it sunk in that the poor lifeless figure in the cloak was supposed to have been her! But for a reckless fall, it would have been. Such vile mockery!

Branwen reeled away, retching violently until there was nothing left to lose. What manner of blasphemy was this that her prospective groom had committed? It was too unseemly, even for an Englishman. And what had he to gain by this public execution? It could be called nothing but that, when no attempt had been made to remove the bodies of those who had fallen under the swords of her father's men. Their orange and blue mantles lay scattered here and there among the black and red, identifying them as bold as the attack itself. And it surely was an execution, for their numbers alone demanded that description.

One of the bolder birds gathering about dove down from its perch above and landed near the bodies of Lord Owen and his lady. Shouting and waving her arms, Branwen raced toward it, driving it back. Why shouldn't she cross it? she reasoned in wild indignation. She was named after it, wasn't she? Branwen . . . fair raven. One bird might cross another. She'd seen them fight among themselves over the dried bread she cast out of her window. She had nothing to fear from them, as long as she didn't kill one. God forbid she kill the legendary Arthur!

Nay, she would save her killing for a flesh and blood murder, not a spiritual one. She would rise above this and bring down the mighty Ulric of Kent. Branwen's eyes began to burn brightly as she savored the idea. Every man had his weakness and she would find his. Surprise, of course, would be her only hope, she thought feverishly. And why couldn't she surprise him? After all, he thought she was dead.

By God, she'd expose him and force Edward to acknowledge his mistake in choosing Ulric to insure peace. The evidence was here, she thought, walking over to where a blue and orange soldier lay. Without heed to his bulging unseeing eyes, she yanked off the incriminating colors. His sheathed dagger, a loathsome and imposing weapon, catching her eye, she removed it as well. She would expose him, but first she'd drive her knife into Ulric's treacherous heart.

A cynical smile lifted one corner of her thinned lips and her gaze took on a feral glow. After all, *it was bad luck to cross the raven.*

Chapter Two

With night fast approaching, Branwen tried her hand at starting a fire with the flint and steel belonging to the slain captain, but after better than an hour of curses that would have incurred the wrath of Satan himself, she sat cold in the clearing. Not even the layers of men's clothing, which she'd borrowed from some of the dead soldiers' sacks as a measure of caution against being found a lone woman on the road, kept away the chill that made her teeth chatter. And with the night would come wolves, she thought miserably, animals that would not be driven away from the bodies by her shouting and arm waving.

She observed the bodies, which she had covered with blankets from the cart that held her dowry and provisions for the journey, in dismay. She might go for help but could not bring herself to leave her parents to the cruel ravages of nature. Perhaps she'd simply go to sleep and join them. She'd heard that's what freezing to death was like and, at present, it seemed the lesser of evils. Except that death would prevent her revenge, and by all that was holy, revenge would not be denied her.

Her thought was far from pious, yet when Branwen looked up at a stirring down the road, she was startled that her oath had won her consideration. There in a large cart, with rails of woven grapevine that made it appear a basket on wheels, were four friars, garbed in drab brown. Better yet, in the front of each corner were pitch torches, burning brightly. Grateful for the blessing, Branwen offered a quick prayer of thanks—first, that the disturbance was not the brigands returning to loot their victims, and second, that here was the solution to part of her quandary. Making a cross over the silver one that lay against her breast beneath her layers of clothing, she jumped up and hailed them.

"May God be praised!" she shouted in as deep a voice as she could muster, running toward them and waving frantically. If they knew she was a girl, much less who she really was, it was not likely that they would permit her to strike out for London alone. "Good friars, see this horrible carnage to which I was witness!"

A tall and thin man, swimming in his woolen robes, stopped the pair of oxen at the edge of the clearing, his pale gaze sweeping over the bodies as Branwen had implored. "It is true, brothers. The poor woman wasn't mad but overwrought with grief."

Woman? Branwen looked back at the bodies blankly. *Aunt Agnéis!* she thought in relief. How could she not have missed her maiden aunt? Again the girl offered a fervent prayer of thanks.

"You, boy! Have you per chance seen the Lady Branwen? The woman kept repeating over and over that her niece was still alive but missing."

Branwen shook her head. "Nay, sir. I'm sorry to say the lady lies over there, murdered most vilely."

"How came you to survive?" one of the others asked curiously.

Branwen pointed across the lake. "I'd gone over there to collect some wood. When I heard the battle start, I ran hard as I could back here, but slipped and hit me head on a rock." She raised a demonstrating hand to

24

the back of her head. "When the fog of it cleared, 'twas all over." She pointed to the birds overhead. "I've been trying to keep the animals away, but I'm glad the good Lord sent someone to help me. The mad woman, is she hurt?"

The friar hopped down from the cart with his fellows. "No more than few scratches. I fear her wounds are much deeper . . . of the spirit."

Branwen lowered her head, well able to comprehend what her aunt must be going through. "Will you see her back to the commote of Caradoc? That is where all these are from."

"Her, you, and them," the man assured her, putting out his hand. "I am Brother Damien. Brothers Timothy, Jonathan, and Peter have come with me for the dead and the living. By the look of it, we've a large task ahead of us and dark threatening fast."

"I'll be going on to London with the news of what has happened to my lord and his lady. Perhaps 'twill open Edward's eyes to the nature of the men he entrusts with his lands and subjects."

The apparent leader of the group lifted a thinly defined brow in skeptical disapproval. "And what will you tell them, lad?"

"That Ulric of Kent is a treacherous knave who threatens peace by murdering his bride, her family, and their retinue."

"You saw him?" the holy man asked in surprise.

Branwen pointed to one of the orange- and blue-clad corpses. "They are his colors, sir, the same that fly over Caradoc e'en as we speak, so bold and impatient is his lust and greed."

The priest clapped Branwen on the shoulder. "Then you have a hard path to pursue, son, for our liege Edward will not take kindly to your news."

"Neither will Prince Llewelyn."

"War just barely buried and now something else flares to spark it again. This can only mean ill for all," the man sighed despondently. "You as well, lad. There is bloodlust in your eyes. Take care that it does not mean your end."

Again the snowy silence of the glen was broken, this time by the low murmurs chanted in Latin over the bodies as they were laboriously loaded onto the cart. Its reverence, however, did not penetrate the hard shell Branwen had raised around her emotions, which burned as hot as the campfire they'd built to afford temporary warmth and light until their task was done.

The last to go on were Lord Owen, Lady Gwendolyn, and their *daughter*. The few horses that had not run off were gathered and tethered on a lead, and one pair of friars took over the driving of the provision cart bearing Branwen's dowry. All that remained of the massacre was the bloodstained snow and a few scattered weapons. Yet, as Branwen surveyed the scene one last time, she could still see them there—her parents with their heads severed and poor Caryn mutilated almost beyond recognition.

It was best that everyone thought her dead. That would leave her the freedom to execute her vague plan of revenge. She had men's clothing in her sack, the colors to prove her story, and her father's dagger and determination. Should she fail, the Lady Branwen was dead and buried—beyond the reach of her murdering groom. She didn't want Caradoc, not if it meant being wife to the English knight.

Besides, a boy could find his way into many places that a girl could not, making her chances of succeeding better in her disguise. Now that the friars were seeing to her aunt and family properly, she was free to take care of Ulric in the manner he deserved.

"I recommend that you come with us to the monastery, son," the leader of the group spoke up, breaking into Branwen's chain of thought. "Night is on us now and it is an hour ahead in the right direction."

"Besides, there is a man at the monastery claiming to be on his way to London as well ... a mercenary, I think," his companion chimed in in concern. "You two might travel together."

"I told you, I'm for London now." Branwen looked about her uneasily. "But if you've a torch to spare, I'd be grateful."

"Of course," the friar told her, adding cautiously, "but 'twill not last out the night."

With the reins of her father's stallion in one hand and the flickering and smoking torch in the other, Branwen stood and watched the cart loaded with the dead take the lead ahead of their provision cart. She could have used one of the tents that had had no chance to be unpacked, but would need help to erect it. If she found a sheltered place from the north wind that was picking up and bedded down close to the campfire she intended to light with the torch, however, she could make do. Meanwhile, she would travel as far as the torch would take her before she risked the danger of it burning out.

A sizzling sound of water striking fire drew her attention to the large snowflakes that were starting to fall, and her adventurous spirit wavered. Armed with fire was one thing. Left alone in the dark without it for light, warmth, and protection was entirely another. She fitted her foot into the stirrups of the saddle and swung up, keeping the torch away from the animal lest she spook it. McShane, named after her maternal grandfather, was a warrior's horse, but there was no point to putting him to the test of an open flame. Nor was there any point in her testing her courage before necessary, she thought, kicking the animal in the ribs to catch up with the others.

27

* * *

The monastery was practically a village in itself. Clustered in a manner so as to enclose it were all the shops and buildings necessary to support the holy order there. As they rode through the gate between the almonry and the building where the poorer pilgrims were sheltered, Branwen found herself wishing that her father had put aside his contempt for the church and sought refuge there for the night.

This was the first time Owen ap Caradoc has been inside a holy place since the death of his infant son, born but a year after Branwen. Her mother often prayed that God would forgive him, in spite of the fact that her husband would not forgive God. Tonight, she would pray for her father's soul, she decided, dismounting as another robed brother hustled out of the stables to take her horse. Her mother wouldn't need her intervention. Lady Gwendolyn was already in heaven, Branwen was sure.

"The Lady Agnéis is in there, if you would see her."

Branwen shook her head as she glanced at the lighted window of the lodging reserved for merchants and noble guests. "Nay, I would not risk the upset again . . . nor would I allow her to view the bodies. You know the three atop there. The others can be identified by the carpenter at Caradoc. You will have coffins made for the transport of his lordship and family?" she challenged matter-of-factly.

"I am certain the lady will have it no other way," Brother Damien replied in a tone meant to remind her of her place.

" 'Twas only of the lady I was thinking, sir." She would have to watch her speech and manner. A mere servant boy would not assume airs as she had.

"Of course you were, son. I suppose this gruesome

deed has us all on edge." Like Branwen's, it was all the apology he intended, but it sufficed. "We'll see the family put in such wood and cloth as we have. The rest will have to do with sewn blankets. You can join the mercenary in the alms quarters there, unless you prefer oxen and horses for company. I'll send Brother Thomas in with some bread from the kitchen."

Branwen nodded mutely. The idea of spending the night alone with a strange man in an alms quarters was certainly a novelty and, as adventurous as she was frequently accused of being, not at all to her taste. The ride to the monastery, however, had given her time and experience to think of the journey still ahead, and a companion would be most helpful, especially one accustomed to being on his own like a mercenary. Even if he were lewd and lascivious, as a boy she would hardly be threatened.

The idea did not settle convincingly as she walked slowly toward the dark quarters, where poor pilgrims and wayfarers were put up at the hospice. After all, there were men who preferred boys, she'd heard, although she was never at liberty to disclose that such shameful knowledge existed in her innocent maiden's mind. It was the sort of thing young women talked about under the blankets, out of earshot of their matrons and, certainly, of the menfolk. It was there that she'd learned how she came to be, for her genteel and easily flustered mother would never have told her.

Branwen paused, her hand on the wooden latch of the door. The reminder of her mother's sweet character assaulted her with grief, as the presence of the stranger inflicted wariness. The combination made her hold the bar suspended until she could steady herself. Then an image of Lady Gwendolyn's lifeless face, frozen in terror, forced a steeling of the determination she had in-

29

herited from her slain father. Not this man, nor any man, would keep her from her task.

The room was pitch black compared to the torch-lit compound. In the center of it was a small fire, banked for the night. She could hear someone breathing with the heavy regularity of sleep and was grateful that at least she would not be kept awake with snoring. As her eyes adjusted, she made out the sleeping figure wrapped tightly in a blanket, like a giant cocoon.

Thick locks of fair hair that ran to his broad shoulders matched that of a longer beard. Both were in need of trimming. It was difficult to make out his face, considering the ragged bristle and the big arm half slung over it. No doubt he could wield a broadsword with one hand! she marveled, not the least put at ease by the thought. Summoning her nerve, she tiptoed closer, trying to make out his features.

A long nose, she noted, of Roman character, bold and not unattractive. His body appeared as lean and hard as it was large, indicating a life of sparse luxury and comfort. Aye, he looked the mercenary, she agreed with the monks' estimation of him—a nomad, self-supporting and sufficing. Like as not, she would know something of his character before she stepped out of the monastery with him alone.

"What the devil are you staring at?"

Her hand was not fast enough to stifle the startled gasp that sent her back a step. Narrowed eyes peered out from under the raised arm in suspicion.

"N . . . nothing!" Branwen murmured dryly. She shrugged in an attempt to affect an attitude of nonchalance. "I got a right to see what sort I'm sharin' a room with, don't I?"

Something akin to a growl escaped the hairy beard. "The name's Wolf. I ain't used to sharin' with nobody and I'm tryin' to sleep! Now get you down, lad, or I'll eat you alive for breakfast?"

Branwen clenched her teeth but could muster no further objection. The brute looked mean enough to do just that. Picking up the bedroll and sack she'd taken from McShane's back, she made a place for herself on the opposite side of the fire. It seemed she'd traded one kind of wolf for another, she thought, wrapping the blanket around her and huddling as close to the heat source as she dared.

"Tho', like as not, from the size of ye, I'd be picking naught but bones and cloth from my teeth for weeks," her companion snorted, rising up to give her an appraising glance, as if to confirm his statement, then turning over with a rough jerk of his covers.

She was saved a game reply by the opening of the door. Another friar, who looked like all the others, entered the room with a half loaf of bread in one hand a flagon of ale in the other. "Brother Damien said you might be hungry, lad. 'Tis cold but filling," he whispered with a wary glance at the other guest. "God bless you and good night."

The bread was stale as well as cold, but as the man had said, it was filling. Not that Branwen had much of an appetite. All she wanted to do at the moment was get warm. After devouring a chunk of bread and chasing it with the weak ale, Branwen lay down, her hand resting on the handle of her father's dagger. Just as her eyelids began to droop, she heard what sounded like a boar feasting on a treasure of tasty roots. She sighed in exasperation. Damnation, she had counted her meager blessings too soon. The hairy beast snored!

Not even that, however, could keep her from the lulling warmth of the fire and her blankets. Such was her exhaustion that even dreams failed to invade her slumber. When morning came, however, something made

31

her stir. It wasn't the sun, which was just climbing to its heavenly throne for the day, nor any sound that she was aware of. It was just an uneasy feeling, causing her to open her eyes a cautious crack.

Sitting across from her and staring impudently was the hairy stranger. "The brothers say you're headed to London with a message for the king."

Branwen rose, smothering a yawn with the back of her hand, and tried to shake the fog from her mind. "I am," she answered sleepily.

"They say ye saw the massacre of Lord Caradoc and his retinue."

How long had the devil been up? She watched as he picked up her flagon of ale and washed down the last of the bread she'd left aside for morning. Long enough to steal her breakfast, she thought grumpily.

"I don't want to talk about it."

"If ye'll travel with me, ye'll tell me what happened and be quick about it. I ain't too fond of travelin' with cold-blooded murderers about."

"Or you'll eat me alive, as well as my breakfast?" Branwen charged, her bravado spawned from annoyance.

It laughed. Or rather, he laughed. It was a loud, boisterous sound that filled the room and assaulted her ears. "Ye've more pluck than size, lad!" The man climbed to his feet to tower over her and started to unfasten his breeches. "So, out with it, lad. Ye say it was Kent's colors the men were wearin'?"

Branwen felt the fire that crawled up her neck to inflame her face, fire that had nothing to do with the one in the circular hearth. "O . . . orange and blue," she mumbled, dropping her gaze and concentrating on stirring the embers. "Same as flies on Caradoc's keep."

Thankfully, the man stepped away from her and over to the wall, where a chamber pot stood. "I ain't never met the man, but ambush just don't seem to be Kent's style of fightin'."

Hardly believing the sound she heard, she cast her eyes sideways and to her utter embarrassment confirmed it. She was about to tell the oaf just how uncouth he was, when she recalled that he thought her to be one of his own sex. Men were not bothered by lack of privacy among men, so she'd heard. At least not this one. "I'll get some wood for the fire," she offered, seizing an opportunity to escape the humiliating predicament.

"Hold, boy," the mercenary ordered, turning as he refastened his trousers. " 'Twould be a waste of good wood when I'm off in a few moments."

"I thought I was to travel with you."

"I don't want no peach-faced, wet-nursin' babe holding me back. I'm fresh from Ulster and eager to be employed again. I hear the king pays good coin."

"So you're from Ireland."

"Ireland, Scotland, Wales, France, Germany . . . I've lived in all them countries at one time or other since my weanin'."

Branwen picked up her blanket and folded it. "Well, I may be peach-faced, but I am weaned. I'll be no bother to you. In fact, I'm rather good at gathering firewood and cooking."

"Are you *rather?*" Wolf drew out the word in challenge. "Where did you get an education for rich words like that?"

"I served as a page at Canador." Damnation, Branwen chastised herself sternly. She would have to watch herself. Oaf that he was, this Wolf was no fool.

"And whose noble born are you?" the man derided sourly, exhibiting a mercenary's lack of respect for the politics and show of knighthood.

"You'll tell no one?"

"If I've reason."

33

"Your word as a gentleman?"

Again Branwen suffered as the source of her companion's amusement. "Aye, my word as a *gentleman* ought to put your mind right at ease, lad. I might even pledge my silence in Latin!"

"To hell with you then!" Branwen grated out irritably. She dropped to her knees to pack her sack.

"Gogsblood, I might have you for breakfast yet, you little wart of a man!"

Branwen grasped at the choking collar by which she was hauled off the floor and pinned to the wall above the urinal. "Or maybe what ye need is a little washin' to bring out the manners ye been taught in the keep."

"You son of a bitch-whore!"

"Instead of your feet, mayhaps your mouth should be washed out!"

To Branwen's horror, he reached down with his long arm for the chamber pot that he'd just used. "All right!" she cried out hoarsely. "I apologize!"

"Whose whelp are ye?"

"I'm Edwin ... of Caradoc ... milord's bastard, if you must know."

"So I've a runt of red and blue blood," the bearded man grunted in surprise. "Are ye an heir?"

Branwen shook her head and tried to force the answer out, but the choking hold would not allow it. "Na ..." She closed her eyes and fought the dizziness that washed over her. God forbid she faint and fall in the chamber pot.

"Here ye go, wart," her captor cajoled, setting her down away from her dreaded fate and slapping her on the back, so that what little wind was trapped within her breast came flying out in a strangled cough. "Well, well, what have we here?" The hand that had gone about her waist to steady her found the hilt of her father's dagger and drew it from its sheath.

"It belongs to my father! I needed something to defend myself with," Branwen admitted grudgingly. "I've his horse as well to transport me to the king with the news of his death."

"Do ye know how to use this piece, aside from cutting up food with it?" the mercenary taunted, balancing it in his hand. Before she knew what he was about, he let it loose with a reckless sling, sending it straight into the center of a knot on the middle plank of the door. Grinning widely, he swaggered over and removed it. "Here ye go, lad. Let's see what you can do."

Branwen stepped forward to claim the blade but did not return to where Wolf had stood. She intended to make use of all the advantage the overgrown bully would allow. Balancing it, hilt out, she pretended to study the target for a moment and then let it fly. To her alarm, the knife struck the door, handle first, and bounced back to her, hastily driving her into her howling opponent.

"Seems to me you ought to take me along, sir."

"And . . ." the man gasped, trying to regain his breath, "and why is that, wart?"

" 'Twould save you the ill effects of overdrink and make you just as silly drunk with laughter at *my* expense."

Slinging her sack and bedroll over her shoulder, Branwen picked up her knife and sheathed it. Hand on the latch, she gave it a tug, only to be thwarted again, for it seemed to be frozen and as much against her as the rest of the world.

"Don't you think you ought to get something to eat?"

"What do you care?" she blurted out, blue eyes simmering beneath thick sooty lashes the color of her disheveled hair. To her chagrin, her bottom lip began to tremble threateningly. She bit it and attacked the latch

35

again, but Wolf bullied the door open with a callused hand twice the size of her own.

"Because I'll not be caught having to deliver your starven bony corpse and damned message!"

"You'll go with me, then?"

"Nay, *you'll* go with me. I'll not put up with no baby. You'll keep up like a man or be left behind, is that understood?"

With what she thought was relief, Branwen nodded. For all she knew, this was a murderer, one of those renegade knights expelled from the order or worse.

"Now give me your things, and I'll saddle your horse while you fetch something to carry from the kitchen."

"How do I know you won't steal my horse?"

"Gogsbreath, boy, this is a church! Even a lowly cur like meself has *some* sense of character!"

Sense of character, the girl echoed in silent disdain, for fear of incensing him again. He wouldn't steal, but he would bully a helpless boy about and threaten to wash his mouth out with chamber slop!

Branwen pivoted and strode toward the kitchen, where tempting smells emerged to fill the stable yard from the slanted chimney vent in its back wall. The ringing of the chapel bell brought her to a halt, long enough to cross herself and ask forgiveness for not attending the morning vespers, but she dared not keep Wolf waiting long. He would, like as not, leave without her.

"Boy! You there!"

At the familiar high-pitched voice, Branwen halted in her tracks. *Aunt Agnéis!* What if the woman recognized her? Seeing no chance of escape, the girl turned as the woman ran toward her, heavy bosom bouncing beneath the layers of her woolen dresses. It was some moments before her aunt regained her breath enough to speak.

"Brother Damien said you were one of Owen's men,

but I vow, I don't remember a callow youth like yourself among them."

"I helped with the horses, milady."

"I knew something terrible was going to happen. I saw the blackbirds in number and my bones ached three days." Her silvering hair, once chestnut like her younger sister's, was matted and tangled, protruding from her loose barbette to frame a face that was gaunt for a woman of her size. Eyes enfolded in aged and sagging lids kept switching about, as if she expected at any moment to see some fearful apparition. "Have you seen my niece?"

Her question was so pitiful, Branwen almost gave in to her urge to admit who she was and offer the distraught woman comfort. "She's dead, milady."

"Oh, no," her aunt contradicted certainly. "I saw her last night. She was dressed in a fine gown and stood with the handsomest knight before a priest. I never saw her more lovely. Her wedding will make up for all this sorrow."

"Then she's likely gone off with her new husband for privacy, milady." Poor dear. The friar was right. Her aunt had gone quite mad. Perhaps returning to Caradoc would restore her, both physically and mentally, for Branwen had never seen her aunt's round, cherubic face so drawn and frightened.

"That knife! You've got Owen's knife! What right has a stableboy to the lord's knife?"

Branwen thought quickly. "I am no mere stableboy, milady. I hate to say anything now, but I am the lord's bastard, born of a fisherman's daughter. He just invited me to Caradoc to train as page, and now this has happened." Crossing her fingers, the girl withstood a narrowed inspection.

"My God, the resemblance is startling! You've got Owen's wild hair, well enough. Why, you could almost be a twin of my niece, but that she's much fairer than you, as well a girl should be."

"I intend to avenge Tâd's death."

"For his wealth?"

"Nay, milady, for his honor. I need none but these two hands to provide for me, although the horse and knife will afford me transport and defense for London."

"Owen's *son!*" Agnéis repeated in a daze. "So he had a son after all. Odd that I didn't see it. I usually see such things." She looked at Branwen again. "Well, I suppose it can't hurt for you to take the horse and knife, but I will tell you now, I feel no attachment to you. I usually feel attachment to kin."

"Perhaps if you had the time to know me, milady . . ." Branwen answered, shifting uncomfortably beneath her aunt's scrutiny. "But I must be off. I've a mission of import to accomplish."

Agnéis patted her on the shoulder. "As do I, lad. I've to bury my beloved sister and her husband. It's best done before Branwen returns with her husband. The child needs nothing else to burden her shoulders."

"Then God's speed, milady."

"And the same to you, lad." The woman reached out and fingered a black curl sticking out from beneath Branwen's cap, before letting it go with a puzzled sigh. "Owen's son!" she echoed, turning to wander toward the chapel with her familiar shuffling gate. "Now, why didn't I know it?"

Again relief was marred, this time by grief, as Branwen made her way to the kitchen. She was both grateful her aunt had not recognized her and upset that the poor dear had lost her wit. That Aunt Agnéis had seen Branwen marry and believed her to be off with her bridegroom only drove home the extent of her shock. It was a wonder that the woman had escaped at all. Knowing her aunt, she'd wandered off in search of either some herb reputed to grow in that particular region or mistletoe. She was greatly distressed to embark on the journey without the mistletoe, which Lord Owen had been too impatient to fetch for her.

Branwen's suspicion was confirmed when she returned to the stable yard, her shirt stuffed with small loaves of bread fresh from the oven. Tied to her saddle was a sprig of the white-berried evergreen.

"Some crazy woman came running out here and insisted on tying this switch to your saddle," her grizzly companion informed her dryly. "Says it will bring Lord Owen's son good luck."

That was exactly where Aunt Agnéis had been. The mistletoe had saved her aunt's life. Who was to say it might not insure her safe return to Caradoc as well? Smiling, Branwen handed over a few loaves from the sack formed by the upper part of her belted shirt, before swinging gingerly up into McShane's saddle.

"You don't believe in that gibberish!"

"It doesn't pay to make fun of that which we don't understand, good fellow." Branwen reined in the stallion and motioned for Wolf to take the lead. "Lead on, sir."

Anyone foolish enough to tackle the hauberk-clad giant would never get past him to her, she thought, wondering at the expanse of his shoulders and the thickness of his sturdy leather-protected thighs. No doubt, beneath those worn and faded clothes was a body scarred from a multitude of clashes with the enemy of whatever lord had employed him at the time. His first loyalty was to himself. That was the way of his breed. His second, to the man with the highest bid.

Odd that she somehow felt safe, regardless of their earlier encounter. She knew now it was a test. She'd seen squires and knights alike put new fellows to the same. Like roosters in the barnyard, she thought in wry amusement, establishing a pecking order. That she had passed was evidenced in the fact that he was permitting her to go with him. It was immensely satisfying, even if he was established at the top of command.

As long as he got her there, she didn't mind the cooking and gathering wood. He might even show her how to use her father's knife with a degree of skill beyond that which he'd mocked. Then she'd really stand a chance to avenge a man who was motivated by honor, rather than money; one who had thought himself to be dealing with one of his kind, instead of a lowly, greedy murderer; the only man who would ever have her respect and love ... Owen ap Caradoc.

Chapter Three

As the day passed, Branwen realized with more and more discomfort that her companion's ability to travel for miles without the frequent rests to which she was accustomed was limitless. At one point, when nature would hear no reason, she was forced to drop behind to afford herself the privacy she needed. Then, thus relieved, she urged McShane on at a full gallop to make up the distance lost, falling in once again behind the man who acted as if he had not so much as missed her. Hence, the milk the good friar had given her upon request, in lieu of ale, remained untouched in its goatskin, lest it prove more stimulating than the hard pace would permit.

It wasn't surprising that not only did they reach Chester before the day's end, but to Branwen's dismay, they bypassed the tempting smells from cookhouses there and sustained themselves, for several miles beyond, with the bread she'd brought along. The scant villages along the way tempted her sorely to abandon her companion altogether, but the dense and intimidating forests between were sufficient argument to maintain his silent and demanding company. By the time they finally stopped, as she feared, in the cover of a thick woodland, she was too numb with exhaustion to care.

"Wake up, lad. We'll stay here for the night!"

"We might have stayed in a stable of that last village we passed and tasted some of that delicious stew wafting on the wind," Branwen complained dourly.

"Oh, so ye've a pocket full of coined comfort, have ye?"

"Nay, just a raw bottom and a jaundiced eye from lack of sufficient rest stops!"

Wolf laughed with a clarity as fresh as the air and just as biting to Branwen's wounded pride. "Ye'll need to over that modesty of yours, lad, or ye'll never fare well as the knight ye intend to be."

"Maybe I won't be a knight now."

"It seems to me, there's more raw than your ass! Ye've been around women too long, lad. Stick with me and I'll make a man of ye yet."

Branwen slid off McShane's back, her knees nearly buckling as she hit the ground. "I don't exactly aspire to be like you, either."

Wolf snorted and tethered his horse to a tree. It was every bit as fine as the golden McShane, strong-necked and bred for warfare. Wherever the mercenary was from, it was clear that his skill had served him well enough to outfit him with a steed to match any knight's charger. There were noblemen who rode lesser animals.

"Take care of Pendragon and set up the campfire over there near that thicket. 'Twill break the wind and keep the wolves away from our back."

Branwen couldn't help the involuntary shudder that ran through her. "And what will *you* do while I play the servant?"

Wolf took down a long bow from Pendragon's back, one Branwen instantly recognized as of Welsh design. Perhaps he was from all those places. "I intend to *play* the hunter, unless you can provide a plump squirrel or rabbit for my fire."

With her dogs and falcon she could do better than that, but Branwen held her tongue. She didn't have them, and if they were to eat more than the remnant of bread from the monastery, she was obliged to Wolf for her supper.

"Then by all means get thee gone, for I'm fairly starved as I am sore."

"Ah, now I see how ye survived yesterday's bloody deed. Your complaints drove them off! Ye've a tongue as finely hewn as a nag's!"

"Must you be unkind as well as uncouth?"

For a moment, Branwen thought she'd gone too far. Wolf glared at her from beneath thick golden brows, all but hidden by his untrimmed hair. A man-bear, capable of tearing her limb from limb, she thought, shrinking under his warning gaze. "Over there, you say?" she asked, pointing to where he instructed the fire be built.

An aggravating gleam of satisfaction settled in his gaze as he snatched up a quiver of arrows and slung it over his shoulder. "Aye, and make it well, for you're not the only one whose belly's sore and bellerin'."

The caring for the horses was no problem. Branwen loved to spend time in the stables when her mother would allow, brushing their coats and manes to a healthy sheen and helping with the feeding. She knew almost as much about keeping the tack in good shape as the stable master himself, and she could ride like the wind, with or without it, on her own spirited blue roan, which had been lost in the ambush. Aladin, she'd named him, his sire from the East.

Her father's golden McShane was a stark contrast to the dark Pendragon. The latter seemed to embody the nature of its owner, impatient and unimpressed with anything . . . except the grain bag Branwen pulled over its head. As for her careful grooming of its rich black coat, the horse seemed to care less. Even the presence of

43

the other stallion failed to cause more than a laid-back ear now and then. The two noble steeds served to keep her occupied and at ease with their companionship, in spite of the growing number of sounds to which she'd been listening as she went about her labors.

Dogs or wolves? she wondered, stacking the wood she'd gathered by the circle of stones she'd formed for the campfire. The ground was hard and made it difficult to drive in the two forked pieces of green oak she'd hacked off with her knife to form a cradle for the spit of the same wood. When there was nothing left to do but kindle the fire, Branwen reluctantly took the tinderbox and flint and steel from her father's saddle pouch.

Perhaps luck would be with her this time, she thought brightly. After all, she'd been overwrought yesterday when the blasted charred linen wouldn't catch. She might have gotten it wet in her frantic attempt to light a fire. Today, she'd take her time and do exactly as she'd often seen her father do, for the hearth fires in the hall and kitchen were never allowed to go out. Hence, there was always a source of fire for the torches and tallow dips.

Taking the driest of the brush she could find, Branwen made a little pyramid in the center of the circle and carefully placed a small piece of the tinder on top. Then holding the steel in one hand, she struck the flint against it. It seemed at first that the tiny sparks flew everywhere, except to the waiting linen, but finally a small corner of the bit of cloth began to glow with promise. Cupping her hand to either side of it to protect it from the wind that managed to penetrate the thorny thicket at her back, Branwen blew gently on it to encourage it to catch.

The glow flickered briefly and then a flame burst on one corner of the cloth. Beneath it, the kindling crackled with the spreading warmth. Afraid to breathe and yet having to act the bellows to coax it along, Branwen all but dropped facedown on the ground and puffed until she felt dizzy with her success. She watched as the brush beneath began to char and then burst into fragile flame as well, reflecting the burst of delight that imitated it within her chest.

"There!" she whispered, as if to cheer too loudly would put out the fire.

Slowly, she climbed to her feet and started to reach for more substantial wood, when she heard a loud sizzling splat. Her heart collapsed within her breast at the sight of the clump of snow, which rapidly turned to water and snuffed out her victory with a dying hiss. To her dismay, the tinderbox, which she'd foolishly left open, was also buried in the landslide from the tree branches overhead.

Branwen swore in her despair. Now what? she wondered, glancing over at Pendragon in hopes of finding another tinderbox among her companion's things. Seeing that he had not taken his sack with him, she immediately rummaged through it, but to no avail. More than likely, he kept it on his person in one of the little pouches tied to his belt. Gogsblood, she thought, borrowing from Wolf's vocabulary without realizing it. He would think her the useless dolt, and he would be justified in doing so!

Miserable and cold, Branwen unfurled one of her blankets and wrapped herself up in it, so that when the mercenary returned, he found her aborted attempt at a fire waiting and the girl herself sandwiched and shivering between the two horses.

"Where's the fire, lad?"

Branwen peered over the folded arms resting on her knees. "Put out by an overhead snowslide."

"And ye let the rest of your tinder get wet?" he exclaimed, picking up the small box and staring at it with incredulity.

"If you're as hungry as you are observant, you'll make up for the lost time soon enough," Branwen informed him grudgingly. "I've collected enough wood for the night and seen to the animals."

As Branwen suspected, Wolf kept his tinder and flint on his belt. Chuckling to himself, he glanced overhead and then moved the stones she'd arranged a yard or so with his booted feet. "It always pays to start a fire in the clear, lad, in case a tree overhead be tempted to spit on it and put it out."

Branwen would have made some cocky reply, but for the fact that she was bone-cold and anxious to have a roaring fire going to warm herself. By the time her appetite thawed enough, perhaps the meal would be done.

"Can ye skin a rabbit?"

She'd seen one skinned, Branwen conceded, before making a verbal commitment. One disaster in one day was enough, however. Instead, she admitted the truth. "I've only seen it done . . . *sir*," she finished apologetically.

Wolf motioned her over. "Then get over here and pay attention."

The mercenary made quick work of preparing the rabbit for the spit she'd moved. It seemed as though he'd made a few well-considered slashes and the soft fur peeled off as easily as she slipped off her shift for bathing. The gutting and the cleaning, however, made Branwen's stomach churn threateningly. Suddenly, it was no longer the rabbit's blood she saw soaking the ground, but that of poor Caryn's as she'd pulled out the spears, sometimes with the girl's entrails coming with them.

With a small strangling sound, Branwen staggered as far away as her legs would carry her, before her stomach heaved viciously. She felt the blood drain from her face, leaving her weak, so that it was only her grasp on a low growing tree branch that kept her from pitching forward.

"Faith, ye can't start a fire, ye can't stand the sight o' blood . . . what is it ye *can* do?"

Branwen swallowed the sob that rose to the back of her throat, tasting of bile. Damn the heartless and annoyingly able villain! "Get out of your way."

She'd point McShane in the right direction, wrap herself up in her blanket, and pray the heat from the stallion would keep her warm. Eyes stinging with tears that she refused to free, she stumbled toward the horse that had been her father's. It turned doleful eyes toward her as she approached, and Branwen suddenly found herself clinging to the stallion's thick neck as though it were Owen himself.

She was not the son he wanted and never would be! She was a helpless, good-for-nothing girl. Instead of skewering his murderer, she was only fit to embroider his shirts. Instead of forcing the hand of justice, she was to suffer its slight. Anger and frustration built to an unbearable proportion, so that when Wolf laid a sympathetic hand on her shoulder, she responded with raw emotion and flew into the man, growling and striking at him as if he represented all that overwhelmed her.

"I'll kill you, you heartless bastard!" she cried hoarsely, her blows falling futilely against his ringed hauberk until her knuckles bled from the abuse.

"Here, here now! Stop before I have to hurt ye, lad!"

Two arms stilled her, pinning hers helplessly to her side and crushing the breath from her against his mail-clad body, so that her only recourse was to continue her anguished growling to cover her tear-ridden sobs. Branwen felt his breath blow warm against the top of her head as he expelled his own brand of exasperation.

47

"Gogsblood, I ain't used to travelin' companions at all, much less the company of a house-trained pup! Now stop your snivelin' and pull yourself together, boy! 'Tis time ye became a man, and if ye'll put up with my coarse ways, I'll try to tolerate your ignorance of things that come natural to me. All that fancy talk and Latin ain't goin' to help you a bit now."

Somehow placated by the awkward admission and assuaged by this unexpected source of strength, Branwen ceased to struggle in defeat. She found herself wishing that her grizzly companion would hold her a while longer, but Wolf let her go and cleared his throat.

"Now, were ye lyin' about bein' able to cook or not? I'll know now, sooner than have me supper spoilt."

Keeping her eyes on her feet, Branwen shook her head. "I c . . . can cook. If you've salt, 'twill help."

It was obvious that Wolf considered the use of seasoning unnecessary opulence, but he was at least verbally gracious. "I might have a sack of it someplace. Ye put the hare on the fire and I'll see if I can find it."

Head still lowered, Branwen returned to the fire and put the skinned and cleaned rabbit on the spit she'd sharpened earlier with her father's knife. She wished she hadn't cried . . . or at least, that the tough mercenary hadn't seen her. But she felt like the rabbit, gutted and empty with grief. Brother Damien had warned her about her lust for revenge, but that was all that filled her now, all that kept her going.

At the appearance of Wolf's boots next to her, she accepted the handful of salt he passed over to her and rubbed it in the rabbit as her mother had taught her to do. There were crushed herbs that would have added an even better flavor in the kitchen at Caradoc, but the larder of the winter forest was barren of such luxuries. So much she'd taken for granted, she realized, trying to swallow her blade of self-pity—her bed, screened off from that of her parents and the scattered bedrolls of servants sleeping on the floor of the great hall, the safety and love she'd enjoyed. *Gone . . . all gone.*

"Humph!" Wolf grunted, squatting beside the fire and warming his hands over it. "It's been so long since hair wouldn't grow on my face and my voice wouldn't drop deep enough to suit my ambition, I damned near forgot what it's like."

"I'd say it's been a good while, considering that mangy mat on your face."

"You're just jealous, lad." Her companion chuckled, and even Branwen's thinned lips twitched threateningly. " 'Twas awful, the way folks talked about me pretty curls and said I had the face of a girl . . . just like yourself, I'd wager. I couldn't wait for manly hair to show them wrong, 'specially the ones what whistled at me and made crude propositions."

Eyes wide with wonder, Branwen looked up to see if the man was having fun with her or was serious. Somehow, she could not picture anyone purposely invoking the rage of her beastly companion. At his understanding wink, she hastily focused on turning the spit. So he did have a heart, she mused in surprise, one like that of Owen ap Caradoc, hidden beneath bluster and bull.

"The good friar told me somethin' else about ye, boy, somethin' I'm thinkin' we might as well get out in the open. He thinks ye might try to avenge your folks' death against Kent."

"I will."

"Kent ain't gonna roll over and let ye knife 'im, lad. He ain't lived this long bein' the fool."

"I have a few tricks he won't expect." Branwen could just imagine the knight's face when his bride showed up very much alive and armed to kill.

"Ye'd best have more than a few. Ye ain't cut out for

49

the life of an outlaw, and that's what ye'd be if'n ye was to succeed."

"I have proof of his treachery. I'd be doing the king a favor to dispose of him."

"And just how do you intend to do that?"

Branwen shrugged. "I'll think of something before we get to Westminster."

The rabbit was delicious and Wolf told her so. Beaming with pride that, at least, one thing had gone right, Branwen held her own in appetite. Following Wolf's suit, she wiped her hands on her clothing instead of washing them as she ate, but unlike the mercenary, when the meal was over, she felt compelled to use the snow to cleanse them. With what was left over of the rabbit moved to the edge of the fire to keep until morning, Branwen excused herself to find more firewood.

"Ye've already collected enough for the night," Wolf objected. " 'Tis black as pitch out there, and if a pack of wolves take a notion to make ye their supper, don't start hollerin' for me."

Trying to discount his threat, Branwen reached the edge of the clearing, only to hear him make a strangling noise. She looked back in time to see him spit a mouthful of her milk at the fire.

"Gogsbreath, 'tis milk!" he exclaimed in an accusing tone.

"And 'tis mine," Branwen pointed out.

"Milk?"

"For the love of heaven, 'tis not poison! Besides, that's what you get for being so greedy."

" 'Twasn't greed but a mistake," Wolf retorted indignantly. "Ye needn't worry, it will not happen again. 'Tis no wonder ye've a babe's capacity to hold your water! Ye haven't been weaned yet!"

"You don't drink milk?" Branwen questioned in surprise, trying futilely to keep the rush of blood from her neck from reaching her cheeks. Men were so . . . crude!

"Not when there's good alé to be had . . . *or bad, for that matter.* A milk-drinkin' babe what thinks he's got more in his breeches than should be flaunted!" her companion snorted disdainfully. "Or maybe your pisser ain't grown yet!"

Face fully flushed with fire, Branwen turned and marched into the trees. There was no point in trying to explain modesty. The mercenary not only scoffed it, but he possessed not a whit. When nature called, he made no attempt to move more than a few feet from the campfire to seek relief, a most disgusting habit Branwen had not thought of when she'd elected to keep her charade to herself. She made a mental note of his selected place, so that when she put down her bedroll for the night, she was nowhere near it.

Nor did she want to be on the outward edge of the fire. If the god-awful demons that howled and screamed in the night were to brave the fire, it was only fair that the experienced and armed mercenary be the one they crossed first. Later, after he observed that she made more over picking a spot to sleep than a hen did making its nest, she eagerly wrapped herself up in her blankets and dropped down to the pile of leaves the two of them had collected. With only the fire-lit ceiling of the tree branches overhead to occupy her, for it was as dark as her snoring companion had warned, her fatigue finally rose victorious over the noises of the forest.

Sometime in the night, the logs on the fire collapsed, shaking Branwen from her slumber. Reluctantly, she climbed from her warm nest of leaves to put more wood on it. She waited until the flames caught up again, lest the newer logs smother it out, and stared across its warming glower at the sleeping face of her companion.

It was hard to imagine that under that unkempt and

unwashed hair lurked a face that people mistook as feminine. Maybe he kept it that way to look fiercer, she mused. Like his gruff manner, it was a front. Front or no, however, it was extremely effective. Not liking to bear the brunt of his amusement, Branwen pushed up to her feet to seek relief in the dark quiet and avoid the urgency usually associated with morning.

She did, however, take Wolf's warning into account and didn't venture far from the glow of the campfire. It was times like this that she so envied men. As she rearranged her clothing upon completion of her mission, a sharp, loud noise cut through the forest night. Her fingers froze and she glanced back at the campsite, where through the brush of her cover, she saw Wolf sleeping peacefully. Although she was tempted to burst from her cover and race back to the safety of his company, instinct bade her be still.

Her reward was the sight of three shadows moving stealthily toward the campfire. No four-legged beasts were these. They moved on toward the place where McShane and Pendragon whinnied uneasily. *Horse thieves!*

"Wolf! The horses!"

Branwen's shout startled her as much as it did the thieves themselves. Freezing in their tracks, they looked about, as if trying to figure where it had come from. Time, however, would not permit, for Wolf sprang up from his bed, throwing his blankets aside with one hand like a caped marauder while brandishing his sword with the other.

All three turned to fend off the ferocious charge, and for a moment, Branwen merely stood watching in awe. Then, as one of the men broke away to make for the horses, she sprang into action. Unlike Wolf, she made no sound but for that of her running feet, and also unlike him, she had not divested herself of her blankets, so that when she emerged from the thicket, they were spread about her like darkwings. Such was the sight that the man reaching for the horses' reins backed away toward their haunches in shock.

"Kick, Pendragon!"

Branwen stopped short as the dark stallion lowered its head and launched both feet backward, sending the man sprawling onto the frozen ground, grasping his ribs and moaning fiercely. The angry clashing of swords drew her back to the ensuing battle between Wolf and the other two thieves. They had separated, like wolves attacking a common prey, requiring all his skill to keep them at bay. As he engaged one, the other started at him from behind, spurring Branwen forward.

She leapt upon his back, throwing her blankets over his head so that he could not see. Thus disabled, the man stumbled about blindly, trying to shake his unseen attacker from his back. Branwen held on with her legs and arms, choking him at the neck and riding his back so closely that he dared not try to strike her with his weapon for fear of hitting himself.

Her expertise at staying on so effectively, developed at that precious age before her mother banned her from the war games of the squires and pages, gave rise to a barrage of curses, not very well smothered beneath the wool of her blanket. Throwing his sword aside, he reached for her and grabbed her hair. With a pained yelp, she bit at what she thought was his ear and was rewarded by an equally agonized cry.

Her elbow grazed a tree as the man staggered past it, and before she knew what he was about, she found herself slammed bodily against it. Her hold loosened with the breath-robbing blow. A second one enabled the man to escape her clutches. Slinging the blanket aside, he gave her a murderous look and snatched up the sword he'd dropped.

Blood chilling in her chest, Branwen ducked behind the tree as he lunged at her. The blade shot past her cover on one side, driving her to the opposite.

"Come outta there, ye little wisp of a man, or I'll . . ."

The remainder of her assailant's threat erupted in a startled, strangled scream. The blade dropped to the ground before her eyes, followed by the thudding crash of its owner's body. Buried in his back was a dagger, surrounded by a growing dark stain on his coarse shirt. Branwen leaned against the tree for support, when Wolf stepped into her range of view and bent over to retrieve his knife. Lips trembling, she managed a weak attempt at a smile as he straightened and wiped the blade on the man's back.

"You all right, wart?"

Branwen nodded mutely. At least, she thought she was all right. At that moment, she wasn't sure if her legs would carry her to her bed if she let go the tree. "Are they gone?"

"The one still breathin' is. This one and the one who tried my blade won't be goin' anywhere."

Peeking around the tree, Branwen saw the other man's body lying lifeless by the campfire.

"Did it ever occur to you to use that knife on your belt, or do you just wear it to look like you can defend yourself?"

Branwen's hand went to the hilt of her knife involuntarily. "I . . . in all the excitement, I forgot about it."

Wolf snorted. "Ye don't have it in ye to kill Kent! Ye best hop on that horse o' your daddy's tomorrow and head back to that fishin' village ye came from. Fish are a lot safer to kill."

Heat flared in Branwen's cheeks as she recovered. "I saved your bloody life, in case you didn't know it. That villain was going at you from the back with his sword and I jumped him!"

54

"With a *blanket!*"

"But it saved your life, nonetheless!" Her lips set in stubborn challenge. "Admit it, Wolf!"

"Aye, it did, but . . ."

"So you owe me," Branwen announced smugly.

"What?"

"You owe me! I saved your life, and the least you can do is show me how to use this knife in return. I can be your squire."

"Just what I need!" he laughed scornfully. "A milk-fed, pissy-pants squire."

Her temper pushed beyond endurance, Branwen drew her knife. "You swaggering ass, if I hadn't gone into the woods, we'd have both been food for the buzzards by now and you know it!"

"Then pardon me, Sir Aspiration. 'Twas a pissin' sword and not a blanket what save our hides."

Instead of a man, it felt as if she'd charged into a tree, but Branwen was so angry now it didn't matter. Not only was she robbed of her breath by the impact, but her knife was painfully removed from her hand in one sharp twist of her wrist. Then, to her humiliation, she was seized by the waist of her trousers and hauled up like a piece of baggage, swinging furiously in the cold air. Her assailant stopped long enough to sheathe his own knife and snatch up her blankets, before carrying her over to the bed of leaves she'd abandoned earlier.

"Bastard!" Branwen grunted as she was dropped unceremoniously in them. "I ought to . . ." The blankets struck her face, silencing her momentarily. "If you're so damned good, then teach me!" she challenged as he grabbed the dead thief and dragged him by his feet to the tree where the other fellow had been left. "You owe me that!"

Wolf shoved them our of sight with his feet and then picked up her blade. Branwen opened her mouth to issue the challenge again, when he spun about and let the knife fly. A gasp was all she managed as it landed only inches from her, burying into the dirt. "You enjoy intimidating helpless men, don't you?"

"Oh, I don't think that feller over there would say you were exactly helpless." Wolf dropped down on his own pallet and rearranged his blankets. "Ye got more courage per pound than I'd give most men. All ye need to do is show me ye've the wit to go with it, and I'll teach ye what ye need to know."

"I'll learn quicker than anybody you've ever seen!" Branwen told him. "I can do anything I set my mind to."

"Ah, such modesty. 'Tis more than a man can stand!"

Branwen stared at the wide back presented her. "How do you know I won't stab you in the back while you're sleeping?"

"Because you ain't a murderer, boy," Wolf grunted impatiently. " 'Sides, you won't stand a chance without me showin' ye a thing or two. Now get to sleep! I ain't gonna listen to no whinin' about ye being tired tomorrow. We've a long journey and it ain't gettin' no warmer."

Branwen rubbed her arms briskly before rolling up in her own blankets as she'd seen Wolf do. At least that was one thing about which they both agreed: It wasn't getting any warmer.

Chapter Four

Branwen was awakened abruptly the following morning by an angry knee thudding into her buttocks and a hostile push, which sent her rolling over in her tightly wrapped blankets away from the warmth she'd enjoyed and onto the cold, hard earth beyond the leaf and pine needle pallet.

"By thunder, if I ever catch you easing up to me like that again, boy, I'll break your simple neck!"

It took a moment for the reason for her companion's indignation to sink in, although to say Wolf was indignant was a rigorous understatement. What she could see of his face was a mottled red, a stark contrast to his dark golden hair. He shot up to his feet in what appeared a single motion and snatched his blankets up to roll them for the journey ahead.

"I . . . I didn't realize I'd rolled over," Branwen stammered defensively, a matching color coming to her cheeks.

"Boy, if I was of the right leanin's, you might have found yourself the sow to a ruttin' boar, rubbin' your ass against a man like that."

"I'm *sorry!*"

Mortified at the very thought and not knowing what else to say, Branwen climbed to her feet and plunged into the trees, hoping the cold air striking her chapped cheeks would help to assuage the heat in them. As if she'd intentionally snuggled up to him! she fumed.

"Where the devil are you off to now?"

"To get more wood!" she shouted over her shoulder.

"Forget that. We'll eat what's left of the hare and be on our way. We've got a lot of miles to cover, and I'd have a roof over my head tonight."

"Then go ahead and I'll catch up!"

"What if that other villain comes back for his friends?"

"He might be kinder than you!" Branwen gritted, her steps slowing at the reminder of their dastardly visitors.

That morning she'd been so warm and comfortable, she'd almost thought the excitement of the night before a dream. Since it wasn't, she tarried no longer than she had to and scampered back to the campsite. While the horses ate their morning ration of grain, she hurriedly choked down a small piece of cold rabbit and chased it with a swallow of milk. By the time she'd made up her bedroll and saddled McShane, her companion had put out the remains of the fire and waited upon the pawing Pendragon with the same patience as his steed.

The landscape to the south toward London became more gentle, enabling them to cover a better distance than the day before. The sun ventured out around mid-morning and made waste of the thinning snow, rendering the roads a quagmire of mud to vex cart and carriage. For a fee, Wolf volunteered to help free a number of them, which slowed them down but, as he pointed out, put a few coins in their pocket. True to his word, when evening fell, they stopped over at an ale house and spent the night in the shedlike barn behind it.

To avoid making that morning's same mistake again, Branwen wedged her haversack between them and fully enjoyed the warm stack of hay for bedding. A parson and a traveling band of entertainers shared their quarters, the first retiring early and the second later, after they'd earned a few coins for their songs and dances from the local patrons. Rowdy as they were, having spent a goodly portion on ale for their thirsts, they eventually settled down in a corner, men and women alike, and went to sleep.

By the end of the third day in the saddle, Branwen was not nearly as exhausted. Perhaps she was becoming accustomed to Wolf's driving pace, she mused as she saw to the horses, a chore that had become hers as part of their bargain. Or maybe it was because her companion was following through with his word to teach her the use of a knife. The lessons were something she looked forward to, not because of Brother Damien's predicted bloodlust but because of the challenge.

At least she could bury it blade first into a board now, instead of having it bounce back at her. The moment she was finished with the animals, she practiced outside by the torchlight until she became too chilled and retired within the walls of the hostelry to join her companion. She had a knack for a blade, Wolf had complimented when she came close to her given target on the second day. Small-built people were usually more agile and skilled with a knife, so he'd informed her, meaning no insult at all, which was a refreshing change.

Theirs was a prickly camaraderie, but in spite of their barbed exchanges, each was becoming more accustomed to the other's way. It secretly amused her when the mercenary would smack her on the back heartily and tell her he'd make a man of her yet, and it outwardly delighted her when he complimented her on her increasing skill.

"You're not ready to take on a seasoned warrior like Kent, but you'll do in an alehouse scuffle, if ye don't get too big for them baggy breeches."

The third night on the road, like all those since the robbers' attempt to steal their horses, was spent at an alehouse at one of the local crossroads half a day north of Coventry. The bush hanging from the pole over the entrance waved in the wind that had been, thankfully, at their backs all day. Branwen's pocket jingled with coin from their new enterprise of rescuing stuck carts and wagons, but her clothes were shamefully caked with mud. Glad that it was only the outer layer, she made the best of it and laughed about hoping it would rain to wash away some of the grime.

Privately, she longed for a bath and a clean gown, but those days seemed so far behind her as she sat, elbow to elbow, with Wolf and sipped a wooden noggin of ale. The last of the milk from the monastery had run out and she hadn't been about to ask for it after the mockery and merriment she'd caused the night before. Without much stomach for brew, she found herself unusually contented and warm with the fire near the center of the room a few feet away.

As one of the locals decided it was time to leave his good fellows and go home to his wife and cottage, a large group of travelers entered. Branwen looked up, expecting to see the minstrels and dancers who'd also been on the road to London, but instead, these were all men, alarmingly familiar. When the leader shouted for ale and slid onto the bench opposite the one she and Wolf occupied, Branwen knew instantly who it was before he yanked back his hood to reveal straight dark hair that had never been manageable.

Dafydd ap Elwaid! Of all the people to meet on all the roads in England, she had to meet her ex-fiancé on this one! Gogsbreath, she thought he was with Llewelyn's retinue. There were other lads from Anglesey and neighboring commotes to Traeth Caradoc who knew her as well, some newly knighted and strutting proud by the way they treated their comrades who were still lowly squires. Branwen shrunk into her clothes, grateful for the mud and dirt that hopefully, with her hat, would conceal her identity.

"Clear this table!" Dafydd ordered boldly. " 'Tis for knights only and not the likes of *that.*"

Another prayer answered! Upon seeing that the newly knighted man was pointing at her, Branwen started to slide off the bench to retreat to the barn, when Wolf put a restraining hand on her shoulder.

"The lad stays. He was here first."

"Look you, sir! I've no quarrel with drinking at the same table as a man of equal merit, but this wisp of an excuse for one will not do. Let him join our squires over there!"

"Or better yet, put him in the stable by the look of him!" another spoke up at Dafydd's elbow.

Branwen recognized John of Erwodd, a year her senior and also knighted during the short war, although for what, she was at a loss to guess. He was hot-tempered and a poor sport who hated to lose. Bringing him along to London was not the smartest of ideas, but then Dafydd was not the brightest squire her father had trained. Boldness was his forte, and that, she thought, glancing at Wolf's unimpressed countenance, could be his undoing. The idea wasn't wholly disagreeable.

"He's my squire and he stays with me." Her companion's voice was thunderously quiet, but there was no question in anyone's mind that he would not be backed down without issue.

Not even Dafydd was foolish enough to push the hairy-faced mountain of a man further. He took his seat and motioned his companions to do the same, while the squires settled on the packed dirt floor around the fire. "You look the warrior, sir. How come you take such a peace-faced lad as squire? Was he orphaned?"

61

"In a manner of speakin'."

"Then it speaks well of you to take him in, considering a broad sword would never leave the ground in his hand."

"He'll do."

"Wench, where the devil is that ale?"

The plump tavern wench who had been eyeing Wolf all evening stepped between Dafydd and John to place a pitcher on the table, along with a stack of wooden noggins. " 'Twill only come so fast from the barrel, 'ansome," she quipped, leaning over as she poured, so that all had a prime view of her mounded breasts.

"Faith, I've changed my mind! 'Tis milk I'll have and right now!"

Dafydd grabbed the wench and pulled her down into his lap, nearly spilling the ale. With a growl, he buried his face in her bosom, exacting a shrill fit of giggles and a halfhearted struggle.

" 'Ere now, sir! I've work to do for the next few hours."

"And then?" Dafydd asked, picking up on the leading trail of her words.

"That all depends on how much coin ye lay in me hand. Ruthie does 'ave room for one more in me little cottage out back, but the lodgin' will cost ye, seein's 'ow it's better than a barn."

Branwen stared after the girl as she twisted her way back to the stack of barrels where the proprietor stood. Twisting was the only description she could come up with for the brazen sway of hips that commanded attention all around.

What did Dafydd see in the likes of that? she wondered in annoyance. She was unkempt, unwashed, and common as they came! Branwen doubted her hair had seen a comb since her mother last attended it, and chances were the most formidable vermin had made their home in it.

"What the devil are you staring at, runt?"

"It seems as though your choice of women is unseemly for a man of your station."

"Ho, where did you learn to speak so high and mighty?"

" 'Tis my own business," Branwen retorted smugly.

"And my women are mine!"

To think that she almost married this man! Branwen fumed silently. God only knew what infestations his indiscretions could have inflicted upon her! If her father knew of his wanton ways, he would surely have broken the engagement instantly.

"This man cannot help himself. The love of his life has been snatched from his very fingers," John pointed out wryly. He lifted his noggin high. "To the late and lovely Lady Branwen of Caradoc!"

"At least Kent will not have her," Dafydd muttered, joining in the toast.

Branwen took a sip of the ale, uneasy at toasting her own demise. Evidently, the news of the massacre had spread faster than she thought possible, given the time of year. Sparks of rebellion were undoubtedly already flying, if that were the case.

But it was Dafydd's reaction that shocked her the most, considering that the plea she'd sent to him to come to her aid and rescue her from the king's order had gone unanswered. Were his pledges of love and promises of marriage upon leaving at the beginning of the war sincere? Had he really pledged his heart to her? At the time, she had simply considered them more of Dafydd's meaningless rhetoric, for she already knew his interpretation of love was lust.

"Now there was a spirit, if ever there was one!" Dafydd went on.

" 'Twas not her spirit that interested you, young knight, but her body!"

Dafydd grinned widely. "Passion, good fellow. It fairly burned in her. My word, to turn it to the bed, rather than the games she was so fond of, might have made marriage well worth the wait."

"A fiery beauty, was she?" Wolf echoed thoughtfully.

"Aye, with a body that begged *come hither* and a temper that could flay a man alive! Not like yon wench there, mind you. She was sleek and firm, with ripe breasts that would just fit in a man's hand, not smother him alive."

"You speak as if you would know," John remarked skeptically.

"I spent long enough time in her father's castle to discover such things."

"That's a lie!" Branwen didn't realize she'd spoken her thoughts aloud until it was too late. All heads swung toward her.

"That's a big challenge for such a little man, boy," Dafydd charged irritably. From the glance he gave Wolf, the big mercenary at the boy's side weighed heavily in his decision not to cuff the youngster as deserved.

"I guess the lad don't take kindly to folks slanderin' his dead sister's name."

"Branwen has no brother! Damnation, why do you think she was such a prize? She had looks *and* land." Dafydd examined Branwen more closely. "Who the devil are you, boy?"

"Owen's bastard by a fisherwoman from Anglesey . . . Edwin, by name." Branwen swallowed, her mouth suddenly dry. The charade was over and at her own foolish invitation, if her ex-fiancé studied her too closely.

Dafydd laughed at the idea. "Owen ap Caradoc ne'er glanced at another woman."

" 'Twas no glance that conceived me, sir."

"He does look something like Branwen," the man beside Dafydd conceded.

"Maybe. He's as troublesome and outspoken," Dafydd replied dubiously. "You've no claim, you realize, boy. Owen's never acknowledged you. 'Twas me that should have inherited his daughter and his lands."

"I make no claims, save one: the right to bury my dagger in the heart of the man who killed Caradoc and his family." Branwen stopped and took a healthy sip of her ale as the entire room bust into laughter.

"Aye, he must be related to Branwen!" Dafydd guffawed loudly. "Looks, fire, and little wit!"

Branwen would have taken exception, but for the heavy hand that clenched her thigh, staying her. Wincing, she shot a furious look at Wolf, only to meet his warning one.

"And he does have her eyes, now that you mention it," the other man acknowledged, sobering. "They could set fire to a man's loins. You'd best be careful how you bat those long lashes of yours, boy. Were it not for yon wench, you'd serve well enough."

"In a dress, he'd be right pretty!" John chimed in with a wicked snicker.

"But I'd rather spread a pair of soft thighs than hard cheeks!" her ex-fiancé retorted, reaching behind him where Ruthie was putting more wood on the fire and running his hand up her dress familiarly.

"Ooh! I'd see your coin first, love!"

"Knew you the treat you had in store, sweet thing, you might pay me!"

To Branwen's further mortification, the woman ran her hand down the front of Dafydd's trousers and winked boldly. "We'll haggle this out later, love."

She'd never seen anything so disgusting, the way the woman's hand lingered. That Dafydd enjoyed it was even worse. Branwen had naively thought that smoldering light in his eye was reserved for her alone, but it seemed it was for anything with a skirt ... or without, she realized, recalling his comment about her. The very idea was as sickening as it was repugnant.

"Disgusting!" she muttered, tugging away from Wolf and climbing to her feet. "I'll be in the barn with the horses."

"They're not as good as a woman, boy!" Dafydd taunted, grinding his hips against the wench he pressed to the table.

"From the color of his face, he doesn't know, either," John of Erwodd joined in. "Which is best, lad? A warm wench or a braying—?"

Branwen stumbled out the door and into the cold night air, gasping deeply to quell her nausea. Behind her she could hear Dafydd ap Elwaid's "I think we've got us a virgin among us!" but her stomach was too queasy to muster further annoyance. Men were the most vile creatures in God's creation, she thought, making her way toward the stables in the moonlight, and Dafydd, for all his education, was more uncouth than even Wolf!

To Branwen's dismay, the following morning she discovered that Dafydd ap Elwaid and his entourage were traveling the rest of the way to London with them. Her only consolation was that the entire lot, Wolf included, suffered from too much ale and, after finding out all the details of Dafydd's night with Ruthie, retired to a relative silence.

It was humiliating enough to listen to the degrading description of what her aunt had called a beautiful act of love between two people, but the excess ale they'd consumed the night before demanded they stop so often, that by the end of the day, Branwen paid it no heed when one of the men jumped off his horse and tore open his drawers then and there. That, added to a juvenile contest among the squires to see who could belch the loudest or break wind the longest, was all the entertainment she could stand. For once in her life, she was glad to be a girl and above the crudity to which she was exposed.

It would have become unbearable, if not for Wolf. When the squires would not leave her be, he called them down. When she excused herself from the group with a scarlet face after some lurid and lascivious tale, he discouraged the taunts that followed. He explained her unorthodox behavior to the group as the result of seeing her family brutally murdered. As long as her peculiarities didn't bother anyone, they were to leave her be.

Nonetheless, Branwen could see them talking in low tones and watching her, which made privacy scarce and set her nerves on edge. The way they went on about needing a woman and the occasional winks they sent her way was enough to rob her of sleep each night until Wolf was settled by her side, her saddle pack wedged between them lest she relax and offend him as well.

The positive aspect of their travel, however, was the wonderful scenery. Accustomed to the rocky traeths and sharp jagged peaks of northwestern Cymry, this gentler country with its wattle and daub villages and commons was picturesque, even in winter. Stone fences showed the effort that went into clearing the fields for farming and pastureland. Fortresses, both new and in ruin, crowned hills and proclaimed a glory past and present.

The roads improved once they passed Coventry, some of them built by the Romans, according to Wolf, the only one who had traveled in this part of England before. Forests of hawthorn, elm, and oak spread out for miles at a span, cut by rivers and streams and cleared spaces marked by cathedrals, monasteries, and abbeys.

Peddlers bearing all manner of trinkets, ribbons, and other fancies to tempt a maid to part with her coin, minstrels and dancers, men of the cloth, and noblemen with their provision carts, pans clanging and banging on the sides, passed with more and more frequency the farther south they journeyed.

With London a day and a half away, they stopped at the small village of St. Bride. Located at the top of a gentle slope was an abbey, and below the village and commons itself was a crescent of buildings built of wood, mud, and stone. The street wound through it, no more than two carts' width, overhung by the second story of the structures on either side, so that its shadows simulated darkness when the sun dropped to the upper edge of the western horizon. At the southernmost edge, an old structure Branwen first thought a ruin boasted the traditional bush overhead proclaiming an ale house and a sign promising food, lodging and, of all things, baths!

Not believing her eyes, she followed her equally enthusiastic companions inside the first and most recently constructed part of the sprawling building, where food and drink abounded on each table. Serving girls, dressed well by most standards, flitted about from table to table to see that the trenchers and noggins were kept full. Wolf and Dafydd called one of the girls to the side and, after a short conversation, followed her through the door into another room.

Branwen was so intrigued by the uniqueness of the tavern that she hardly noticed the squires gathering together behind her, whispering in low conspiratorial tones. At the opposite end, built in stone, was a hearth as big as that of the great hall at Caradoc. On a giant spit turned a carcass of beef, enough to feed an army. Down the wall were stacked barrels of ale and mead, as well as bottles of wine. The opposite wall was lined with small perpendicular booths, raised like the dais in the hall and curtained for privacy. so that, short of peering around the edge of the curtains, it was impossible to see the diners within.

Surely, London itself could have nothing this grand, she thought, her attention drawn to the doorway where one of the servant girls motioned at her group to follow. Branwen stumbled forward at the ungentle push given by one of the worst of her tormentors, a squire called Tom Black, but righted herself before crashing into a group of foresters in brown and green enjoying wooden porringers of some sort of stew. Ignoring the amused chuckles behind her, she stepped into the next room and came to an abrupt halt.

There was no fireplace and yet the room, lit by a line of cressets around its perimeter, was warm. The domed ceiling, with cracked and indiscernible frescoes, had once had an opening in it, but appeared to have been covered with beams and thatching, reducing the loss of the heat rising visibly from the water in the great pool below it to a small vent she could make out. There, in the shallow man-made pool, men and women alike soaked in the steaming water, their goblets of wine and ale resting on the ledge along with towels and clothing.

"Be you the squires of yon gentlemen?"

"That we are, mistress!" Tom answered, assuming the role of speaker for the group.

"Then you are to come with me," the servant girl informed them, flashing a particularly winning smile at the tall, fair Tom. "Ye got yourselves good knights to see to your comfort like this. Me 'n' Katie will scrub ye from head to toe and see ye tucked in content as little lambs before the night's out. Now you just step in here and strip off your clothes whilst I fetch some towels."

"I don't want a bath!" Branwen asserted, backing away.

"Sure you do, wart!" Tom encouraged, grabbing her

69

arm with long, bruising fingers. "Anybody talks as fancy as you must be dying to scrub off that mud and dirt."

Branwen's heart swelled with the panic growing in her chest. "You go! I'll wait with the horses!"

"We *all* go, wart! Don't we lads?"

As if on cue, the other three boys latched on to Branwen's flailing limbs, laughing as she cried out for her mercenary friend.

"Him and Sir Dafydd and John got a woman each, but we're willin' to share our two with you, this bein' your first ti . . . ouch! Damn you, little beggar, I'll knock your teeth in if you bite me again!"

Branwen yelped as Tom cuffed her against the side of the head. "Wolf! Wooolllfff!" she screamed, kicking at the boys trying to yank off her trousers while the other two held her down.

"She said strip, and by God, you're not gonna ruin it for all of us!" Tom said, shoving one of her stockings in her mouth viciously.

"Hell, you ain't got nothin' we ain't got ourselves, Edwin."

Branwen drew back a free foot and sent one of her assailants flying back through the curtained wall into the main bathing room. She felt for the handle of her knife.

"You little bastard!" Tom growled, straddling her at the waist to hold her hips down. "I ought to knock you senseless and go on without . . . Gogsblood!"

"Tell them to get back!" Branwen warned, pressing the blade of the knife against his straddle threateningly. Her voice grew shrill with her hysteria, but her eyes burned with sheer fury, leaving no doubt that she would think nothing of making the young man astride her a eunuch with a single stroke of the blade she'd been practicing with each day.

"Get back!" Tom croaked, his own voice reaching a higher pitch than usual.

"Now get off me, you lily-livered dungheap, or you'll talk that way for the rest of your life!"

Branwen's breath was ragged as Tom eased up from her, his hands held high to show he meant no threat. Gradually, she sat up and scrambled back to the curtained wall. "I said I don't want a bath and I meant it, you lop-eared sons a' bitches. Now you can strip and whore all you want, but leave me the hell alone!" Her simmering gaze shifted from one to the other of the dumbfounded youths. "The Black Sow curse you all and all your seed!" she hissed.

As she stepped backward, instead of the swinging curtain that had been there before, Branwen struck an ungiving wall of muscle. Thinking yet another conspirator had sneaked up behind her, she swung about, only to have her waist captured by Wolf.

"Easy there, wart!" he warned good-naturedly. "I thought ye needed some help, but I can see ye've done fine without me. Now what's the problem? I thought ye might enjoy the luxury of a bath and a handsome wench to scrub your back."

"I am not taking my clothes off in front of the likes of them." Branwen glanced uneasily at Wolf. "Or you, for that matter. I . . . I have an affliction," she mumbled lowly.

Wolf exhaled with forced patience. "Ye are a queer one! What say ye to using my bath water, once me 'n' my scrubwoman are done with it?"

Branwen struggled with the temptation, her thoughts racing. "The water'll be cold."

"This water is from a hot spring, lad. Mother Earth keeps it warm. Who knows, maybe there's somethin' to the legend that it's healin' and your *affliction* will go away."

"Or at least his stench!" Tom derided irritably.

Branwen shrugged. "I guess it can't hurt."

"Then come with me," Wolf cajoled, his big hand resting on her shoulder as he ushered her out of the small enclosure. "Ye can wait outside the chamber till me 'n' the lady are finished. Then ye can bathe and dress and join the others in the tavern loft."

"Aren't you coming, too?"

Wolf leaned down and whispered wickedly. "She's a comely and warmhearted wench, lad. What do ye think?"

Branwen's lips thinned as her companion slapped her on the back heartily and chuckled. She seriously doubted that he wanted to know what she really thought, and even though his prospective night did not sit well with her, she dared not voice her opinion. After all, the big, brawny bear was her only friend in a hostile world where even her fellow Cymru seemed against her.

Chapter Five

Surrounding the main chamber were several lesser ones. It was beyond Branwen how the servants were spared carrying the water from one to the other, until Wolf pointed out to her the ingenious system of piping that made use of the central source of the mineral spring. It was also beyond her why the eroding columns that once bespoke great architecture did not fold and allow the entire ceiling to fall on the shameless goings-on. It seemed a pity that such a marvel as this was wasted on whoremongers.

From outside the curtained door of Wolf's chamber, she listened with interest to the conversation between him and his scrubwoman concerning the proprietor. A barber by trade, he had returned from the Holy Land and discovered what he'd thought at first a cave beneath the hill on which the monastery had been constructed. Inspired by his discovery and his exposure to the eastern baths, he set about reconstructing and shoring up, as best his means would allow, the original bath.

Everyone had laughed at him at first and called him mad, but the old adage of the one laughing last laughing the loudest proved true. With the bath at the crossing of three main roads, word of mouth had done the rest and he'd not had to work a day since, except to make certain his managers were not stealing from him.

"The good priests at the top of the hill sent word, I hear, to the Pope 'imself, callin' us blasphermers, but since the master started givin' regular to the church, we ain't 'eard no complaints since! Word is, some of the brothers themselves come down 'ere for medicinal reasons, seein's how the hill is blessed with the church atop it."

Corruption, Branwen thought, the word leaving a sour taste in her mouth. There was no end to it. It thrived in the church as well as in the courts and palaces. Had her father been the only just man left on this earth?

"Ooh, ain't we the bull now? Is all that for me?"

"If you're woman enough," came the husky reply.

"You just lay back, love, and I'll show ye, once'd I've scrubbed 'im clean."

Blushing profusely, Branwen looked away from the curtain. Gogsdeath, surely they weren't going to do what she thought they were talking about in the bath! A splash followed by a squeal of delight confirmed her suspicion and made her nose wrinkle in disgust.

" 'Ere now, ye've wet me clothes! I'd have taken 'em off!" the woman scolded halfheartedly.

"Then be quick about it, wench. 'Tis been too long since I've known a woman's comfort, and he'll not wait much more."

A good smack would teach the mangy beast some manners, Branwen mused in disdain. Wolf sounded as if it were on death's door, rather than eager for mischief. This was no bath house but a breeding stall! She pushed to her feet and walked down the length of the dimly lit corridor, where titters of laughter, both high and deep, erupted from time to time. There was nothing holy at all about this custom brought back from the Holy Land.

'Twas the devil's own work and none other, Branwen thought, crossing herself for protection.

A servant girl carrying a tray with remnant loaves of bread, chunks of cheese, and wine jugs nearly ran into Branwen at the intersection of the next corridor, ending her fervent prayer in a startled gasp. "Gogsbreath!"

"Here now, what takes you spying outside the bathin' chambers like this?"

"I'm waiting for my master as he told me to do . . . the big hairy bull in that one over there!" Branwen informed her, pointing a scornful finger toward the curtain of Wolf's chamber. "They were making so much noise, I thought I'd come down here where it was quieter."

A knowing smile graced the girl's lips. "I'll bet you're hungry."

Branwen looked at the tray, her stomach rumbling in response. In their haste to satisfy their more base hungers, the men had evidently forgotten food. She retrieved a small pouch containing the coins she'd earned with Wolf over the last few days. "How much?"

"Well, let's see what you got there."

"Is it enough for a bath *and* food?"

"Since your master's already paid his full fare, you can pay but half. I'll take two and leave you two," the girl answered, picking up half the coins and dropping them into a pouch tucked in her cleavage. "Step right in here, young sir."

Pleased that she was paying her own way, Branwen followed the girl inside the small chamber. Like the wall of private tables, it was canopied and enclosed, but instead of a table commanding the space beneath, a sunken pool did. Curious, Branwen rolled up her sleeve and stuck her hand in the water. It was more than elbow deep and warm. She felt around a little more until she found the pipe that, according to Wolf, fed off the main pool.

"Here you go, boy. I believe there's a bit of wine left in this cask to chase down the food." To Branwen's surprise, the girl plopped down in a mound of skirts by a small plank that served as a table, evidently designed for the bathers. "I ain't ate yet, neither. We been awful busy with travelers headed for London to see the Prince of Wales give his due to the king. There's goin' to be a tournament and a weddin', too. Seems like all the knights in the kingdom have been through here. Is your master one?"

"He's a mercenary," Branwen informed her, taking a seat on the masonry floor beside her. She broke off a piece of the bread and bit into it hungrily.

"You look Welsh, you know, with that dark hair and pretty blue eyes. Would you rather me fetch you some milk?"

Branwen dipped a used goblet into the water and swished it about to clean it before slapping it on the plank. "The wine will do."

Her voice had grown hoarse from keeping it low, so that her husky tone was no longer an effort but natural. In truth, she didn't mind the company of her own kind. At least she might relax a while. She wiped her hands on her pants while the girl filled the glass.

"We have a hot spring in a cave near Traeth Caradoc. I'd bet we could pipe the water into the castle from it and save having to heat it for baths."

The girl shook her head. "Not if it's very far. These here pools are built right over the spring. The further away the baths are, the cooler the water gets, leastways, in winter. You know," she giggled, her eyes raking over Branwen with interest, "you're supposed to undress before you eat. That's why the table is put to the edge of the tub."

Branwen scowled. "I do not eat naked!" She drew out her knife and carved a piece of cheese.

"Such pretty talk and manners! You've been brought up in the Great Hall, I'll wager."

"Aye."

"And you're traveling as squire for a mercenary? Where's he from?"

"Everywhere." Branwen appreciated the girl's kindness, but her incessant questions were beginning to wear thin.

"You ain't like the usual squire. Gawd, there's a bunch in a main pool raisin' all sorts of ruckus with Mary and Jeannie. You'd never know they had one bone of education save the one they're anxious to try on the girls."

"Heathens!"

"Like as not!" the girl chuckled, popping a piece of crust into her mouth. "Oh, the name's Mary Marie."

"Do people ever come here *just* to bathe, Mary Marie?"

The girl brushed her damp brown hair out of her face and grinned at Branwen smugly. "I thought so. That's why you put up such a fight a while ago, wasn't it? You ain't never had a woman."

"I've not missed it."

Branwen drained the wine from her goblet, a welcome change from the fermented ale and almost as warming as the water that heated the place. She couldn't think why it had never occurred to her to use the pool in the cave for a bath, rather than heat pots of water to fill the screened-in wooden tub she usually resorted to. The hot spring would be perfect, even in winter when it was impossible to find the great hall empty enough to suit her. That is, if she ever found her way home again.

"I'm surprised some lusty maid hasn't treated you to

one of life's sweetest pleasures, handsome as that face is."

"Good cheese." Branwen was beginning to feel uncomfortable with the way Mary Marie was ogling her.

"More wine, love?"

She shoved her goblet forward, trying to think of something to change the subject. Sweet Jesus, she'd not counted on *this!* "You got a family?"

"Aye, a father. He runs this place for Master James. Me an' me sisters usually do the cookin', but I help in the baths sometimes. You want me to help you undress?"

"I'll do it myself when I'm finished eatin'."

"Well now ... what is your name, boy?"

"Edwin."

"Well now, Edwin," Mary Marie began, uncommonly pleased about something. "Where will you be sleeping tonight?"

"With the others in the loft."

Actually, Branwen intended to sneak out to the barn. She had no intention of sharing a loft with Tom and his cohorts without Wolf nearby.

Mary Marie leaned forward, her full breasts teetering precariously at the edge of her loosely gathered bodice. "Tell me, Edwin, do you like ... *girls?*"

Warily, Branwen backed away from the foul breath that assaulted her nostrils as the girl all but crawled over the table. "They'll do." She shoved the forward servant backward and snatched up the last of the cheese attempting to finish it before she made the wench angry enough to take it away.

"I don't think you do. I think you left your master's chamber because you were jealous."

"You're crazy!" Branwen derided. "Jealous of *that* giggling tart?"

"A boy like you could make good money here,

78

Edwin. There's plenty men would pay well to get at a pretty peach-faced lad such as yourself." Mary Marie snickered as Branwen choked on the wine she'd just sipped. "It ain't no shame. Papa says a lot of men . . ."

Branwen jumped to her feet and slung the goblet down. Wiping her mouth with the back of her hand, as if her companion's suggestion had not only insulted her but left a contemptible taste as well, she glared at the girl. "A pox on you, bitch!"

"If you've such a distaste for men, then prove yourself to me . . . *boy,*" Mary Marie challenged, reaching down and lifting her skirt to reveal a slender white thigh.

"Go to hell!" Branwen spat, slinging aside the curtain and marching outside the close quarters.

Jealous! By God, all she felt was pure contempt for the likes that frequented this place. She had no need of a man and she sure as the devil didn't want a woman! The high laughter that echoed behind her followed her down the corridor to where Wolf had been. She hesitated at the curtained entry, faced with yet another quandary, when it was yanked aside abruptly.

"Where the devil have you been? I've had to stay here to keep the chamber for you!"

Branwen stood agape at the gleaming rugged male torso standing before her with naught but a towel girded about his waist, until she heard the taunting voice of Mary Marie a short distance away.

"Good night, *Edwin!*"

Her face fairly burned with the fire of embarrassment as Wolf looked beyond her to the retreating figure of the servant girl and erupted in amusement. "Ho, so there is more of you than meets the eye!"

"Laugh, will you?" she charged irritably, brushing by. "From the noise you were making, I couldn't tell if you were enjoying yourself or dying, so I went to fetch a bloody priest!"

The enclosure was much the same as the one she'd just left. There was even food and wine on the plank. A single candle provided light, not a tallow dip but one of real wax, indicative of the success of the establishment. Only on the most special of occasions did her mother use the wax candles!

"Ha, you're craftier than I thought, lad!"

"If you are in such a hurry to get back to your whore, then get you gone and leave me be! I've had all the debauchery I can stand for one day."

Wolf stood magnificent, legs braced and arms crossed as he mocked, "Don't tell me. You're bound for the monastic life *after* you murder Ulric of Kent, that is."

"Better that than what *she* was suggesting!" Branwen blurted out, denouncing the *she* as if it were a curse. "She thought . . . that is, I . . . she wanted me to *work* here, and I do not mean serving the wine and food, either!" Her fury only added fuel to her companion's amusement. "You hairy bastard, it's not funny . . . it . . . it's debauched!"

Wolf made an attempt to sober and poured a goblet of wine. "Drink this and calm down, lad. I promise to rescue ye from this pit of passion when mornin' comes."

"And I won't sleep with those mangy squires, either! I'll be in the barn when you're finished and ready to travel again."

Her companion shrugged. "Suit yourself, lad. I'll be ready to go with the rising of the sun."

The parting glance Branwen gave him was enough to convince her that he was capable of keeping a woman company all night and being fit for travel the next day. Wolf was exactly as she'd imagined, all muscle and sinew, devoid of excess flesh. This Wolf of Everywhere was a man's man . . . and a woman's, she thought, her face growing warm as she recalled the servant wench's reference to another part of his anatomy that must have been just as well proportioned.

She banished the thought instantly with an oath. This den of inequity was beginning to infect her with its moral decay. After making certain that the curtain was fixed so that no one passing by might glance in, she began to strip off the clothes she'd donned too many days ago. Ideally, she would launder at least the outer and innermost layer, but that was out of the question. Instead, she wiped off the mud with one of the damp towels Wolf must have used, until it was presentable. After hanging it up on the curtain, she slipped out of the shift she'd kept stuffed in her trousers and into the water.

It was delightfully warm compared to the cooler air that assaulted her naked skin, but before she would sit down, she held the candle over it for an inspection, unable to dismiss from her mind what had gone on in it less than a hour earlier. It was remarkably clear, swept in through a pipe at one end and out through the same at the opposite. Amazed at the ingenuity, she sank down into the tiled pool and sighed contentedly.

In order to soak, Branwen had to slide down the tilted back with bent knees so that her back and shoulders might experience the healing qualities of the warm mineral water. Her breasts, round and erect, rose above the surface like rose-tipped islands, hardly enough to smother a man, she thought, recalling Dafydd's lewd description of her. How on earth had he known that?

Branwen dropped down lower so that she was able to wet her hair, discovering as she did the soap that had grazed her thigh beneath the water. It was obvious the servant didn't care that the soap would waste away in the water. She'd been too busy placating Wolf to return it to the crude marble bowl designed to hold it.

It was indeed a treat after the plain concoction made by the servants at Caradoc. Pleasantly scented with spices rather than the flowers of a gift Tâd had once brought her from France, she worked it into a lather and placed it in the dish to rinse off. Much the same as the plainer bar, however, some of the lather managed to get in her eyes when she washed her hair, forcing Branwen to reach for the one remaining clean towel that had been left folded by the tub.

Naturally, her blind groping found the bar of soap, requiring her to rinse her hand off before continuing along the ledge toward the linen. Instead of soft dry toweling, however, she found the unmistakeable flesh of a foot—a rather large foot and not of the stone belonging to some of the broken statues that graced the main chamber. Before she could reason out the consequences of her discovery, a downpour of water washed over her head, bringing her upright in shock!

"What the devil . . . ?"

Blinking the water from her eyes, she squinted upward, preparing to give the servant a piece of her mind, but instead of a female, the unmistakably masculine form of Wolf hovered over her. The flickering candle behind him made him seem twice his size.

" 'Tis some *affliction* ye've got, lad," he enunciated wryly. "What are ye, one o' them half-man half-woman creatures?"

Branwen snatched up her knees and hugged them to her chest as the mercenary peered over the edge of the tile to check out the half beneath the water. "Have you no regard for privacy!"

His voice still full of wonder, Wolf held out the bucket he'd dumped over her head. "I brought this back thinkin' ye could use it. I thought for a minute you were drownin', and then I saw two of the finest breasts I've been privileged to witness . . . ripe, firm . . . *just big enough to fit in a man's hand.*"

Branwen glared at him as he dropped to his knees,

showing no inclination to leave. "*Lady* Branwen, I am most honored to make your acquaintance. It explains many things, I can tell ye. I eagerly await to hear the rest of your explanation."

"You'll hear naught from me, sir, until you quit this room and leave me to bathe in peace. 'Tis the least you owe me after driving me like a slave these past days and acting the crude oaf. I vow a man will relieve himself anywhere, anytime! Never have I . . ." Her voice trailed off as the big man stepped into the tub. "Wh . . . what do you think you are doing?"

"Penance, milady. Far be it from me to have ye suffer to bathe without assistance."

Branwen huddled against the wall of the tub as small as she could make herself. She wished one of the cracks running along the edge of the tiles in the floor would open up and swallow her, or she'd be sucked into one of the aqueducts. Anything was better than the position she found herself in. The water level rose, indicating her companion not only intended to scrub her, but join her as well!

"I am done, sir!" she whispered urgently, scrambling in panic to get out and wrap the towel she grabbed about her, before all semblance of dignity was denied.

"Faith, 'tis true!" Wolf exclaimed, one hand securing Branwen by the waist and the other clamping over her mouth as she screamed in outrage. "Shush, milady, or your secret will be out for all to see! I can't help but wonder what yon Dafydd would think to see his beloved so very much alive and kicking!"

Branwen shook with the dour amusement of the man who settled against the slight incline of the tub with her back pressed to his ridged and sinewy torso. He at least had a towel about him, while she was as mother naked as she'd been at birth!

"Now will ye keep a civil tongue or will you have witnesses to the *unveiling* of your charade?"

Unable to answer for the smothering hand, Branwen nodded and ceased to struggle.

"Ah, Edwin, Edwin, Edwin . . ." Wolf tutted, keeping his arm about her waist lest she attempt to escape before he was done with her. "Ye make a finer woman than a boy any day. What possessed ye, *lad?"*

Arms crossed over her breasts, Branwen mumbled lowly, "I thought 'twas the safest way to travel, but I have had more than one occasion to see the error of my decision since our first meeting."

It was some moments before her companion regained his composure from the body-shaking mirth that rocked them both. Branwen was torn between being relieved the anger she'd seen lurking amidst his utter astonishment had seemingly faded and furious that he found her predicament so damned amusing.

"If you were any kind of gentleman, sir, you would unhand me and permit me to make myself decent."

"But, as you well know, milady, I am not. Faith no, I expect to make the most of this delightful surprise."

"You've already had a woman!" Branwen reminded him acidly as he began to rub the soap on her back briskly. "And I don't need help!" Her skin shriveled at the touch of his rough hand upon her back as he vigorously worked the soap into a lather.

"Ah, but by your own admission, you do, milady," Wolf reminded her. "You have yet to polish your skill with your father's blade."

Her heart beat so rapidly, she could hardly summon her voice. No man had ever treated her so . . . so boldly. She felt self-conscious enough with the women servants who drew her bath! "Then at least afford me the dignity of a towel, sir. I am not accustomed to sharing a bath with anyone, let alone a big bully of a man! If . . ."

The appearance of a towel in front of her face cut her off abruptly. "Lift your arms and I'll wrap it about you."

The breath warming the back of her neck made her shiver as she spoke. It was no taunt, this, but a devastating caress without so much as a touch. A man's man, she recalled . . . and a woman's. With the indifference of her maidservant, Wolf shook the towel out and wrapped it about her snugly, but the deep seductive quality of his voice was far from indifferent.

"Ye've skin soft as a babe's cheek, lass, but I suppose ye know it."

"Save your sweet words for your tavern wenches, sir. I'll talk naught but business with you." As if she had a choice, Branwen realized in frustration. He'd made it plain she was not to escape until he was done with this sense-riddling madness.

He rubbed the soap up and down her arms, evoking charges of unsolicited delight that spread throughout her body. Her loins were flushed with a new and disconcerting warmth. Never in her life had she felt so . . . so vulnerable. It was as if the closeness of his virile body and bold manner were awakening a woman in her she hardly knew.

"Business, ye say. Well, I'm a man of business. What is it ye'd discuss?"

Branwen forced herself to think, seizing upon the first thing that came to mind. "I want you to kill Ulric of Kent for me."

His fingers began a mind-boggling massage that under any other circumstances might have been most welcome to her tense neck and shoulders. "And what will you pay me?"

"I . . . um. . . . I will have money later. I have proof of his treachery." Damn the wine and a stomach pitifully teased with tidbits of food that resulted in her head lolling back, as if she were enjoying this insulting outrage!

"So you can marry Dafydd as planned, and then he'll own you *and* your possessions? Perhaps we should discuss this with him first."

Branwen jerked away, clinging to her towel, but Wolf was quicker. His fingers managed to grasp her shoulders in spite of the slick lather. "Damn Dafydd ap Elwaid and all the Welsh knights! They would not help me when I sent for them. They speak of me as if I were some tavern slut in lies that foul the very breath with which they tell them. Dafydd . . . Dafydd doesn't know me anymore!"

A sob caught in her throat, taking her unawares. Was she always to be the victim? First, fate's wicked plan to marry an enemy, then Dafydd's cowardice and the murder of her family, and now this shameful body that would not heed her fierce orders to ignore the delicious sensations sweeping through her! Gogsbreath, she would not cry! Turning to face her companion, she swallowed her frustration and grief bravely.

"I have no one, sir, to stand for me . . . no one."

Having no one on which to lean was as new to her as having to beg for help. She fixed a beseeching gaze on his face, noticing for the first time that her companion's straggly beard and hair had been trimmed. Now the beard conformed to the masculine taper of his chin, and his dark golden locks curled at his wide, unencumbered shoulders. Across a furred chest was a ragged scar, delivered no doubt by the blade of a sword. Smaller ones were raised here and there, telling of punctures that may have downed a lesser man. Had he shown any of his victims mercy? she wondered.

She tucked her wet hair behind her ears self-consciously and cleared her throat. "I held my parents' heads in my lap. I wrapped my maid in my cloak to hide her nakedness, but first . . ." She sniffed and looked away. "First, I had to remove the spears with which they'd impaled her to the ground for sport. Of course, that was after they'd slit her throat and raped her. They thought . . ." Branwen shuddered violently. "They thought she was me. They . . . they'd even put my bridal veil on her in the vilest mockery." Branwen's fists clenched on the edge of the towel, an outward sign of the inner struggle that held tears suspended in her eyes. "Can you not see why I want the man responsible brought to justice for this, sir?"

For just the slightest span of time, Branwen thought she had at last won an ally. Was it the flame of the candle that reflected in his eyes, or had she struck a sympathetic nerve? She looked away, again nervous, as the same gaze raked over her not once, but twice, as if he still needed to confirm what he saw.

"My only obligation to you, milady, is to teach ye to use the knife as I promised. But I am not fool enough to let a tearful confession, much as it touched my heart, send me off to fight a man of Kent's repute. Not without payment in advance."

Branwen climbed to her feet, her chin tilted in defiance. She should have known better than to appeal to his sympathy. No doubt he'd traded that off long ago to keep it from interfering with his sense of survival. "Then I'll do it myself, sir, for I am not lacking in courage."

"Only good sense." Wolf motioned her to sit back down. "Relax, milady. This may well be the last bath you ever enjoy."

" 'Tis hard to enjoy with the likes of you fouling the water. Can I trust you to keep my charade a secret but one more day, or will you brag as yon Dafydd that you, too, are privy to my charms?"

"What gives me pleasure is no one else's business, milady. Your secret is safe with me."

"At what price?" Branwen sneered skeptically.

Wolf hooked his finger in the front of her towel and pulled her forward. "A kiss . . . to seal the secret."

Branwen felt as if the wine she'd consumed had dropped to the lowermost part of her body, infecting her with a most wanton reaction to a suggestion her mind found ludicrous. She'd been a fool to trust this man who was on his way to sell himself to the king. Who was to say he wouldn't kill her and claim some prize for it . . . after satisfying the hunger that had begun to glow in his assessing gaze?

She kept her towel pulled tightly to her breast as he eased her toward him. The water between them was warm, but warmer still was the body that grazed her tensed one and coaxed her against it, until only the arms she stretched out to brace herself on either side of the sunken tub kept her from total surrender. She was unaware of the fetching view presented by the drooping towel, only of the amber-green eyes that had taken on a glow brighter than the flickering candle mirrored in them.

A tongue, just the very tip, appeared to moisten the anxious lips framed by mustache and beard, jolting her with a shudder not unlike anticipation. Branwen clenched her teeth to stop the reaction before it carried her off, when her knees slipped on the bottom tile and she plunged face first against his broad chest.

"Oh!" Losing her hold on the tub, she found herself with her arms wrapped about Wolf's neck and his banded about her waist, so that she knew the full extent of his need pressing hard against her abdomen through the wet towels. "Damn you, if you think to claim more than a kiss, think twice, sir!"

" 'Tis for you to decide, milady, after I've shown you what it's like to be kissed by a real man and not one who needs brag of his conquests to appear one."

A real man. The words rang true to the woman within her, beckoning unreasonably for her to test his word and frightening her with its powerful persuasion. There were two camps battling in her mind for supremacy, and the one she recognized was weakening with each passing moment, each word of promise, each birdlike beat of her heart.

Hypnotized by the spell she watched until his lips claimed hers in a hungry caress that demanded surrender . . . a surrender she could not afford, she told herself in a panic. He had scorned her for asking him to fight for her and yet expected her to submit to his manliness without question, like the wench he'd just taken earlier. Nay, worse, he intended to pay with naught but his own satisfied lust.

The parting of her lips to the sweet, tenacious assault of Wolf's tongue sent flares of warning and promise to every nerve center, invoking panic and confusion in Branwen's bedeviled brain until she, too, felt the urgency he was imparting to her. It was now or never, she thought, reaching clumsily for the soap dish. Her fingers closed on it as if it were a lifeline, and reason took heart. Without warning, she brought the dish down on the back of Wolf's damp head with a flesh-crunching thud.

Branwen gasped as the heavy dish fell away from her hand but she remained frozen, her eyes widening before his startled ones. At first, she'd thought she'd seen her own death burst into flames within the dark orbs, and then, like a curtain, his eyelids fell and he collapsed against the tiled incline with a groan. As his arms dropped away from her, she scrambled to her feet and stepped out of the tub.

What in heaven's name was she going to do now? she wondered, drying off briskly with a semi-damp towel she found lying near the table. She hadn't meant to hurt him, but had she not stopped his bone-melting seduction when she did . . .

In the corner of her eye, Branwen spied Wolf moving. Thinking him about to retaliate she stepped back in alarm, only to exhale in relief upon realizing it was only his dead weight carrying him down into the water. Gogsbreath! she swore silently, moving to the edge of the tub to stop him from drowning, when his feet lodged against the opposite end of the tub. The uncommon length of his outstretched legs prevented him from going down further. Hands trembling visibly, she set about donning her clothing.

If she were still there when he came around, he'd kill her, she thought, panicked. She dared not stay, but leaving in the middle of the night was not much more appealing. Neither was trying to explain why she'd done such a thing, when she didn't understand it herself. She'd felt so out of control, so helpless and yet eager at the same time. He'd spoken of the danger of her carrying out her plan to kill Kent, but Wolf had posed a far more dangerous adversary. Ulric of Kent might claim her body and lands, but this mercenary had somehow unlocked the way to her very soul.

Chapter Six

Blood! God, if she never saw another drop of it, it would be too soon! Unless it was Ulric of Kent's, Branwen reasoned, summoning the thirst for vengeance that had kept her going the last three days to renew her fatigued state of mind and body. Damnation, Wolf had been breathing when she left him. She'd bandaged the back of his head where the marble dish had left a bloody gash. That was all the devil deserved for his bold treatment of her.

So why did he keep haunting the little bit of sleep she'd stolen the last three nights, making the day travel all the more trying? She'd had to catch herself more than once to keep from falling off McShane's back after nodding off. Gogsbreath, he even haunted her daydreams, those moments of stupor when McShane instinctively made his own way because she was too spent to think beyond staying in the saddle. He deserved more than a knot on the head, she decided once again, having lost count of the times she'd come to the same conclusion.

It was hard enough being a stranger in a strange land without the haunting guilt she felt over Wolf robbing her of the rest. There were many similarities to Wales, but there were many differences, too. At least at home, she knew the people and felt able to judge their intentions. Here, everyone appeared suspect.

McShane, a fine horse by any standard, drew many curious eyes, particularly since a mere boy rode him. She'd finally had to resort to yet another lie to maintain her charade. The horse was not hers but that of her master's. She was to deliver him to London for the tournament. So far, it had gotten her by, but not without dubious looks.

Had she taken a lesser horse, things surely would have gone easier. Once she'd convinced those who questioned her that she had not stolen the animal, Branwen had to be wary of those who eyed the magnificent charger with greed. Hence, at night, after using the last of her coins to pay for food, she slept with McShane in whatever shelter the ale or cook houses afforded, her hand resting on the hilt of the knife she still practiced with.

The stallion was more than just a means of transportation. He was her father's horse, the only living thing left of Owen ap Caradoc. It was childish sentiment born of the desperation of her plight, perhaps, but she could talk to McShane, rely on his strength, and see understanding and sympathy in his doe-brown eyes. Her companion sustained her when fear threatened to leave her undone.

A group of entertainers bound for the Christmastide pageant, whom she met the second day on the road when her funds were expended, offered to keep her company until they reached London. In exchange for gathering wood and helping with their horses, they shared their sparse food and camaraderie. They were a gay lot with an ounce of pity for a lone youth, surprising Branwen, who had heard of their profession's lowly character. Now, however, they were on their way to the northwest side of the Tower walls where they intended to camp, leaving her to oblige her story of taking McShane to Smithfield, where the stables usually set aside for livestock sale were filled with the steeds of the knights who had come for the tournament.

Over a scatter of huts, buildings, and tents, the walls of London loomed, holding her fate within. It was so vast compared to the villages near Caradoc. In the midst of the lowliest hovels, complete with pungent pigsties and livestock sheds, were walled-in gardens and orchards belonging to noble houses, miniatures of keeps that looked far more hospitable in comfort and accommodation than their larger models. The very idea of such a thing only confirmed her opinion that the English nobility had more money than good judgment and a decided impairment of their sense of smell. Faith, if she ever found her way home to Caradoc again, she hoped Ulric's men had not moved the livestock pens next to the keep.

Her sense of superiority was not sufficient, however, to ward off the intimidation of the great city. While she knew English as well as her own language, there were tongues being spoken about her that were totally foreign! Branwen fought increasing anxiety as she sought anything familiar. Where was the Welsh entourage that had arrived a week earlier? she wondered, scanning the banners flying over the tents for familiar heraldry or colors.

It had never occurred to her that London would be so big. She'd thought finding the king and Llewelyn would be as easy as spotting Caradoc's keep in the distance. Buildings as large as the castle with its bailey rose along the entire southern horizon. They couldn't all be cathedrals, she mused, appalled at the idea that English could be that pious. London looked as if every village in the cantref, perhaps in all of Wales, had been thrown together. Gogsbreath, she'd never seen such an impressive sight! And the people! Every noble in England must be there, his vassals as well!

Excitement began to replace her anxiety as she became lost in the chaos surrounding the outer walls of the city. Near the edge of what appeared a fairlike green, browned and spotted with winter-stripped trees and iced-over ponds, was a group of young men skimming over a frozen marsh, just as she and her friends were wont to do in her homeland. Drawn by the familiar sight, Branwen rode McShane over to a tree and tethered the stallion to watch the curious play they were about.

Strapped to their feet were shinbones of animals, and in their hands were iron-shod poles with which the more daring propelled themselves headlong into each other. The clashes were ferocious, often sending both adversaries sprawling on their backs and skidding apart like curled stones. Nearby, spectators watched and cheered, seated on great chunks of stone resembling mill wheels.

Bonfires and cressets here and there offered warmth, which Branwen sought out immediately. Her stomach rumbled as the smells of the hot bread and pastries drifted over from a small cluster of buildings inhabited by bakers, spicers, and pepperers. A cookhouse added the aroma of roasting beef and fowl, no doubt purchased from the slaughterhouses she'd passed at Newgate or the hovels belonging to the poulterers and skinners. Next to that, an alehouse boomed with revelry, which contributed to the festive air.

It would be dark soon, and Branwen was going to have to find some place that would take in a penniless boy. Trying to ignore the pangs of hunger that assaulted her stomach, she looked around the panorama of activity, her gaze returning to the fields beyond, where tents were set up for the attendants to the chargers stabled for the tournament. As she considered the possibilities, a familiar whinny drew her attention to the tree where she'd tethered McShane.

There, two soldiers were admiring the stallion and looking about, as if seeking its owner. Or checking to see if they might walk off with as handsome a horse as money could buy, Branwen thought, breaking away from the group around the fire to make her presence known. By the time she reached the horse, the men had already untied the leather reins.

"Hello there! Where are you off to with my horse?"

The two men stopped and stared at the breathless, flushed-faced youth standing obstinately before them.

"*Your* horse, ye say?" one of them challenged.

Branwen nodded. "Aye, mine . . . that is, my master's horse. I'm to take care of it until he arrives."

"And just who is this master, lad?"

"Lord Owen of Caradoc."

"A *Welshman!*" the other derided under his breath.

Branwen checked the rise of indignation in her veins. "On his way to join his prince. I would be obliged if you gentlemen would show me where Prince Llewelyn and his entourage are keeping their steeds."

"Anywhere they can, like as not. Most folks about here are particular about the kind of *animals* they'll keep."

"If that be so, sirs, how come the likes of you are allowed about?"

Dodging the backhand that swung awkwardly toward her, Branwen sprang onto McShane's back and kicked the stallion urgently. Responding to her plight, the horse reared at the soldier trying to hold its reins, its hooves pawing dangerously in the air until the man darted out of the way with a curse, abandoning his attempt altogether.

"Stop that thief!" the first man shouted, as McShane pivoted on his hind feet and bolted off away from the thickness of the hubbub around the outer wall of the city.

Until that moment, Branwen hadn't realized how many soldiers were milling about, enjoying the Christmastide celebration and keeping order. Before she could turn the stallion away from a group that charged her head-on, another jumped from out of nowhere and snatched her by her belt from McShane's back. Her angry gasp was cut off in a pained grunt as he slung her down on the hard ground. Suddenly, her hair was being pulled viciously, bringing her up to her feet in a blaze of pain.

"Where'd you get a horse like this, boy?"

"I . . . I told you! It belongs to Owen of Caradoc!" Tears stung her eyes and burned her cheeks, in spite of her efforts to hold them back. Gogsbreath, she'd be bald at this rate!

"Why would he part with a steed like this?" her tormentor sneered skeptically.

Branwen was on the verge of blurting out the real reason her father did not accompany his beloved horse, but it was too soon. She needed the chance to get at Kent before the news of his treachery was out and mutual suspicion made English and Welsh alike wary. "It's a gift!"

"A gift? Whose gift?"

Branwen closed her eyes, her teeth clenched to keep from crying out. "To Ulric of Kent . . . his future son-in-law!" To her relief, the pressure on her hair was released. It was obvious, when she could bring herself to observe her captors, that they had heard of Kent, if not the wedding.

"Kent's horse, ye say?"

"A gift . . . to be presented at the wedding. I'm to care for it until then."

One of the others laughed in the background. "When

96

them milk-drinkers surrender, they do it right enough! This'll match any English charger."

"It probably *is* one . . . stolen from a marcher lord," another quipped. "Ye know how them Welsh'll steal."

"If you English knew the meaning of hospitality, we might not be so forced. I've just arrived in a strange town with Kent's wedding gift and been treated like a thief, rather than offered a hot meal and a warm place to bed down until my master and the bride arrive. 'Twas the warmth of yon fire I was seeking when you tried to take my horse."

"How do we know ye speak the truth?"

"Caradoc's crest is a raven on a scepter," Branwen answered stiffly. "Look on the horse's coat." Her mother had embroidered the insignia on McShane's scarlet and black blanket.

"It's some kind a' black bird. I guess it's a raven."

" 'Tis bad luck to cross a raven, bad as that of the black sow."

The man fingering the finely woven cloth dropped it as if it had burned him, giving rise to laughter amongst his peers. "That's a lot of wash, Wilfred! Ye know how superstitious these Welsh are."

"The black sow ain't just Welsh. My mother . . ."

"What will it be, gentleman? Will you show me where to quarter the horse and fill my belly, or will the bridegroom hear how his father-in-law's envoy was insulted by the sheriff's men?"

The soldier who had avoided the pawing stallion's hooves, exchanged an uneasy look with his companion. "He does speak awful fittin' to be a common thief. He's been raised with books, proper as he is."

"With Welsh princes, outspoken and bold to boot!" another agreed derisively.

"I ain't gonna make Kent mad. If there was anythin'

left of me when 'e was done, the King would finish it off."

"But we'll be keepin' an eye on ye, boy," the one called Wilfred warned her. "If ye try to take that horse away from here, your head'll be hangin' on the tower gate before sundown of the next day. Understand?"

Relief flooding through her, Branwen nodded. Once again, she'd survived by sheer wit and determination. She'd managed to travel from the wilds of Snowdonia to the great city of London intact, despite crossing an ill-tempered and woman-starved mercenary and the King's guards.

That awful night she had left Wolf behind and traveled by moonlight, she'd wondered if she'd ever see daylight again, much less make it to London. Yet, somehow, she'd been spared the attack of the wolves howling in the distance and the preying bands of human ones to whom life held no value. She offered a quick prayer of thanks and fell in behind Wilfred, who led her north toward the livestock area that would be her quarters for the night.

"I . . . I hate to cause you more trouble after our misunderstanding, but I haven't eaten since early this morning and am fair starved. I was set upon by villains last night who robbed me of my last pence." As if to demonstrate, Branwen shook out her empty purse. "I would remember you well to Lord Owen, Wilfred sir, if you would remedy my hunger."

The soldier stopped so abruptly that Branwen nearly ran into him. With a scowl that showed his displeasure, he stomped over to where a woman with a tray of some sort of pastry hawked her wares. Her shrill voice resounded in protest as he snatched one of the small pies up and offered her a rough "King's business!" for compensation.

"Ye'll get your own drink, lad. I've work to do besides wet-nursin' the likes of you."

Finding drink proved easier than Branwen thought. Once McShane had been stabled in a lean-to shelter filled with hay, she wandered over to another shelter where cows had been brought in for the auction to take place the following day. There a young boy about her own age was busy milking. Branwen offered to help in exchange for filling her goatskin, a deal that provided each of them company into the night.

The boy, named Nathan, worked for the seller who owned the stables and kept the animals while their owners sought lodging in the hovels nearby. He was to keep the lanterns burning throughout the night and watch for thieves, although the sheriff assigned men to the grounds the day before the sale was to take place. It was just the beginning of activities scheduled for Christmastide.

Balls, parties, and pageants would occupy the nobility from the Tower to Westminster, while the common folk would enjoy their share of entertainment as well. It was like walking from one fair to another and another with costumed mummers raising as much devilish revelry as the carolers raised holy spirit. Every kind of entertainer within traveling distance was in London for the following fortnight or so.

As Branwen listened, she could hardly imagine such pageantry on the scale the boy described. There were small fairs in the different commotes around Caradoc, but this was as large as the city of London itself. Even at night, the cluster of buildings outside the great wall was alive with people making their way from tavern to tavern. Surely people from all over the world lived there.

"There's people from everywhere 'ere," Nathan confirmed. "We got Italians, French, Germans, and some I don't think kin even understand each other!"

Off in the distance, laughter and singing had replaced the hawking noises of the street vendors, and a few lanterns cast scant light on the alleys between the shacks and buildings. Shops were boarded up and dark, their proprietors resting for the next day of business. From the stables, contented whinnies and snorts of the horses blended with the mournful sound of cows bound for sale at daybreak.

In the midst of it all, eager as she was to hear all about this novel town and its inhabitants, Branwen began to feel the oppression of her fatigue gaining on her. She was just about to tell her new friend good night and retire to the shed where McShane was stabled, when she heard an outbreak of shouts coming from a tavern on the edge of the township.

"Clubs! Clubs!"

"Oh, boy, c'mon!" Nathan exclaimed, abandoning his stool and bucket in a mad dash toward the ruckus.

More wary, Branwen followed, keeping her distance. Her caution proved wise, for just as Nathan reached the tavern door, it burst open with a wave of men entangled in what appeared a full-fledged brawl. The boy barely escaped the moving multi-headed monster with its flailing arms, kicking legs, and clubs, which consisted of any cudgel that could be broken off and wielded against an opponent.

The soldiers who had so readily apprehended her earlier that day took longer to appear to break up the fight. At first it seemed that they were merely adding to the fury, until their mounted counterparts emerged from within the walls of the city brandishing swords and riding right into the mass to bring the fray to an end. To the ringing of church bells, which Nathan told her upon returning marked the curfew to be off the streets, the

100

soldiers hauled the small group of pepperers and spicers, who had come to blows and started the brawl, off to the Tower, while the luckier combatants who had taken sides made their way home.

With all the thrills she could bear in one day behind her, Branwen bade her friend good night and wandered into the stable, where McShane waited patiently. At one end was a large haystack, where she made up a bed with her blankets for the night. She had no right to find the enemy's capital so intriguing, she thought guiltily as she tried to unwind from all that had happened the last few hours. Yet, for a short while she had been so diverted that she'd nearly forgotten her purpose in being there.

She had a task to do, a mission of vengeance to complete. Her mother and father were cold as the hard ground beneath her mattress of musty-smelling hay, murdered by a man who no doubt made merry in the luxury of an elegant hall, warmed by a hearthfire, strong ale, and a willing wench. He was likely drinking to the family he had betrayed as if he looked forward to their arrival, all the while knowing it would not happen. Gogsdeath, just think of the uproar when the news arrived about Owen!

All she had to do was get to Ulric of Kent before Dafydd, not to mention the undoubtedly retaliation-starved Wolf, arrived to put everyone on guard against treachery from any quarter. She glanced over at her father's stallion, its sturdy muscled hindquarters outlined in the flickering torchlight outside. Perhaps McShane would provide the means. She'd send word to Kent in the morning to come see the gift his father-in-law had sent in advance of his arrival . . . before the overlord's murderous blasphemy had been carried out. Her hand went to the hilt of her dagger. It would work, she told herself tiredly. It had to. Time was running out.

Had she been conscious, it wouldn't have surprised her that Wolf came to haunt her dreams again, nor that guilt accompanied him. This time, however, it was guilt of a different nature, for instead of bloodying his head with a soap dish, she hadn't stopped his soul-robbing kiss. She'd allowed him to continue, and the result had left her a quivering mass of surrender to his manly advances.

Or was it the cold of the night that helped her to shake off the dream before it carried her into the unknown? Regardless, she burrowed deep in the warm pocket of hay, smothered in her blankets, and left Wolf adrift somewhere in the warm, sweet fog. Even his whispered "Come here, milady" failed to rouse her from the cozy enveloping cradle into which she fit so snugly when he came back, this time not to seduce but to hold her.

Yet, when the first stirrings of the animals hailing their keeper for food and the bright chatter of the early marketers setting up their booths began to lift her exhaustion-induced sleep, the weight of his arms, the magnetism of his strong, heat-giving body, did not go with it. Loath to give it up, Branwen resisted until McShane's impatient snickering could be ignored no longer. Cocking one eye open at the hungry horse, she moaned in protest and snuggled deeper into the cocoon she'd made, when she caught a glimpse of a second set of fetlocks, black compared to McShane's golden ones.

Her body reacted, tensing in alarm, before her mind registered Pendragon's presence. Then a voice removed all confusion between dream and reality, a deep voice that rumbled warm against her ear. "Good morrow, milady."

Her head clearing instantly, Branwen threw herself away from the cozy nest she'd made, only to find herself trapped in it. Instead of hay snuggled against her back, it was Wolf's curled body and it was arms, not blankets that held her so snugly wrapped. The how of it eluded her as she began to thrash and pull against ungiving arms. All she knew was that retribution was surely at hand, a terrible one at that. The idea gave rise to a scream that was muffled even as she inhaled to force it out.

"Easy, milady! I mean ye no harm!" Wolf cooed in her ear as soft as her grip was firm. "If I had, 'twould have been done by now."

Branwen froze, trying to reason out his words in the midst of her panic. Was his sincerity as real as he was, or were they both spawned from some bizarre dream in which she was trapped? As if to confirm that this was really happening, that it was indeed Wolf who held her, she pushed her head against his chest and peered hesitantly over her shoulder. There was no mistaking the golden beard conforming to a noble jawline, nor the white flash of teeth that grinned down at her in irritating satisfaction. It was her mercenary. With little alternative, she surrendered the tenseness of her body and closed her eyes in defeat.

"Will you kill me now with your bare hands or hand me over to Kent for a fat purse?" she queried, throwing herself at his mercy.

"That depends on you, milady."

"What then, sir? Would you tumble me in the hay in this blasted cold for all the world to see? You well know you have the advantage," she accused grudgingly.

"Ho, I would not make the mistake of thinking that again, considering the lump on the back of my head."

Branwen looked over her shoulder again. "I didn't mean to hurt you. You ... you frightened me, carrying on so."

"If I thought that you meant me ill, lass, I'd not have kept your shiverin' bones warm last night, but put ye out of your misery for good." A shudder ran through her as her imagination embroidered on the threatening suggestion. "But for that towel wrapped around me head, I'd have been sorely angered."

"You weren't?" Branwen echoed aloud, eyes widening in wonder. He loosened his hold so that she could turn within the confines of his grasp to face him.

"Well, I was at first," he admitted, sucking in his cheeks as if enjoying some private thought. "But ye did go out of your way to see that I didn't drown or bleed to death. There's plenty of mischief to spare, but not one murderous bone in that lovely body ye keep hidden in a boy's clothes."

Fire crept to Branwen's cheeks in full profusion. Heaven knew this unshaven and crude oaf had seen all of her there was to see, without and within. But she did have one murderous inclination, one she had to see fulfilled and quickly. "Give me but a moment alone with Ulric of Kent and I'll prove you wrong, sir," she whispered fiercely under her breath.

"Give it up, lass. Ye're no match for him!" His emphatic hug nearly crushed the breath from her.

Branwen wanted to react in anger, but somehow she sensed that Wolf was not against her, only her plan. Indeed, he'd called her *lovely*. It was odd that she'd received compliments far more polished and smoothly delivered, but his had actually made her blush like wildfire. Arms that she initially feared offered untold comfort and reassurance in a strange world that threatened to swallow her up. Was his constantly recurring memory not a sign of guilt, but of actually missing his boisterous and driving company?

He was a man, she told herself, shaking the sentimentality that threatened her senses, a mercenary who thought of himself first. To warm to the idea that he'd come after her and held her during the cold night was sheer folly. Had it been more temperate, it was hard to tell what pleasures he might have taken with her. Were she a man, he might have killed her. As a woman, there was a worse fate likely in store.

"If you won't help me, sir, all I ask is that you keep silent until I can tempt Kent down here to the stables."

"Oh? And how might you do that?"

"I'll send word that my father has sent a wedding gift ... McShane. If Kent is half the warrior he'd reputed to be, he'll hasten to see such a prize." .

"And you'll confront a man who has fought more battles than you've years on this earth and kill him in hand-to-hand combat?"

Branwen shrank beneath the scornful gaze directed at her. "I'll take him by surprise," she mumbled uneasily. Remembering, out of the blue, her reason for haste, she abruptly queried, "Where is Dafydd?"

"A day behind. His horse lost a shoe a day's ride from here. There was a fine tavern ..."

"And plenty of warm ale and wenches."

Wolf lifted a hairy brow. "Ye act the jealous woman!"

"Don't be absurd!" Branwen scoffed. "It's only that I've learned a lot about men since traveling as one among them. There are no gentlemen in this world ... only hypocrites who present one face to a lady and quite another among their own. I have never been so humiliated in all my days!"

"All eighteen years of them, eh?" Wolf chuckled, still holding her in a fatherly fashion.

Yet, whatever assurance his embrace imparted, it was far from fatherly. Her entire body was aware of his and seemed to be communicating in a primitive manner. "How do you know my age? I do not recall telling you."

"Dafydd speaks of you often."

How well she could imagine! Branwen grimaced. "Tell me no more, sir, or I shall take two lives before I part this place."

105

"So there's a growing list. Am I to be added to it?"

"Only if you try to stop me." Her voice implied her determination, yet there was an unwitting plea in the eyes she lifted to his. "My cause is just, Wolf."

"And senseless, lass."

"No more so than the murder of my parents. Don't you see, there can never be peace between Wales and England as long as such treachery is allowed to go unpunished. 'Twill burn and fester until it erupts again in another rebellion. I will not submit to a murderer for husband, nor will my people do so for the man who killed their lord."

He was worried, truly worried about her, Branwen thought, distracted as he straightened her cap and brushed a wild, dark length of hair away from her face. What was this compelling attraction that permitted him to hold her now, almost effortlessly? Did he feel it, too? It almost made her want to forget it all and take to the road with him as his companion.

"Then if ye insist on seein' this through, I'll help ye. I'll not draw your vengeance blood, mind ye, but I'll help ye get Kent where ye'll stand a chance of escapin' alive."

"Oh, Wolf!"

Impulsively, she wrapped her arms about her companion's neck and hugged him, sharing her relief and joy. "I know I can win with you helping me!' We'll make a great team with my cunning and your brawn!"

"Ye've a winnin' way with words, lass," Wolf remarked wryly. "Makes a man proud, it does."

Branwen's smile faltered. The last thing she needed was to insult the mercenary now that she'd somehow enlisted his help. "I . . . I didn't mean to imply that you were dull-witted. . . . I only meant . . ."

Her words trailed off as Wolf lowered his lips to hers. Time and all but her beating heart, within and without her, stilled. She could feel it thrusting against her chest, thundering loudly, as the tender caress deepened to a heady invasion. It was a sneak attack, scattering her defenses before she even thought to summon them. Yet the burst of hot madness that it released in her veins spread through her as though it had been waiting, ready for the triggering advance.

That they were utterly incompatible, from totally opposite worlds, never occurred in Branwen's staggered mind. That he was motivated by lust rather than the growing respect and, oddly enough, affection she was beginning to feel for him was no more effective in chilling the heat wave rippling through her than the cold morning air. The little bursts of steam escaping their nostrils was more reflective of the flames within rather than the cold without.

And when their lips parted, halting the expression of unspoken words between two hearts, Branwen clung to Wolf as if her next breath depended on it. As she looked at him in the charged silence that drowned out the noise of the awakening city, confusion darted about the kindled glow of desire he had stirred in her gaze. At that moment, it felt as if they were the only two people on earth, locked in a mutually dependent embrace of survival.

"Why?" Branwen breathed, voicing the doubts assaulting her passion-dazed thoughts. "Why did you do that?"

"To see if 'twas true that the same lips that could flay a man alive could promise a heavenly reward after."

Dafydd! It was another of her ex-fiancé's unfounded boasts! Aye, she'd flayed him alive on more than one occasion, but he'd only tasted her lips in the most chaste of kisses at Christmas, when mistletoe granted the privilege.

" 'Tis no mistletoe here, sir, but hay! I would warn

107

you, should you force your attentions on me again, you may find yourself at the sharp end of my blade!"

To her horror, it took her a moment more to muster sufficient resolve to give up the warm haven Wolf offered. Unencumbered, she rolled away and to her feet, her cheeks stinging with blood.

"Aye, you're the female, all right!" Wolf grunted, undaunted by her sudden change of heart. "Ye've lips that cry yea and nay at the same time."

The worst part of the damnable situation was that Wolf's statement was true! He'd heard both factions battling for dominance in her traitorous body. Unable to argue and reluctant to remain too near the inviting warmth of her companion, Branwen backed away. But damned if she'd give him the full satisfaction of her confusion.

"You, sir, are deaf as a post, then, and twice as thick!"

His responding chuckle offered no absolution and only served to deepen her blush to the furthermost reaches of her body. Yet, there was nothing for her to do to dissuade it except to walk out of earshot. Somewhere down the line a donkey brayed and a wicked grin tugged at Branwen's lips. Perhaps she'd just trade one jackass for another until she could regain her senses.

Chapter Seven

The meat pastry she had purchased from the baker's wife with the money Wolf had given her was better than it smelled. That, added to the wine being distributed from the public water cisterns at the city gate, compliments of Christmastide, was as warming as the fire next to which Branwen sat. The mercenary left her after a breakfast of hot bread and warm milk from one of Nathan's cows, to make his way to Westminster, where they'd discovered the king was in residence. As he'd pointed out, it was difficult to kill a man when his whereabouts were unknown to them.

She supposed that was the advantage of having a mercenary as a partner. He was not subject to the emotional onslaughts that left her reckless with frustration and grief. Her emotional trauma had turned her into a different girl from the dreamy innocent who had left Caradoc last spring. The most violent inclination she'd known then was to slap Dafydd, although she had, when younger, given him good chase with a lighter sword. That was before she was forced to become the future lady of Caradoc and was more her father's pet than Lady Gwendolyn's.

Branwen laughed, unamused, at the irony. All those years her mother had worked to make her a lady and now she was acting the man, the son out to avenge his parents' death. Perhaps it was the wine, but it all seemed so ridiculous. *Caradoc's lady!* Gogsdeath, this was a jest at fate if there ever were one! A single tear ventured from glazed eyes and she was grateful there was no mirror or glass in which to see her reflection. Somehow she didn't think she'd make either of her parents proud.

She had finished off the wine and wiped her lips with the back of her sleeve, when she spied a commotion coming from the direction of the Tower. Curious at all the strange sights and happenings, Branwen meandered to the well-packed road leading to Smithfield's yards and fell in behind the crowd. Soldiers on horseback were dragging two prisoners by the feet. The unfortunates were to be executed, she overheard, for treason against Edward, although she wondered if their present treatment would allow them to live long enough for the hanging everyone seemed to anticipate with the same fervor as a pageant.

Her first thought was that the king had gone back on his word to accept Llewelyn's surrender. That in mind, she pushed to the front of the crowd until she could see the poor devils. There were two of fair coloring, one short and sturdy of build and the other pitifully malnourished. Both were filthy and in rags, which the rough frozen ground tore away from their flesh in places. Hardly anyone she knew, Branwen decided, thinking to drop away.

Yet, once caught, she found herself being carried along with the jeering crowd toward Smithfield proper. There they came to a halt before a large scaffold Branwen had not noticed yesterday. To her wonder, pie sellers and ballad sellers infiltrated the group, calling out as though at the marketplace, while she was roughly pushed this way and that by latecomers who wanted a good view of the grisly proceedings.

" 'Ere now, the lad was 'ere first!" A big man beside her shouted at a uniformed footman who shoved her deep into the throng.

His intentions were good, but Branwen's feet nearly left the ground as the butcher by trade, judging from the blood staining the filthy apron around his ample girth, hauled her in front of him, affording her a prime view none dared to challenge. At least, she hoped he was a butcher. If not, he belonged more on the scaffolding than the two men who had to be helped up the steep steps by their jailers.

"This is what 'appens ta traitors, son! See that ye keep yerself loyal to 'is Majesty an' ye'll not suffer the same."

"Aye, sir!" she agreed heartily, trying not to notice the scent of fresh blood and meat about him. The pie she'd just finished churned uneasily in her stomach as she watched the hangman slip a noose over each of the prisoner's heads. It wasn't that men weren't executed in Wales, but her father would never have allowed her to be present, nor did she care to be.

"Edwin!" Branwen turned to see Nathan working his way toward her. " 'Tis more than a hangin', this one," the boy informed her, his eyes bright as they focused on the scaffold. "Master'll fetch high prices today for sure. Folk are here from all over the shire."

"They can only kill them once and they're near dead as it is," she observed dryly. "What more can they do?"

Nathan grinned, revealing teeth blackened with rot that she'd not seen the night before; but then, the lighting had been dim and he'd spent most of their time together with his face pressed to a cow's belly. "Just watch, lad. Ye'll see."

See she did, more than she wanted to. The prisoners

111

were hanged until they nearly lost consciousness, jerking at the end of the ropes to the cheers and jeers of the crowd. Then to her horror, they were disemboweled before her eyes and their bodies cut into quarters, so that they were carried away in pieces by a black-cloaked gentleman and his assistants. Their anguished screams, she knew, would haunt her till her dying day.

Branwen stood frozen by the sight of the blood-soaked platform, unable to move when the crowd backed away to find other excitement. She didn't think she'd ever seen anything so barbaric and gruesome in the making. She'd only seen the aftermath of such bloodthirsty madness.

"What do ye thin, Edwin?" Nathan beamed at her side, as if proud of the spectacle. *"Edwin?"*

Branwen blinked at the moving image of her companion as her own blood left her face and knees at the same time.

"Are ye goin' to be sick?" he taunted, cocking his head sideways to stare at her in disdain.

Behind him, the stables and the walls of the city were moving, too. Everything was moving, except her feet. Her stomach fell in with the circuitous motion and nausea rose to the back of her throat. She *was* going to be sick, Branwen thought dizzily, waving her companion aside in warning. Instead of retching, however, as she leaned over and swayed back and forth on unsteady knees, she plunged headfirst into a pool of swirling darkness that suddenly opened up in the hard frozen earth.

Branwen had never fainted in her life, hence this netherworld was as new to her as the English city of London. She heard voices, or at least thought she did. There was Nathan's panic-stricken one. Then there were others that seemed to lift her in the air, so that she floated not on, but *in* a dark enveloping cloud. Her nostrils registered the musty smell of the hay that had been her bed the night before, comfortable in the blackness . . . so much so, that she seemed to sink deeper and deeper into it, where the scarlet of blood and stench of death could not reach her.

How long she remained there, she didn't know. What she did know was that she was reluctant to leave it. She wouldn't have, either, had Wolf's voice not coaxed her out of it. He was the only one with whom she felt safe in this strange place where bloodlust provided entertainment.

He held her hand. She could feel the rough sandwich of his own about it, warm and inviting compared to the cold temperature that suddenly registered in the netherworld.

"Wolf?"

"Aye, lass. I'm here."

But where was here? She opened her eyes warily. She was in a bed, not the haystack, and in a room, not the stable. A fine room it was, too. The ceiling rose two stories where shuttered windows battled to keep the winter air at bay. The bed was massive, large enough for a lord *and* his lady, and well packed with rush. Over it was a drapery of tasseled damask that hung from a half canopy. The light that filled the room came from a brisk fire in a shallow hearth a few feet away. What manner of place was this? she wondered, for it was too small to be a great hall, and who ever heard of a private bedroom set aside for any but a king or maybe the Pope!

"Where are we?"

"The palace at Westminster," Wolf informed her, his wry grin widening at her gasp.

"Faith, have ye put me in the king's own bed?"

"Hay, 'tis one of the lesser rooms set aside for his guests."

"What have you done to me?" Branwen blanched whiter than the pallor she'd awakened with, giving the man at

113

her bedside cause for concern. Had he revealed her secret? Did Kent or the king know she was here? Gogsbreath, would she die the horrible death those poor devils had on the scaffold. The frantic questions bombarded her mind too quickly for expression.

"I've found ye shelter more fit for the lady that ye are. Ye did want to get into the palace where Kent is keeping the king's company, didn't ye?"

"I hadn't thought to be a guest!" she snapped in irritation. "What have you told him?"

"Who?"

"The king! Do they know about my father?"

Wolf shrugged. "How should I know? I haven't had an audience with the man. This," he said, waving his arm around the spacious room, "is a favor owed me by a friend in Edward's retinue of judges. There are few of Edward's knights that I have not fought with these last eight years in the Holy Land."

"Who?" Branwen asked suspiciously. It seemed incredible that she could be in the king's own palace and him not know.

"Rodrick of Berkley. I plucked an arrow from his thigh and dragged him across a sandy hell to safety after a Saracen attack on the pilgrim caravan he was part of."

"Were you wounded?"

"Here and there, I suppose." Wolf made the admission casually, as if he spoke of no more than an insect bite. But Branwen had seen his scars—scars from wounds that might have finished a lesser man. "I lost track. Would ye mind tellin' me what the devil happened to ye back there in the field?"

Branwen pushed herself upright on the bed and swung her legs over the side. "They executed two men in a way I've never witnessed." She shivered as the memory rose fresh in her mind. "I . . . I'm not normally squeamish, but there was blood running everywhere and suddenly I saw Father, lying in a scarlet pool by Mam . . . and poor Caryn . . ." She sighed as her hand was retrieved once more. "I don't think I've ever felt so tired . . . or defeated. Do you know I'm *mistress* of Caradoc?"

Wolf chuckled gently. "Aye, milady. 'Tis I that's been tryin' to convince ye of it since I discovered your . . . *affliction.*"

A hint of a smile settled on Branwen's lips, while her cheeks regained their color. "My father wanted a son," she confessed miserably. "I tried hard for years to make it up to him and fared well enough until I turned twelve. Then I was plucked from the company of the schoolmaster and squires and forced to wield a needle rather than a sword. 'Twas not nearly as entertaining."

"But wielding a sword results in bloodshed, and that doesn't seem to agree with your gentle nature."

"Ulric of Kent's blood will be different," she rallied, seeing the direction in which her self-appointed mentor was manipulating her. "Where is the devil? In this tower?"

"In the king's tower. We are but lowly knights."

"You, a *knight?*"

Wolf shook his head. "I meant mere friends of one of his lowly knights."

"We all sleep in the hall of Caradoc." Her home seemed so backward in comparison to this place. It was still hard to imagine anyone with a room of their own.

"I think you'll find London more civilized than your Welsh castles and villages."

"Aye, I saw evidence of such civilization today," Branwen scoffed bitterly.

" 'Tis but a small part ye saw, lass. After ye're rested, I'll show ye about."

"You know London well?"

115

"As well as I know Florence and Paris and Jerusalem and . . ."

"Sir Wolf of Everywhere."

She tried to maintain a smug countenance, but could not help but join Wolf's boisterous mirth. It was infectious when it wasn't at her expense. Besides, she had to admit, London was the most intriguing place she'd ever been, and there was so much more she had not seen beyond those walls and along the river. "I'm rested now!" she announced, leaping from the bed gingerly in eager anticipation. The city awaited her and she'd wasted enough time already.

It amazed Branwen that Westminster was not in the walled city around the Tower. It was a palace with its own walled-in courtyards and gardens, elegant even in winter's bleakness. Sprigs of evergreen adorned every arch, pronouncing the season of Christmastide, and lords and ladies in rich attire meandered about the grounds watching mimes, mummers, strolling balladeers, and theatre performed in brightly painted pageant wagons. She kept an eye out for her traveling companions, but they had set up to entertain at the Tower rather than at Westminster.

There were evidence of poorhouses and ramshackle buildings interspersed along the gravel stretch paralleling the river called the Strand, but wealthy manors with enclosed courtyards and orchards dominated it. Built for comfort rather than for protection, their terraced lawns sloped down toward the river in places, beyond which vessels of every description struggled in the wind and icy currents.

Branwen was fascinated by the barges that picked up and let off people at stations up and down the muddy banks. Oars protruded from the sides of them, giving them the appearance of large squat centipedes stroking their way against the current in one direction and riding

116

leisurely downriver in the other. The latest to board were huddled on the top decks, which would have been pleasant on a less blustery day, but when the barges tied up at the small docks, they disembarked eagerly to seek warmer quarters.

Accustomed to the damp cold along the waterfront, Branwen, however, thrilled at the sights and the wind that whipped her short curls around her face in spite of the hat pulled down over her ears. At the first sight of London Bridge, she squealed in delight. Wales was lucky to have a bridge wide enough for a cart to cross, but this one housed buildings along its sides. "Faith, you can fish out of your own window!" she marveled, her effervescent gaze a bright blue. "Can we walk across it?"

Wolf made a face but indulged her. "Why not? It may be your last day in this world, and I'd have it be a good one."

Refusing to let his taunt spoil the wonderful afternoon, she danced ahead, peering through the shop windows and stopping to watch the street entertainers who were on every corner. "Every ship in the world must be here to see Llewelyn surrender!" Branwen exclaimed upon seeing the sea of masts and furled canvas that marked Billingsgate. "And I know there must be at least one person from every country!"

"What say ye to a taste of good German ale? There's a tavern a few blocks away on Cheapside. We've seen all of London but the market, and God forbid ye miss a thing!"

"Why not?"

In her enthusiasm, Branwen linked arms with the big man and skipped ahead, only to have him jerk away with a scowl. "Damnation, *lad,* have ye taken leave of your senses?"

Her heart sobered long enough to see a devilish twin-

117

kling in his eye that gave her leave to laugh. "Sorry, sir. I forgot! I'll buy!"

It was Wolf's money, but it seemed the least she could do. He was being so thoughtful now that he knew she was a *she*. For the last few hours she had almost forgotten her plight and the dread mission planned after the king and his guests retired for the night. Most of the attention she'd received from her suitors at Caradoc she'd taken as her due, but Wolf's was different. Even though he was a mercenary, there was something in his eyes, something warm and wonderful that bespoke sincerity. His concern was heartfelt and so was his remark that she was lovely, even if he did say so to make her blush. Her face had flashed red and white like the banners snapping along the street since they'd left the gargantuan palace at Westminster.

As they made the turn onto Cheapside, a panorama of shops and stalls unfolded before her. They walked along, taking in the tempting smells and sights. Wolf pointed ahead to a bush hanging on a pole that stretched almost across the street, announcing the presence of an ale house, and Branwen felt her belt for the money pouch Wolf had supplemented earlier.

"It's gone!" she exclaimed upon coming up empty-handed. Disbelief riddled her face. "I've been robbed!"

"I've coin enough for us both."

"But someone robbed me!"

"So it appears. London boasts some of the finest pickpockets in the world. Can ye tell me when ye last had it?"

Branwen tried to think. "I had it when I bought that pie just before noon."

"Faith, lad, 'tis not only stolen, but spent thrice by now!" Wolf slapped her back in consolation. "We'll have a draft of ale to ease your loss. 'Twill be my treat! Besides," he added in a voice dropped for her benefit alone, "it's unseemly for the mistress of Caradoc to carry on so over a few pence."

" 'Tis not the money, 'tis the principle!" she flashed back, glancing up as she followed the man into the tavern.

Above the door hung a sprig of evergreen with small white berries. Gogsdeath, *mistletoe!* Branwen jumped back as if she'd seen a ghost. "Wolf, what day is it?"

"Three days until Christmas. Now for the love of God, close the door and come in!"

Branwen shook her head. Mistletoe boiled for medicine was one matter. Hanging over the door was another. "I'll not step foot in that place. Not with *that* over the door."

Upon seeing that she was not about to cooperate, Wolf went back out and appeased the patrons inside by closing the door behind him. "What is wrong with mistletoe?"

" 'Tis foul luck to hang it before Christmas Eve. I need no more ill luck today."

"Well, ye needn't fear me stealin' a kiss, here before all and ye lookin' like a boy."

Branwen grimaced with impatience. "It's bad luck, man! 'Twill curse ye for the year, like as not. Mistletoe is good for many things, but bad if hung . . ."

"Before Christmas Eve, is it?" her companion echoed skeptically. "Ye don't believe in such nonsense!"

"Your ignorance will not protect you! 'Tis not well to make jest at that which you do not understand," she quoted Aunt Agnéis.

"Then follow this street to Ludgate and take the Strand back to Westminster. I'll catch up with ye there."

At her fallen face, her companion repented. "I'll meet you at the gate in half an hour. Ye can watch the water until I catch up with ye. I've someone to see here on business."

119

"Then tell them to take down the mistletoe and pray for mercy," Branwen told him somberly. "They like as not don't know such, being from Germany."

"I've heard the Welsh were a superstitious lot," Wolf observed dourly, "but I tell ye 'tis tomfoolery and naught else."

" 'Tis caution and naught else. There's spirits none understand besides the Almighty, and it doesn't pay to anger them recklessly."

"Aye, an ye be one of 'em . . . thick and stubborn as a tree!"

Annoyed to the point of exasperation, Wolf stepped inside and closed the door, ending the argument abruptly before Branwen had the chance to rally. Shaking her head, she started off down the street toward Ludgate. Men didn't understand, she supposed, reflecting on Aunt Agnéis's observation of Owen ap Caradoc. He was a good man, but her aunt worried that he didn't respect tree spirits enough and her mother fretted over his conspicuous absence at the keep's masses. Owen had considered it enough to build a chapel for those who wished to put it to use.

A group of young people bundled in rich fur-lined cloaks were gathered near Ludgate, their attention fixed on two rowboats a short distance from the bank. Banners of red flew from one of the small boats, while blue waved over the other. In the front of each a young man stood, braced with, of all things, a blunted lance! Upon positioning the boats opposite each other, both teams of oarsmen began to row with all their might toward each other. Fascinated by the tournament activity on the water, Branwen gasped as the red leader knocked the blue solidly overboard, nearly upsetting his crew as well.

A shiver ran through her at the thought of falling into the icy water, but the young man was pulled out of the murky river almost as soon as he hit it and wrapped in blankets while his teammates rowed toward shore. Already, another team was on its way out to challenge the winner and the drama took place again. It took four teams before the boy at the front of the red boat finally took his turn in the water. His friends on the shore roared with laughter and cheers as he was hauled aboard and brought to land to warm by a bonfire along the riverbank.

" 'Tis a hard way to impress a lady." Branwen turned at the sound of the wry observation, to see Wolf holding out a wooden noggin of steaming cider to her. "This ought to warm your insides at least."

Gratefully, Branwen accepted the treat, noting with curiosity a packaged tucked under Wolf's arm. "I don't mind. Mam used to fret over my riding along Traeth Caradoc on a low January tide, but the wind blowing across my face and the freedom . . ." She took a sip of the cider and gazed across the river dreamily. "It made my blood race through my veins and made me feel more alive than a dozen afternoons in the solar, working on one of her tapestries."

She was totally unaware of the winter blush that made her cheeks glow or the hidden fires that burned with sapphire flame in her wistful gaze. Wolf knew instinctively where she was at that very moment—riding along a stretch of wet sand, daring the tide to come in before her pent-up spirit had spent itself. He'd admired her spunk when he thought her a lad, reminded of himself at the same age, trapped by circumstances not of his making. When he'd discovered her, naked as Mother Nature had masterfully made her, he'd been shocked, angered, and awed.

If ever a woman had been born to suit him, it was this impish creature with a face of innocence, eyes of mischief, a heart full of courage and compassion, and a body made to pleasure a man. At least, as he recalled

121

from that startling night it was. At the moment, it was very well concealed beneath layers of clothing. What would the thin silk he'd purchased from Frau Hilda look like clinging to . . ."

"What's wrong?"

Wolf shook the spell that had held him captive and he grinned. " 'Tis getting dark, and I'd be within the walls before curfew bells are sounded."

Branwen felt it, too, the disappointment that registered in the unfathomable gaze that had been fixed on her when she returned from the past and a happier, more carefree time. "Me, too."

Silent, she fell into step beside her companion and walked the remaining distance along the Strand, past noble houses and slums, toward the looming towers of the white palace framed against the winter red horizon. Inside the walls were costumed entertainers circulating in the crowds to arouse interest in the scheduled evening performances. Flags and banners hung from windows, and parapets and garlands of evergreen were draped wherever they could be hung. Bonfires and cressets burned in the streets, filling the air with light-charred debris that was carried up in the draft overhead.

"Could we watch one of the pageant wagons?" Branwen asked as Wolf protectively ushered her through the crowd ahead of him.

"Not this night. I've a supper to attend in the hall. 'Tis best if ye stay in the room until I return after the revelry is done and Kent retires. Ye stay in my room and I'll send you some supper, since it's not likely ye'll be wantin' to join the rest of the squires in the hall."

Branwen shook her head. "I'll sleep outside your door . . . *afterward,*" she added meaningfully.

"Ye still wish to go through with it?"

"I must."

Their conversation ended as they approached the

stairs to the tower containing Wolf's quarters. Wolf took the lead, passing the guards at the foot of the stairwell, and Branwen fell in behind him, the obedient squire. By the time they reached the third level, Branwen no longer felt the affects of the coming night chill that had fallen over the town, and she was actually perspiring! Dutifully beating him to the door, she stepped back to let Wolf in first and then followed.

"Wolf?" Branwen leaned against the closing door as the mercenary turned expectantly. The question had been on her mind all day and now she could keep it no longer. "Why haven't you handed me over to Kent? You are a man motivated by money. There's surely some value on my head."

Wolf shrugged off his great cloak, revealing the finer hunter-green one she'd seen in his sack while searching for a tinderbox days earlier. "There's even a code of honor among thieves, lass. I gave ye my word I'd help ye."

"You said you'd teach me to use *this.*" Branwen rested her hand on the hilt of her knife. "I'm pretty good."

"Put it in that knot behind ye," Wolf dared dubiously.

Branwen walked over to where her companion stood and drew out the blade. She hadn't practiced since arriving in London, she thought nervously, balancing it in her hand as Wolf had shown her to do. Suddenly, she flicked her wrist and, with a smooth follow-through, sent the knife flying straight toward the knot. It landed a few inches down and to the left.

"Give it up, lass."

"It was close!"

Unconvinced, Wolf turned her to him and shook her roughly. "Close enough to see ye ripped limb from limb. No man would take such a nasty prick lightly."

"He'd bleed to death!" Branwen stammered.

"Is that so?" He let her go, stripping off his shirt and

123

cloak in a single angry motion. "Well *this* didn't stop me from taking off the head of the man who buried his knife here," he growled, pointing to one of his scars. "Nor did *this* keep me from running through the bastard that heaved his spear into my shoulder."

"You're no normal man!" Branwen covered the scars with splayed fingers as she struggled to keep from losing what little courage she had left. "Can't you understand why I must avenge my parents' death."

"Because you still want to be the son they never had! Well, damn it, lass, you're a woman . . . made for *this!*"

Branwen cried out, startled, as Wolf yanked her to him and claimed her lips roughly. One arm banded at her waist, he held her head captive with his free hand, so that there was no escaping the demanding imprisonment without total and absolute surrender. Her fists clenched with the best of intentions to drive him away, before the melting tumult generated in her lower body by the grinding of his hips robbed her of all semblance of reason. She meant to offer protest but instead parted her lips to a heady invasion that would give no quarter.

Her senses swam in the frantic tide he masterfully whipped up with each stroke of his hand moving up and down the curves of her back, edging her closer and closer until not even breath separated them. "This is how the fire that burns within ye should be put to use, milady," Wolf mumbled huskily into the unwittingly exposed hollow of her throat. The brush of his beard against her soft skin coaxed her head back even further until her hat, loosened in the first assault, fell to the floor. *"This* is what ye were made so soft and gentle for."

Burrowing his face into her hair, he sought out her ear with devastating expertise, distracting her from the hand that somehow had found the shape of her breast through the layers of clothing. Branwen closed her eyes, but lights of desire still flashed, blinding her to all but the sweet torment of his fingertips. When she forced her eyelids open, the pattern of the ceiling plaster gradually came into focus and she realized that she was no longer standing, but lying on the large bed with Wolf hovering over her, the aggressive predator closing in on his weakened prey.

If there was any order to the chaos he had evoked within her, it resembled the jumbled swirls that filled the spaces between thick oak beams. Her blood pounded in her ears, deafening at first, but upon the realization that the forceful seduction had stopped, it gradually subsided, so that reason might struggle to the surface. She licked her lips as if savoring the remains of Wolf's kiss, then exhaled shakily. Shame that it was, she had this wanton yearning for more.

"Stay with me tonight and forget this vengeful madness, fair raven. I vow I will see your parents' murderer brought to justice!"

More tempting words had never been spoken. They only heightened the degree of inner turmoil brewing within Branwen's chest. If any man could make her forget, it was this one. For the first time, she *wanted* to be a woman, to dance to the wild seductive melody his fingers played on her skin until she knew the mysterious fulfillment that would satiate them both.

"I have more reason than ever to return here tonight, sir," she whispered with all the volume she could summon. "I swear I will . . . *after Kent is dead.*"

The explosive oath that erupted at her side gave her a start as Wolf threw himself from the mattress and stalked to the hearth, nostrils flaring in anger as he peered at the fire. "Then God have mercy on your stubborn soul, lass!"

He bent over and snatched up the shirt he'd divested himself of earlier. Branwen rose up on one elbow to

125

watch as he pulled it roughly over his head, covering the scarred and rippling flesh stretched over sinew.

"You're leaving *now?*" she asked timidly.

"I told ye I had an obligation to sup with the man responsible for this room."

She looked away to hide her disappointment. "But you'll be back when the king retires?"

"If not, I'll send ye notice of where Kent is. 'Tis best we say our farewells here and now."

Branwen's heart stumbled over the implication. He didn't think he'd have a reason to return. "Have you no faith in me, sir?"

Wolf combed his shoulder-length hair with his fingers and straightened his cloak before coming over to the edge of the bed. "I did, lass, but I see I misplaced it. Ye've a heart poisoned with a hunger for revenge and a mind addled by it."

But she would be back! She knew it! Branwen scrambled to her feet as her companion spun away from the bed and started for the door. "Wolf, wait!"

The door creaked with the tug that opened it. Torn between the urge to run after him and injured pride, she wavered in silence.

Turning a sneering countenance toward her, he bowed mockingly. "I'll see you in hell with the rest of us mercenary souls, *milady,*" he derided.

The slamming of the door made Branwen flinch in the midst of her confusion and despair. Never had anything sounded so painfully final or echoed so much with the ringing of forever.

Chapter Eight

She knew everything about the room by the time a page knocked with her supper and a message from the disgruntled Wolf. In view of the tournament scheduled tomorrow, there was a midnight curfew. Hours away, she thought dismally—hours in which to lose her resolve, hours in which to dwell on what might have been, hours to recall the sweet torture of Wolf's angry kiss and his cruel parting salute.

Branwen supposed a man like him, a mercenary, wouldn't understand honor. Money was his primary motivation. Whichever side had the most money was the right one, regardless of whether it represented justice. In this case, the king and Kent had the money and power, but they were not just.

Her father had swallowed his pride to surrender and persuaded her to do the same to agree to this political mismatch. On their honor they'd embarked on the trip to London, fully prepared to pledge allegiance to Edward and to accept his newly appointed lord as master of their ancestral lands. To keep peace, she would bear this overlord a son, an English and Welsh heir to govern the lands.

It spoke of courage, not cowardice, to surrender with such dignity, keeping the welfare of their people in mind; and in one despicable act of cowardice, it had all been put asunder. How could she not make this villain pay for his treachery? By all that was just and holy, not even God could expect her to willingly submit to the pawing of hands stained by the blood of her parents! To do so would make her a fool as well as a coward! Who was to say Kent wouldn't try to take her life a second time . . . *after* the wedding? It wouldn't be hard, considering the depth of his disregard for life and honor.

Take it to the king? she wondered, her lips thinning to a bloodless line. Not after seeing his brand of justice today! True, she'd heard from the page that he had accepted Llewelyn's allegiance that very day but stripped him of more than half his holdings. The title he'd been allowed to keep as Prince of Wales was as shallow as his pardon. Further, Edward had yet to release the bride he'd snatched from Llewelyn's hand. If all were forgiven, why had Eleanore not been handed over to her groom?

Nay, she dared not trust the king to right this wrong, she decided, finishing the last of the ale the page had brought her. Her supper of roast venison, duckling, breads of a variety, and a number of dishes that appeared suspect to her lay hardly touched on the imported porcelain plate. The mixture of emotions churning in her stomach made eating impossible. If only there were someone to talk to, someone she trusted. But they were all gone.

The time that passed before midnight crept by painstakingly slow. The distant revelry from the great hall was occasionally broken by a passing party of knights and their ladies bound for guest chambers. From the sound of it all, the castle had to be almost as large as London itself to accommodate the vast number of guests, not to mention the servants! It would be all she'd need to get lost.

Ignoring the fact Wolf had no further words for her, Branwen repeatedly studied the rough map he'd sent, trying to memorize the directions to the royal tower. Kent's high position was underscored by a private room at the opposite end of a main corridor from the king's own quarters, which meant more guards than would ordinarily be about a mere knight. She'd even considered making her way there before the curfew hour, but thought the wait there to be even more unbearable than the one she faced.

The noise outside the room quieted down to the passing of servants who would work a good deal of the night to prepare the great hall for morning breakfast. From the window, she'd heard the sergeant at arms call the eleventh hour, pronouncing all was well, and listened as it echoed from parapet to parapet within the walls of the royal residence. The courtyards and inner bailey below were empty of the Christmastide diversions that had taken place earlier, the only present stirrings that of dogs, a few harried servants, and the poor shivering souls assigned to guard duty outside.

When it appeared that Wolf was not going to return to the room at all that night, Branwen picked up a French porcelain commode and stepped out into the hall. She'd hoped the least he would have done was come back to see if she'd changed her mind. She thought he cared that much. With a sense of purpose in the midst of her disappointment and trepidation, she walked toward the winding steps leading down to the main floor where the banquet had taken place in the great hall. The whole of Caradoc might have fit in it!

At the late hour, it was mostly servants who shuffled in and out with platters and half-eaten trays of food. Upon slowing her step, however, she was astonished to note that there were a number of lesser noblemen still there, most likely not wealthy enough to participate in the games. They were, however, not making merry but were snoring indelicately, oblivious to the clean up going on around them. A pair of legs sticking out from under one table indicated the probable presence of others unseen, providing an explanation for Wolf's absence. Like as not, he'd gotten drunk and passed out, as had some of his comrades.

At least, Branwen preferred to think so, rather than to admit that he might have been one of the boisterous lords keeping the company of the giggling serving wenches who had staggered through the halls earlier in search of their rooms. A man like him would have his needs, and like as not, they'd not keep for her. Either that, or they were enough to satisfy two wenches, she thought, recalling the arousal she'd felt beneath his towel after he'd pleasured the scrubwoman and joined her in the mineral bath.

One of the servants called out to her to help move a table, but she pretended not to hear and kept on a singular path toward the opposite tower from the one she'd just left. As she expected, the guards were doubled at the base of the steps. She kept her arm casually across her abdomen, holding the hidden hilt of her dagger as she stepped behind a woman carrying linens.

"Boy, where are you headed?"

It was no servant but a soldier calling after her this time. Her heart lodged still against her chest, Branwen turned and grinned sheepishly. " 'Is lordship has a bit of the grip. Seems one commode ain't enough, since 'e needs one for 'is 'ead, too."

"No small wonder, the way they been puttin' the food and drink away like tomorrow won't come!" one of the men snorted in envious disdain. "Which 'un is it? Kent or Berkley? Neither of them could walk up the steps earlier. Me 'n' Giles had to carry Kent and that was no small task, I tell ye!"

"It was Kent sent for the extra commode."

The man snickered. "'E'll be in fine shape for the games tomorrow. Get on with ye, then!"

"I might be back, if ye know what I mean," Branwen explained, wrinkling her nose in demonstration. "'Tis a fearsome smell to endure the night."

"There be a lavatory chute below this tower and a water barrel."

"Then I'll see ye gents later."

"Just keep your distance!" one of the guards called after her as she started back up the steps again.

The royal corridor stretched before her when Branwen emerged from the stairwell. Hanging overhead from the great Roman-style arches were flags and banners, tasseled in gold, while royal crests were boasted on escutcheons along the stone walls. A series of beautiful carpets ran the length of it, leading to the double doors of the king's chamber beyond. They were well lit with flickering torches and flanked on either side by uniformed guards.

She'd never seen the likes of this place! Aside from the royal dais in the great hall, it was the first carpeting she'd ever seen on a floor! The landed gentry she knew put the colorful treasures on the walls sooner than risk ruining them by constant traffic, animals, and filth. But then, her experience to date had proven King Edward not prone to spare a pence when it came to luxury. Rush was probably too common for the royal foot.

Grateful that Ulric of Kent's room was immediately on this end rather than that of the grandiose royal side, Branwen smiled at the guards in the distance and pretended to knock, striking her knuckles on the stone rather than the wood of the door and praying her intended victim was not a light sleeper. After listening carefully for any sound, she eased the latch of the door open and stepped inside.

131

Although the light in the corridor had been dim, that of the bedchamber was dimmer. Easing the door to, Branwen stood breathless for a moment, allowing her eyes to focus on the glow of the embers in the hearth near a magnificent bed completely curtained. From inside, snoring echoed, low and regular. He was asleep!

She let out her breath slowly and felt her heart make an attempt to beat. All she had to do was put down the commode silently and steal over to the curtains with knife in hand. The rest was in the hands of fate. Her leather boots made no noise against the stone floor as she approached in the shadow of the bed. Hand shaking visibly, she eased upon one of the drapes and, summoning her courage, peeped inside.

Gogsdeath, he was big! She stared, with wide eyes, at the broad shoulders turned back to her and sniffed cautiously, inhaling the stale and reassuring scent of liquor. And as the guards had said, she derided in relief, *in a drunken stupor.*

There would be no need to throw the knife at all. All she had to do was drive it into his back, upward, as Wolf had shown her, so that the bone would not impair her thrust. Swiftly in and then twist to cut the base of the spine. If he didn't die right away, at least he'd be immobilized and she could slit his throat.

A vile lump rose in the back of Branwen's throat as she contemplated the mechanical procedure she'd worked out earlier without any repercussion. But Ulric of Kent had not been an arm's length away from losing his life's blood, indeed his life itself, then. Nor had she heard his guileless breathing or made out the shape of his head against the pillow, encased in a nightcap, both which now brought the scheme to reality.

He ... Branwen's thought became muddled with emotion. He looked like her father, sleeping there. Owen was just as broad-shouldered although not as tall.

She believed she could see Kent partially sprawled upon the bed, one booted foot resting on the floor, a matter of course considering his drunkenness. But her father had worn a cap just like that, claiming it made up for the loss of his thinning black hair. Instead of dark curls, it was fair ones that peeked out from under the cap and dipped into the loose collar of his nightshirt. And instead of her father, it was his murderer, she reminded herself sternly.

Branwen grasped the knife by the handle and drew it from the sheath tucked inside her outer leggings. In the dim light and shadows, it seemed to look larger, more lethal than before when she'd practiced with it. And it quivered. Gogsdeath, did it quiver! Just as did she. The knife blurred and she blinked fiercely. All she had to do was drive it into the dip at his waist. All she had to do was *do it!*

She raised her hand and held it poised, as if some invisible barrier would not let it pass. He'd killed her father and mother. He'd mutilated Caryn. God only knew how many innocents' blood stained his battle-toughened hands! He was so drunk he would never know what happened to him!

The arguments for bringing the knife down continued to pile up in her tormented brain, but the hand was stayed in midair. She had every reason to kill this man. *Every reason!*

Yet, for one she could not fathom, she lowered the knife and returned it to its hiding place. Her eyes stung with shame as she let the curtain fall and backed away in defeat. Wolf was right. She was an emotion-crippled female not an honor-driven son. She was not now, nor would she ever be, the son Owen had wanted. She'd not only failed her father in life but in death as well.

Hardly able to see it, she fumbled with the latch with shaking hands. It clicked, sounding like the loud snap of wet wood on a hot fire, and her breath caught. Fearfully, she glanced over her shoulder toward the bed, but Kent was as still as her heart. Dead to the world, she thought bitterly, but not nearly dead enough.

She cracked open the door and slipped outside, remembering at the last moment to reach back through for her passport to Wolf's chamber—the commode. Her emotions bordering on hysteria, Branwen had to force herself to walk toward the steps, holding the pot away from her as if its potent aroma were as sickening as her cowardice. Yet, once she started down the steps, her feet took flight and would not be stopped. As she fled past the guards who had stopped her earlier, a sob strangled in her throat.

"Keep away, lad. No cause of us all gettin' sick!" one shouted after her as she sped down the corridor leading to the other tower.

"That's it, use the lavatory on the other side!" his companion chimed in with an amused hoot.

It was not by design, but her frantic expression and pallor, combined with the swaying chamber pot, provided her unquestioned, unhampered progress to the opposite side and up the steps. Only then did she slow to a walk, for all the arched doors looming in the dark recesses of the hall looked alarmingly the same. Which was Wolf's, the second or third from the stair? She closed her eyes and swallowed the hysterical lump in her throat as far as her fluttering heart would allow.

Eyes wide with panic, she looked at first one and then the other, unaware of the pot slipping from her hand until it bounced and rolled off her foot. The noise made her start. She was groping madly for the escaped article and had seized it before it rolled away from her clumsy kick, when one of the doors flew open and Wolf stood before her, silhouetted in its arched frame. For a moment, neither of them moved, and when they did, it was at the same time.

"Wo . . . olf!" Branwen hiccupped, her voice shrill to the point of breaking. She ran into him and threw her arms about his waist, as if she were at last safe and sound.

A second sob erupted against his chest and then another and another, until there was no stopping them. Branwen felt him ease the handle of the commode out of her hand and put it down, all the while whispering reassurances against the top of her head. Then his arms were around her, holding her so tightly, it was all she could do to breathe. She didn't mind at all. She was exactly where she wanted to be, the only place left in the world for her to go.

"Shush, lass. Tell me, are ye hurt?"

Branwen shook her head, unable to assemble a simple *no*. She felt him exhale in relief and crush her again to him. "I . . . I . . ." Her shoulders shook with the weight of her trauma, her cries racking them as if to unload the burden she'd carried too long. Tears saved from that nightmarish day when she'd helped the brothers from the monastery load her family's bodies on the cart, along with tears of fear and frustration that she'd held back as she made the daring journey to London, found their escape, drawing what little strength she had left with them, until Wolf bore the brunt of her slight weight.

"Lass, ye had your reasons to do it," Wolf soothed, when she was reduced to gasping breaths and swollen eyes.

"But . . . but . . ." Branwen tried to breath evenly. "I did . . . didn't do . . . do it!" she stammered brokenly. "You . . . you were r . . . right! I . . . I . . ."

"You *didn't* kill Kent?"

Branwen shook her head. "I let my father down in life

135

and now . . . now I . . . I couldn't be his son in . . . in death, either! I'm a cow . . . coward, Wolf!" she sobbed, tears coming from nowhere to scald her reddened cheeks. "I'm a good-for-no . . . nothing woma . . . aan!"

Her eyes widened as Wolf grasped her face between his large hands and shook her. "Now, that notion belongs with that mistletoe nonsense of yours!"

"I need y . . . you, Wolf!" Branwen implored shakily. "I need you to do it! 'Tis the least I can do to see it done, if not by my hand!"

The tenderness in her companion's hazel eyes iced over instantly. "I told you once: I don't kill for other people without payment!"

Branwen pressed against him, her neck arched so that she might look him in the eye. "I'll pay you! I'll marry you! You can have my lands . . . everything!"

Her body grew cold as Wolf set her back firmly and walked away. "Why would I want your lands? I'm not the farmer, lass, I'm a warrior."

"You could have the finest armor in the kingdom. You . . ." Branwen swallowed the bad taste her coming concession made in her mouth. "You don't even have to remain home. I can run the estate."

" 'Tis bondage to a man like me . . . and what reason do I have to think the king won't keep your land, if I can even best Kent on the field?"

"Because I've proof! I've Kent's colors, bold and despicable as he is!" Branwen ran to the sack containing her scant belongings and pulled them out. "This will prove him the traitor to the King's arrangement! Edward would not dare ignore this before all the Welsh knights he's promised equal favor! 'Twould be seed for another uprising!" Heartened that a dissuading retort did not come, Branwen went on, her color heightening. "And you said yourself I was lovely. I vow I would be an obedient wife."

"Obedient is a hard word to accept, coming from you,

lass. . . . And what would keep you from driving a dagger into my heart some night while I slept?"

Branwen's gaze softened in the firelight. "If I could not kill my enemy, how could I do so to my champion?" At the skeptical rise of Wolf's thick brow, she confessed, "And as I stand here now, sir, may God strike me dead if I lie. You are the first man who ever made me want to be a woman . . . made me feel like a woman." She looked away in embarrassment. "I know not what else to say, sir. I am not accustomed to such an unseemly feminine proposition."

"Are you proposing marriage to me, a mercenary, milady?"

A raking gaze settled on Branwen, moving up and down her, as if considering the prospect in the basest of terms.

"I . . . yes, providing you champion me against Ulric of Kent. My word, he's senseless from liquor now and will not be at his best tomorrow. I heard the guards say so."

Its long sweep from her feet to the crown of her head not enough to satisfy that which he looked for, Wolf's amber-green gaze started down again. More slowly this time, it dropped from her face to her breasts, where it hovered, as if he could see through the layers of cloth all but hiding them. His tongue slipped between his lips, moistening them, and Branwen's insides curled in response, sending another heat rash of color from her neck to the crown of her head. Gogsbreath, he acted the animal and she reacted the same, she thought, disconcerted by both responses.

"I'd see the merchandise first." He waved at her imperiously. "Take off those clothes. I've something more fitting for a woman to wear."

The crudity of the man! "As I recall," Branwen reminded him stiffly, "you have seen the . . . *merchandise.*"

"Aye, but 'tis the sampling I'm thinkin' of now, lass,"

he suggested with a low rumble that skittered unnervingly along her spine. "I told ye once I'd not take the risk of challengin' Kent without that. Should I not survive, 'tis the least ye owe me."

What Wolf was proposing was exactly what Branwen had dreamed about earlier, but for the way he did so. She had wanted him to show her once again what she had been born to be, the warm, willing woman to his virile, eager man, a mate and lover, not a sampling.

He knew no better, she assuaged herself. Better a crude-spoken and admitted rake than a silver-tongued deceiver in noble clothing. There was hope to add polish to the honest heart of the first, but one could not clean and brighten a soul that was black-hearted to the core. Inhaling deeply and praying for patience, she looked around. "You have something more feminine for me to wear, then?"

Wolf was as doused in ale as Kent, she realized. Although, it did look as if he'd spilled more than he'd consumed, judging from the stains on his green shirt, which bore as well some tidbits from his supper. If she stalled long enough, he might pass out like Kent. If she would have him, she wanted him warm and caring, not cold and drunk.

His step seemed steady enough as he walked over to the bed and retrieved from underneath the package he'd purchased earlier that day. Branwen had all but forgotten it in her turbulent state of mind. The large hands that snapped its binding cord and shook out the contents of ivory silk were sure as well—capable in battle and in lovemaking. Embarrassment at the base bent of her own observation made it impossible to look him directly in the eye.

"Frau Hilda picked this out for me personally . . . just in case the need for such a thing should arise," he added, one corner of his mouth twitching smugly.

She ought to act indignant that he'd presumed he'd need such a thing . . . particularly with her. "It's *Italian!*" Branwen remarked, ineffectively keeping the admiration from her tone, for she'd never seen a shift too lovely to cover up. The lace alone was worthy of a ballgown, not an undergarment.

"Her sister married an Italian banker on Lombard Street."

She caught herself and lifted her chin with a reproving tilt. "Don't you think you were being a bit presumptuous?"

White teeth flashed in a wry grin. "Not now, I don't."

The truth could not have been more plainly spoken, nor more undermining. It was as undeniable as the electricity that charged between them. A shiver swept through her, raising the gooseflesh on her skin, yet she was far from cold. It was happening again. Somehow their bodies were carrying on their own courtship, eager to be done with the games of innuendo the mind found so stimulating. Enough was enough.

"Do you want me, Wolf?" Branwen blurted out boldly.

The very suggestion kindled a light in his gaze that warmed her to the core. "Aye, I do, milady."

"As a wife?"

"Aye, as a wife . . . tonight." On the last word, his voice dropped to a velvet tone that all but stroked her. "Are we agreed, woman?"

Branwen nodded. Summoning her nerve with a deep breath, she unfastened her belt and dropped it to the floor at her feet. Accustomed to having help, she waited a moment, but the mercenary showed no inclination to assist her and she had no intention of asking. She reached up under her shirts and unfastened the trousers. Then, sitting on the edge of the bed, she peeled them off, along with her boots, to reveal a shapely pair of legs and delicately formed feet.

"Do you intend to bed me with your clothes on, sir?"

she challenged, erecting a brave front to cover an unanticipated attack of nerves. She'd felt nothing of the kind when she'd wistfully thought about her and Wolf earlier.

" 'Tis the bride's choice," he rallied. "What say ye, woman?"

How the words ever got out of her dry throat, Branwen would never know. *"Take them off!"*

At least if he was preoccupied with his own clothes, he wouldn't keep staring at her like the hungry cat at a tempting banquet table. Turning her back to him, Branwen pulled her shirts over her head, taking care to keep her plain wrinkled shift on in doing so. Once free of the tangled layers, she tugged it down over her hips, only to feel resistance. As she pulled harder, however, she felt the heat of Wolf's naked body press against her buttocks, melting the taut gooseflesh covering them on contact.

"At your service, milady." The hands that had kept her from lowering her shift tugged it up over her head and slung it aside.

"Where's the nightdress?" she asked, crossing her hands over her breasts as if chilled.

"Why risk tearin' such a pretty thing as that, when I'd have ye know now, 'twill come off the moment we're in the bed. Now turn around, lass, and let these eyes see 'twas no figment of imagination I saw in that bath, but a raven-haired Aphrodite rising from the water."

A raven-haired Aphrodite! The same words spoken by a pimple-faced Dafydd had once made her laugh, but laughter never entered her mind as Wolf turned her to face him. Indeed, it was her knees they affected this time, weakening them so that it was only prudent to lean into the inviting male body. She lifted her fingers to test the coarseness of his beard and trace the strong line of his jaw.

" 'Tis like a blunt broom!" she observed, not unaffected. "You would fare handsomer without it, I'd wager."

"More like your *Dafydd?*" He cupped her buttocks,

one in each hand, and closed the scant distance she'd instinctively maintained between them, so that not only were her breasts crushed against his chest, but her abdomen knew the full extent of his hard arousal.

Branwen inhaled sharply and lifted startled eyes to his. "Does *that* mean *now?*"

Wolf chuckled wickedly and began a sensuous massage of her back. He brushed his lips across the top of her head. "It means, milady, whenever you are ready." He felt her shoulder muscles let go in relief, her acceptance of his word as hard to resist as her naivete. Lifting her chin, he kissed her gently. "Do ye think ye can tell me when?" he teased, revealing a new and intensely beguiling feature of his continuously unfolding personality.

It would be so easy to throw her on the bed and ease this burning torment in his loins, but his aggression had frightened her once, and Wolf never wanted Branwen to fear him again. He'd have sworn it was revenge that drove him to ride into the night in order to catch up with her after she'd rendered him unconscious and left him, bandaged and covered chastely with towels, to come to alone. Perhaps it *had* been. After all, a little wisp of a girl like her outwitting a seasoned warrior as himself was a bit hard on his male ego.

But then, his anger turned to concern when he had not caught up with her. He'd begun to think she'd disappeared altogether to some ungodly fate, when a tavernkeeper recalled a young dark-haired boy who had joined a troupe of entertainers bound for London. Wolf had found the group putting on a nativity play in the Tower and discovered the clever ruse under which his charge was traveling. By the time he'd found her, wrapped in blankets snug as a babe in a cradle of hay, all he felt was relief.

There was more to her parents' death than what had been revealed, of that he was certain. He was also sure

141

that once she was discovered alive, she'd be endangered again. The only other thing concerning Lady Branwen of Caradoc that he knew without doubt was that he would make her his, body and soul. The soul would require more wooing, but the soft body molding to his as he sought the sweetness of her lips once more was as good a place as any to start.

Wolf's manner as a companion was as crude and inconsiderate as his tender lovemaking was the opposite. *Polished* hardly described the masterful way he paid homage to Branwen's body with his hands, his lips, his tongue. . . . What started off as slow and teasing, permitting her to savor each of the new responses racing eagerly to register in her mind—as well as places that could not think but were perfectly capable of feeling—became more and more urgent, until there was no question as to who was the master of the game and who was the novice.

It occurred to her through the passion-filled haze that enveloped her to repay some of this exquisite seduction, but the fleeting pangs of obligation were all too quickly drowned in wave after wave of the liquid fire melting her into complete and total submission. No longer was thinking even possible. Each caress, each kiss, each breath increased the dominance of the demanding need in her lower abdomen, until Branwen was breathlessly pleading his name against his perspiration-damp skin.

She knew no embarrassment as he drew away from her and stared down at her white skin, glistening from his fevered enticement. It took only a brush of his hands against the quivering flesh of her inner thighs to open the way to their mutual fulfillment. Instead of fear at the sight of his full and pulsing arousal, she felt a shiver of excitement rock her to her innermost being.

"Wolf!" she half-pleaded, half-commanded, stretching out her arms to him.

He answered with an animallike sound from deep

within his throat, and a swift and merciful thrust that finished the paltry defense of her maidenhood and occupied the heretofore forbidden sanctuary of her femininity. The fortifying breath Branwen had taken was expelled in a sharp cry, not so much from the discomfort he'd taken fiendish measures to minimize, but from the wonder of the experience itself. She could not contain the emotional swell that rose within her—that sweet magic of needing and being needed, of giving and receiving as man and woman.

"Wolf!"

Although he had not moved, allowing her time to adjust to his conquest, he looked down at her in concern. " 'Twill only pain you for a while, sweet Branwen. 'Tis all part of becoming a woman."

Her laughter smote his face with confusion. "Nay, sir, 'tis *wonderful!* I've had skinned knees twice as painful and not nearly as pleasant in the preparation. I vow, I think I've stood all a woman can take." She splayed her fingers on his chest, running them through the light fur there. "Might I enjoy this for a while before you quit me to sleep? I shouldn't mind your weight, if you wish to relieve your arms."

As if to leave him no alternative, she wrapped her legs around his hips and wriggled closer, so that Wolf wondered if he could oblige this beguiling creature's naive request without losing himself and his control. "I promise you, milady, I shall endeavor to make the most of this for you before sleep enters this mind."

Whether it was the wickedness of his chuckle that widened her eyes or the resulting vibration within her, Branwen didn't know. It was as unexpected as the slow, gyrating motion of the lean hips trapped within the confines of her legs. She tightened them, not to stop him, but to knit the union that threatened to explode with unbearable pleasure. Smiling, as if privately amused, he bent down and with his lips seized a quivering breast by

143

its rosy peak. His beard tickled the smooth surface of the soft, pliable mound, while a devilish tongue played with more sensitive tip.

Another tide began to churn and gain momentum, causing her to shudder uncontrollably. "Wolf!"

"Would you have me stop, milady?" he whispered huskily, his dancing eyes full of mischief.

"I . . ." Branwen smiled. "Nay, sir, I would know everything you are capable of, so that I might do my best to match it."

The invitation evoked another riddling chuckle, the source of which Branwen quickly came to understand. She had thought she knew everything about what a man did to a woman, but all she had understood was the physical part. Nay, she thought as a riptide of renewed desire raked through her, promising even more, 'twas the mechanics, no more, for never had she thought so many dizzying sensations could erupt in so many places at one time. If it was like this with every man, then for the first time, Branwen understood the tarts who haunted the slews and taverns.

Yet, even as Wolf drew up from the bed, her hips riding with him, she knew this was special, different from anything she could ever know with another man. Wolf was . . .

His downward thrust cut through her desire-dazed thoughts and freed him from her hold to launch a fierce, rocking assault. From daze to domination, his hunger-driven passion infected her, roaring in her veins, thundering in her ears, and driving out all but the fiery spell that swept not only Branwen, but also her virile golden lover, away to a sensual paradise.

Chapter Nine

"Their high feast was love, who gilded all their joys. Love brought them as homage the round table and all its company a thousand times a day. What better food could they have for body or soul? Man was there with woman, and woman there with man. What else should they be needing? They had what they were meant to have. They had reached the goal of their desire."

Gottfried von Strassburg

Warm, cozy, complete. Branwen felt all those things when she opened her eyes in the scant light afforded by the shuttered windows. It was what she was born for, Wolf had whispered in her ear. They were like Tristan and Isolde, he rumbled against the top of her head, proceeding to quote the poem with the eloquence of a bard as he held her in his arms after the turbulence of their sweet union had subsided and languor drugged them both. She'd closed her eyes to the sweet, husky conclusion. *They had reached the goal of their desire.*

It was almost sinful, she thought, that she should have found such happiness with her parents dead only a few short weeks. But they'd wanted her happy. Her mother had promised before they left that all Branwen's despair was but the precedent to a long, happy life as mistress of her ancestral lands. She would bear its heir, her aunt had reassured her. Her marriage meant peace.

Fate had somehow brightened her despair over her parents' tragedy by matching her with Wolf. She knew they would never have approved of this mercenary of questionable lineage, which her husband-to-be was, but it didn't matter. Before she hadn't cared if Kent killed her, but now she had every reason to live. If only they could know her mother's gentle prophesy had come true! Their daughter had taken fate by the collar and restored hope for Caradoc . . . their *daughter,* not their son.

Wolf would make a fine lord. He could hardly be the illiterate oaf he'd first seemed, any more than he was heartless and mercenary. Last night had opened her eyes to the real Wolf—a knight as chivalrous and gallant as the king himself. *Lady Branwen of Everywhere.* Somehow the title suited the more unorthodox side of her, which had so often driven her mother to her wits' end. They would be happy, she mused, a touch of melancholy sobering her as the sleep faded from her eyes. Perhaps, even now, she carried their grandchild and the future heir of Caradoc.

"Do you like children, Wolf?" she asked. Having forgotten the protective green stone which prevented such a possibility, she innocently ran her palm over her stomach to see if she felt any different.

She looked expectantly over her shoulder, her smile wavering as she discovered not Wolf, but a pile of pillows tucked at her back that had lulled her into sleeping longer than usual. With a gasp, she pulled back the covers, as if to be certain he wasn't hiding under them, up to more mischief, but the empty bed only confirmed what she knew. *He was gone.*

It hadn't been a dream, she argued at the onslaught of doubt that plagued her mind. He had surely made

146

love to her. Not only was she naked as the day of her birth, but her body still tingled with the aftermath of his passionate possession. If he were but half the warrior he was lover, Ulric of Kent would be a dead man before the day was out.

The morning chill raised gooseflesh on her bare skin, forcing her to seek out her clothing in haste. She was tired of these boyish rags, Branwen thought, tugging them on in disdain. When she and Wolf returned to Caradoc, she would wear her finest so that he would never make the mistake of thinking her a male again. She might even let her hair grow. Before she hadn't cared whether she was attractive or not, but now . . .

A round of laughter drew her attention to the activity in the hallway, and Branwen tiptoed over to the door to listen. She had no idea of the time, except that it had to be late or Wolf would have brought up breakfast . . . or at least sent it, she mused, glancing over at the tray the servant had delivered last night with the remains of her supper still on it. Beside the food was the note he'd sent telling her of Kent's whereabouts.

Voices outside the door drew her attention back to the conversation in the hall. Challenges had been made last night at the banquet as the knights paired off against each other. Already the betting was taking place by servants who would not even be able to attend.

"Who'd have thought Kent would even be about yet, much less working out his charger in the fields? My money's on him! Ain't knight nor knave what can best him on a bad day!"

"Bet all ye want, ain't nobody fool enough to challenge 'im yet!"

"He's the king's favorite. He'll fight the winner of the other jousts," the more enthusiastic of the two scoffed. "I hear he's got enough suits of armor and chargers to outfit an army of his own."

" 'Twill be a novel sight for the likes of them Welsh-men. Ain't many have respect for a knight's trappin's. By the by, where's Ollie?"

"Gone with the king and his stewards to the tourna-ment."

The other servant bellowed in outrage. "You mean 'e's left us to get these chambers aired and cleaned be-fore the none day feast whilst he watches the games with the gentry?" An explosion of expletives faded down the hall as the men moved on.

Gogsbreath, it must be later than she thought! Wolf had left her to sleep to go on to the games without her! As if she'd miss this! She lived and breathed seeing Ulric of Kent on the bloodied end of a lance, and now that it was about to be, Branwen surely wanted to be there. She wanted to see Wolf triumphant!

Her Tristan of courage, she reflected warmly, picking up the directions he'd put down for her the night before and staring at them blankly. Now she lived and breathed for another purpose, and her rough-mannered mercenary had made her want it for the first time. She wanted to be his wife and mother of his son. Of course it would be a boy. A man of Wolf's capabilities could have nothing else as firstborn.

Her aunt had once told her, it was only halfhearted lovemaking that made a girl, although Branwen was the exception. Considering the boldness of her father and her mother's warm glow whenever he was about, Branwen had barely made the female sex. It explained her own bold and stubborn resolve. Both women had fretted from time to time that they wondered if a man existed who would ever tame their *fair raven*. If only they had seen Wolf. Again her heart twinged with the sup-pressed grief buried deep inside.

However, something about the note she held in her hand shook her from the melancholy. It wasn't last night's note. It was another, written on the back of the miniature map of the castle. Eagerly, she scanned the lines, but as she did so, her heart seized in her chest.

"My lusty little raven,

'Tis best if you remain in my room till the challenge is done. With Providence's blessing I shall return to you 'ere the day is out and bring you forth as the lady you deserve to be. I am securing armor for the fight from my good fellows, for to face Kent in anything less would be pure folly. My heart is yours, no matter what fate has in store for us.

Wolf"

What could he mean, *no matter what fate has in store?* Surely he could defeat the pampered and liquor-dulled Kent! Unbidden, the conversation she'd overheard between the servants came back to her. *Ain't knight nor knave what can best him on a bad day!* But Wolf could do anything, she thought resolutely, The words rang more hollow with each repetition meant to hold on to her opinion. Just like she'd believed her father could . . . except that Owen ap Caradoc lay dead with his wife in the family vaults now.

"Wolf!" she exclaimed in a tortured whisper, grabbing up her boots to don them.

She had to get to the tournament field, to stop him from issuing the challenge she'd begged him only last night to make. Life would not be worth living without him. Caradoc would mean nothing. By God, she would kill herself if anything happened to the mercenary who had won her heart, Branwen vowed, tugging down her hat over her dark, disheveled hair and making for the door.

"Hey there, boy! Come help us with—"

"I have to deliver a weapon to the tourney me master left," Branwen shouted, producing the blade strapped to her waist as evidence. "He'll kill me now for sure for borrowin' it to practice and not puttin' it back with his pack!"

149

It didn't matter, she told herself, breathlessly running across the inner bailey. Kent could have Caradoc and think her dead and gone. Let Edward deal with it. She and Wolf could take to on the road as Lord and Lady of Everywhere. Her needs were not large and the adventure appealed to her impetuous nature. Nothing mattered as long as he was alive and by her side.

The tournament field lay beyond the large abbey near the palace, a royal defiance of the church, which frowned on such games and diversion. Pageant wagons abounded, with plays of the most pious and ribald nature. There were puppeteers to amuse the children, as well as a host of mimes, mummers, and jugglers to keep the crowds satisfied until the heralds announced the next contestants in the bannered enclosure in front of the royal dais.

People of noble status were afforded a view of the field according to their rank, leaving scant room for the commoners who placed wagers just as vigorously as their betters. Boys cheered from the top of tall posts where the festive banners fluttered in the bright winter sun. Horses snorted clouds of steam, pawing impatiently, while their tack and armor were put on by busy squires. Small tents dotted the area, each boasting the colors of the noble warriors who were inside being fitted for battle like their chargers.

Wolf had no colors, no way to identify him. Frantic, Branwen raced in and out of the people, the horses, and the tents, searching for his familiar face or someone of his stature. If he had fought Kent while she still slept, warm from his lovemaking, she would never forgive herself. It was love that had launched her on this vendetta against Kent and love that would satisfy it. She only prayed she would not be too late.

Her eyes were wide with fear and her chest ached from her frantic search as the heralds blew trumpets to announce the next joust. Berkley was to take on a knight from Saxony. *Berkley!* Branwen raced around to where the contestants entered at the opposite end of the field from the dais, in time to see them trot toward the field to pay their respects to the king. Wolf would surely be watching his friend.

To her dismay, however, there was no sign of that yellow-bearded face anywhere in the shouting masses. None! In desperation, she tugged on the sleeve of the squire wearing Berkley's colors. "Boy, where is your master's friend . . . the mercenary called Wolf?"

"Unless your master is in the games, *boy,*" the squire retorted patronizingly, "get ye gone! I know of no Wolf but the kind that haunts the forests!"

Oblivious to his greater size, Branwen flushed with anger and grabbed the squire roughly by his scarlet mantle. "I said where—"

The fists that struck her chest knocked the rest of her demand out of her and sent her sprawling backward on the frozen earth, steaming with the fresh addition of manure from the impressive chargers who had preceeded them.

"Ho, there! Out of the way, or neither of you will ever know how it feels to sit a charger!"

Branwen tucked her feet under her as a horse and knight forced their way between her and the bullying squire. The bright orange skirt trimmed in royal waved the scent of horseflesh toward her nose, drawing her gaze after it. *Orange and blue,* the same colors as those she had left in Wolf's chambers to prove Kent's guilt. The rider pulled his magnificent steed over to a holding area to await the victor of the current joust.

It was Kent! Where was Wolf? she thought, glancing around the crowd frantically. Perhaps it was the armor, but never had she seen a fiercer-looking warrior—a demon in shining metal and flamboyant plumage. Painted on his notched jousting shield was a black dog in midleap against orange and blue quarters. Barely visible above a rich mantle of royal, the golden curls she'd seen peeking out from a nightcap glistened in the sunlight.

The roar of the crowd drew her attention to where Berkley unseated his challenger in the first charge. In a clash of metal, the loser crashed to the ground. It sounded as if every silver plate in London had struck a stone floor at the same time. The man just lay there for a moment, recovering from the wind-robbing fall. Gradually, his metal-clad limbs began to quiver and then thrust in an attempt to get up, while Berkley rode forward to the cheers of the crowd as victor.

When the loser's squires rushed forward to assist their master, Ulric of Kent spurred the black-eyed horse toward the dais to join his challenger as the heralds announced his entry to the field of combat. The clamor of the spectators was enhanced by the thunder of hooves coming from behind Branwen.

Wolf! she thought, pivoting in time to see, not one, but three knights in full regalia race onto the field, bringing the king to his feet in spite of the guards, who rushed readily to fix themselves between the intruders and the royal leader. None of them rode a black charger, confusing her as much as the familiar colors of Elwaid. *Dafydd ap Elwaid and his companions!*

Her ex-fiancé's identity registered at the same time as Edward, in a voice as imperious as his position dictated, demanded, "What is the meaning of this, good knights? The preliminary games are done. This is the King's joust and we await our champion."

Dafydd threw back his helmet and shouted defiantly, *"Champion,* sire? Does His Majesty acknowledge a murderer and traitor to the alliance of Wales and England as a *champion?"*

Stunned, Branwen made her way into the ring in front of the ropes holding back the crowds, oblivious to the irritated whispers of complaint behind, whispers that were the only sound breaking the sudden stillness as everyone awaited the king's reply. Was this the Dafydd who had ignored her request for aid?

"Explain yourself, sirs, for these are grave charges you make against Sir Ulric, as well as our royal favor."

"My fellows and I came to pay homage to Your Majesty, sire, as did my good friend Owen ap Caradoc and his family. But on the road to London, my friend and all his retinue, including this scoundrel's bride-to-be, were ruthlessly ambushed and murdered."

A murmur flared from both nobles and commoners as the outrage was repeated in shocked whispers around the arena. It grew until the king found it necessary to raise his hand to the trumpeteers to summon silence with their instruments.

"And what does this have to do with Kent?"

"The murderer's men, those who were felled by brave Owen before he and his soldiers were overcome, wore the orange and blue of yon knight, and somewhere in this city is an eyewitness to the slaughter . . . a young boy by the name of Edwin!"

The king turned to the accused. "We would hear what you have to say to this, sir. You know the fate of traitors to our cause, be it war or peace. You told us but yesterday that your bride was here and would be presented to us this night at the banquet."

The knight bowed his head. "Aye, Your Grace, and I spoke the truth."

"Then *produce* her, sir!" Dafydd sneered boldly.

Unable to tear herself from the drama unfolding before her eyes, Branwen stared at Ulric of Kent as he swung his snorting stallion's head round and rode toward the exit. What was he up to? she wondered, knowing full well he could not produce the Lady Branwen. There was only one who knew she was alive.

153

Color drained from her face and settled in her feet, weighing them so that she could not move, even when she dropped her astonished gaze to the sleek black legs and fetlocks that seemed to carry horse and rider smoothly toward her. Thunder burst in her ears, echoing her heartbeat, as everything seemed to commense in slow motion.

The metal-clad giant with bright orange and blue plumage reached for her, his gloved hand hooking in her belt, so that when Pendragon swung around, she was flung out toward the onlookers, arms and legs flailing in midair. It felt as though she were flying, but for the cinch that cut her in half with her own weight. The clatter of the armor rang in her ears, like tin clashes above her pounding pulse, and then it squeaked to a halt before the royal dais.

"*There*, Your Majesty," Dafydd cried out in triumph. "There is the very boy of whom I spoke!"

Branwen dropped to her knees when Ulric loosened his hold, but before she could assemble her wits and climb to her feet, the knight was on the ground beside her, resuming his grip on her belt. Eyes wide with fear, she looked from the stern-faced king to the faceless man behind the helmet holding her. Then, with his free hand, he flung up the visor, where a familiar hazel gaze met hers.

"*Here* is my bride, Your Majesty, alive and well, by God's good grace . . . orphaned by brigands on the road here as I rode out to meet her."

"What jest is this?" Dafydd derided behind them. "This is Edwin, Owen's bastard!"

Ulric of Kent snatched the hat off Branwen's hair and turned her so that the angry young Welshman might see her. "She misled us both, Elwaid. 'Twas not until our night at Bath that I discovered the young lady's . . ." Branwen whirled around, her eyes glowering up into a mischievous gaze. "Identity," the knight finished gallantly.

154

"Gogsbreath!"

Dafydd's shocked expression fell on deaf ears, for at that very moment, Ulric tugged off his helmet and revealed himself to Branwen. Unable to believe she'd been so taken in, Branwen studied his clean-shaven face. The golden curls were the same, but the beard . . .

"I heard it on good word, I'd be more appealing with a lad's face."

Gone with the beard was the ruffian's accent. It was all a ruse, all an act of treachery as base as that which led to her parents' death, for he had surely slain her heart. At least, it felt as though the crushing pain it suffered was killing it. Her voice broke in a tortured, disbelieving, "Wolf!"

"Ulric means *wolf*, milady. I am one and the same man, beard or nay, to be your husband 'ere the week is out as you proposed only last night."

Branwen struggled with the blade cutting her throat from the inside out. It would not be swallowed, but simply wedged itself so that words were shakily delivered. "Nay, sir. I was tricked into thinking noble a conscienceless demon cloaked in deceit."

"Milady . . ."

"Get your hand away from me!" Branwen growled, knocking away his hand as it moved to catch the single tear that had escaped her control. Anger and hurt were but a few of the emotions that filled her voice with body-shaking passion. "I would not marry you if you were the last man on this earth! *I won't!*" she reiterated, turning defiantly to the King. "You can hang me and cut out my insides while I watch, but I will not be wife to this murdering, deceitful . . ." To her humiliation, her voice cracked with a sob. "I saw his men, Your Majesty!" she cried, rushing out of Kent's reach toward the dais. "They wore *his* colors! They . . . they beheaded my

155

parents and committed unspeakable atrocities to the maid they thought 'twas me."

"Then why did yon knight offer his protection to you to see you safely brought to London?" Edward asked, his brow knitted beneath his royal crown.

"Who knows the workings of a fiendish mind such as his? He killed my parents! I will not submit myself to his likes. Surely Your Majesty can see . . ."

The man in the blue mantle swung Branwen about and shook her roughly. "I did not kill your parents, milady! As I stand here before God and these witnesses, I knew nothing of this treachery! The pledges we made last night are—"

He broke off as Branwen spat at him, the spittle running down his clean-shaven cheek. "That is what I think of your word, Ulric of Kent!" His name came out as the lowest of oaths. "*His colors*, Your Majesty. The dead attackers were cloaked in orange and blue!"

Before she realized what was happening, the heavy blue mantle Kent wore over his armor was pulled over her head. She screeched and fought to shake it off, only to be caught up in the ironclad embrace of the angry warrior.

"Look you, Your Majesty. This woman wears my colors! This, according to her word, makes her mine!" Ulric bellowed, roaring like the lion he appeared with his golden mane blowing in the light breeze.

The King motioned for his company to rise. "We will hear more of this at the hall." Raising his voice, he addressed the waiting crowd. "We declare Berkley champion of the day! The tournament is over!"

Sounds of disappointment and exhortation echoed in Branwen's ears as her captor turned her loose to follow Edward and his retinue back to the palace. Without looking back, she slung off the mantle and spat on it, before walking proudly over it and straight ahead. She clenched her teeth tightly until the tears that threatened

156

were bullied back into hiding. How ironic that the man who had made her want to be a woman was the very one whom she must battle as an equal.

"Branwen, wait!"

She heard Dafydd call after her but kept on going.

"Branwen!"

"How is it your courage comes to you when you think me dead, but to find me alive turns you back into the weak coward you always were?"

"Branwen, had I known, I would have personally seen you to London and confronted Kent with you."

Branwen stopped. "Then do it now, Elwaid!" she averred dispassionately. "There he is, being stripped of his armor, even as we speak. You have the advantage. Take the deceiver for me!"

"I can not defy the king, milady."

"I heard no order not to spill his blood. Only to tell more at the royal court."

Dafydd glanced back uneasily at Wolf, who walked, half out of his armor and surrounded by attending squires trying to remove it in passage.

"I *thought* so," Branwen scoffed bitterly. "Well, *I* have no fear of death!"

Leaving Dafydd standing dumbstruck, she whipped out the blade hidden in her shirt and charged with a fiendish yell at the paused knight, who waited impatiently for his leg armor of cuir-bouilli to be removed. So startling was the sight of her small figure rushing the giant warrior that his squires looked on with frozen stares.

Branwen threw her body into Wolf, catching him off balance, then continued on, her momentum carrying them both over in a pile of armor and tangled limbs. "You lying bastard!" she grunted, crawling up his front and shoving the blade at his throat, so that it indented skin, pinkened from the new shave he'd received earlier. "How does it feel to be on the bleeding end of a knife for a change?"

157

"Stop her!" the king commanded in the background.

However, the only words that penetrated were those of the man beneath her. "Be done with it, *if you can*, milady."

Branwen stared down into Wolf's murky gaze and felt as if her heart were being pulled by it from her very chest. He saw beyond her anger, beyond the cold steel of the blade he'd taught her to use, to her very soul—an ordinarily gentle soul, tormented and tortured into reckless and impulsive behavior. Cold-blooded murder, however, was not within the realm of it. He knew that after last night.

She sniffed back her emotion. " 'Twas you in Kent's room, wasn't it, Wolf?"

"I had to see how deeply your ability to hate ran, milady. We both know now, 'tis love that you need more than revenge."

"Not from *you!*"

Wolf's doubt was evident before he even voiced it. "I am the same man you vowed to marry and offered your love. 'Tis only the name that is different, for I am Ulric of Kent. Wolf is but a namesake as the raven is to you."

Branwen's grip on the knife loosened with her wavering emotions. "I may spare your life, milord, but your treachery has slain me as surely as it did my mother and father. I will never forgive you so long as I draw breath. I curse you and all you are. Heed you well this, Ulric of Kent. Fate's favor is fleeting, but wolf or no, 'tis always bad luck to cross the raven."

She saw Wolf's expression change, sharpening in warning, but before she could react or register his loud "No!" one of the guards struck her a blinding blow, knocking her forward, face slamming into his chest. Blackness rushed in, like a dizzying anesthetic, as she tried to hold on to the handle of the knife, which had somehow disappeared . . . disappeared just like her awareness of the man she instinctively clung to as she was swallowed in the senseless void.

Chapter Ten

The great hall in the palace was buzzing with speculation. Those who had missed the bizarre confrontation
at the tournament listened eagerly to those who hadn't.
All the while, inside the king's private council chamber,
the two factions squared off, separated by the table at
which His Majesty sat. Edward heard each side in turn,
but it was obvious to Branwen that he had only listened
to Dafydd and herself as a courtesy. His royal mind had
been made up . . . in favor of Kent.

She would not look at the man who had so deviously
won her heart and body, lest she fall victim to those
warm eyes she could feel watching her intently. It was
humiliating enough to awaken from the blow that had
rendered her unconscious in his arms, much less to lose
her temper and the scant credulity her rash behavior
had left her with. While she struggled to regain her wits
amidst the sore ache from the assault, Wolf, or rather,
Ulric, had spoken to His Majesty on her behalf, blaming
her reaction, indeed her entire charade as a boy, on the
trauma of her parents' death.

So convincing was he that Branwen nearly believed
him. Lord knew, she had been through hell since she'd
left Snowdonia with her parents. She'd seen and experienced things far beyond her protected upbringing. But

159

for the mercenary . . . her *enemy*, she reiterated sternly, she'd might not have made it. Yet, Kent hadn't helped her the last leg of the journey. She'd ventured that alone, at the mercy of the forests and all its howling spirits. More than once during that horrible night, she'd questioned her sanity.

"We hardly think the presence of Kent's colors at the scene of your family's death is solid evidence of his guilt. As Ulric so aptly demonstrated when he wrapped milady in his mantle, the colors did not make her his."

"But does it not seem odd that Kent was traveling on the same road at the same time as my father?" Branwen challenged.

The royal appraisal made her want to shrink under the table, for she was aware of her filthy and disheveled appearance—hardly befitting her true station. She hadn't combed her hair. It crowned her head with untamed raven curls that made her white pallor almost sickly in comparison. Even her wind-chapped lips were bloodless, for standing in front of the man who had brought Llewelyn to his knees was, at the least, intimidating. Even sitting down, Edward was a commanding presence. Nonetheless, she kept her chin at a noble tilt, doing her best to act the lady of Caradoc, regardless of her common and unseemly attire.

Ulric of Kent's voice, oddly velvet with patience, provided the answer to her query. "Your Majesty is well aware of my business in Wales. There has been much amiss at Caradoc that has slowed the building of the new fortress. I was hastening from there to my wedding, when I happened upon Lady Branwen at the monastery. In view of her distress, I thought it best to keep my identity a secret."

"Hear you the logic of yon knight's words, milady?"

"I have heard much from yon knight that was not true. Why should I believe him now?" Branwen rallied.

"Although, I am curious to know the nature of the need that demanded he visit my *father's* keep."

She hadn't meant to sway, but the blurred vision of the room that swept past her would not be denied. It passed as quickly as it came, but not before it was noticed. Ulric of Kent started for her, but Dafydd, standing at her side, steadied her beneath a protective and possessive arm. With the snap of Edward's imperial fingers, a chair was brought forth for her to sit upon.

"Your Majesty, perhaps this had best wait until the lady has recovered. As you can see, she is overwrought."

Tempting as Ulric's suggestion was, because it was his, Branwen would not have it. "I am fine, Your Majesty, and I would hear of what is amiss at Caradoc."

His momentary compassion hardening, Ulric obliged her tersely. "Three of my builders and masons have met with a most gruesome death, abducted in the midnight hours and found with their throats slit the following day. Warnings to cease construction have been written in their blood on Caradoc's new walls. This has so spooked the laborers that they will not work."

"Did you expect to be welcomed with open arms, sir?" Branwen demanded wryly.

"I expect my due as the new lord of Caradoc, no more, no less."

"So what was your solution, milord? Did you lock up every Welshman?

Ulric's countenance grew grim. "Nay, milady, I had one Welshman executed for each of my slaughtered men and will continue to do so until this madness stops."

Branwen leaned against the leather back of her chair, weak with dismay. "Gogsdeath, my people are at the mercy of injustice all around! How know you the men you execute are guilty, sir?"

"If they are not, those who are will suffer the condemnation of their fellow men. Then the Welsh can punish the Welsh. This senseless loss of lives must be stopped."

"Is it the loss of life that concerns you, Ulric of Kent, or the delay in the building of your grand castle?"

Branwen jumped as Ulric brought his fist down on the King's table. "Damn you, woman, I am sick of being accused the murderer, when it is obvious there is a fanatical plot to undermine the peace we seek! Can you not see, even *your* life is in danger?"

"Kent is right, milady," Edward affirmed thoughtfully. "There is a plot about to avoid the peace between our peoples. You and Kent are but victims of it."

"If that is so, it is not a Welsh plot. My family was on its way to pay homage, yea, myself, even to marry Kent to protect our people, yet all I have seen is bloodshed in return for our good faith."

The King nodded in understanding. "So, if you were to ferret out this vermin that seeks to avoid peace and drive a wedge between us, you would see justice done?"

"Wholeheartedly, sir! Send me back to Caradoc and I will rout him out and swing him from a scaffold . . . with *evidence*, that is, of his guilt."

Ulric leaned forward on his hands, his drilling look refusing to allow Branwen escape from her challenge. "Then return as my bride, milady, and we shall administer justice together. Do so if for no other reason than to protect your people's interest, since you think me so unjust an administrator."

How neatly the trap had been laid! Branwen shifted under the fathomless appraisal of both the King and his knight. She felt the trembling rabbit in the snare, half sick with fright and half with despair.

"Or shall I depart from London to take this matter into my own hands as I see fit, without your gentle council?" Ulric went on.

"As if you would heed my word!" Branwen sneered, mustering a skeptical tone. "Nay, Kent, more likely you'd make me the next example!"

"Milady!" Edward warned, a raised hand bringing down the volume of her voice, which had risen as the snare tightened in her throat. "You will return with our blessing and protection. Your father came to offer us his allegiance and his daughter. 'Tis our obligation to him to see her so protected as well as properly wed. The wedding will proceed as planned."

"But Your Majesty!" Branwen objected.

"Once your people see themselves represented by you in the administration hall of their cantref, their minds will be put at ease as to the justice to their kind."

"But! . . ."

"The marriage is a sign of permanence. Like you and yon knight, England and Wales will be as one." As if pronouncing a judgment, the king tapped his scepter on the table, silencing further protest. "We have every trust that the two of you will make a noble pair, just and fruitful to the benefit of the Crown."

"Dafydd!" Branwen turned in desperation to her last pillar of support, only to see it crumble.

"There is much wisdom in His Majesty's decision, milady. I hereby pledge my assistance to Sir Ulric to end this senseless shedding of Welsh and English blood."

"Well said, good knight!" the king acknowledged in satisfaction. "Now let us make merry in the hall, for a wedding is a joyous occasion to anticipate."

While the men rose, Branwen continued to sit at the table, numbed with her helplessness and frustration. They each moved with purpose, while she felt left in limbo. She could not go back to a happier time, and going forward held no attraction. What *was* she to do? Wander around the palace halls begging handouts until the wedding, then march on His Majesty's arm to her groom in these rags?

Self-pity and desolation blurred her eyes, but she refused to spill their evidence in front of her tormentors. If only she had died with her family! Then she would not face this travesty of royal justice and her heart would not feel as though it were being wrung in half within her bosom.

But what would her people do, those hard-working souls who depended on her family for support and protection? They still needed her, not as an avenging son, but as a protective daughter of Cymry. They needed her with all her wits about her, not charging about recklessly seeking blood for blood. The task before her could only be accomplished by a woman.

"Excuse me, milady, but His Majesty has instructed that I show you to your quarters."

Shaken from her thoughts, Branwen rose and followed the steward out of the private chamber and into the great hall. Dozens of pairs of eyes followed her, but she kept her head erect and walked as if bedecked in satin, rather than coarse and ragged wool. To her surprise, she was shown to the room she had shared with Wolf the night before. Another means of torture? she wondered bitterly.

When she was alone, she wandered aimlessly about the room. At least the bed had been newly made and there was fresh water in a bowl on the table by the bed. A fire danced merrily in the hearth, reflecting the sounds of laughter coming from the great hall a floor below and the merriment echoing up from the inner bailey over which her window looked. It was comfortable, she admitted, *for a prison.*

After all, that was what it was, wasn't it? She was there, not by choice, but by royal order. Unless the door was left unguarded, she thought suddenly. She crossed the room and tested the latch, which gave way freely. However, the noise of the opening door brought to his feet a servant seated on a bench across the hall.

"Is there somethin' wrong, milady?" Branwen needed no imagination to sense the disdain in the man's voice, for it showed on his face as well. By now, she supposed the entire kingdom knew of the confrontation at the tourney and the wild Welshwoman who had attacked Ulric of Kent.

"Nay, I was just looking about."

Inside the room again, Branwen went to the window seat and forced open one of the wooden shutters. The cold air blasted her in the face, but it felt refreshing compared to the smoky inner chambers of the palace. The pageant wagons were there in the bailey, gaily bedecked in reds, greens, blues, and yellows. The townspeople flocked in numbers around them, seeking the Christmastide entertainment, while the tempting aromas of the wares carried by the piemen wafted upward toward her lofty perch.

Peering directly down, Branwen could see the thatched canopy of an open shop below, fitted tightly against the turret wall to keep thieves from robbing from the rear as well as from the front. It appeared sturdy enough to break a fall, she mused, her mind beginning to formulate a way out of this damnable predicament. If she could make it to Caradoc on her own and assemble a company of loyal servants, it was possible she could find out the meaning of these murders by the time Ulric caught up with her. At that time, she could swear allegiance to him, in lieu of matrimony. She saw no reason why that would not do.

Her heartened gaze moved to the bed, where strong woven linens were tucked snugly around the plump mattress on which, only hours before, she had given herself completely to her deceiver. How well he'd disguised hell as heaven, wrong as right, and manipulation as love. Tristan and Isolde! she sneered in silent disdain.

By all that was holy, Tristan had not been able to help his love for Isolde. He was bewitched by love, not filled with greed and lust as Wolf ... Ulric, she reminded herself again, trying to keep the two separate, in spite of the fact that they were one and the same. Honey-dipped lies, so easy to swallow and too binding to escape.

Making up her mind, Branwen closed the shutter. As she approached the bed to relieve it of its linens, a sharp knock sounded at the door, giving her a guilty start. "Yes?"

"His Majesty has ordered you a bath, milady! May we come in?"

Left with little choice, Branwen opened the door for the servants, who entered carrying a wooden tub just large enough for her to sit in with her knees drawn up under her. Following them were more servants carrying buckets of water with which they filled the bath. The water carriers repeated their trip twice more before the tub was filled halfway, affording a decent if not luxurious bath like the one she'd experienced at the slew.

And she did need one, Branwen thought, taking the towels from the servant woman to dismiss her. She smelled like horses and God only knew what else! Besides, how could it hurt to escape clean? She couldn't make it away in the daylight hour, anyway, for fear of drawing attention. After sundown, when only the lights of the torches in the inner bailey and on the pageant wagons flickered against the darkness, she would make her move.

"My name is Miriam, milady. His Majesty's chamberlain assigned me to your service."

Aside from the episode with Wolf, which was far from relaxing, when *was* the last time she'd been helped to dress or bathe? Branwen gave in to the indulgence. "That would be lovely, Miriam. I am too tired to lift a finger, much less attend to the scrubbing I sorely need. I've acted the boy too long for even *my* liking!"

Miriam was a pleasant sort. She was a farm girl from the west country bordering Wales, who had sought the more glamorous life at the palace waiting on His Majesty's lady guests. Only recently arrived, she had yet to be assigned to a permanent position with one of the ladies of the court. Her speech and manners were a cut above the ordinary attendant, a deliberate effort on her part. With dark brown hair, stylishly hanging in waves down her back from beneath a ruffled bonnet, and clothing that bespoke some noble gentleman's favor, she was a pretty addition to Edward's court.

"What happened to your hair, milady? 'Tis more like a page's than a maid's." the servant asked in guileless concern as she worked it into a lather with delicately scented soap. "Did the villains who killed your parents cut it off?"

Branwen winced as Miriam's thumbs assaulted the swelling at the base of her neck. Instead of berating the servant, who apologized the moment she realized what she'd done, she relaxed against the side of tub. " 'Tis easier to manage so. My grandmother wore her hair this way."

"But long hair is a woman's glory, milady."

"Some man told you that, no doubt."

"Nay, milady, 'twas my own grandmother. Still, I'd wager I could do something to make it look . . . more feminine," Miriam tactfully speculated. "With those natural curls and ribbons or a small braid perhaps . . ."

Branwen chuckled without humor. "Aye, 'twould do wonders for those rags."

"Well, you're too pretty to hide your beauty under a man's clothes! The fact is, you'll need all your wiles to

167

keep your husband-to-be in your bed once the wedding knot is tied."

"As if I'd want that!"

Miriam's doll-like face grew incredulous. "My word, milady, are you blind? Why, Sir Ulric is sorely sought after by all the ladies, wed or not. 'Tis been a sad time since the announcement of the wedding. I wouldn't be surprised if some jealous lady in the court had not tried to keep you and your family from arriving safely."

"Then she has a perverted sense of accomplishment to leave Ulric's colors behind to indicate his guilt."

The servant girl made a grimace. "Aye, I hadn't thought of that." Her round face brightened again. "Maybe it was a jealous husband! Lord knows there were enough . . ." Upon seeing Branwen's sharpening interest, Miriam covered her mouth with her hand. "Oh, blessed Mary, I'm sorry, milady! Naturally I'm speakin', I mean, speak*ing* of affairs that happened *before* your betrothal."

"The knave has the morals of a tomcat, Miriam. I've seen that for myself."

"Ohh," Miriam acknowledged uneasily. "Then I'm sorry, milady. I'll say no more."

Miriam did not say any more. It was Branwen who found herself talking instead to a complete stranger. Perhaps it was guilt for taking her frustration out on the innocent girl or the fact that here was someone almost as unfamiliar with this English noble world as she, a sympathetic ear, that led her to tell the story of her travels with the mercenary she'd met at the monastery. As she did so, there were times she joined Miriam in amusement at the discomfiting positions Branwen had found herself in, being treated like one of the men.

"Aye, there are surely two sides to men," the servant agreed as she scrubbed Branwen's back briskly. "I've seen it with my stepbrothers. I'm glad to be free of them and their crude ways, and pity the poor girl taken in by their put-on manners."

"Or good looks!" Branwen added scornfully.

There was silence for a moment, broken finally by Miriam. "He *is* handsome, isn't he, milady ... Lord Ulric, that is? At least he isn't like most of the gents. He doesn't force attentions on a maid that doesn't want them. 'Tis the women that do the chasing in his case. By the saints, how I would have liked to see his lordship's face when he found you a girl and not the lad he'd bullied about."

Well, *she* certainly had not chased Wolf! Branwen thought, distracted from the conversation by the revelation of Ulric's pursuit by the opposite gender. 'Twas *he* that had climbed in the bath with her and coaxed her into kissing him. 'Twas *he* that had followed her to London and slept at her side in the hay. 'Twas *he* that ... She glanced uneasily at the bed. The blame of last night's rapture, she could not clearly define. If she admitted the truth, she had been as eager as he. A step into heaven, a plunge into hell, she mused, trying to swallow the lump that wedged in her throat. Damnation, no doubt it was Caradoc that had made him take up the chase!

"There's some here at the palace that make it hard for a maid to keep her innocence, if you know what I mean," Miriam chattered on, continuing with the woman-to-woman talk without noticing Branwen's withdrawal. "They think a pretty dress or a handful of ribbons is fair exchange for a warm roll in bed. Gifts ease their conscience, I suppose. I thought when I left the farm, it would be different at court, where there were gentlemen, but I vow, they're the worst! Like you said, a face for the ladies and a face for the poor servant girl ..." Miriam broke off at the interrupting knock on the door. "That would be the seamstresses his lordship sent for."

"Seamstresses?"

"Give us a few more moments and the lady will be ready!" Miriam shouted, taking charge of the situation. "His lordship wants to see his bride clothed in keepin' . . . *keeping* with her station, milady. I'd wager them . . . *those* clothes," she emphasized with a purposeful nod toward the boy's clothing, "have made your fair skin cringe with the itch."

"By God, if he thinks to buy me with . . ." Branwen choked off her rebuttal as the servant dumped a bucket of rinse water over her head.

"There now, milady, it isn't as if his lordship isn't going to marry you. At least there's *some* honor to your gifts."

Upon seeing the girl fingering the figured pink cloth of her dress, Branwen bit off her tirade. She'd been so caught up in her own quandary that she had paid no attention to what Miriam was saying. Nonetheless, the girl's circumstances were clear. "You've been forced, haven't you, Miriam?"

The maid's fair complexion surpassed the color of her dress. " 'Tis the lot of us common girls, milady. I'm not complaining, mind you. Someday a steward may take me to wife, and then I'll be safe from such advances. Now let's dry you off before you take a chill. I vow, it feels as if the window has been opened!"

Branwen was wrapped in a blanket, submitting to Miriam's comb, when the seamstresses dutifully returned. For a full half an hour she was pinched, pinned, and perturbed by the impertinence of the head seamstress, who acted as if she were condescending to work with Branwen at all. Worse, the women chattered to each other about her as if she could not hear them.

Finally, she could endure no more. It was bad enough

170

to stand through fittings for clothing she wanted. She was tired, her head ached, and her patience was at its very end. With an angry jerk, she tugged away from the woman turning up the hem of the garment they were refitting to her figure.

"Milady, please!" the head seamstress reprimanded sharply.

"Out!" Branwen growled, ignoring the raking pins that had held the garment to her delicate curves. "I'll have no more of this affront! Tell Ulric of Kent he'll take me in one dress or not at all! Caradoc has provided me with ample clothing. I need none, save one for the journey there!"

"But, milady, your wedding dress has yet! . . ."

"Out!" Branwen stepped out of the dress and slung it at the head seamstress. "I'll choose what I wear to my wedding!"

"But . . ."

The woman broke off with a shriek as Branwen, wearing nothing but the single shift left of her feminine possessions, dipped the rinse bucket into the cool bath water. Seeing the wild Welshman's intention, the seamstresses gathered up their tools and garments and, screaming, made for the door. At the banging of the door clothing behind them, she lowered her loaded weapon to the floor, oblivious to the water that splashed over the edge.

"It won't work, you know."

Branwen had all but forgotten the maidservant who sat by the fire, a hint of a smile on her face, as if the mistress's display of temper had given her some satisfaction. "What's that?"

Miriam got up and brushed off her skirts. "I've an extra gown you can borrow, if those provided by Sir Ulric offend you, but 'twill do no good to ignore the man's gifts, except to anger him. You can't go naked and you

171

can't wear those rags," she pointed out practically. "Let me fetch my dress and I'll do your hair."

Branwen shook he head. "I appreciate it, Miriam, I truly do, but all I wish to do is rest. My head feels as though I've been kicked by a horse."

"Then I'll bring you some warm wine and—"

"You've done enough! I would sleep now . . . *please!*"

Miriam curtsied obligingly. "Very well, milady. Shall I bring you supper?"

She would need food, Branwen thought tiredly. "Aye, and plenty of bread. I love bread and I'll be fairly starved by then."

After the servant put more wood on the fire and left, Branwen sank down on the plump mattress, exhausted both physically and emotionally. She was too tired to even hurt properly, she thought, tugging the coverlet over her. A nap would restore her humor and resolve. Then, after supper, she'd fill her pockets with all the food she could, tie together by sheets, and lower herself out the turret window. By the time she was missed the following morning, she would be well on her way home.

Chapter Eleven

It took the noise of thunder itself to shake Branwen from the exhausted sleep that had claimed her. At least, that's what she thought had invaded her dim room. Bemused by the presence of such a storm in the month of December, she threw off the covers and flew, barefoot, to the window to see the phenomenon. To her chagrin, however, the shutters would not bulge. Furthermore, the source of the sound, narrowed down to the barrel-vaulted opening, came to her, shaking the last of her fatigue from her mind.

Branwen cut loose with a curse meant to singe the ears of the men barricading the shutters from the outside, but her heartfelt dissertation was directed solely at Ulric of Kent. Angered that her escape route had been so easily diverted, she snatched up the rags she'd worn and threw them at the window, gaining pitiful relief of her outrage. By all the saints, the knaves *would* hear her protest! In frustration, she spun about to fetch her bath bucket for a more substantial bombardment, when she saw a familiar figure lounged against the wall, watching her curiously.

"Bastard! I ought to . . ."

"I ought to turn you over my knee like the recalcitrant that you are and beat that temper out of you for

173

good, but if you can find the means to calm yourself, milady, I shall restrain from such a drastic measure."

Fists clenched to her sides, Branwen checked the wild urge that begged her feet take her across the room to the bane of her existence. *Damn the fiendish knave!* "Why don't you simply have me hanged and be done with me? That seems the meat of your justice."

"You'll serve me better *alive,* milady."

If Branwen doubted Ulric's tone, there was no mistaking the nature of the long inspection that raked her over from head to toe. She pulled her shift about her for cover, unaware that she only enhanced the curves, which before had been just tempting shadows highlighted within the folds of the thin material by the hearthfire behind her. Somehow fire crept along the stone hearth beneath her feet, spreading from her toes to the crown of her head, and the gooseflesh that had risen on her skin, chilled from the abrupt abandonment of the cozy bed, melted under Ulric's quiet study.

"Have you rested well enough?"

"Hah, 'tis jest that you act concerned for my health, now that your plot to see me dead has been fouled by fate."

Ulric climbed to his feet from the leather bench he'd been resting on. His shadow grew even larger than the man himself as he approached Branwen. "Fate has fouled someone's plot to murder you, milady, but I swear, 'twas not mine. I'd have a warm and willing bride, not a stone-dead one."

"If I have my way, you'll have neither."

"Which is why I ordered your window boarded." While his words offended her to the core, his smile managed to annul their effort. It was that wicked one Wolf had brandished so effectively in coaxing her into the very bed against which she backed. At the mere sight of it, a thousand places on her body remembered the sweet

174

torment it preceded and came to life at once. " 'Tis too lovely a neck to be broken in a reckless act when it can be worshipped like this."

"No!"

Branwen grabbed a pillow and thrust it between them, but Ulric, his gaze as ethereal as the golden bristle of his masculine jawline in the fire's glow, was just as quick to dispose of it. How could such a demon seem so heavenly? He looked like one of the avenging archangels in the cathedral, with his leonine mane swept away from handsome and noble features.

"I'll scream!" she threatened, twisting in his grasp as he caught her by the waist and hauled her upright.

Her heart beating like the wings of a trapped bird, Branwen arched backward as this younger, more polished version of Wolf bent down to silence her with his lips. Even as she mustered an assault with her fists, her knees were buckling in involuntary surrender against the pressure of the mattress behind her. Her breath held, she locked gazes with the one in which the smoldering coals of the fire seemed to snap. A bolt of bone-melting lightning charged between them, only to be snuffed out abruptly by the deep roar of the conquering lion's voice.

"All right, ladies, you may come in! Lady Branwen is in a mellower mood, *aren't* you, beloved?"

Branwen's upper lip curled as she struggled to emerge from the heady closeness of the virile body pressed against her. "Why, you . . ."

"And you're more than willing to stand for the fittings as the lady you are, and not the heathen who would make it necessary for me to stand over you and hold you still whilst these good women go about their work, aren't you?"

Her nostrils flared and her eyes flashed with the blue fire of a summer storm. The cooling of the air that filled the space between them as Ulric stepped back to present her to the timidly approaching seamstresses helped her assemble some semblance of dignity. With an unmitigated glare, she stepped before them.

"Be done with it, lest you fit me a dress that will accommodate both bride and groom!"

One of the girls dared to let a snicker escape her mask of sobriety, but was silenced by Branwen's stabbing look. "As you wish, milady," she conceded hastily.

Branwen looked over her shoulder. "Haven't you anything else to do, sir? An after-supper stabbing, perhaps?"

"Not when the fire of your temper sets me ablaze with equal burning. I've a mind to send the women away after all."

Branwen was relieved of her tormentor's unnerving appraisal and the biting reply his taunt demanded, by the loud clatter of dishes crashing and scattering on the stone floor. Staring at the prospective groom in disbelief, the servant Miriam stood aghast in the doorway, the remains of her mistress's supper spread around her feet.

"Sir, what madness is this? Know you not, it is bad luck to see the bride in such estate before the wedding?"

"Who the devil are you to question me, wench?" Ulric bellowed, unaccustomed to the disapproving tone of anyone, much less a mere handmaiden. He needed no meager distraction when it came to the battle yet to be won with his future bride, although he was pleased with his victory thus far.

"She's my new servant!" Branwen retorted in defiant defense of the girl cowering beneath the overlord's glare. "The king assigned her to me." She lifted a finely lined brow in an imperious challenge. "If I would be your lady, 'tis the least I should be afforded, since you *murdered* mine own!"

Ulric's golden complexion flushed hot scarlet. One moment's diversion and his bride-to-be had regained

176

her defiance with a most annoying justification. Nay, he would not slit that soft white throat, but the idea of wrenching it was sorely tempting! "Damn you, woman, I . . ."

Before Branwen could move beyond the circle of women scrambling to get out of the way of the lumbering giant, Miriam shoved herself into his path. "Hold, sir, I beg you! Surely you can see my mistress is not herself! What woman *would* be, so recently robbed of her parents and forced to live like a common lad among full-grown men?" His patience tested to its limit, Ulric reached for the impudent maid, only to have her fall prostrate at his feet in a heap of pink skirts. "Patience, milord! That is all milady needs."

"Milady would test the patience of Job! What milady needs, wench, is a strong hand—"

"And a kind heart, sir. 'Tis no secret hereabouts that you have that."

One ill-tempered woman was curse enough, but add one with a voice as sweet as it was practical, and it was more than the seasoned warrior would take on. Where in God's creation had this troublesome betrothed managed to find this ally?

"Gogsbreath, get you away from my knees before I trample you asunder, wench! I've no intention of harming the lady."

"Then leave her to me, sir," Miriam responded as she accepted Ulric's polite assistance to rise. "Who can understand a woman better than one of her own, milord?"

Ulric peered over the servant's head at the renewed and mutinous Branwen. Despite the plainness of her shift and the half-made dress draped over her slender frame, she was every inch the new Lady of Caradoc. "I doubt the Almighty understands the workings of *that* mind, but have at it, wench. I warn you, however, the first I hear of your mistress blowing up like a northeast gale, I'll take you both to task! Is that understood?"

Miriam nodded eagerly, but Branwen merely returned her fiancé's ominous glare in unsettling silence.

"Milady!"

At Miriam's plea, the girl acquiesced, but her tone undermined the acceptance she succinctly delivered. "Aye, 'tis understood."

In anticipation of his upcoming wedding, the seventh son of Kent had ordered a dozen new gowns made from materials he had purchased from the East. Once resigned to the fittings, Branwen could not help but admire the beautiful combinations of velvets, brocaded cloth, and fustians, not to mention taffetas and silks. In truth, it was a wardrobe fit for a queen! Her wedding dress of perse with gold embroidery, to match the filigree veil that poor Caryn had been forced to wear in death, was paltry compared to the day dresses the women had sewn based on preliminary measurements provided upon the taking of Caradoc by its ladies' own head seamstress.

The reminder of her previous maidservant sobered Branwen's thoughts, so that when it came time to choose the trimmings of the gowns from the wide assortment provided, she had lost her enthusiasm. Leaving it to the head seamstress's discretion, she picked at the new supper tray Miriam had brought up, loaded with the bread she professed to crave. Like a soldier regrouping from a setback in battle, she assessed her situation.

She had lost her parents and the man she had been tricked into loving, but she was still Lady Branwen of Caradoc. While she did not trust Ulric of Kent, he was under the king's order to take her advice into consideration . . . provided she was the knave's wife. If not convinced of anything else, she was certain that this

English king, for all his faults, wanted peace between England and Wales.

Although Llewelyn's title existed only for the duration of his lifetime and his dominion was reduced to less than half of what it had been, the Welsh prince had his head, and word from the chattering of the seamstresses was that he and the king were coming to an agreement concerning the release of Llewelyn's hostage bride, pending his honoring his word and homage.

They had lost the war, she reasoned, but all was not lost. She still had the means to help her people at Caradoc . . . and she had a new friend. Instead of her fellow Welshmen coming to her aid, it was a poor English handservant who had thrown herself in Ulric's angry path on Branwen's behalf. It was a mark of courage Branwen could not help but admire, for even she was readying to flee—pins, folds of material, and all—to the other side of the bed when he charged across the room like a snorting bull. She would ask His Majesty if she might take Miriam with her to Caradoc . . . that is, if the girl was willing to go.

"Faith yes!" the handmaiden answered the following morning when Branwen made the suggestion. " 'Twould be an honor to await a brave lady such as yourself." To Branwen's astonishment, the girl dropped to her knees and grasped her charge's hands. "We've much in common, milady, for though our stations are different, we've each been victims of two-faced gentlemen."

"Get up, girl! I've no need of a groveling servant. When one grovels, it makes me suspect they bear some secret guilt that plagues their soul." Branwen helped Miriam to her feet, a heartfelt smile betraying the first sign of hope in the tide of fate that had swept her from beloved Caradoc by the sea.

The servant girl returned it sheepishly. "If I've a secret guilt, milady, 'tis only to want to better myself."

"There's no shame in that, Miriam. 'Tis what we all should aspire to, though I've slipped backward wearing the likes of those." Branwen nodded to the boy's clothes she'd thrown at the nailed shutters the night before. "I suppose I'm at your mercy for a dress . . ."

"Oh, no, milady!" Miriam corrected, her brown eyes brightening. "I forgot to tell you. I'm to stop by the seamstress's chamber and fetch your first gown. They've worked all night so that you might have something decent to wear at tonight's banquet, when milord will present you to his family!"

Branwen blanched. *A seventh son!* "Gogsdeath, how many are there of them?" she whispered, as if speaking of demons rather than of her future relatives by marriage.

" 'Tis quite a clan, but they can not help but like you . . . provided you can control your temper."

"I can well imagine." Indeed, Branwen could imagine that Ulric's family would think of her—a sacrificial Welsh calf, endured for the sake of their knighted son acquiring lands of his own. Although she realized the merit of Miriam's advice, Branwen nearly choked on her words. "But I will do my utmost to impress them favorably."

"And I'll make you look like a raven-haired angel!"

A few hours later, Branwen was more impressed than ever with Miriam. The girl had worked wonders with her unmanageable curls, so that Branwen disdained to wear the wimple and cap that had been sent along with her new gown. Indeed, her shift was so lovely, it troubled her to cover it with the pale blue perse of her trained kirtle, richly trimmed in a white fur and peppered with grey, around the draped neckline and narrow cuffs of the sleeves. Faith, she looked like a princess, even with her short and unstylish hair! These Englishwomen certainly knew how to make the most of their beauty, or lack of it. If only her mother could see her!

Yet, pleased as she was with Miriam's work, Branwen was nervous as the afternoon passed without summons. Had there been a carpet on the floor, she'd have worn it out, pacing back and forth in soft kid shoes scavenged by Miriam from one of the seamstresses who was most anxious to impress Lady Kent with her handiwork. Such was her state of nerves that she feared ruining her dress with perspiration, in spite of the scented talc that she'd applied and the cool temperature of the room. For the sake of wrinkling the same, she would not sit . . . not that she could be still, anyway.

Finally, Miriam reappeared, her face beaming. "Lady Kent has sent for you, milady!"

Branwen felt as if her stomach had suddenly shriveled and dropped to the cold floor, dragging her heart with it. "How do I look . . . I mean, not that I care what Wolf's . . . I mean, Ulric's mother thinks, but I would have the ladies of the court think me . . ."

"You look the ravishing raven, milady," the handmaiden assured her, leaning forward to pinch Branwen's cheeks unnecessarily for added color.

Ravishing raven, Branwen echoed hopefully as she accompanied Miriam along a maze of torch-lit corridors. She supposed Miriam knew the Cymry meaning of her name from living so close to the Welsh borderland. She smiled, grateful again for someone with whom she had something in common—a friendly face in a foreign world.

Although the open shutters of the windows afforded light, they also permitted in uncommonly cold drafts that made Branwen's perspiration draw into gooseflesh. Yet, she was grateful for it, for the smoky torches lining the corridors made her forced breath even more difficult. Her heart pounded with each sharp knock Miriam delivered to one of a pair of doors filling an archway to an inner chamber, obviously larger than her own. If there was an insult intended, it did not register. Branwen could only think of the impending meeting with the mother of the golden knight who was to become the lord of Caradoc.

"Enter!"

It wasn't the voice of a monster, but there was as much warmth in the command as there had been in the drafty hallways. Miriam stepped into the room first to announce her new mistress.

"Lady Branwen of Caradoc to see you, milady."

"Well, come in, child! We would have a look at you!"

We, Branwen bristled, wondering at the woman's gall to suggest the same deification as the king. She swallowed her indignation, however, and walked into the room with as regal a carriage as she could assume. The *we* the lady of the room had referred to was instantly made clear. There were at least a dozen women in the room, all as richly attired as she and all staring at Branwen as if she had horns.

It was the lady herself, who needed no introduction, to whom Branwen addressed a polite curtsy. For once, she was glad her mother had insisted on her learning the more courtly manners seldom used at what was becoming increasingly apparent to Branwen was a rather backward Caradoc. All the woman needed was a spear and a shield, and she'd intimidate the legendary Boudicca, the fierce heroine of the Celts, who was a worthy adversary of the invading Romans.

From her smooth forehead, etched with fine golden brows now arched in speculation, all the way down her towering frame to velvet slippered feet, she was Ulric of Kent's mother, sturdily built yet devoid of excess flesh. The wimple that covered her doubtless golden hair accentuated a pointed chin with an indentation in it to match that which surely plagued her more square-jawed son in shaving. There was a no-nonsense air about her that made it difficult to assemble a verbal greeting.

"Faith, she is but a child! Have you a tongue, girl?"

The condescension was exactly what Branwen needed to cure her dumb silence. "Aye, milady, though not as sharpened as your years have made your own."

"Such impertinence!" one of the other ladies scoffed, stepping forward from the ranks to address Branwen. "But what can one expect of a *Welshwoman.*"

"Aye," Branwen rebounded sharply. "We are known to give as good as we get." For a moment, she thought she saw the stonelike countenance of Kent's mother waver, as if her face might shatter with a slip of amusement.

"This is my Ulric's aunt, Maive. These other women are my daughters-in-law, Elizabeth, Anne, Caroline, Eleanor, Anna ..."

The introductions were rattled off so quickly that the rank of females, each dipping at the mention of their name, reminded Branwen of a rippling wave. All that she could gather from the count was that Ulric was the sixth of the seven boys of Kent to marry. There were other women relatives, but Branwen could no more recall their names than those of the daughters-in-law. Only Lady Kent and Lady Maive managed to register with any permanence.

"You may disrobe behind that screen, if you wish, milady. Help your mistress," Lady Kent commanded Miriam, "then you may take your leave."

Branwen would have protested then and there had Miriam not ushered her behind the painted privacy screen before she could recover from her shock at the woman's suggestion. "Here, what is this?" she demanded of the girl, who started to unfasten the dress

Branwen had taken such uncharacteristic pains to keep presentable.

" 'Tis nothing, milady! Surely you can't expect to marry Lord Ulric without being inspected by his mother and relatives?"

"The devil I can't!"

"Milady," Miriam whispered, trying to set an example for her mistress. " 'Tis a normal practice! It's only natural for her ladyship to be certain you are capable of producing heirs for her son."

The nerve of the man! Branwen fumed, her ire mounting in spite of her submission to Miriam's gentle persuasion. He hadn't needed a soul to inspect her when he made love to her! She was fit enough for that! Gogsdeath, what further humiliation would he have her bear?

It took all her willpower to quit the privacy of the screen at Miriam's encouragement and walk as if fully dressed, instead of mother naked, up to Ulric's mother. A poorly smothered snicker, which echoed from the group of future "sisters" who had, according to Miriam, suffered the same examination, did not help Branwen's growing impatience. She flinched as Ulric's aunt pinched the skin at her waist.

"Thin little thing. Are you weaned from milk yet, girl?"

"I would be addressed as milady, since my station is no less than your own, Lady Maive." Branwen felt ridiculous demanding respect in her current state of undress, particularly since the women surrounding her were swathed in winter coats and mantles. She wondered that they weren't all faint from the heat provided by the leaping fire in the hearth, but then, she was hardened to the winters of wild Wales and felt discomfort only from the attention, rather than from the nip in the air.

"I think my son will be well pleased." Lady Kent motioned for Branwen to turn. "Let me see your back."

Teeth clenched, Branwen obeyed, fixing her glower on the line of young women who had yet to step out of rank, as if seeking the perpetrator of the embarrassing giggle for revenge. The placement of ice-cold hands on her hips, however, made her jerk away instinctively. Gogsbreath, the woman was a walking corpse! she thought, staring at Lady Kent in indignation.

"Your hips are proportionately wide. You should bear children rather easily."

" 'Tis just as well, considering the size of Ulric," the aunt observed in practical agreement.

"All my boys were big babies."

Branwen bit off the caustic *"Small wonder!"* that teetered on the tip of her tongue.

"But they gained in size with each birth, Dianna," Maive pointed out.

"Hush, Maive. You'll frighten the child unnecessarily. Anyone can see she was made for bearing children. What think you, daughters?"

To Branwen's utter embarrassment, she was submitted to further inspection and comment, until she had stood all her spirited nature would allow. "Enough!" she shouted, sending two of the girls scampering out of her reach. "Be you satisfied or nay, I am done with this nonsense."

Without Miriam, who had quietly taken her leave, Branwen marched behind the screen and tugged on her clothes as best she could, considering her impatience with the whole affair. Damn Ulric of Kent, his female relatives, and his prospective giant babes! She had a green stone from Anglesey that would make this issue a moot point, anyway. For now, it was safely tucked in her sack with her other scant belongings, including the useless orange and blue mantles she'd hope would bring justice. If justice were to be done, it would be up to her, and right now, she owed Ulric of Kent and his Amazon mother more than a good share of it!

Lady Kent's account of her first meeting with Branwen left Ulric less than easy as he awaited the arrival of his future bride in the great hall of the palace. He could have easily told his relatives that the lady of Caradoc was perfectly proportioned for all his purposes, but had thought to save Branwen that much embarrassment concerning their previous intimacy. His mother had nearly strangled with amusement as she'd relayed the saucy banter his Welsh maid had rallied with in the face of his numerous sisters-in-law and aunts. Although her disapproval would not keep him from marrying Branwen, it gave Ulric pleasure that Lady Kent considered the girl a worthy bride in character as well as in wealth. His father, the late Earl of Kent, would have liked her as well, he thought, and there could be no doubt that his brothers would find her as engaging as . . .

"Lady Branwen of Caradoc!"

Ulric climbed to his feet, suddenly nervous as a high-strung pup, and directed his attention to the entrance, where the herald announced the arrival of his future bride. He blinked at first, refusing to believe the apparent reason for the collective gasp that arose from the lords and ladies gathered at the long rows of tables set up on either side of the hall. He should have known, he chastised himself sternly.

There, pausing to wash her hands in the silver bowl presented to her by one of the stewards, was his bride-to-be garbed in nothing but the shamefully thin linen of her shift. Belted at her waist, it clung most revealingly to the ripe swell of her breasts, peaked proudly from the chill in the air. With all the grace of a queen, she dismissed the steward and, head erect, marched toward the royal dais as if swathed in the richest of raiment. Even in the flickering light of the torches and candles, little was left to the imagination as to her perfect proportions.

"My word, what a prize you have, brother!" his eldest brother remarked wryly at his side.

"Have you lost your mind?" Ulric raged as he vaulted over the table to meet her halfway.

Gogsbreath, was it his imagination or was it but a triangular shadow centered at the widest span of her round hips? He snatched off his fur-lined mantle of scarlet en route and wrapped it about her milk-white shoulders roughly. Oaths unfit for the ears of the already-aghast ladies mingled with words that would not come together, so that the only sounds he made were unintelligible.

"Milord!" Branwen addressed him with wide-eyed innocence. "Perhaps you should take back your cloak, for you look on the verge of a fit."

"What . . ." Ulric choked on his own rage. "What is the meaning of this, woman?"

With a cursory glance at the royal dais, where undivided attention was afforded her, she shrugged. "I thought to banish all question that I am fit to bear the heir to Caradoc, lest your lordship require further opinion than that of your women relatives." With a perfectly wicked smile, she stepped out of Ulric's dumbfounded possession and swung his mantle around, affording the assembly a provocative peep at what it endeavored to cover. "What think you, Your Majesty? Am I not woman enough to meet a good wife's requirements?"

If the king replied, Branwen did not hear him. All she heard was the leonine roar of her prospective husband as he snatched her up unceremoniously under his arm and thundered out of the hall. The eruption of laughter

187

behind them grew as his outburst faded with his spent breath, giving her the exact response she'd sought. Not the least intimidated, she made no attempt to escape the bearlike grip about her waist that held her suspended backward, like a battering ram. If humiliation were to be dealt out, then it was only fitting that Ulric of Kent have his equal share.

As the enraged knight started up the winding steps to the corridor where her room was located, they met a frightened Miriam. "Here, sir, I tried to talk her out of this madness, but she was so overwrought . . ."

"Get you out of my way, woman, or I'll take you to task as well!"

"Ho!" Branwen chortled as they swept past the cowering maidservant. "Milord can't bear the taste of his own medicine!" The stinging smack of Ulric's hand across her buttocks raised her voice to a shriek. "Is it not enough to submit me to humiliation without adding assault to your growing list of vices!"

"Silence, woman, lest you provoke me beyond my patience!"

"*Patience?* You call this *patience?* Gogsdeath, I should hate to see your example of annoyance!"

"Faith, I should be delighted to show you, you shameless vixen!"

Instead of opening the door, Ulric kicked it, sending the latch flying out of its cradle from the impact. It struck the wall and bounced to, narrowly missing Branwen's head. Because the latch did not fasten, the door received another angry boot. She thought the planks would split from the crash, but not even the oak would cross the incensed knight.

Branwen grunted as she was tossed roughly on the bed. Instinctively, she rolled over to the other side and sprang to her feet, but instead of following her onto the mattress as she'd first thought Ulric would do, he stood, legs braced while unfastening his tooled leather girdle. The blood that had rushed to her face from hanging upside-down drained instantly, in spite of the frantic beating of her heart.

Was it firelight glowering in her companion's gaze, or had some red-eyed demon possessed him? Gogsblood, he was trembling as if Satan himself were bursting to be loosed. Crossing her arms defensively, she backed against the plaster of the wall. Cold as it was, it was warm compared to the chill that ran through her as he coiled the belt around his fist.

"Strip!" Was that her voice barking orders at the giant fury?

Ulric was as taken aback by her outburst as she. *"What?"*

Branwen swallowed dryly. "I said strip . . . just as mother naked as I was today! Only I will not ask you to submit to the curious eyes of strange women, who poke and pinch you to see if you're fit to sire Caradoc's heir, as you so expected me to. I shall see to the task myself."

What manner of creature was this with oversized eyes, brimming with unadmitted fear, and wild black hair framing a face of the same alabaster as the shoulder bared by her struggle to escape him? What power did she wield that could fire his rage so easily and then disarm it with a look, a quiver in her voice, or the capture of a trembling lip between her teeth. So wild, so bold, so vulnerable . . . so lovely, he thought, admiring for the first time the way her shift caressed her curves. Faith, he'd have her no other way, he thought, utterly disarmed.

"I should have told you, milady, but 'tis the first time I've been betrothed, much less come this close to a wedding."

Branwen's bravado faltered at the soft-spoken apology. "You're not angry any more?"

189

" 'Twas not so much anger, but jealousy that your charms were viewed by eyes other than mine. In truth, I've cause to be proud to have such a woman as my future bride. You've made me the envy of every man in the court, from the lowest swain to His Majesty himself."

A narrowed gaze met his. "You mean to say you're not humiliated?"

Ulric absently toyed with the belt on his hand. "Oh, I was at first, but now that I've had a second look at you, I can do no more than appreciate what's soon to be mine."

"Damn you, Kent, you're fickle as a fly!"

" 'Tis you that makes me so, milady." The belt unraveled, he tossed it on the bed between them. "And I would gladly strip for your inspection. The very idea makes me burn in anticipation of the possibilities of such an opportunity."

"I'd have you burn, all right, but not . . ." She glanced at the front of his trousers and looked away, discomfited. "Get you back to your family, sir! You know full well I've no interest in you, with or without your clothes!"

" 'Tis another challenge I'll take up upon the exchange of our vows, milady." With a perfectly devilish grin, he snatched up the belt and donned it. "In the meantime, I think I will join my family and my liege. You may join me if you wish, milady, with or without the clothes I have provided you. I leave the matter to you." He slung his mantle over one shoulder in a roguish fashion and paused at the door. "I look forward to our wedding, fair raven." His jaunty "Good night" was punctuated by the timid click of the latch in his wake.

Nonetheless, Branwen shivered in silent response, although whether it was from heat or from cold was impossible to tell.

Chapter Twelve

The ringing of the twelfth hour at the abbey a short distance from the palace at Westminster made Branwen's stomach flutter nervously, despite the fact that she had forced some bread down before the ordeal of dressing for her wedding commenced. Her dress of white figured silk, edged with black sable, was a credit to the seamstresses who had worked each day and night to finish her wardrobe. A hooded cloak, lined with the same fur provided ample warmth as she was escorted in the royal carriage to the church, where Sir Ulric of Kent awaited her. Unaccustomed to such finery, she fidgeted most of the short journey beneath the fatherly eye of King Edward himself. The carriage was surrounded by royal guards as elegantly attired, to Branwen's notion, as she. Banners of every hue known to man snapped in the winter breeze, brightening an otherwise cloudy day that earlier produced a light dusting of snow.

"You do your family and your people ample justice, Lady Branwen."

Branwen found herself blushing from the royal compliment. "And you do us honor, my liege, to act in my murdered father's stead."

"You still entertain the idea that your groom is behind all this?"

Branwen met the royal question with aplomb. "I have seen no evidence to the contrary, sir. 'Tis only your order that bids me see this through . . . and, of course, my wish to protect my people from Kent's tyranny."

The king smiled wistfully. "We do not doubt your ability to see that done. In truth, this has been a most entertaining courtship."

The coach slowed as the crowd thickened approaching the abbey, and Branwen clutched the open window frame to maintain her balance. 'Twould be all she needed to sprawl like the backward oaf she felt before His Majesty! Never in her life had she traveled in a closed vehicle such as this! At home, she rode astride in her father's retinue. If the trip was a long one, a two-wheeled cart containing their belongings accompanied them. This was extravagance at its royal best!

So many things she might have enjoyed the last few days, had not the hour of her forced wedding to Sir Ulric of Kent loomed ahead! The King's banquet tables held foods she never dreamed of, and the lords and ladies of the court were the most elegant she had ever seen! It awed her just to watch them. They supped with the same grace with which they danced, as if each move had been instilled in them since birth.

Lady Gwendolyn's tutoring in such arts, combined with Branwen's natural grace, served her well enough, but she found herself spending more time imitating the ladies about her than actually eating. Faith, only that morning, she'd had Miriam act the steward for her, so that she might practice the art of dining, even if nerves would not allow her to actually swallow the food.

"Your Majesty, I would ask a favor of you," she spoke up, reminded of the maidservant who had made the last few days bearable as her confidante and tutor.

"We are listening."

Seated on the dais, King Edward was an impressive

figure, but in the confines of the coach, dressed in ermine-trimmed raiment, he was even more so. He was as tall and sturdy of build as Ulric, leaving little doubt as to his ability on the battlefield, or in tournament, for that matter. Yet, there was more than mere physical presence to the man. There was a certain air of possession about him that bespoke wisdom and determination, leaving Branwen to no longer wonder how this particular Englishman had brought about the defeat of the brash Prince of Wales.

"The handmaiden whom you have assigned to me . . ." she began hesitantly. "I would have her continue in my service and accompany me to Caradoc, if it pleases Your Grace. She tells me she has no assignment as yet."

"Her name?"

"Miriam . . . of the west country. I know not exactly the name of her commote."

"We shall instruct our chief steward upon our return to the palace."

Relief flooded Branwen's face in the form of a smile. "My thanks, Your Grace."

"My privilege, milady," Edward responded with a gallantry far above her expectation, for his promise was sealed with a royal kiss on the trembling hand he fetched from her lap. "And now, we are arrived."

The coach came to a halt with the pronouncement, and Branwen felt her strength fade with her color as she looked out at the towering spires of the cathedral. The king emerged first to the cheers of the onlookers and turned to help Branwen out personally. As she stepped down on the packed dirt of the street, skirts lifted to avoid soiling the rich sable-trimmed hem and train of her dress, her knees refused to support her for just the flash of a second.

"Here, milady, 'tis not an execution, but a wedding!"

193

the king chided gently, a supporting arm about her waist remaining until she had regained her footing. "We would see that beautiful smile of yours, which, were I not bound by matrimony to the queen, would tempt me sorely."

Were all Englishmen this courtly? Branwen wondered, smiling in spite of her trepidation. If so, it was a wonder they hadn't been able to charm Llewelyn into surrender! Her experience with gentlemen was limited, of course, to those in proximity to Caradoc, whose compliments were often stumbled over as if in Latin or some other tongue foreign to them. The art of battle seemed of greater import than that of love.

Branwen clasped her fingers tightly on Edward's arm. "I would have your word again, my liege, that you will vouch for my safety?"

Somehow, even as she spoke the words, part of her refused to believe Ulric meant her harm. Yet, there was another part that stirred her insecurities to the point of near hysteria and made her doubt her judgment entirely.

"Would it ease milady's mind for me to charge one of your fellow Welshmen as your protector?"

"It would, Your Majesty!" Her throat felt as if it were closing in rebellion to the pending vows to be made.

"Have you any in mind?"

To her dismay, she could not think of the name of one Welshman, so scrambled were her thoughts. Branwen climbed the steps of the cathedral, clinging to the royal arm as though it were a lifeline to sanity. Her future sisters-in-law converged on her at the back of the church like a rushing covey of quail. As they chattered in urgent whispers and pecked at her gown until it felt just right, Branwen's unfocused gaze narrowed on the guests lining the aisle before her, until she made out Dafydd ap Elwaid among them.

"Elwaid, Your Majesty! I would have Dafydd ap Elwaid assigned to Caradoc."

Coward that he was, Dafydd was as close to a relative as she had, barring Aunt Agnéis on her mother's side, for her father had been an only child. She had practically grown up with Dafydd serving as page and then squire under her father's supervision.

"Done!" Edward indulged her. He covered her hand with his jewel-bedecked one. "Shall we proceed?"

Branwen nodded, her voice too constricted to speak as Ulric's sisters marched off ahead of her in a hasty flutter toward the front of the church, where six tawny-haired men awaited.

Ulric stood at the fore, garbed in royal and gold. Next to him, at shoulder height, was his eldest brother, the Earl of Kent. James, was it? she puzzled in distraction as the distance closed between them. She'd been introduced to them all during the pre-wedding festivities but had yet to master their names, much less which of the convey of women ahead belonged to whom.

Leopold, Ronald, Conrad, and Hugh! Branwen recalled with a degree of satisfaction. They were, as Ulric's aunt had pointed out, progressively taller from James to Hugh, who could have been Ulric's twin, but for his neatly trimmed beard. The sixth brother, Thomas, actually the third son in order of birth, stood to Ulric's right, garbed in the robes of a priest. It was with no small amount of pride that Lady Kent stood in the first row of onlookers, her gaze softer than Branwen would have thought possible, moving from the groom to the bride and back again to Ulric.

Such was Branwen's state of emotions when the king brought her to a halt before the altar and priest that she dared not meet the somber study of her prospective husband. If she did, she might swoon in his arms or retch, neither of which would help restore the dignity she had painstakingly groomed since her bold protest against the Kent women's examination.

Paler than the winter-white of her gown, Branwen listened as the priest began the ceremony. Her attention wandered from the cathedral's gilded icons to the masterful sculptures of saints that were as frozen in life as she, so that she barely registered the exact nature of what the man was saying, except to note that his voice was deep and husky, like his brother's, and did not possess that dronelike quality to which she was generally accustomed. It wasn't until she felt the cold abandonment of her hand by Edward that she was pulled back to the moment at hand.

"So I give you my daughter of Wales," Edward proclaimed loudly, his voice ringing in the arched ceiling above where yet more examples of masterful artistry were evident. "To honor," he continued, "and wife and half of the bed, the locks and keys, and every third penny and all the right, land, and title, which is hers after the law."

Her hands were damp and shaking as they were claimed by Ulric. Branwen fought the panic welling in her breast. She heard her voice repeat the vows, yet it was as if some other woman stood within her body carrying on for her. Her eyes were too wide and dilated to even spring a glaze of sentiment as Ulric slipped a jeweled ring on her finger after his fervently spoken pledge. The strange woman who had taken over for her responded in kind at the prompt of the robed version of the groom, and suddenly her hands were wrapped together with her husband's in a satin stole of white and gold.

"Let the yoke she is to bear be a yoke of love and peace."

Regardless of what sort of yoke the priest spoke of so reverently, it was already weighing heavily upon her.

Coaxed into turning toward Ulric, Branwen could no longer avoid his handsome, smiling face. Nor could she evade the lips that swept down to claim her own as husbandly right, any more than she could the strong arms that encircled her—arms that seemed to lift the pressing burden in her chest. The background noise of shuffling feet and hushed whispers faded until only their pronouncement as man and wife rang in her ears.

"May this union be blessed and fruitful," the priest finished, adding in a loud voice that all might hear, "Congratulations, *Lord* and Lady Caradoc!"

The wedding banquet and festivities took place in the great hall at the palace. Branwen noticed little difference in the decoration, for the room was already bedecked in Christmastide laurels of evergreen. Draped over the canopied dais were similar garlands, interspersed with mistletoe. This time, however, Branwen did not balk, for she had been startled only the day before into realizing that Christmas Eve was to be her wedding day. The king had attended a mass first thing that morning in the midst of the light snowfall that only seemed fitting for both occasions, while Branwen had worshipped at the private palace chapel, having no wish to set foot in the abbey before the dictated hour of the wedding.

She had to admit that life at the king's palace was gloriously distracting, so much so that she hardly heeded her husband, seated at her right. With the clanging of cymbals at the dais and a blast of trumpets, the master steward entered the hall, clad in scarlet and waving a white wand. Following him were squires and upper servants, each carrying large platters on their shoulders. After one set a great shank of stag on the royal table, the king's carver set about with great aplomb to slice it, while cupbearers filled the silver flagons before each guest with the finest wines and ales.

Minstrels, bards, and dancers in gay costume made it

impossible to give proper attention to the lavish fare brought out, after the blessing given by Ulric's priestly brother. It was served by a host of young women, most of nobility, who did honor to both the king and the wedding couple by their service. Seated in pairs to share a plate, the guests could not keep up with the endless supply of food being brought to the official servitors by young boys from the cookhouses.

Another blast of trumpets brought silence to the chatter-filled hall and the king rose to his feet. "Milords and ladies, a toast to the newly wed Lord and Lady Caradoc."

Branwen's attention was deterred by the possessive hand that covered her own and the brush of Ulric's thigh beneath the table. Until now, she'd been able to remain aloof, for the king had commanded most of Ulric's attention on the ride back from the abbey in the royal coach.

Goblets and cups were lifted from one end of the room to the other, prompting Edward to continue. "May their union, like that of England and Wales, be prosperous and blessed with everlasting love and good will."

"'Tis insult not to drink to the king's toasts," Ulric whispered, taking up his goblet with the other hand. "Especially to one so worthy."

The wine was a red one, heavy-bodied and dry, so that Branwen could not decide if it was the toast or the refreshment that caused the resulting shudder as it went down. "Even His Majesty is given to flights of fancy," she whispered back through a fixed smile. "Just keep you in mind, sir, 'tis not love that makes this union, but royal order."

"And keep you in mind, milady," Ulric returned, as he took up a loaf of bread set out for them and sliced it with his dining dagger onto the silver plates afforded those on the dais and on the tables of the highest-ranking nobility, "regardless of how the union was made, 'tis made with all the rights and privileges afforded man and his wife that go with it."

Branwen's knife slipped, cutting a small gash across her forefinger, which was as attention-grabbing as his implied meaning. She gasped, the utensil clattering to the table, but before she could attend to the wound, Ulric seized her hand. "My word, milady, all I have endeavored to teach you and you still are a novice with a knife!"

An annoyed retort was on the tip of her tongue, when the handsome man at her side popped her finger into his mouth. As he gently suckled it, Branwen looked about guiltily. Surely everyone could see the resulting hot flush sweeping over her, leaving a scarlet singe from her head to the tips of her toes in its wake! When he was satisfied that the slight bleeding had stopped, he kissed it, as tenderly as a mother would her child's cuts and scratches. "Permit me to serve you, milady, for contrary to your belief, I would not have one drop of your blood spilled on my account, save that which I have already drawn in our intimate prelude to this occasion."

Again, Branwen glanced around, but no one was interested in the velvet conversation her husband carried on single-handedly. Gogsdeath, he *would* remind her of that which she'd tried these last days to pretend had never happened. She took another sip of the wine to fortify her painstakingly erected defenses, while he placed two succulent slices of meat on the bread trencher. As he did everything, he masterfully cut it into bite-sized portions, some more dainty than others for her benefit. It was clear that hers was not the first plate he'd shared with a lady.

Branwen took a quick survey of the room to see if Ulric's command of their plate was common practice and found that it was no exception. What was the exception was that the royal table had actual plates on which to eat from. Those seated farther away from them, the lesser members of Edward's court, ate directly from the tablecloth as she was accustomed to at Caradoc. She sighed at the shameful disregard of it all. It was such a crime to scratch the beautiful silver plate, when the bread formed an equitable trencher and provided food for the alms baskets and dogs later. Stains on the linen itself would be far easier to remedy.

"Milady?"

Drawn back to her own luxury, Branwen turned to see her new husband holding a piece of meat out to her, as if to feed her. She would have checked to see if that were proper, too, but for the imprisoning gaze that captured her own unawares. "How do I know it isn't poisoned?"

Ulric smiled, but the amber sparks, which flared in his hazel gaze and just as quickly were snuffed by sheer will, belied his indulgent manner. "It came from the king's own platters, milady, but I will take half to prove my innocence of any malice." He bit the morsel in half, chewed it, and swallowed, the smile returning as he put the other half to her lips.

Branwen accepted it in resignation, but the lingering trace of his fingers caused her to jerk away instinctively. Something in his steadfast scrutiny made her feel like the main course of the feast, about to be devoured by the hungry wolf. Wolf! she reflected wryly. How aptly his mother had named him!

At the next tidbit he offered, she shook her head in denial. It had been all she could do to swallow the first with Ulric watching her like that. Instead, she concentrated on the jongleurs playing the flute above the general voice of the crowd. Miserable as she was at present with her groom's unsettling devotion, she still prayed the festivities would continue.

The royal cookhouse certainly did its part to answer her silent plea. Course after course kept coming, boar's head larded with herb sauce following the stag, and after that beef, mutton, legs of pork, swan, roasted rabbit, pastry tarts . . . Meat after fowl, after meat, after cheese and egg concoctions, after meat, all interspersed with meat pastries and pies. The capacity of these English to eat exceeded their ability to dress and act the noblest of all peoples. Even up to par, her appetite was too spartan to do justice to a portion of it.

Just when Branwen thought she would be ill if one more train of servants came in, the heralds called the crowd to a hush. At the opposite end of the room, large double arched doors opened to admit what at first looked like a large flying swan, carried by a richly bedecked squire on a tray of green pastry, raked to resemble grass. It looked as if it were still alive and swimming with its beak gilt and its body silvered!

It was placed on one end of the royal table, but already it was upstaged by the entry of four squires bearing a giant pastry. This was put before Edward, who stood up to acknowledge its creators. With a large knife, the king himself, rather than his meat server, addressed the curious dish with two quick slashes. Branwen could not help her gasp of amazement as a score of little birds spilled from it and scattered on the floor.

"Faith, have you ever seen the like!" she blurted out, inadvertently shaking her husband's arm as if wanting him to confirm this incredible scene unfolding before her eyes.

" 'Tis just the beginning," Ulric whispered, utterly captivated by Branwen's naive charm. There was much he wanted to show her, to share with her. If only Providence would give him the patience to win her trust, he thought dryly.

As soon as the birds were loosed, the king's falconers appeared in the doorway, simultaneously unhooding their score of hawks, which, in a twinkling, pounced after their prey to the entertainment of all, save Branwen. Never had she seen anything quite so spectacular or sadistic! She was all for the hunt in the field, but to bake those poor creatures alive and turn them loose, stunned and disoriented, within the confines of a hall at the mercy of their predators nearly made her livid!

While the other guests scampered to get out of the way, laughing merrily at the chase, she scrambled to rescue one of the small birds, snatching it up as its predator dashed down after it. With an angry flourish, she snapped a large napkin of royal scarlet at the hawk and then began twirling it, all the while wrapping it about her wrist.

"Gogsdeath, woman, have you lost your wits?" Ulric demanded, rushing to her protection along with two of the king's falconers.

"Hold this!" Branwen shoved the quivering bird into her husband's hands and stepped forward with a sharp whistle, her other arm extended.

Dumbfounded and amazed, Ulric watched as the hawk came to her arm, exactly as trained, and took a bloody piece of meat from the table as a peace offering. He teetered between rushing to beat the hawk away before Branwen lost a finger and staring in openmouthed admiration as she soothingly spoke to the bird and fed it another tidbit from the table.

"Llewelyn has indeed paid you tribute, Your Majesty."

The king, amazed and intrigued by the lady's unexpected action, found his voice. "How does milady know this goshawk is from the Welsh prince?"

"I trained her myself, Your Majesty," she announced proudly, slipping on the embroidered hood, which the falconer handed her with deference. "Isn't that right, Morgana?" she cooed to the bird, whose blue-grey feathers had yet to settle. After stroking them into a calm, she handed the falcon over to its new trainer and faced the king with a short bow. "And, Your Majesty permitting, I should like to keep this poor creature for a pet. . . ." Knowing better than to insult her royal host, Branwen added, with a beguiling smile that made Ulric's heart step up to send a rush of animal arousal to his loins, "As a memento of my wedding feast. 'Tis a fair enough trade, is it not, Sire?"

"By the saints, you've a prize worth every bit of the land and title that comes with her hand," Edward congratulated Ulric enthusiastically, before ordering his falconer to fetch a cage for his quest's new pet.

Branwen unwrapped the napkin and tossed it on the table, which servants were beginning to clear, before gently taking the quivering bird from Ulric's hands. It was only then that her husband saw the small bloodstains dotting the fitted cuff of her gown. What manner of woman was this? he wondered, for surely she'd felt the piercing nails of the goshwak. Had she not had the napkin wrapped about her . . .

"Come, I will see to those wounds," he told her, taking her arm to escort her away from the table.

Going anywhere with Ulric was something Branwen hoped to avoid as long as possible. " 'Tis nothing but a few scratches, milord, hardly worth missing but one moment of our wedding celebration. I would have a goblet of wine and forget them."

"You must tell us and Lady Kent of the mews at Caradoc!" Edward encouraged her, taking her at her word that she was unharmed. "You two ladies have much in common. She, too, has amazing skill, and her birds have outshone my royal ones without conscience on more than one occasion."

For the first time finding a subject on which she might converse comfortably, Branwen obliged the king with more than the cursory answers that had become habit for the day. Perhaps it was the wine that loosened her tongue, but once she started talking about Caradoc, she could not stop until her heart was bared of all those things that held her affection. She told total strangers about the smell of the salt air, the kiss of the shore breezes, and the spirit of her favorite mare, whom thankfully, she had not taken on the journey to England.

"My word, it hardly sounds like the same place my brother described!" the Earl of Kent remarked, as bewitched by the wholesome glow of the bride's face as he was by her descriptions. "We must visit you this summer! I should love to see the improvements Ulric has told us about and ride this traeth you speak so highly of."

"So would I, daughter," Lady Kent chimed in with a smile that actually changed her whole presence. "I will bring two of my best birds."

Had the wedding thawed the woman, or was it the wine she'd been enjoying heartily with the king? "You are most welcome, milady. All of you." And had *she* taken leave of her senses? Branwen queried of herself. These were the relatives of her family's murderer!

"Come, Ulric, join us for a drink, whilst the women refresh themselves for the dancing," Hugh cajoled, dragging his brother from his bride's side with a heavy clap on the back.

"And I would have a word with you, Branwen," Lady Kent spoke up, taking her new daughter-in-law in tow.

After turning her rescued bird over to the falconer, who returned with a small cage, Branwen washed her hands in a silver laver and followed Ulric's mother into one of the large exterior corridors, where many of the guests milled while the hall was being readied for the dance to follow. They were stopped for congratulations all along the way up the stairs to Lady Kent's private chamber, so that Branwen, suddenly shy again in the midst of so many strangers, was relieved for the quiet respite.

Her mother-in-law beckoned her to take a seat and marched over to one of the shuttered windows, as if searching for the right words to express what she had to say. "My son is a good man, milady, and incapable of the treachery that you insist he committed."

Branwen was so taken aback by the direct confrontation, she had to struggle for an answer. At her hesitation, the lady's stern countenance softened.

"As you can see, I am a direct person. I know no other way, but this trait has served me well in raising seven sons. Believe it or nay, you are of the same mettle as myself, Lady Branwen of Caradoc. Much as I love the other wives of my sons, I suspect that you are special. I look forward to getting to know you and visiting with your offspring. I admire your spirit and have seen you've a heart as kind as it is proud. If my grandchildren possess but a portion of the qualities of their parents, they can not help but make a grandmother proud."

"You are most kind, milady." Was this another way of hammering home the point that she was expected to be Ulric's broodmare? Branwen wondered suspiciously.

"All I ask is that you listen to your heart where my son is concerned, for I have watched you these last days. There is a certain glow that tells me Ulric has won a place there, despite your suspicions of him."

"I have pledged to be a good wife, milady. What more can I do?"

"Word is not enough for Ulric. Like his father, he will demand body and soul."

"You do not strike me as the subservient wife, milady."

"I was not. I stood at my husband's side and worked with him to build Kent into a prosperous estate. I ran it in his stead, when battle carried him away; I bore his sons and raised them to upright young men, loyal to the king and country; and I comforted him in every way a woman could. In exchange, I knew a loving worship and respect few women are privileged to experience.

"Ulric is more like his father than all the other boys," she sighed, her eyes taking on an affectionate glow. "Both were seventh sons, you know, and both have fought and earned recognition from their king. Like his dear father, Ulric also possesses great sensitivity."

"*Sensitivity?*" Branwen asked, intrigued.

Her mother-in-law offered a charitable smile. "Let us say, seventh sons have many lives and an uncanny instinct for survival. But that is not what I wish to tell you," she said, waving the matter aside with a slender jeweled hand. " 'Tis the man himself that I would have you know. My Ulric will teach you what it is like to be cherished, but he is also a man's man, more at ease with rowdy knights and squires than ladies, and more at home in a tent on the edge of some godforsaken battlefield than in a castle. To settle at Caradoc will be as difficult a trial for him as accepting him as your husband will be for you."

Branwen started to mention that her wealth and land would surely ease his pain, but she refrained. The real Lady Kent was speaking to her now, from the heart, as a mother concerned for her child, even though he be a grown man. Like the crusty front presented by Wolf, her initial aloofness was but a cover for a heart capable of selfless love. Did her son's front hide the same, or was it but another personality revolving around that of a murderer and a deceiver?

Lady Kent reached down and squeezed Branwen's hands. "You both have your devils to fight. I vow as I stand, that you will take my blessings and my prayers with you! I know that together you can overcome them all, including this murderer who would have my Ulric take his blame and drive a wedge of hate between you. Whoever this is, they are no friend to England or Wales. All I ask is that you keep your eyes and your heart open, child! *The truth will out.*"

Chapter Thirteen

"For indeed I know
Of no more subtle passion under heaven
Than is the maiden passion for a maid;
Not only to keep down the base within a man,
But teach high thought and amiable words,
And courtliness and the desire of fame
And love of truth, and all that makes a man!"

Bernart De Ventadoun

The minstrel's words echoed sweetly at the bridal table, which now was the only one left intact. All others had been cleared, board and trestle, for the dancing, which was anticipated by all with great enthusiasm. Branwen, relieved of her veil and silver and gold coronet, gave polite attention to the singer and sipped the heavy red wine in her goblet to steady her nerves. She loved to dance, but would these English gad about the floor differently? They did everything else with such flair!

A troupe of jongleurs entered in colorful costume, forming a line that the minstrel joined, harp in hand. Five in all, they played, in addition to the harp, flutes, castanets, and a drumlike instrument resembling a giant tambour, beat upon with a stick padded at each end. Couples rushed, ready, to the edge of the giant space that had been cleared for them, but it wasn't until Ulric took her hand that Branwen realized they were waiting for the bride and groom.

Stirring the floral scent of the dried flowers strewn over the floor of the hall in honor of the occasion, Branwen accompanied her new husband, her fingers biting into his muscled arm to betray her anxiety. If Ulric were ill at ease, it didn't show. Indeed, there was a sympathetic nature to his gaze as he squeezed her shaking hand reassuringly and listened for the right beat of the music to begin.

"Just follow me, milady."

His smile was like a lifeline to a drowning victim. Seizing upon it, Branwen rewarded him with a like one, which was also grateful and shy. His hands were warm to her icy ones when he claimed them, and suddenly she found herself drawn into movement. With a keen sense of rhythm, her feet found their own pace, keeping up with her partner's as he swung her around and around, establishing a large circle for the other guests to follow.

With her train looped to one wrist, Branwen's dress was no impediment to her whirling progress around the room. Cheeks that had lost color upon arriving at the dance floor now blossomed a rosy hue. Matching lips actually widened their smile to reflect the infectious lightening of her heart as the lively music played on. It was nothing at all! she thought buoyantly. She'd done the same with Dafydd and his fellow squires on many occasions, although occasionally they'd tripped or fallen out of step, something her groom avoided with a grace that belied his size.

Ulric was remarkably light of foot, she mused in reluctant admiration, and as masterful at dance as he was at everything else. Branwen felt her shameful blush darken her face as a result of the intimate speculation to which her mind took, and she looked up to see, to her dismay, that it had not escaped her observant partner. Yet its source was missed entirely, which offered more reprieve than the jongleurs, who brought the first dance to an end amidst clapping and cheers.

"My step is too long for you, milady. Come back to the table and refresh yourself, lest you repair to our marriage bed spent in exhaustion."

Branwen drew back as if the bed itself awaited her instead of the canopied dais. "Nonsense, sir! I am most fond of dancing."

"That's good to hear, brother," the Earl of Kent boomed at her side, "for I am about to claim your lovely bride for just that."

"Watch your feet, milady," Ulric warned good-naturedly, "for James is more at ease with a ledger than a lady."

"What my brother means to say, Lady Branwen, is that I am more at ease with hard work than he!" The earl tossed a troublesome forelock of golden hair, flecked with silver, out of his face and seized Branwen's hand. "But I'd wager your Caradoc will remedy that soon enough! 'Tis time someone anchored Ulric's wandering feet to the ground."

Anchored? Branwen repeated silently as she was swept away by her eldest brother-in-law. Odd, but she never thought of Caradoc as an anchor but as a home, a place to belong to and love. Wolf had disdained the idea when initially put to him. He'd said he had no need of land to tie him down. As *Ulric,* he accepted it as his right as her husband, indeed connived to lure her into begging him to wed her, all the while trying to wipe the blood of her parents off the hands with which, as his alter ego, he seduced her.

Gogsdeath, she'd married two men! One she thought she loved, the other she knew she despised. But which of

210

the two was real? Until she knew, she could not let herself be taken in by those hazel eyes and that ruggedly chiseled face, softened with the babelike smoothness of shaven cheeks. Nor could she give rein to the desire that, even now, stirred at the thought of his tender lovemaking. She mustn't give in, no matter how much part of her longed to. It would be like spitting on her parents' grave.

If only his family and fellow knights were not going out of their way to be kind to her, to make her feel a part of their circle! For once in her life, Branwen had to ask for respite from the endless line of nobles and brothers, who danced her around and around the room until her head continued to spin when her feet had come to a standstill. If her cheeks were red at all, it was from the chaste kisses she'd received from men and women alike!

All the while, the *covey*, as she'd privately named the aunts and sisters-in-law, gathered about Lady Kent in chattering observation, when not dancing with their own handsome husbands. For all the speculation in their eyes, some smacking of a greenish tint, there was nothing in the gaze of Ulric's mother except the joyous blessing she had declared to Branwen earlier. Again, she had been fully prepared to hate her mother-in-law by forced marriage but was vexed by reluctant admiration for her. Until James had come of age, she had administered her late husband's lands for two years with a strong and just hand, or so King Edward had informed Branwen during the long banquet.

When Edward's father required an army, Kent's armed and able forces were there, led by Leopold, Conrad, and Ronald. All three brothers were knighted by Henry and were now lords in their own right across the channel. Hugh and Ulric had risen to their favored station in the Welsh uprising, although Hugh remained in His Majesty's royal army at present. Like his youngest

211

brother, however, Hugh had accumulated considerable wealth, which was combined with his wife's lands to their mutual prosperity.

However, wealth did not mean happiness, Branwen philosophized as the gentleman in her thoughts spun her to the end of the simple dance. There was more to overcome in her situation than marriage to a stranger. Surely Ulric could see this and not expect her to honor her vows, at least not all of them, until her mind had been put at ease concerning his guilt in her parents' death! Surely . . .

"You look as if you are about to take flight, milady, like the bird you rescued earlier. There is a fine carol at hand and I would dance it with you, if you would so honor your fellow Cymri. 'Tis of a slow enough pace to catch your breath, though in truth, the glow of your face shames all attempts to light this hall."

Untouched by his gallantry, Branwen accepted Dafydd ap Elwaid's hand and stepped back into the circle of dancers with an air of condescension. He had a knack of making himself scarce when needed and a nuisance when not. "So your courage has risen again, Elwaid."

"Does this travesty of marriage mean you will not call me *Daffy Dafydd* hence, milady?" he teased with a roguish tilt of his lips.

Dafydd was still part boy for all his manly inclinations, she thought, her demeanor softening slightly toward her childhood friend. To encourage her to call him by the nickname she'd given him years ago was surely a sacrifice to his male ego. Dafydd always tried too hard, thinking that louder, larger, longer, farther, harder, and so on always meant better.

Moderation was a word foreign to him. Lady Gwendolyn had, on more than one occasion, appealed to Branwen's sense of sympathy by pointing out the lad's insecurities as the reason behind some outrage he'd committed. Sympathy be damned, however, there were those foundless boasts he'd made when he thought her dead and gone, instead of in his very presence.

"Speak you of me again as you did on our journey and I shall dub you Dead Dafydd! How *could* you spread such lies, impart such as you knew nothing about?"

Dafydd's hands tightened on hers. "Milady, I spoke of you as a—"

"Tavern slut with whom you'd been most familiar!"

"Nay, a . . . a goddess," he decided urgently under her snapping reproval, "whom I'd imagined in my dreams . . . one I have been appointed by His Majesty to serve as protector and confidant in lieu of husband. 'Tis not at all what I had hoped, Branwen."

"Ah, Dafydd, 'tis your breeches speaking again!" Branwen denounced with a dismissing laugh.

Yet, there was a certain fervor in her partner's pale grey gaze that almost struck her as sincere. Gogsbreath, she dared not trust her judgment of any man, since Wolf's disarming seduction! It had robbed her of her ability to think as well as of her innocence.

"Is *that* where my heart fell when I heard you had been brutally disposed of? Faith, milady, you've helped me find it again with just the light of your smile. . . ."

He was incorrigible! Branwen could not help but laugh.

"The sounds of your laughter . . ."

"Dafydd!" she warned with a snicker.

"The sweetness of your kiss."

Before Branwen realized what he was about, he pointed overhead to a berried sprig of mistletoe and tasted her lips. The kiss was gentle but lingered longer than propriety demanded. She was so shocked, it never occurred to her to break away. She simply stared up at the bold young man.

"No summer sky was ever so blue as your eyes, Branwen."

"Gogsdeath, Dafydd, you sound as if you swallowed a poetry book! It's unnatural and I don't like it, coming from you." It was odd how similar phrases seemed like music to her ears when Wolf ... *Ulric*, she amended pointedly, had whispered them.

Aware that the music had stopped, Branwen glanced toward the dais, where her husband and three of his brothers had joined together in a raucous song for the delight of the king. His mother, back turned, pretended she was engrossed in conversation with the surrounding women, but it was apparent she did not miss the gist of the lyrics. Her lips lingered between amusement and reproval.

"Does Kent ... pardon me, I mean *Caradoc*," the young man revised, "say such sweet things to you, Branwen?"

Instead of waiting for an answer, he placed a hand at her back and ushered her through the open doors into an adjacent corridor, where they might hear above the merriment within the hall. Servants rushed by, back and forth from the kitchens and cellars to the hall, oblivious to the lord and lady who stepped into the privacy of one of the barrel-vaulted windows.

"Our time together has been scarce since I discovered who he really was," Branwen informed her companion in complete candor. "I only hope to keep it so, even though he and his mother profess his innocence of my parents' murder."

"So you still think him guilty?"

"There's more to indicate yes than nay, although ..." Branwen broke off from finishing that she hoped Ulric was indeed innocent. It was so selfish, considering her family's fate. "Why did you not come to my aid when I sent for you?" she demanded, taking her frustration out on Dafydd. "Had you and your men been with Tâd—"

"We'd have been dead as well, no doubt. These English leave little to chance. They do everything with extravagance," Dafydd remarked, a trace of envy in his tone.

That aspect of English philosophy would appeal to Dafydd, Branwen mused dourly. And it was impressive, she had to admit. But at whose expense was all this? Llewelyn and Wales certainly were obligated to pay their share of it. The terms of the surrender saw to that. Then there were the ragged poor who had begged on the streets and fields in London proper and along the way to Westminster.

Caradoc's people were not wealthy by any means, but they were robust and well fed. Good management of the family lands and livestock saw to that. But then, Branwen's family had not required such luxury as she had seen here.

"Never think I have deserted you, Branwen. I swear my allegiance to you as I did to Lord Owen, not to your new lord and husband. We are Cymri and, as fellow Welshmen, must stick together. The king told me of your request that I stay on at Caradoc and I want you to know that I am honored to do so, milady."

Branwen could not help but shiver at the ominous note in Dafydd's vow and prayed she'd not made a mistake in requesting his presence. Were he to be the overzealous defender . . . but then, Dafydd had yet to show signs of that, when going against Ulric himself was required.

"You must be my eyes and ears, Dafydd. We shall investigate the circumstances of my family's murder and discover the coward lurking behind this mysterious curtain of Kent's colors."

" 'Twill be harder to unveil him now that his colors are the scarlet and raven of Caradoc."

"Ulric professes there is murder at Caradoc as well . . . of his laborers. Perhaps the enemy lies in neither the Welsh nor the English camp. Perhaps . . ."

"That is what he would have you think, fair raven. How better to divert attention from oneself than to make the blame out to belong to others? The less cooperative our people appear, the more they will suffer." Dafydd lifted her chin so that their gazes met. "Surely that polished charm of his had not turned your head that you cannot see his faults? 'Twas his men who invaded Angelesey and destroyed our food and crops. 'Twill be a hard winter for all our people this year."

Would that she hadn't heard that! 'Twas bad enough to know Ulric had earned the king's favor in suppressing the rebellion, without the bloody specifics. It was the crowning piece to a condemnation sturdily built upon her parents' murder. Branwen's lips thinned, undermined by the plaguing turmoil in her heart and mind.

"Nay, sir, I know them too well and fear to learn even more of them ere the night is out. Oh, damnation, not *this!*" she averred, her voice breaking in the overwhelming tide. She looked away, embarrassed by the sudden crack in her composure.

In a clumsy but well-meaning consolation, Dafydd put his arms about her and squeezed until she thought her shoulder blades would overlap. "The very idea of him touching you makes me burn for vengeance. You were meant to be mine, Branwen . . . this night to be ours."

Branwen rebelled instinctively against the hands that encircled her waist, as well as the body that pushed her farther into the shadows of the wind vault. *"Dafydd!"* With little success at that endeavor, she brought the heel of her slipper down hard across his instep, sending him back against the arched wall with a pained grunt. It was a tried and true assault where Dafydd was concerned.

"Damn you, Branwen, you'd vex the great Merlin himself!" the young man swore, holding a throbbing foot in his hand.

"You never learn, Dafydd!" Branwen chastised, making an irritated dash around him.

Where she should have gained freedom, however, a wall of muscle endowed with arms of steel appeared from nowhere, enveloping her within their realm. With a gasp, she glanced up in the dim lighting from the sconces along the corridor wall to see the handsome face of her bridegroom contorted in a look as fierce as thunder itself.

"Wolf!"

"You'll call me by my proper name, woman!"

"Ulric," Branwen hastily obliged, observing that the former was more apt at the moment. No amount of polish or fine raiment could diminish the animal quality glittering in Ulric's eyes as they peered past her at Dafydd ap Elwaid.

"Your bride was nervous, milord. I thought to comfort her. . . ."

"Do you think me the fool, Elwaid?" Ulric growled lowly.

Gogsdeath, this *was* Wolf! An angry one at that, Branwen thought, springing to Dafydd's defense. "I was distraught, sir. The king assigned Dafydd to Caradoc as my protector and he—"

"Protector!" Ulric's voice boomed inside the narrow arched vault, deafening.

"There *is* a murderer there," she rallied. "You said so yourself, sir. When you are not there, would you have me left alone? Dafydd is like a brother to me, and one with whom I am most comfortable."

There was no doubt in Branwen's mind that an oath,

perhaps a string of them, built up behind her new husband's clenched jaw, now twitching in betrayal of the storm raging within. A few words escaped the trap, but they were so maimed by his fury that she could not make them out.

"I beg your pardon, milord?" she asked, trying to keep some semblance of reserve in the face of the threatening explosion.

"I said, *the priest is ready to bless the nuptial couch.*"

Had Ulric not been holding on to her, Branwen might have collapsed then and there at his feet. All the trepidation that had been nipping at her composure throughout the evening quickly washed the color from her face and widened her eyes to a disproportionate size.

The priest! The announcement of Satan could have had no less effect. There would be the blessing of the nuptial couch, and then she'd be handed over to the Kent covey of women to be *put to bed.* Where had the night gone? Surely it was only an hour since the dancing had begun!

"But the musicians . . ."

"Will play the night out for the guests, but not for the bride and groom."

"You have not heard my congratulations as yet, sir," Dafydd interrupted boldly behind her. "I would lie to say that I do not envy you and even resent your privilege, but such is life. May I serve you both as loyal knight and pledge my service to Caradoc!"

Ignoring Dafydd's conciliatory declaration, Ulric turned Branwen in the crook of his arm and ushered her firmly toward the hall. "Smile, beloved, or I vow, I will give you reason to regret it later."

The wine blush on her cheeks, put together with her forced smile, was a masterful facade. To look at the tall nobleman escorting his new bride toward the dais where his brother awaited, robed in the cloth of a priest, one would have thought them both dizzy with happiness. They'd have had no idea how hard it was for Branwen to keep her knees from giving way as they followed Father Thomas up the steps, with an entourage of family and friends in tow, to watch the last ceremony of the night.

At the room, where she had pitifully failed to carry out her murderous intent, the crowd lingered outside, while she and Ulric accompanied the priest to the great canopied bed, now turned back and strewn with flowers. After they knelt at its side, the priest solemnly blessed the marriage bed while proceeding to light the incense and candles placed around it until it looked and smelled like an altar.

And she was the sacrifice, Branwen thought as the prayer came to an end. But for Ulric's assistance, she could not have regained her feet. When he abandoned her to the womenfolk, she held on to the thick carved post of the canopy and stared at the closed door through which he'd disappeared, an odd mixture of relief and dismay overtaking her.

The women converged on her all at once, so distracting Branwen that it seemed a matter of moments before she was stripped of her wedding clothes and swatched in a thin silk chemise, over which she wore a matching robe of ice-blue. Then Lady Kent, who had supervised the ritual with an air of expertise well earned from the previous weddings of her sons, embraced her warmly and planted a motherly kiss on her cheek.

"A girl needs a mother at such a time as this. I hope that I will suffice, for though I bore naught but boys, each of their wives are daughters to me."

The mention of her mother was all Branwen could endure. Her eyes were aching with tears as she hugged the woman back, then leaned against the pillows stuffed between her and the massive headboard to watch them

219

all depart with pleasant wishes. Confusion ran rampant in the myriad of emotions tearing at her as the door clicked shut, pronouncing her *ready* for her groom. Yes, she wanted her mother! She wanted her father as well, to face the man who would soon come to her. But the most damnable part of her quandary was that she wanted Wolf . . . a man who existed only as a front for her enemy.

The sickeningly sweet scent of incense combined with that of the roses now gathered in a vase on a table near the bed filled Branwen's nostrils, and suddenly all she could picture in her mind was a slab of stone, in lieu of the plump bed, and the effigies of her parents laid upon it. Leaping to the floor in her bared feet, she lifted her skirts and scampered to the shuttered window. Unlike her own room, Ulric had not had it barred from the outside. Grateful, she threw it open and deeply inhaled the cold night air, praying it would relieve the pounding ache that assaulted her temples and the churning that made her stomach weak.

The moon was out, bathing Branwen in its ethereal glow and brightening the patches of snow left from that morning's dusting. She could make out the figures of guards in the inner bailey, marching back and forth at their assigned posts to keep warm until their replacements relieved them of their duty. Everything she saw bespoke strength and security, yet she was trembling inside from the opposite.

In the distance, the bells of the abbey began to ring, and Branwen could have sworn she heard voices singing joyously of peace on earth in Latin verse. She counted. *One, two, three* . . . A single tear escaped her glazed eyes. *Four, five, six* . . . She folded her hands against the low gather of her bodice and stared at the star-spangled night. *Seven, eight, nine* . . . Peace, she prayed with each clear note that cut through the Christmas Eve sky. *Ten, eleven . . .*

"Gogsdeath, have you lost your wits, woman!"

"The bed smells like a funeral pyre! I'm . . . I'm half sick from the stench!"

"Then blow out the candles!" Ulric thundered, the tempest blown in to disrupt the blessed calm that had enveloped her.

He slammed the flagon of wine he'd brought with him on the table and made quick work of all lights, save one wax candle, which flickered in the draft from the window where Branwen sat still as stone, as if frozen emotionally and physically. Even when he turned away from the bed and approached her, she refused to move. It was as if some sedative had been administered to equip her for the inevitable confrontation.

"You're cold as a corpse!" he swore, reaching past her to secure the shutters in the window. He scooped her up in his arms like a recalcitrant child and carried her over to the bed, where he deposited her in a less than gentle manner. "What was on that unpredictable mind of yours, woman? Did you think to leap to your death, or wait for the chill and fever to set in?"

Branwen submitted in silence as he wrapped her in a woolen blanket, like a snug little babe, and then turned his attention to the small hearth, which was painted with a diamond pattern to match that on the walls not covered with eastern tapestries. The sparks flew up the chimney as Ulric stoked the fire and added additional wood until it blazed brightly.

"There!" he pronounced in satisfaction.

Branwen followed him with her gaze as he fetched the flagon of wine he'd brought up and poured a delicate stemmed goblet full for her. "Mam always warmed milk and fortified it with water of gold to sleep off a chill," she observed solemnly, wriggling into an upright position.

Ulric handed her the glass. " 'Tis not sleep that was on my mind, milady."

The insinuation halted the cup at her lips. With sheer will, she forced a sip and steadied the vessel with both hands. "I did not sleep well last night with all the noise you and your king's men kept, and today has been most demanding. Faith, your brothers have worn me out!"

The mattress swayed with Ulric's weight as he sat down beside her. "Is this why you were praying in the window? That I would leave this union unconsummated?"

" 'Twas consummated most heartily, if prematurely, as I recall, milord," Branwen reminded him in a heated flush. "But that was not what I sought in prayer."

"Oh?"

" 'Twas peace I prayed for." She took another sip, distasteful as the wine was, for it was a stronger brew than that which she'd consumed earlier and she needed fortification. "I vow, I am so bewildered by all this, I know not what to think or how to act!"

Ulric wrapped his hands over hers, steadying the glass that threatened to spill wine on the blanket. "Think and act *my wife*, Branwen, as you were born to be." He brushed the tips of her fingers with his lips.

She would have him the bellowing bull, rather than the silver-tongued devil. "Noo!"

As if his touch had unstrung her pent-up emotions, she threw his hands, as well as the cup, away from her. The red wine splashed to soak in the white linens. She made to roll away, but the confines of the tightly wrapped blanket would not permit her to escape Ulric's long reach in time.

"You test my patience like none I've ever met, woman!" he averred, dragging her back to him.

"I know how that little bird felt!" Branwen blurted out, on the brink of loosening the tears dammed in her eyes. "I've been staggered and trapped by treachery, with nowhere to run but to a predator far larger and stronger than I!"

"I seek not to harm you, but to love you, milady."

"As I did that bird I rescued, but that did not cease its trembling. It does not know me. That will take time ... time I so desperately need," Branwen whispered brokenly. "Time to learn to trust you, milord ... and ... and get to know who you really are."

The snap of the glass stem in Ulric's hand, where he had retrieved it, gave her a start. The goblet fell away in two pieces as the knight opened his palm to expose an ugly gas, spilling scarlet.

"Milord!" Instinctively, Branwen reached for the wounded hand, only to have it snatched away from her.

"What?" he snarled contemptuously, through clenched teeth. "Doesn't this spill enough of my blood to satisfy your vengeful appetite?"

His accusation checked Branwen from further show of concern. Instead, she sank against the pillows and watched as he retrieved the pieces of the glass and disposed of them with an angry sling into the hearth, where the remains shattered against the undaunted brick.

"What are you doing?" she gasped, as he marched to the bed and held his bleeding hand over it.

"I would give the servants no cause to insinuate our vows have not been consummated, *wife,*" Ulric spat, allowing a few droplets of his blood to join the stains of the wine on the linens. That done, he wrapped his hand in a towel placed by a painted bowl of rose water on the table by the bed. "By all that's holy, Elwaid was right. You would vex even your great Merlin, for 'tis certain this man of simple flesh and blood knows not how to handle you! I'd wager 'twould take a greater magician than him to understand the likes of you, Branwen of Caradoc!"

Relief flooding her face upon realizing he intended to honor her wish, Branwen scrambled off the bed, leaving the blanket in her wake. "I would be a good wife in every *other* way, milord."

She stopped a few feet from the man, halted by Ulric's heated appraisal. Unaware of the way her disheveled robe and gown had slipped off one shoulder, hanging on the swell of her bosom for decency's sake, or of the twisted silk that clung to the ripe curves of her body, she reached out expectantly.

"Let me tend to that, Ulric of Kent."

Instead of offering his wounded hand, Ulric seized Branwen's extended one and yanked her forcefully toward him. Her feet tangled in the dragging silk hem of her garments, so that she fell into his arms, her own outstretched.

"Ulric of *Caradoc,* milady," he corrected huskily. "With every right to do this!"

There was no escaping the lips that swept down to plunder her own, even though their descent was slow enough to afford it. It was the amber flecks of desire dancing amidst the hazel coloring of his eyes that held Branwen frozen, like an animal blinded by light. Once the angry kiss ensued, a belated thawing commenced, her limbs faltering from one extreme to the other.

There was no denial of his assertion that he was her lord and master in theory, any more than she could deny the physical possession of the invading tongue that somehow managed to flay her for her insubordination and caress her all at the same time. His bruising lips sealed off her breath, demanding further penitence, until Branwen felt light-headed with the traitorous desire

MORE PASSION AND ADVENTURE AWAIT... YOUR TRIP TO A BIG ADVENTUROUS WORLD BEGINS WHEN YOU ACCEPT YOUR FIRST 4 NOVELS ABSOLUTELY *FREE*
(AN $18.00 VALUE)

4 FREE BOOKS

TO GET YOUR 4 FREE BOOKS WORTH $18.00 — MAIL IN THE FREE BOOK CERTIFICATE T O D A Y

Fill in the Free Book Certificate below, and we'll send your FREE BOOKS to you as soon as we receive it.

If the certificate is missing below, write to: Zebra Home Subscription Service, Inc., P.O. Box 5214, 120 Brighton Road, Clifton, New Jersey 07015-5214.

FREE BOOK CERTIFICATE

4 FREE BOOKS

ZEBRA HOME SUBSCRIPTION SERVICE, INC.

YES! Please start my subscription to Zebra Historical Romances and send me my first 4 books absolutely FREE. I understand that each month I may preview four new Zebra Historical Romances free for 10 days. If I'm not satisfied with them, I may return the four books within 10 days and owe nothing. Otherwise, I will pay the low preferred subscriber's price of just $3.75 each; a total of $15.00, *a savings off the publisher's price of $3.00.* I may return any shipment and I may cancel this subscription at any time. There is no obligation to buy any shipment and there are no shipping, handling or other hidden charges. Regardless of what I decide, the four free books are mine to keep.

ZB0494

NAME

ADDRESS   APT

CITY   STATE   ZIP

(   )
TELEPHONE

SIGNATURE   (if under 18, parent or guardian must sign)

Terms, offer and prices subject to change without notice. Subscription subject to acceptance by Zebra Books. Zebra Books reserves the right to reject any order or cancel any subscription.

coursing through her veins. Only then did they offer pardon for the initial reticence of her own.

A double-edged blade tore at her insides, leaving her aching to know more of this bittersweet retribution for her insolence and at the same time overcome with shame that its source was her beloved parents' murderer. *"Please,* milord!" she implored, begging for relief from at least one as she trembled with want and weakness within his strong embrace.

"My needs are sore, milady, and if you will not satisfy them, you will not utter one word if another does?"

Branwen shook her head. "Just leave me be! Please!"

She caught herself as Ulric let her go and turned away without further ado. She should have been grateful that he'd made the decision easier for her, but she wasn't. Gathering the silk up over her shoulders, still hot from his touch, she watched as he slipped silently through the door and cringed at its prophetic slam. With that, the dam of tears building in her eyes burst, driving her to the bed with an overpowering sweep of despair and desolation . . . alone.

Chapter Fourteen

January's wind through the rising hills marking the holdings of the marcher lords made even Branwen shiver. Grateful for her fur-lined cloak, a deep smoke-blue wool from the wardrobe her husband ordered for her, she drew the hood closer, so that only her face showed, framed in silver fox. So many were her dresses that it was impossible to wear them all. Consequently, she and Miriam had packed her things after the twelfth night celebration at Westminster, which marked the end of their stay at the palace, and rode close to the cart bearing her new trunk, another wedding gift.

The last three weeks had been wearing on Branwen's nerves, acting the happy bride for the sake of appearances and suffering the long hours Ulric spent in her bedchamber each night for the same, before abandoning her to pursue whatever pleasured him afterward. One morning she'd found him sleeping off the result of too much ale under the table on the dais! She'd never known such embarrassment, having to impose upon his brothers to carry him to their room.

Oddly enough, however, there was also a touch of relief in the midst of her embarrassment, for her mind was relieved of the troubling suspicion that one of the flirtatious noblewomen serving at the court had entertained the knight, while his bride tossed and turned alone in her room. Her life had been a series of contradictory emotions since Wolf had become Ulric, none of which made sense for any length of time before the opposite rose to challenge it.

She loved him; she hated him. She could not wait for the brooding lord to take his leave of her bedchamber, and then spent the night speculating about his whereabouts and companions. She gladly gave him leave to satisfy his many appetites with another wench, yet she literally ached for him at the thought of his stirring kisses and tender touch. His fierce temperament frightened her, but when she became overwhelmed by the English court and her surroundings, it was her husband she wanted at her side for reassurance.

It was no wonder she'd lost weight and looked as if she could sleep for a fortnight, Branwen mused grudgingly, staring ahead at the source of her quandary. Ulric rode with his knights, who saw more of him these last weeks than she, behind a division of soldiers and flag bearers. Among them was Dafydd of Elwaid and a few other Welsh lords who'd sworn fealty to Ulric and the king. They resembled a parade, she observed, oddly detached. The wolf on orange and blue followed the wild raven clutching a scepter on the black and red of the newly married lord, proclaiming the retinue to be of Welsh and English composition. Impervious to the weather, the new overlord rode as befit his station, his rich russet cloak fluttering from his broad shoulders, its hood back. His golden hair whipped about his ruddy face as he laughed and conversed with his comrades, as if on a hunting frolic or pilgrimage of pleasure. Occasionally, a gust of wind would reveal the mail hauberk worn beneath his shirt, his armor packed away under the care of his squires. Looking more an accessory than a threat, his sword hung peacefully at his side, sheathed in tooled leather the same hue as that of Pendragon's ornate saddle and tack.

Behind Branwen, her maidservant, and the carts bearing their supplies and belongings, another platoon of armed men rode. These were more obviously bedecked for battle, which belied the initial harmless appearance of the entourage. The king's battle-hardened rear guard would return upon seeing the new lord and his lady to Caradoc, but neither Edward nor Ulric were taking chances of a repeat of Caradoc's previous lord's fate.

The last three nights they had stayed at the homes of men of their overlord's station. As he had at Westminster, Ulric spent a respectable amount of time in the room assigned them by their host and his good wife, and then left. Where he slept, Branwen had no idea, except that he seemed well rested and refreshed for the morning's departure, which was more than she was. But for Miriam, she'd go mad, Branwen thought, glancing fondly at the girl who was wrapped not only in a cloak but in a blanket as well.

"I shouldn't think we'll continue much longer. My husband must know ever knight and knave in the kingdom!" she remarked to her shivering companion.

"Milord *is* well liked," Miriam agreed with a sigh. "I've yet to hear a single harsh word concerning him, but that his sword is fierce and his heart is noble. The king has made a good match."

"You know my feelings, Miriam. I would have you respect them."

Not for the first time since they'd been on the road, she checked her late father's spirited golden stallion, which was annoyingly restless after spending so much time in the royal stables, from rushing ahead to catch up with its peers, the chargers ridden by Ulric's knights. Poor McShane's pride must be wounded, forced to keep company with women and cart horses, Branwen thought sympathetically, but she'd make it up to him once they were on the wet sands of Traeth Caradoc.

"I do, milady. Indeed, you have my deepest sympathy for the plight in which you find yourself. I pray each day that you will sort out your troubles and reconcile your heart's desire."

"I pray day *and* night for that, but alas, to no avail."

Miriam smiled reassuringly. "It will work out, milady. I just know it will, once you're home and no longer on parade for all to see."

Home, Branwen thought wistfully. Caradoc's winters might be harsher, but its hearthfires were warmer, its people a stouthearted lot. *There* she could at least put aside one set of insecurities. She would know how to act and what to say in her own hall without fear of appearing from the backward end of the earth, which so many Londoners dubbed Wales. *There* would be people she knew and trusted. It was a place where trust might grow . . . as well as love.

The ringing of vesper bells heralded their arrival at the abbey where they would spend the night. It hovered on the crest of a hill like a giant stone fortress, yet within its walls, the voices of the monks proclaimed naught but peace and praise. Branwen's brief elation that there would be no long drawn-out supper requiring a paralyzed smile faltered when the guest master who welcomed them in the stable yard showed her and her husband to a private chamber.

It was a small cell with a lifeless hearth, shaped much like a beehive, in the corner. Two mattresses, which were meagerly stuffed with rush, lined the two adjacent walls joined at the fireplace, one on either side. Ulric's squires immediately kindled a fire in it, borrowing a tallow dip from the kitchen for a source, while Miriam unpacked blankets from their cart to make up the beds of the lord and lady. When the maid had finished, Branwen watched her cross the courtyard to the hospitium, where those travelers of lesser means were assigned.

She didn't have to feign fatigue to beg off joining the group at the dining hall for the evening meal. She could not recall the last night she had slept through without interruption. This night did not promise any better, with Ulric forced to remain with her after the curfew bell. The nap the warming fire implored her to take might be the only untroubled time she would have.

Left to herself, Branwen uncovered the cage containing the blackbird she'd rescued from certain death at Westminster Palace and dutifully fed it a biscuit she'd saved from breakfast that morning. It was a ritual that had been established over the last few weeks. She would place a trail of crumbs from the middle of the cage to the door, where the balance of its meal she held in her fingers. Then Eddy, named after His Majesty, would gradually eat his way toward her until faced with the decision of whether or not to take the food directly from Branwen's fingers.

There, he faced the same quandary she did—to trust or not to trust. At first, he'd simply done without. Now, he would venture close enough to peck at the food in her hand and then scurry to the opposite end of the cage to devour it. With an ironic smile at their similar behavior, Branwen popped the dried remainder of the bread in her mouth and lay down on the mattress. After a few moments, the bird began to chirp contentedly at her head, another ritual they'd developed since his rescue from the talons of death. Tonight, however, she would have her new master share her cage with her, if not her bed.

At each foreign sound, she started into wakefulness, so that when Ulric finally entered the cell, gallantly following Miriam, who bore her supper tray, Branwen bolted upright, clutching her chest.

"At ease, milady. The modest stew has satisfied my appetite and yon bed will rest these aching bones tonight," her husband answered her dourly. Without a second glance at her, he attended the fire, while Miriam set down her supper tray. "You've naught to fear, milady," she whispered in a conspiratorial fashion. "He was most mindful of seeing to your repast, when I, in truth, nearly forgot in my fatigue and retired to the hospitium."

"For all the rest I've gotten, I would have been as well off to join you! How I look forward to my own bed again!" Branwen averred lowly.

She ventured a glance at the figure made larger than life by the shadow-casting firelight, only to receive a speculative appraisal that confirmed her husband's ears were as sharp as his sword. Gogsdeath, how was she going to bear this? This palace and nobel entertainment had been a much-needed, if troublesome, buffer.

"Will there be anything else, milady?"

Branwen shook her head. "Thank you, Miriam. Sleep well."

"Milord Ulric," Miriam curtsied at the door in parting, depriving Branwen of Ulric's attention briefly, before stepping outside in a rush to keep the scant heat in the room.

"What's wrong with the food? I vow, you've had the appetite of a bird of late."

Branwen rallied stiffly. " 'Tis not the food, but the company I've been keeping. Nonetheless, I will keep up my strength."

She helped herself to a scoop of the stew with a chunk of the bread Miriam had brought along to accompany it. It was more gravy than meat or potatoes, yet it squelched the gnawing that had begun in her

231

stomach. Surprisingly enough, bland as it was, she finished off the ample portion in short order, while her husband settled on the opposite bed, evidently stung into silence by her declaration. With a sigh, she broke up the remaining crust of her bread over Eddy's cage, only to have her conclusion that Ulric slept without a care proved in error even as she reached it.

"Is it too soon to tell if you're with child?"

The dish in Branwen's hand clattered against the tray upon which it had been delivered. "I am not with child, milord!"

Such was her vehemence that Ulric peered quizzically over his shoulder at her. "I only ask to save the ordeal of additional and unnecessary . . . *siring.*"

Branwen would have told him then and there that he would never sire a child by her without her wish, but that it would give away the secret of the green stone, tucked safely away in her sack at the foot of her bed. Its powers were reputed to work in the proximity of it, if it was not worn personally. No doubt the night she'd spent with Wolf, it had sweated as never before. She had not thought to check it.

"Then we shall both have to wait in suspense," she mumbled, burrowing down in her blankets.

The question hardly seemed to trouble the broad-shouldered man across from her any more than herself, for somewhere between the ringing of the hourly bells, he began to snore softly. She contemplated his sleeping figure for the longest time before she closed her eyes. Even when he was oblivious to her, he affected her. The feel of his coarse golden hair woven in her fingers, the heat of his flesh against her own, the fierce possession he'd taken of her, body and soul, all were indelibly etched in her memory, almost as seductive as the act itself.

Gogsdeath, how could she fight such power as he

held over her without even trying? Was that inclusive of those of a seventh son? she wondered miserably.

Yet, in the midst of one of Ulric's veiled threats, he'd actually given her an idea. If he thought her with child, she might be spared his attentions a bit longer . . . at least until she could sort out this quagmire of fact and emotion about the ambush, as well as her feelings toward him. All she had to do was imitate some of the symptoms and . . .

As if in response, her stomach roiled with a nauseous surge that caught her by surprise. This is ridiculous, Branwen thought, bolting upright and inhaling deeply to thwart it. All she could taste was the bland stew, now embittered with bile. She wiped the filmy weakness from her forehead with her sleeve and looked at the empty plate suspiciously.

Spying a goatskin of ale Ulric kept filled, she eased off the mattress and crawled across the floor to fetch it. Perhaps the ale would chase down the vile taste in her mouth, she mused, pulling the cork and taking a tentative swig. Barely had she time to replace the cork, before she crawled urgently toward the clay commode. She shuddered as the ale came back up, along with a portion of her supper.

This wasn't happening, she told herself sternly. The green stone wouldn't allow it! A rustling from behind alerted her to Ulric's approach, before his growing shadow on the wall in front of her.

"Faith, are you ill?"

Branwen cut a slashing look sideways, afraid to answer lest she be overtaken by another sickening tide. Shuddering as his hands clasped about her shoulders, she leaned over the bowl again with a violent retch.

"You . . . bastard," she swore, wiping her mouth with the back of her hand. "If this is your doing, I'll . . ." She struck him with her fist, but its glancing blow was un-

233

dermined by her weakness. She fell into him, grasping his clothing to keep from sprawling on the floor. *"Gogsdeath!"* she swore, swinging back again, as she lost what little was left of the meager supper she'd taken a few hours prior.

"Is that it? Do you think you're—?"

Branwen would have struck him for his insufferable enthusiasm, had she not needed both arms to keep her from pitching headfirst into the commode. "Get . . . get Miriam!"

"Will you be all right?"

Anger overcoming the nausea that would not leave her be, Branwen grabbed the clay commode and glared at her husband with a snarling curl of her lips.

Ulric needed no words to guess the meaning of her intentions. "I'll be right back!"

The door had no more than slammed when Branwen was overcome again. The pain that had been gradually growing in her abdomen worsened as she heaved dryly, forcing her to grasp her stomach with one hand, so that the other bore her full weight against the cool wall. It wasn't supposed to be like this, she thought, unrelieved as she sank against the plaster and tried to assuage the heat that set her skin afire. At least, she had never heard of a pregnant woman suffering pain, except in birth . . . and miscarriage.

But she couldn't be! There was the stone. Dazed, she crawled over to her sack and rummaged through it until she found the relic, passed down to her from her aunt. Her foot sent her bowl skittering across the room as she tried to climb to her feet unsteadily. However, the razor-sharp cramp that doubled her over brought her hard to her knees with an anguished cry. Nay, this sounded more like the result of a poisoning her aunt had once described to her.

Beads of perspiration dampened her forehead as she

struggled to focus on the dish, now in the center of the room. It was a Saracen concoction laced with ground glass, which would cut a person's insides to bits in the cruelest of deaths. Wasn't that what it felt like? she reasoned through the desperate fog closing in around her. Weren't her insides being slashed in all directions at the same time? Wasn't . . .

Ulric practically pulled a sleepy Miriam off her feet as he raced back toward the cell where he'd left Branwen. He'd face a host of knights on any occasion, but women's matters required women. He'd only meant to prod that spirited temper of Branwen's, nothing more, and this was probably God's vengeance for his ill-conceived humor. She'd been so quiet these last few days, in truth having grown gaunt from not eating, that he'd worried she was ill.

"What manner of illness is it, milord?" Miriam shouted, trying her best to keep up with the long-legged strides of the knight.

"She's sick, woman! How . . ."

At the sight of Branwen laying ashen and still on the floor, his voice hung in his throat. He rushed over to her and scooped her up effortlessly in his arms to carry her back to her bed. At her head, the blackbird thrashed wildly in its cage, as frantic as Ulric felt. Her face was warm and a rapid pulse beat at her throat when he pressed his fingers to it. He closed his eyes in relief. For a moment, he'd thought . . .

"I'll need water and towels, milord," Miriam told him, assuming control of the situation.

She untied the fasteners at Branwen's neck and slipped her cloak off her shoulders. By the time she started tugging at the embroidered laces of her bodice, Ulric was on his way toward the kitchen, where a faint glow in the window indicated someone was still up and about.

The monk banking the cookfires for the night hastily obliged Ulric with his request and sent for the prior. When Brother Gregory arrived with the messenger, Ulric was watching helplessly while Miriam held his now half-conscious wife as she retched again and again to no avail. There was nothing more in her stomach to lose, he thought, certain the convulsions would do the child no good. If there was a child, he amended, recalling Branwen's fervent denial.

Brother Gregory knelt by the women and spoke to them between bouts of nausea. His voice was as gentle as his manner, causing Ulric to have to strain to hear.

"What did milady have for supper?"

"The same as all of us—a half loaf of bread and the stew from the dining hall. Milord dipped it himself," Miriam provided, her voice near trembling with concern.

"Has she had anything to eat different from you?"

"I do not think so. Have you, milady?"

Branwen, who had been leaning against the woman, shook her head weakly. "Dear God, I cannot stand this pain!" she whispered, doubling over as it seized her.

Brother Gregory took Branwen's hand and squeezed it. "I have sent for some tea which should help the poison pass, milady. 'Tis fortunate that you have rid yourself of most of the food before it was digested, although I cannot promise a pleasant night."

"Poison?" Ulric helped the black-robed prior to his feet. "What is this of poison?" he demanded.

"The taste your wife complains of and the stench of the refuse smacks heavily of it, milord. There are no other symptoms to indicate your suspicion of pregnancy. Indeed, you are wed too early to know of such as that. Know you of any who would seek your wife's life?"

"I would speak outside, brother," Ulric replied tersely. He glanced over his shoulder as he held the door open

236

for the prior to precede him and saw Branwen staring up at him. The hurt in her pale blue-grey gaze cut him like a knife, buried in his heart. "I will get to the root of this evil, milady, ere this night is out," he vowed gently.

"Need you . . . need you look further than yourself?"

Had Ulric been told one so weak and pale could deliver so hearty a blow, he would not have believed it. Yet the knight reeled from the impact of the painfully spoken accusation as he closed the door behind him. Gogsbreath, it was bad enough that Branwen believed him responsible for her parents' death, but now *this!*

Milord dipped it himself. The maid Miriam's words rang incriminating in his mind. Aye, he had dipped the stew . . . from the same pot from whence his own had come. Then what? Ulric puzzled. Two of the knights had been arm wrestling, and he'd put it down a moment to watch the contest. Upon noticing his wife's new maidservant making her exit, he hailed her to take up the tray and deliver it while he took on the winner.

But something had made him decline when the opportunity presented itself . . . a strange sense of foreboding, not unlike that which made him take extra precautions before a battle or journey. In spite of the king's offer of a rear guard, which he'd accepted at the last moment, Branwen was still in danger.

"Could your wife have carried some tainted meat from your last lodging?"

Ulric broke away from his tortured thoughts to address the prior. "Nay, all she took was a biscuit from Huntingdon's table for that blasted bird of hers."

The bird! Ulric pivoted and ran back inside the room, where Miriam was helping Branwen into bed.

"Milord!" Miriam exclaimed in surprise, forcing Branwen's eyes open with a start.

Neither of the women had noticed the small creature lying lifeless in the bottom of its cage, for their eyes were on the large knight, who crossed the room in two lumbering strides and snatched it up. As he shook the cage, Branwen came up on her elbow. "Leave Eddy be! Haven't you done . . ."

Ulric's stricken look halted her in mid-question.

Grasping her stomach as if to unleash the clenching fist of muscle within it, Branwen struggled to her feet, Miriam on one arm and Ulric's strong hand under the other. Her husband lowered the cage, so that she could look inside where Eddy rested on an awkwardly spread wing, as if frozen in the midst of a convulsion. Ulric dropped the cage and caught her as she swayed with a despairing groan.

"Eddy!"

He hauled her up in his arms and hugged her closely to his chest. Whoever had poisoned the biscuit evidently thought she'd taken it for herself instead of for the bird, who had hopefully consumed the bulk of it. "He's lived long enough to repay you, milady," Ulric whispered softly.

Branwen winced, gripping her stomach as she buried her face against his chest. "Wolf!" She half-sobbed the name, clenching the material of his cloak in her pain drawn fists, now as white and bloodless as her complexion.

Ulric swore at the cruel twist of fate that made the girl feel naught but contempt for him as her husband and long for the comfort of the crude mercenary he'd pretended to be. Gogsdeath, what a fine corner he'd backed himself into with the best of intentions.

"Am I to die, too?"

He brushed the top of her forehead with his lips. It was damp with perspiration in spite of the chill in the room. "Nay, milady. The good brother will be along with a tea potion to ease the pain and make you sleep."

"I've made her bed ready again, milord."

Ulric nodded, but instead of putting Branwen back on her cot, he carried her over to his and sat down, his back to the wall. If she needed Wolf, then Wolf she would have . . . at least now, when she seemed so vulnerable, clinging to his clothing like a lost and frightened child.

Who would have dreamed when he'd first discovered the half-grown boy with the piercing blue eyes that the orphan would become a she, much less the wife for whom he'd ridden day and night to catch up with in hopes of getting to know her before the wedding. He'd be the first to admit it was love of her land that had made her an attractive bride . . . before he got to know Branwen of Caradoc. Then he'd discovered a spirited woman with a passion equal to his own. No wench had *ever* made such a miserable melt of his soul! By God, he would not part with her now.

"You take her bed, Miriam. She can have mine after she's had the tea."

"And what of you, milord?"

Ulric gave the servant a half-smile. "As a soldier, I've slept upright against walls and trees more than I've slept laid out upon a mattress."

"Then at least take a blanket to put over your legs."

Ulric watched thoughtfully as the maid divested her own bed of one of the covers, to wrap about his long legs. The buffer between them and the packed earthen floor was welcome. "Tell me, woman, do you know where my wife got that biscuit?"

Miriam shrugged sorrowfully. "Faith, *I* packed some to nibble on on the trip with my own hands! I know not if it was one of them or one she picked up herself from his lordship's breakfast table. She's been bringing the wee bird rolls and treats since she saved it. Perhaps it was an accident . . . poor dear," she added, looking at

Branwen's half-conscious figure in frustration. "Who would do such a thing on purpose?"

Before she could pull up the covers, a quiet knock, followed by the entrance of Brother Gregory with the cup of tea he'd ordered, brought her upright again. Miriam jumped up to relieve the prior of it, then knelt dutifully at Branwen's side to coax the dazed woman into taking it. Between her and Ulric, they managed to get Branwen to finish the entire cup, save the leaves floating at the bottom.

"Shall I dispose of the bird?" the prior asked, taking up the cage to examine the still creature inside.

Ulric nodded. "Aye, she needs little else to upset her."

"The lady should sleep out the night now that she's taken her tea. It contains an opiate to relax the body from gripping so fiercely, so that it can rid itself of the remaining poison, if there is any. At worst, she should prove sleepy tomorrow . . . and weak, of course." The prior hesitated, uncertain as to what else to say. "Is there anything else milord might require?"

Ulric pressed Branwen's head against him, tucking it under a square chin, now bristling with golden growth. Never had the Benedictine heard such humility in the voice of a nobleman such as this one. He'd seen men possessed look less haunted and bedeviled. "I would ask for your prayers, brother . . . just your prayers."

Chapter Fifteen

The remainder of the journey to Caradoc was a blur for Branwen. There were moments more memorable than others, such as when her husband held her in his arms, wrapped in cloak and blankets, with Pendragon snorting at the reins beneath them. Then there were the nights, spent in different beds and chambers, draped with luxury beyond her ability to appreciate. Ulric cradled her snugly beneath the covers, his balming hand spread warm over her abdomen, where the horrid pain had wreaked so much havoc. Each place he'd accorded chaste tender kisses still tingled, alive at the very recollection—her forehead, the tip of her nose, the crown of her head, her cheeks, her chin . . . her lips.

How she could feel secure in his embrace against the mounting evidence that he would be rid of her was beyond her ability to reason out when she was clearheaded, much less under the sedation of the tea the good prior at the abbey had sent with them. Ulric had prepared her supper tray. Miriam had said so, although the girl was quick to come to her new lord's defense, insisting the poison had been in the biscuit she'd fed poor Eddy. But Branwen knew she had also given Eddy the crust of the bread that had accompanied the stew.

Ulric's grand show of affection and concern could be

contrived to champion his innocence. Gogsbreath, she realized that; and yet, she could not help but accept his concerned attentions, like a starved urchin after food. How she wished things had been different! She even dreamed of the wedding with her parents there to give her to the fair-haired groom who now carried her on his noble Pendragon along the familiar forest-lined road to Caradoc. What a grand occasion it had been!

The barren tree limbs spread against a winter-grey sky overhead, however, were a grim reminder of what was reality. At least at Caradoc, she would have Aunt Agnéis as an ally against this seventh son. Her aunt, absentminded as she was, would nurse her back to health and enable her to see more clearly the truth of things. Perhaps Aunt Agnéis even knew what manner of evil had beset Caradoc with murders and raids. Perhaps . . .

Branwen's thoughts were interrupted by the widening of the road marking the approach to her home and Ulric's gentle nudge. "Look ahead, milady. There is your Caradoc!"

Whether it was the change in the air that suddenly assaulted her nostrils as they emerged from the distant forest or the sight of the familiar towered keep against the silver-grey horizon that cleared her head, Branwen could not tell. With more strength than she suspected she had, she managed to sit upright and soak in the welcoming sight. At least, the cold blustery sea-swept coast was welcoming to her, if not the estron, or foreign, knights shuddering beside her.

"Might we ride to the cliff, milord?"

In answer, Ulric turned Pendragon away from the group and started across the cleared brown grassland toward the ledge on which Caradoc's keep had been built, a stone lookout over the restless sea that crashed coldly against the pitted rock wall. It was high tide on the traeth, but nonetheless inviting. Unaccustomed to the breaking noise of the waves, the stallion balked as they reached the edge, forcing Ulric to rein him in and speak in a reassuring tone.

Would that she could trust so readily, Branwen thought as she slid off the becalmed stallion's back to her feet. Restoring strength seemed to invade her weakened body from the air as well as from the solid ground, so that her knees were able to carry her to the edge of the sharp embankment. The wind blew back her hood and swept her raven tresses away from her face as the very wildness of it all was absorbed in her coursing blood.

Wild Wales, they called it—cold, lashing, and unfriendly. Yet it was *Mam* Wales to her . . . Mother Wales, nurturing and life-giving. "There, milord, I shall ride McShane tomorrow," she announced as Ulric joined her.

"Gogsdeath woman! Will you swim?"

Branwen laughed at her knight's incredulity, unaware of the way her cheeks had pinkened to a healthy hue and her eyes, now bluer than sapphire, sparkled with miraculous revival. It was magic, Ulric mused, entranced by the change. While fragile, Branwen sustained her beauty even in illness, but now, with the elements dancing about her in a sort of pagan worship, she literally glowed with renewal. He'd never seen such a change.

"When the tide is out, milord, the traeth makes a wonderful ride! None of Caradoc's steeds fear to get their feet wet," she issued in beguiling challenge.

If he'd but suspected it was her home that she needed to restore her humor, he'd have risked offending the king to bring her there sooner. "Even I'd take to the beach with you as my mistress, milady," Ulric complimented huskily.

He could feel it, whatever it was, working on him as

well. What manner of place was this, he wondered, that could so quickly snatch him from a despondency born of helplessness? Or was it the lady? Gogsbreath, she molded his soul at will with her guileless witchery and fired his loins as none other!

The magic that charged between them gradually changed in the hazel eyes devouring her. Branwen saw the amber flare of passion burst amidst the blending of blue and green and brown. Like that of their owner, their absolute nature was impossible to determine. There were but hints, dropped here and there amidst earthly passions of anger and raw desire. Could murder be among them? she wondered, breaking away from her soul seeking search before she became lost in their depths.

It was then that she saw it, that which banished all thoughts of the golden warrior standing before her. The oak grove, which had been planted in centuries past and had flourished in spite of the salty elements, was gone! Nothing remained of it but weathering stumps! What had these estrons, these aliens from England, done?

"Milord!" she gasped, blanching before Ulric's very eyes.

Ulric pivoted at his bride's unbridled alarm, fully prepared to draw the sword he sought instinctively with his hand, but nothing was there to threaten them other than the blasting and wet wind that dampened his hair and cloak.

"Damnation, woman, what is wrong?"

Branwen pointed to the pitiful remains of the once-mighty grove. It was magic, Aunt Agnéis had told her when she was only a child, planted for the fairies to live in amidst the protection of the tree spirits.

"*There* lies the root of your troubles, Ulric of Caradoc! There among the remains of the oak grove your men have so foolishly done away with!"

" 'Twas cut for the new construction," Ulric explained, perplexed by this sudden wave of hysteria. "I gave the order myself last spring. 'Twas being put to use when I left. . . ." Ulric hesitated, reluctant to add further fuel to the suspicion his intriguing bride already had of him. "Before I tried to catch up with your father's entourage to make the trip to London."

Damnation, but fate was playing false with him in those enchanting blue eyes. How could he blame her serious consideration of the fact that he was in the vicinity when her parents were murdered; that the men wore his family colors; and that he had dipped the food she ate the night of her poisoning? But now she was acting as if the cutting of a lot of trees was equally damning!

"They were needed for the framing and doors," he said quietly, trying to hold back his sorely tried temper. How well the lady could revive it, when she was more herself.

"Caradoc needed the blessing of the grove more than it needed your framing and doors! Gogsdeath, man, you've cursed us all!"

"I've cursed no one!" Ulric declared in frustration. He clasped Branwen's shoulders and shook her gently. "This is all a lot of Welsh nonsense! I'm a Christian man and will not have this sort of talk spooking our people!"

"Cymry nonsense, is it?"

Where the girl's strength came from evaded the impatient knight as she tore out of his grasp and stomped off angrily a few yards away. When she turned, she might have been the epitome of the Arthurian Morgan herself, with her cloak whipping about her lithe figure and her raven hair flying wildly about her indignant face. She looked the fairy queen, the enraged enchantress about to conjure the demons from hell itself with the blue fire blazing in her gaze.

"I am Christian also, *Lord Ulric of Caradoc*," she scoffed

245

imperiously, "but I am no fool! Not even the Pope denies the existence of spirits and powers beyond our understanding! Who do you think *you* are, to be immune to such? Gogsdeath, I will not have you turn the dark world against my people because of your pious ignorance!"

Where was the fragile, vulnerable creature who had reposed in his arms these last few days? Ulric pondered amidst his mighty struggle for control. Was all that just a womanly ruse to soften him? Left with but one weapon against his mounting confusion, Ulric seized upon it.

"By all that's holy, woman, you will heed my orders and cease this lunacy! I declare that any and all who dare to even whisper of it shall suffer the lash by mine own hand. *Is that clear?*"

His words had been understood, of that Ulric had no doubt. Yet, it was the smug countenance with which they were received that left him uncertain as to the effectiveness of the threat.

"Beware, milord, for you and yours have already tasted the lash of your due retribution." She lifted her chin in defiance of him and all the elements. "There is a Cymri saying you'd do well to heed, sir: *'Tis bad luck to cross the raven.'*"

It was a simple Welsh saying, as meaningless as the rest of the nonsense his superstitious bride spouted, yet it deftly dropped the last straw upon his overburdened control. In two swift strides, Ulric was upon her, entrapping her within the folds of his cloaked arms, ere she take flight. Like the bird in the cage, she thrashed within his embrace as he met her rebellious gaze.

" 'Tis not *crossing* the bird I have in mind, milady, but *taming.*"

With that, he claimed the thinned lips she presented to him, giving her a taste of the method he intended to use. Her sudden stillness enabled him to be gentle. The unclenching of her teeth seemed to facilitate the victorious plunder of his tongue, yet even as his loins began to burn with the prospect of conquering the soft body he pressed to him, he realized something was wrong. There was an emptiness in it all, heretofore unmet, except on the field of battle when the enemy surrendered without fire.

"*Branwen!*"

Ulric lifted his head at the shout of his bride's name, yet his attention was not for the older woman running across the grassland toward them, but for the stony countenance that met his. He'd seen warmer effigies lying atop a tomb.

"And if the bird will not be tamed, will you resort to *murdering* it?"

Gogsdeath, he wanted to choke the very breath out of the girl's words, yet take the woman herself there and then upon the damp and rocky ground.

"*Branwen child!*"

The steel of her gaze shifted momentarily toward the plump figure crossing the stretch of pastureland between them and the keep, and then back to Ulric with a royal lift of one finely etched brow. "Are we finished for the present, milord?"

A thousand oaths ached to be loosed, but Ulric swallowed them and nodded, mute from the effort. He watched as the girl turned away from him without further ado and started in a brisk but composed walk, toward the woman who called to her. The two met halfway, the older enveloping the younger in her arms. There was joyous crying, but Ulric could not tell if the source was one or both, and then there was but one hysterical scream of alarm.

His feet going into motion before his bewildered and flustered mind, Ulric ran toward the women as the younger of the two collapsed at the elder's feet, despite the woman's attempt to catch her. Branwen looked like death when he reached them, her head cradled in her aunt's lap. Black lashes, dark as her skin was pale, fanned out upon cheeks drained of their indignation.

To his astonishment, as he gathered the unconscious girl up in his arms, the older woman grabbed his sleeve. "What have you done to my niece?"

"Naught but try to tolerate her, madam," Ulric answered tersely. He stepped around his bold accuser and started for the keep in strides that required her to run to catch up with him.

"You cannot tame the raven by force, seventh son of Kent, only by gentleness," she warned him breathlessly. "Listen to your heart!"

Ulric easily outdistanced his accuser turned advisor, leaving her panting and struggling in his wake. How the devil did the hag know what had transpired between him and her niece, for Branwen had certainly not had time to tell of the trouble between them? Were both seers? He dismissed the idea with the same vehemence with which he'd disregarded his bride's superstitious nonsense.

Listen to your heart indeed! Damnation, his heart was the knave that had put him in this prickly situation to begin with! First, he'd wanted the wild land that had captured it and then he'd wanted its equally wild lady. Queer as both were, he now questioned his judgment on both accounts!

"Antidote, my aching toe! 'Tis nothing more than a drug to make a soul weak! How long has she been taking this?" Agnéis of Caradoc demanded of the timid Miriam, shaking the bag of tea at the girl like a weapon in itself.

" 'Twas given to me by the prior at the abbey, Aunt Agnéis," Branwen called from the large bed on which she'd awakened. "Ulric thought to continue it would keep the pain away."

"Then he's not using the good sense he was born with!" Agnéis opened the shutter and tossed the bag out.

"Milady!" Miriam gasped in horror.

"What if . . . what if the pain should come back?" Branwen chimed in.

She could still recall how terrible it had been. In spite of Ulric's insistence that he taste all her food before she attempted it, her stomach still threatened revolt when she ate, as if it remembered and was as nervous as she.

"You'll be taking no poison here!" Aunt Agnéis averred with a degree of certainty, which made the girl on the bed relax once more against the plump pillows at her back. "Welsh nonsense, indeed! 'Tis no wonder, between that pious potion and yon groom's blasphemy, that you were struck down with weakness! 'Twould knock out my stiff knees were I not so stubborn!" The woman pointed at Branwen. "And that one has a streak in her, too, mind you," she warned Miriam with a snort. "It's just that mine's had longer to harden."

Agnéis went over to the hearth and lifted off the small pot of mistletoe tea she was brewing. Oblivious to the heat of the steam assaulting her face, she inhaled it deeply. "Ah, this will do just nicely, even if it wasn't boiled on the hall hearth! Imagine," she scoffed absently, "a separate bedchamber with a hearth! This new lord does have his peculiarities. Like as not, all this privacy will be put to use to get a new heir handsome as himself."

"Milady!"

"Aunt Agnéis!" Branwen exclaimed simultaneously with Miriam in mortification.

A mischievous twinkle sparkled in her aunt's pale grey

gaze. *"You* might have had a brother or sister if Caradoc had had such as this when your dear parents were alive. Now drink this before those big blue eyes roll right off those pale cheeks of yours."

Branwen accepted the tea, wondering if anyone saw her as anything more than a brood sow to Ulric. "You know yourself, dear aunt, that no heir of Caradoc will be born without its lady's wish."

"But how can that be?" Miriam inquired, her curiosity piqued by the knowing exchange of smiles between aunt and niece.

" 'Tis a secret of the Anglesey women."

When it became obvious that it was not to be shared, Miriam set about unpacking Branwen's trunk. With each beautiful garment she produced, Aunt Agnéis clucked and tutted in admiration so much that she resembled a cackling hen. It became increasingly clear to Branwen that the only thing her aunt held against Ulric was his refusal to acknowledge the gifts of a seventh son. Handsome, generous, and manly were just a few of the complimentary observations the woman made.

With Miriam agreeing wholeheartedly, Branwen began to wonder at her own judgment again. But then, her aunt had not heard of all that had transpired between them. That was something Branwen preferred to discuss in private, despite the close relationship that had formed between her and Miriam.

Whether it was the brew of mistletoe leaves or another surge of energy born of her joy to be home, Branwen was not certain. She did, however, feel the need to bathe and don clothes that did not bear the dirt and stench of their days upon the road. After sending Miriam down to inform the steward of her plans, Branwen proceeded to unveil the events that cast suspicion on her new husband.

"Oh," her aunt drawled thoughtfully. " 'Tis worse than I thought."

"Ulric?"

"Nay, the mistakes he's made. But someone's chosen the wrong man to cross. 'Tis bad luck . . ."

"He's no raven!" Branwen derided.

"But he is, child! He is your husband, bound and declared before God and man, and heir to Caradoc as sure as if Owen's own blood flowed through the veins."

"Then *who* makes a murderer of my husband?" Branwen insisted.

Agnéis took Branwen's hand in her own. "Trust no one, niece. It could be the work of possession."

"*Possession?* What is this of possession?" The sight of Ulric standing at the door of the room silenced both women. "Well, has someone stolen your tongues?"

"You forbade anyone to speak of such things, milord, within your earshot. Unless you intend to whip your own wife, or perhaps her frail aunt, I would make my approach known."

Ulric squared his jaw in an attempt to stop the sudden angry rush creeping up from his neck. No one else had died since his departure, but the work on the outer bailey and turrets had been continuously sabotaged. Scaffolding had been weakened, ropes sawed, and mortar ruined with precious salt, no doubt from his own stores. One day's work crumbled beneath the weight of the next one's. His ears had been filled until he could take no more.

"I need not hail my approach to mine own chamber, woman. 'Tis mine as much as you are."

"Ooch, think before you speak, lad."

Branwen had on more than one occasion snickered behind her hand when Aunt Agnéis, in indignation at something her father had said, had clamped her mouth shut so tightly her chin nearly reached her nose. Were

251

it not for her own ire, she might have seen the humor in it. As it was, amusement was far from the girl's mind when her aunt scurried out of the room in a huff. Branwen climbed off the bed and stuck her feet into her slippers.

"*Your* chamber, milord?"

"The *lord's* chamber, milady."

"Are you saying I have no rights in this room?"

"Only those I am willing to accord you as your lord and husband."

Branwen bristled at the man's assertion. "*Half* of everything is *my* right, according to our vows! If justice were done, 'twould be all and you would still be a landless blowtoad with more money than sense!"

"Speaking of *injustice!* It bewilders me, milady, how you fare so weak as to win my favor and then rise against me with the strength of a fury at whim. If you would master womanly wiles, 'twould serve you well to be more consistent."

If she had to, Branwen could not explain away Ulric's insinuation. Indeed, she had no idea where the strength came from to assert her indignation. It was yet another contradiction, for were her husband to quit the room, she felt as if she would collapse from the draining confrontation. As long as he was here, however, she would be damned before she weakened in the blast of his affront.

" 'Tis the very devil in you that conjures my strength, milord!" she rallied haughtily. "I will champion my people against you with my last breath. As for your room, I would not have it! The hall has served my family well enough before, and it will serve me now."

Ulric blocked the door as Branwen started for it. "Don't press my patience, milady! You are my wife and will sleep hither in the room I have prepared for you."

"Like some slave, with no rights? I think not, milord."

"You will have all rights as my wife, when I have all mine as your husband."

"You *had* your rights, milord. 'Tis bullish of you to wish me suffer them more, when my condition is so delicate."

Branwen refused to let the guilt from her misleading words assault her. He did not play fair in his game and only by the same method might she survive at present, she reasoned, placing a gentle hand upon her abdomen. Besides, this was a small deceit compared to that which he'd practiced on her.

Ulric's eyes narrowed in suspicion. "You said nay most heartily when I asked before. *Is* there a child or not?"

"I know not for certain, milord. But if there is, the poison accosted only this body which carries it."

"Then you shall have this room."

"Nay, milord. I am content to sleep in the hall as before. Aunt Agnéis might share my bed and attend to me. I will not bask in luxury at the cost of my people."

Ulric rolled his eyes toward the high ceiling, where artists from Italy had been employed to paint gilt designs to compliment the tiled pattern on the walls. Only the hall and the master bedchamber had received such treatment at the expense of his own coffers. Royal moneys paid for most of the fortification, spent to remind these rebellious peoples, of whom the fiery creature before him was one, of English sovereignty. However, he was not disposed to defend himself in his own castle—a castle earned, if by nothing else, by his efforts to husband Branwen ap Caradoc!

"Gogsdeath, you are an exasperation!" He stepped back with a courtly sweep of his arm. "By all means, milady, sleep where you will, though as you well know, the company of knights can make your fairer and gentler sex most uncomfortable."

"Sleeping with swine would be preferable to your alternative, sir!"

"I have heard no complaint these last nights!"

Branwen turned at the top of the steps. "I was drugged by that tea *you* thought so good for me! But I am now and shall be ever alert hence!"

Ulric literally found himself trembling as he grasped the latch of the plank door, freshly made of oak. Damnation, two could dance to this tune of indifference, which he suspected was falsely sung by those honeyed lips that had accepted his kisses readily when her guard was down. If he could not soothe this ill temper of hers, then, by heaven, he'd use it to bring her to his will. If he could but keep his wits long enough.

"Then be so, woman. 'Twould save me the effort of looking after you and free me to my own diversion as lord of this keep!"

Branwen started at the hostile slam of the door separating them. An effort, was she? she fumed, spinning on her heel to descend the steps still smelling of fresh mortar. By all that was holy, she'd cost him no effort but that which he earned with that thick wit of his.

At the foot of the winding staircase, she halted, astonished that it had deposited her in the part of the keep with which she was familiar. At least, in part, she thought, surveying the pattern painted in royal over the sand color of the smoothed mortared wall. Her mother's tapestries had hung there before, covering the rough masonry wall where the mortar had been squeezed out by the weight of the stones and dried, unstruck.

She glanced to where light filtered in through open windows above, and with it the wind as well. A gallery had been built around the entire perimeter of the room, and the windows widened the width of two shutters to replace the narrow slanted openings affording archers clear shots at approaching villains. While they offered twice the light, brightening the hall, they also offered twice the cold!

Yet, it was only the northwest sea windows that threatened the room, and they were closed . . . with her mother's tapestries hung over them! The inner bailey windows on the lee side of the keep were the only ones open, and only the inner drafts shook the banners decorating the walls. Much as she was tempted to climb to the second-story gallery, where before only a walk wide enough for two men abreast existed, she gave her attention to the hall itself.

The beds that had comforted her parents and herself had been removed, along with the embroidered privacy screens, stalwartly framed in oak. Instead of the hall to which she was accustomed, it reminded her of the great room at Westminster. There was room for naught but dining and entertaining. Even the hearth was empty of the tempting smells that used to awaken Branwen in the morning and lingered to put her to sleep each night.

"You seem at a loss, milady. Perhaps I might be of assistance?"

The appearance of Dafydd ap Elwaid at her side brought a brief smile to her face. At least here was someone familiar. "I *am* lost, Dafydd," she admitted ruefully. "I would have my bed and screen reinstated near the hearth, if I knew where they were."

Thankfully, Elwaid did not question her as he was prone to do, but accepted her wish as command. She had fought enough for one day and would preserve her strength to face Ulric. "I will ask milord's chamberlain. Your aunt tells me he is the one who had overseen this chaos of building."

At that moment, three stewards entered the room bearing the large wooden tub she'd ordered for her bath, followed by a string of servants carrying buckets of steaming water. "I take it the kitchen is now in another building?" she asked tersely.

"Aye, milady. There are many changes. I would escort

you to see them, but would rather have you take a seat for now, until you recuperate from our tiresome journey."

Branwen offered no resistance when Dafydd bodily picked her up and carried her across the room to the dais, raised to the same level as the large hearth. Using his foot to move out the large leather chair that had been her father's, he gallantly deposited her on it. In truth, she was grateful that someone was taking over for her, for her encounter with Ulric had left her drained. Still, she protested mildly.

"You did not have to do that, sir."

"Faith, I near swooned myself with concern when I saw you collapse on yon pasture after that quarrelsome kiss planted before public eyes by your husband. Remember, I am assigned to you, milady—my arm by the king and my heart by my own pledge. Say what you would have and I will do all in my power to see it done." Dafydd lifted her hand and kissed it. "I will speak to the chamberlain and send your maid to you."

"Tell her I would have my things moved . . ." Branwen hesitated, glancing toward the steps leading to the master bedchamber. "Nay, she might fetch only what I need as I need it, I suppose," she reconsidered practically.

There was more room in Ulric's chamber . . . and privacy, she thought, realizing with dismay that her longed-for bath awaited her there in the lion's den. She dared not risk his joining her, which the scoundrel was as likely to do as breathe just to spite her. When her screened-in chamber was set up, she would bathe as best she could there sooner than trouble the servants to fetch another tub of water because of the quarrel with her lord. There was a point to be made—an example to set for the extravagant English estron, and no one but she dared to do it.

Chapter Sixteen

"Sleep in the hall with those estrons? Indeed, there's a foolish tint to that stubborn streak of yours, Branwen ap Caradoc!" her aunt had declared incredulously upon hearing of Branwen's request. "I have my own chamber, small and cozy as an old woman's aching bones could desire. It speaks well of your good knight."

While Branwen didn't know how well it spoke of Ulric, his designs usually contrived for some purpose, she did wish she were in the cozy and, no doubt, quiet room with her aunt, instead of *trying* to sleep above the revelry of Ulric and his visitors. Gogsblood, she had never heard the likes of boasting as to what they were going to do to these brigands who had raided the small village of Brynmorfa on the southwestern-most border of Caradoc! What little grain the Welshmen had hidden from the English invaders was burned along with many homes, and the villagers had come to Ulric seeking their due protection.

It wasn't that the unknown scoundrels didn't deserve everything the knights anticipated for them. It was just that the more the men drank of their overlord's ale, the more they thought of and the bolder they became. If they were half as astute at catching the villains as they were at talking about it, tomorrow night should see their heads hanging on the outer bailey walls.

It had to be well after the midnight hour, she thought, turning restlessly on her side. When her parents had retired for the night so had the castle, but it was evident that her need for sleep had no effect on the new echelon's order. No doubt the new lord was keeping such boisterous company to make her regret her decision. While she had to admit the ploy was working, she would sooner stay awake all night than let him know it. Tomorrow morning she'd have her revenge, she promised herself.

To her chagrin, however, when dawn broke through the shutters in the gallery above, Ulric's men were already stirring. By the time Branwen rose and saw to her toilette behind the thin privacy screen, the lord himself had joined the group of mulling men, any one of which she expected to knock into the screen and topple it.

As she picked up a new rose-colored gown from the things Miriam had fetched for her, she noticed that the maid had inadvertently picked up Ulric's traveling sack instead of Branwen's. While untangling the dress's long, narrow sleeve, which had caught in the strap of the bag, the bag fell to the floor, spilling a few of its contents. Branwen was about to call the maid from wherever she'd wandered off to pick it up and exchange it, when she caught sight of a curious-looking vial, corked on one end.

Perfume? she wondered, picking it up to examine it. One sniff told her in short order that it was not anything one would want to dab on themselves. Its odor was medicinal, more like one of Aunt Agnéis's liniments or potions.

Or poison. Branwen's fingers closed around the vial, as if hiding it might flush this unwelcome suspicion from her mind. But it was too late. The seed had taken root.

After donning her dress, she slipped the potion into a small pouch fastened to her belt to see what Aunt Agnéis thought it was, then carefully repacked Ulric's other belongings—a comb, a shaving kit, and the tinderbox that had afforded them a warm fire on their journey to London. It felt as if she'd lived three lives—one with her parents, one with Wolf, and this third one with Ulric, a man who would feed her sweet words and poison at the same time.

But she didn't know that for certain, part of her argued, the part that had fallen irretrievably in love with her new husband. That remained to be seen. If the vial did contain poison . . .

She'd deal with that then, Branwen decided. She braced herself to face the man in question as she emerged from behind the screen, only to find Ulric and his men missing. Such had been her inner turmoil, she hadn't heard them leave, which gave her further reason to mistrust her hearing when the chamberlain told her where the lord had gone. Owen ap Caradoc had thought the building of the chapel enough penance without actually having to attend it! Chapels were for women and weddings, he'd often declared when Lady Gwendolyn would press him to set a good example for the villains.

"Lord Ulric is a most devout man, milady. His family attends chapel together each morning at Kent and he would keep this tradition here," his chamberlain informed her, as if she were heathen, before excusing himself to consult with the steward. It was also custom, it seemed, for the lord's breakfast to be on the table when he returned from his devotions, and there was not enough progress showing in the hall to suggest that his lordship's wishes were being followed sufficiently.

It was just as well the lot did some penance, she mused dourly, considering the devilish extent of the deeds they'd entertained committing the night before. Besides, it was obvious now that Ulric considered his disgustingly belligerent, belching, and wind-passing companions his family, to which, *thankfully,* she did not belong. Otherwise, he'd have afforded her the courtesy of at least asking her to go with him.

Resolved to see to her own more saintly pursuits later, Branwen decided to seek out Griffin, the former head steward, and find out what other changes had been made in the staff. It was her responsibility to plan the meals, not that of the stiff-necked man Ulric had appointed to take Griffin's place. Now, was his name Harold and the chamberlain's Blanchard, or was it the opposite?

"Did milady sleep well?"

Branwen shook the puzzlement from her mind and addressed her protector from Elwaid, who met her at the entrance to the room with cheeks smitten by the biting outside air. Round apples beneath a pair of black walnuts, she mused, her mind wandering back to a time when Owen had described his cherub-faced squire as such. Except that Dafydd's jaw had grown more square in manhood and the apples sported a shadow of beard, dark as his eyes, despite the fresh shave that contributed to the ruddy hue.

"Fair enough, I suppose, sir. How come you not to be with the others in chapel, Dafydd?"

"I see no more need in it than my mentor, milady," Dafydd disclaimed heartily. "I was checking with my squire to be certain they were seeing properly to my horse."

Even in someone else's keep, Dafydd could not help feeding his need to command someone, if only his squire. Branwen supposed he had suffered great disappointment when he'd had those walnut eyes of his set upon Caradoc, if not his fickle heart. For Dafydd, he'd taken the loss in a most manly fashion. But for that brief flare of temper on the tourney field, he had succumbed to Ulric's lordship over him with great decorum. At his reasons, she could only guess. Somehow, she could not bring herself to believe the young knight felt any more toward her than what stirred in his trousers and would satiate his ambition.

Dafydd motioned toward the table, where the first of the servitors came in with a tray piled high with bread wrapped in linen. "I would consider it an honor if milady would share breakfast with me. It smells most tempting and I would fortify myself for this morning's hearings. I have a feeling the complaints of yesterday were just a hint of what today's will be, now that word is out that the new lord is in residence."

"Oh?" Branwen inquired curiously. "I thought Ulric was riding out this morning to hunt down the plunderers."

Dafydd ap Elwaid shook his head. "Nay, this afternoon, I think, to see for himself the damage done. Ever the soldier, he would know his battlefield before engaging the enemy."

After breaking a loaf of bread in half and tasting the section he gave to Branwen per Ulric's protective decree, Dafydd went on to fill her in on the story of the murders Ulric had referred to the day he revealed his identity. Both men, a master mason and an architect, were found with their throats cut and a warning, written on the wall in their blood, to desist from expanding the outer bailey.

"But this is hardly conversation to have with a lady," Dafydd declared, seeing Branwen put aside an uneaten portion of bread.

"I am still not completely recovered," she confessed, "although I do feel clearer of mind than yesterday."

"Have you any idea what it was that made you ill?"

Branwen was tempted to show the vial to Dafydd, but there was no point in starting rumor unnecessarily. It was likely her stomach twisted in knots for nothing.

"The bread, I suppose," she murmured, backing away for the servant to place a wooden bowl of steaming porridge before her. "But *this* should do wonders for my indisposed stomach!"

With a forced burst of enthusiasm, Branwen stirred in a healthy dip of honey and a dash of fresh milk in the hot cereal, then mixed it with her spoon until it began to cool.

"Ah, yes, good porridge and milk are welcome after so many weeks of beer, ale, and meat of every kind imaginable!" Dafydd observed with a laugh at the English diet. "Faith, 'tis no wonder the English are such a testy, ill-humored lot! I wonder that English babes don't spit their mother's milk out and squall for blood."

Branwen laughed and took a bite of the hot honeyed bread he offered her. She was unaware that Ulric and his entourage had returned from the chapel until the servants hopped to attention to await his lordship and his guests.

Sobering, she greeted her husband coolly. Ulric handed off his mantle to the steward and responded with an equally stiff nod, taking time to level a long, hard look at Dafydd ap Elwaid before sitting down in the leather chair at the opposite end of the table.

"We missed you at chapel, Elwaid."

"When I saw you depart without Lady Branwen, I thought to accompany her after the repast, so that I might taste her food beforehand, milord."

"How noble, sir," Ulric drawled with a forced calm not missed by those at the table.

"I am her devoted servant."

"Devoted enough to be castrated so that you make a *proper* chaperon for my wife?"

"Ulric!" Branwen gasped over the general outbreak of snickers at the table.

A devilish grin, which made her question the degree of success of his visit to the chapel, quirked on his lips. " 'Tis done all the time in the East, milady . . . for *obvious* reasons."

"There are many things they do in the East, milord, as pagan and uncivilized as one can imagine, yet we do not mimic them here."

"True, milady," Ulric rejoindered with a hearty chuckle. "Here we've a harsher way to keep a lecher in his own trousers. We *bury* him in them." The initial amusement died at the implied threat in the overlord's voice.

"Milord," Dafydd spoke up gallantly. " 'Tis unseemly to question your lady's honor so for she would allow naught but the most chaste of relationships between us."

"Oh, desist, Dafydd! He would not know the meaning of a gallant relationship," Branwen averred sharply.

"Ho, woman, you champion the knight you damned as oafish and crude not so long ago, along with all his kinsmen?"

Branwen's cheeks began to tingle with the blood that rushed to them from her neck. "That, sir, was before he learned from you everything he should *not* be."

For a moment, Branwen thought she'd gone too far. Ulric placed his clenched fists on either side of his bowl, poised as if capable of leaping the length of the table at her and Dafydd. Trying to act unaffected, she managed to swallow a spoon of porridge. It went down in a single lump that threatened to hang in her throat.

Ulric's sudden burst of laughter widened her eyes with a start. "Faith, I can see I shall have to practice dueling of a different sort for morning! Perhaps those of you who are married might offer your expertise."

The lord's prodding elicited a range of comments

263

from disclaimers to sympathies, all of which were tinted with like amusement. For all appearances, the storm had passed. Ulric wolfed down the bread and porridge set before him as if famished, all the while taking part in the conversation that ensued on the merits of the various chargers stabled in the outer bailey. Yet Branwen could feel his tension reaching across the table and closing about her throat.

Again she wanted to produce the vial, but this time to throw it into Ulric's face and demand before all to know its contents. Judging from his brooding gaze, which she found upon her whenever she glanced up from her own breakfast, he was quite capable of doing away with her. She heaved a nervous sigh. Biding time was not something she had ever done gracefully, but Branwen knew that was exactly what was required of her.

After her husband emptied his bowl for the second time, he washed his hands and turned to address her again. "A peace offering, milady," he announced. "There will be a service in honor of your late parents at the week's end. Shall I have the chamberlain and steward see to the food, or are you prepared to take over some of your wifely duties?"

Branwen had little alternative but to accept that which would have come as extremely thoughtful from anyone except Ulric of Caradoc. "Oh, I am prepared, milord, to take over as of this moment. I daresay you shall have no complaint on that account. I would also sit in to hear the grievances of our people," she added, a smile belaying the insinuation that justice might not be served without her. "Then I shall see to the sharpening of the stakes upon which you and your company will hang the heads of these nocturnal raiders."

Gogsbreath, how did that get out? Branwen chastised herself sternly. While it reflected her true disdain for all their boastful plans, it was hardly gracious to criticize one's guests, much less speak disparagingly of them. Every grace her mother had ever taught her managed to elude her in Ulric's presence.

"Hanging and stakes are too good for halegrins!"

The locked gazes of blue and hazel broke apart to acknowledge the elderly woman hobbling down the steps on stiff knees. Ulric took up the issue cautiously. "What makes you think these men flesheaters? I have heard of no violations of graves, nor tombs, Milady Agnéis."

Agnéis looked at the young man before tentatively easing down on the bench next to her niece's chair. "You will, milord."

The general conversation at the table died down at the simply stated charge. Ulric leaned forward on his elbows, a scowl betraying his annoyance at the woman's insinuation. "And, pray tell, how do you know this, Agnéis?"

The woman looked up over a cup of warm buttermilk, as if astonished that he should ask. "Why, I saw it!"

There! It was said! Her patronizing tone intimated. Branwen had heard the same employed before Owen, but this was not her aunt's brother-in-law, who held grudging affection for her. Gogsdeath, how the devil was she going to protect Aunt Agnéis from Ulric's decree to refrain from speaking of the spirit world—something that came as natural to the woman as breathing!

"In her dreams," Branwen explained, a shudder creeping up her spine at the very thought of those vilest of outlaws. Never had such plagued Caradoc before. Crimes there were usually of a petty nature, generally the result of a quarrel between neighbors. But if Aunt Agnéis had seen them . . .

"Ah!" Ulric acknowledged, with a mocking glance

sideways to his knights. "In that case, I appreciate the warning, Lady Agnéis."

He was laughing at her, Branwen thought irritably. Her aunt concentrated on her porridge, not the least concerned. Ordinarily, Agnéis would have engaged in a shouting match with Lord Owen by now, bombarding him with all sorts of warnings and blessings to protect him because he was her sister's husband and not because he deserved them. Perhaps her witness of the massacre had left her permanently affected after all. Yet, yesterday she'd seemed so much in charge of her normal wit. Branwen hoped her aunt's mystic instincts had not been dulled to the point that she could not identify the liquid in the vial.

"Excuse me, milady."

Branwen started at the sound of the chamberlain's voice behind her. The mention of halegrins, combined with the tension at the table, had certainly worked their havoc with already-strained nerves. "Yes, Harold?"

"Blanchard, milady," the chamberlain corrected. "There are people gathered at the gates begging alms. Shall I have Harold see to them?"

"I'll do it," Aunt Agnéis asserted authoritatively. She patted Branwen on the hand. "I've known these beggars for years and can spot the cleverest deceiver. 'Twill take you some time to develop the eye Gwen and I have, though I'm sure you will."

Since Ulric did not object, Branwen let her aunt assume the task. Agnéis was gifted at recognizing charlatans who suffered only from laziness and greed. Sometimes the stories her aunt and mother would tell at the supper table had put all in stitches from laughter and, at other times, in tears. Caradoc had never been known to turn away the needy without alms.

The chamberlain's black mantle rustled as he rushed

to help the older woman from her chair. "Shall I accompany you, milady?"

"Faith, no, dear man. I need to keep my mind on modesty in *all* matters when dealing with the likes that *can* work taking the food set aside for those that cannot." Her face softening beyond what Branwen had ever known it to, Agnéis thanked the man.

"If your mother taught you anything, Blanchard, 'twas courtliness. You do her credit."

"It comes natural in the presence of such a fine lady as yourself."

Her aunt snickered. "Such flattery, sir, and you a good score younger!"

" 'Tis said one is as old as one feels, milady."

Gogsdeath, the man *could* smile, Branwen thought, struck dumb by the friendly exchange. To think she'd worried about Aunt Agnéis left at the mercy of the English *estrons*! If she didn't know better, she'd swear the woman was flirting with Ulric's chamberlain and he reciprocating. From the wry looks passed round the table, she was not the only one who had noticed something amiss.

"Well, sir," Agnéis rejoindered readily, "how this old woman feels depends on whether you ask her knees or her heart!"

"I would heed the heart and be damned with the rest, Agnéis," Ulric advised good-naturedly.

Her aunt nodded in approval, making a point of drawing Ulric's proposal to Branwen's attention with the gesture and a telling look. "Well said, seventh son of Kent."

Branwen rose also, assisted by Dafydd, who had retreated into silence in the midst of the crossfire between the lord and lady of the castle. "I would go with you, Aunt, to observe for a while, until the tables are cleared for milord's hearings. Will you accompany us, Dafydd?"

"With milord's permission," Dafydd conceded magnanimously.

"By all means, Elwaid. I would think you'd possess a good eye for charlatans."

Branwen felt the hair raise at the nape of her neck, but instead of allowing Ulric to prod him into anger, Dafydd merely bowed in deference to the lord. "I shall do my utmost to help the lady see more clearly."

She held back her sudden urge to smile at Dafydd's clever parry. Her heart felt as if it had been walking a narrow ledge since Ulric had oafishly launched an attack on her *and* her companion's integrity. The last she needed was to give him time to reassess his thoughts and strike again. Retreat was in order, if ever there was a time for it, she decided, following slowly in her aunt's wake to keep from running over the old woman in her eagerness to escape the wintry gaze following her.

Branwen's lingering doubts that her aunt's faculties had failed her were banished, at least concerning her memory, by the swift work she made of cutting out the pretenders. Having been protected from this aspect of her mother's duties, the girl was shocked at the levels to which some people would stoop for free handouts. It was bad enough to take food that could feed someone really in need, but to soap one's mouth so that there was froth and to throw oneself bodily on the ground, thrashing about, made the theatrics of the pageant actors seem paltry by comparison.

"Alms! For the sake of Christ, alms!" the woman managed between her conjured seizures.

When the charlatans had been given the chance to earn their portion with labor or put to flight by the guards, Aunt Agnéis and Master Harold began to dole out food to those in true need. Branwen recognized some from her mother's concerned stories of them. A blind woman from a nearby farm, afflicted at birth, was

268

led by a child through the gate. A young lad with a withered arm, crushed by a millwheel, waited his turn behind her. One of Caradoc's aging hunters, disfigured by goiter, and a mother of eight whose husband had been slain in a brawl were a few more familiar cases.

Leaving her aunt and the steward to dole out the left-over loaves of bread and broken meats, Branwen was assaulted by contrition over her earlier condemnation of Ulric's steward's flamboyant waste of food. There *was* room for some temperance, she thought in her own defense. After all, there was enough food to fill both arms and every sack of the needy lined up at the gate.

Besides, it was no wonder there seemed an inordinate amount of idlers amongst the needy, if word was being spread of Caradoc's bountiful handouts! Thanks to her husband's forces destroying the grain stores of Anglesey, the winter would be harsh for Wales. No doubt this influx of beggars was yet another backlash of the English victory.

Then there was the plague of the plunderers, she mused, hastening through the black alley, a narrow passage that separated the new outer and the old inner bailey. A flock of chickens scattered from her swishing skirts, while with each step, Branwen's resolve to remedy the situation gained steam. By heaven, if Caradoc's villagers were robbed of their winter stores by pillage, they would all suffer together. This English extravagance would stop!

The vial swinging in the pouch at her waist forgotten, Branwen burst into the hall, prepared to address Ulric right then. The sight of his knights, along with a smattering of vassals who had once served her father, seated at tables on either side of the lord's dais, however, brought her to an abrupt halt. She swallowed her husband's name as all heads turned, including that of the villein speaking before the assembly, to acknowledge the urgency of her entry.

Cheeks coloring, she dipped politely. "My apologies, milord, for the interruption. There was more to the almsgiving than I had anticipated."

"Your chair awaits you, milady." Ulric stood up and held it out for Branwen to take her seat, before sitting back down beside her. "Fear not that I have dispensed any more than the settlement of a boundary dispute and the disposal of one fat sow with six piglets."

Ulric's tongue in cheek expression made the corners of Branwen's' mouth twitch, despite her embarrassment. Such petty cases were hardly worthy of such an assembly's consideration, but usually fell under the jurisdiction of the leather-vested provost seated at the end of the dais.

"This villein, however, is telling us of the latest raid on his village." The fair-haired lord motioned for the plainly attired man to go on.

" 'Ell, milord, they comes sweepin' down from the hills to the east, howlin' like wolves and ridin' through the village like hellions. Even their horses wore devil's masks with big painted eyes. Halegrins, they were, if ever I saw one!"

Branwen's humor vanished instantly. She cut a sideways look at her husband, who leaned forward, arms folded on the table.

"Were your dead disturbed?"

"These devils rode through the graveyard and knocked over tombs and markers like they were doin' battle with 'em!"

"The graves, sir," Ulric specified. "Were the bodies themselves disturbed?"

The villager mopped his brow with his hat nervously. "Nay, milord. There was no time. They were too busy runnin' off our pigs and cattle and firing our stores and cottages. Carried off old Erwin's daughter, but she got away from 'em afore they took to the hills again and hid till they give up lookin' for her."

Ulric straightened. "And where is the girl? I would speak with her as to which way they headed in their retreat . . . or anything else she might tell us of them."

"She ain't spoke a word of sense since she come runnin' back, her dress all tore and face scratched from where the trees beat her when she was slung over one of the heathen's saddles."

"Nonetheless, I would see her."

The man glanced over his shoulder at the gathering of his peers behind him and motioned at them. From the center, there was a commotion of whimpering and a scuffling of feet. The closer the cluster of figures moved to the edge of the crowd, the shriller the protest became. Ulric rose to his feet.

"Bring her forward," he encouraged.

The filthy and tattered creature took one look at the tall knight and collapsed in hysterics, so that her companions had to drag her forward.

"No!"

The men stopped at Ulric's abrupt command. Branwen watched curiously as her husband stepped down off the dais and approached the frightened girl. When he spoke again, it was to her, in ringing syllables, soft and pure. Gogsblood, he was speaking Welsh, Branwen realized in disbelief. All her efforts to curse him in his own language so that he could not help but understand the full extent of her contempt had been for nothing. She could have lapsed into mother Welsh and added a whole new prospective to her angry dissertations. Her wonder was interrupted by the sight of Ulric of Caradoc kneeling down before the girl.

"Come, *geneth*. I am your *noddwn*, your protector, not

271

your enemy." The lord addressed the men. "What's the girl's name?"

"Avala."

The smile Ulric gave the girl was warm enough to melt a statue's resistance to communication. His golden hair, which curled about his shoulders as he reached for the girl's hand gently and lifted it to his lips, combined with his lean, handsome features, reminded Branwen of one of those Roman statues comes to life—Apollo, the sun god.

"Avala," the lord of Caradoc repeated gently. He peered at the girl over her hand, a hint of mischief lighting in his eyes. " 'Tis no wonder they made off with you, sweet apple, for you were surely the choicest pick of the village. Most likely they thought you all beauty with no wit to escape them."

What the blazes was this devil up to? Branwen wondered, pricked by the seductive quality of her husband's tone. Gogsbreath, this was a village wench! By the looks of her, she hadn't bathed since summer, if then! And no doubt her mother's comb had been the last to touch that tangled mass of hair.

"But *I* know better," Ulric went on smoothly. "They didn't think you would notice where they were taking you, but you did, didn't you, Avala?"

The girl, somewhat calmed by Ulric's tone, peered up at him suspiciously through the fingers that covered her face.

"Blanchard, fetch that bowl of fruit from the cupboard!"

The chamberlain hurried to oblige Ulric, presenting him with his request. At the sight of the fruit piled on the bowl, Avala's face brightened. Her tongue slipped from one side of her lips to the others, while shadow-black eyes darted from the apples to Ulric and back to the fruit.

"Go ahead, take one."

The poor child had likely never been inside the castle, much less taken food from the lord's own table. She looked at Ulric as if he might sever her hand were she to obey him. More sensitive to the girl's quandary than Branwen would ever have guessed, the young lord picked a choice one and handed it out to the girl.

"Here then, take it. My gift to you."

Avala snatched the apple greedily from Ulric's hand and clutched it to her chest.

"Can you fool those devils and tell me which way they went upon leaving the village?"

Avala shook her head feverishly. "Swynwr!"

"Wizards?" Ulric questioned. "Wizards, not devils?"

The girl nodded and, keeping her prize possession close to her bosom with one hand, made a sweeping motion with the other. Then, pulling away from the men who had relaxed their hold on her, Avala ran to the northwest wall of the keep, babbling so rapidly that not even Branwen fully understood her.

"She's saying something about them riding into the sea," Branwen informed her bewildered husband.

"The wizard and his men rode along the coast?"

The girl nodded uncertainly and then retreated in haste to her guardians, as if fearful the rogues might ride down upon her at any moment for her betrayal. Again, she began to mumble and point frantically at the wall.

"They didn't go up into the hills!" Branwen exclaimed, affected somewhat by the witness's excitement. "They crossed the lowlands and rode into the sea!"

"On the traeth?" Ulric queried the girl, raising his voice above the murmur of speculation that resulted.

Avala nodded again feverishly.

"Damnation!" the knight swore, swinging about to face his court. "Their tracks were gone with the tide!"

At Ulric's explosion, the girl dropped behind her

273

companions with a squeal. In a masterful struggle, the knight reined in his temper and scooped the remainder of the apples from the bowl. "For you, Avala. You are as brave as you are sweet and pretty. Your lord thanks you and promises to address his anger to the wizard and his men to avenge Caradoc's people." Ulric straightened and faced the crowd. "You all have my word on that. My provost and men will ride the traeth until we find where the rogues took to land again. Blanchard, dismiss the court. I would be on my way at once."

Somehow, Avala managed to carry the eight or so apples in her arms, refusing to permit her companions to help her out of the hall with them. Oddly envious of the compassion her husband had shared with the distraught girl, Branwen continued to watch him from her chair as he began to hand out orders to his various captains for the preparation to depart.

"Three villages, all along the coast," he echoed aloud.

"And three of Caradoc's main food suppliers, milord," the chamberlain reminded him. "The lowlands there are the most fertile land in the cantref."

"Perhaps it's Edward himself." Branwen bit her bottom lip, but it was too late. The blasphemous thought had been voiced audibly enough for all to hear. " 'Twas only a jest, milord."

The cold blast of Ulric's appraisal conveyed all that needed to be said. The irony that he and most of the knights in his company had been the ones to cut off the Welsh food supplies at Anglesey had not been missed.

"My good wife is not herself, gentle knights, since she took the poison. I pray you dismiss her indiscretion and go have your squires prepare your steeds for the ride." He arched a mocking golden brow at Branwen. " 'Twill be a refreshing change, milady. We can warm ourselves from the distinct chill of this room by the wind and spray from the sea."

Chapter Seventeen

The upper windows of the hall had been shuttered and the fire blazed brightly in the massive hearth near the dais, yet Branwen was cold. The vial had contained liniment, Aunt Agnéis informed her after the men had left for the chase of the night raiders. It was good when applied on abrasions or sores on a horse's leg, but was never ingested. It caused violent colicky symptoms known to be fatal to horses. Even the newest squire knew better than to leave it on his hands and not wash them before eating.

"I don't like the looks of this at all," her aunt puzzled aloud as she handed the vial back over to Branwen. "I shall have to think on this."

Think, the girl thought forlornly. It was all that consumed her thoughts as she set about making the arrangements for her first evening meal. How could the same man be capable of such gentleness and compassion as he'd shown that poor frightened village wench and, admittedly, Branwen herself on occasion, and dole this treachery out at the same time? Ulric was two men and one of them terrified her. The other she loved.

Which only added to the frayed state of her nerves, for Ulric and his men had yet to return from riding the coast and night was hanging heavy on the eastern horizon, enhanced by the cloud-shrouded sun that sunk in the west. Perhaps they'd happened upon the halegrins. The English hauberks were no match for a Welsh longbow, which had been known to nail a knight through armor and saddle to his horse.

Tomorrow she would start her own investigation, Branwen mused, cracking open the gallery shutter to peer outside over the baily walls beyond at the grass morfa, or lowland, and on toward the ragged coastline where Ulric's retinue had ridden off late that morning, brightly bannered in scarlet and black. She'd ride to the plundered villages with her aunt and see what might be done for those who had been injured and left without food. While she could not bring in the rogues, a fellow Cymry might be able to find out more than the English knights.

In the distance, Branwen caught sight of a movement, which eventually cleared the shadows of the distant forest, enabling her to identify the return of Caradoc's new lord. An unacknowledged rush of relief escaped her lips as she hurriedly closed the shutter and sprang to the rail overlooking the hall below.

"Master Harold, alert the kitchen. Milord returns and is surely famished!"

The chief steward bowed shortly to Branwen, affording her the barest of civility. He had not taken well to the lady's curbing of his menu, much less her appointment of his predecessor Griffin to see her plans carried out. While lesser in quantity, Branwen was certain the food prepared by Caradoc's cooks was equal to any in England. Lady Gwendolyn had counseled them well on how to make the most of what was available, simultaneously developing Master Maitlen's artistic flair for presentation.

By the time Ulric led his entourage into the great hall, Branwen stood by the table on the dais, overseeing the placement of spiced cheese soup at each setting. To her dismay, he was also surrounded by her father's hounds, which had taken a traitorous liking to their new lord. Out of respect for her mother, Owen had kept the dogs on the lower level of the keep, where they were free to come and go as they pleased into the bailey. Thus, Caradoc's hall was kept cleaner and fresher-smelling than even that at Westminster Palace.

Aunt Agnéis, spirited out of her room by the commotion of barking and laughter, shuffled downstairs and helped herself to one of the baskets of small fingerbreads, which had been intermittently placed along the main table. Preoccupied, she started eating one of the sticks and turned to wander back up the steps, all the while whispering to herself.

"Aunt Agnéis, what of the rest of the meal?" the girl called after the older woman, wounded that her aunt would not share the first supper prepared at her direction as the lady of Caradoc. After all, Agnéis had been all advice earlier.

"It was delicious, dear. Sleep well."

Branwen sighed in resignation. She knew better than to go after her aunt. When Agnéis was in one of those particular humors, it was difficult to intrude on it. It was as if she'd stepped into another dimension, where they could see her but couldn't reach her ... at least not without a violent shaking. It used to drive Owen ap Caradoc to distraction. Perhaps it was just as well, Branwen mused, since her aunt would invariably bring up the dark spirits hovering over Caradoc, and heaven only knew to what that would lead.

While the men sought the use of the lavers on either side of the main entrance to wash their hands, Branwen held the solid brass one her father had once used for Ulric himself and kept a watchful eye on the dogs sniffing along the edge of the table in hopes of finding something tasty within their reach. It was a sight that would have made her mother cringe, despite its wide acceptance in most halls.

Branwen would have made her objection then but thought it, like the matter of the vial she'd found in Ulrick's sack, best for private discussion. Besides, the late night's carousing was now telling under Ulric's eyes, the long hours in the saddle showing in the labored way he eased into his chair. A good meal would put him in a better humor.

"I take it milord's day was fruitless?" she ventured at last, assuming a seat at his left. Branwen actually was rather pleased with her adaptation to this part of her new role. The wifely inquiry might have come from Lady Gwendolyn herself.

Instead of answering, Ulric stirred the soup in his bowl and studied the contents. "What is this?"

"Spice cheese . . ."

"I know 'tis cheese soup, milady, but where is the *rest* of the course? Are we to eat it one dish at a time?"

"If you would be a Welsh lord, Ulric, you would dine like one. There is more to come. You will not starve," she assured him. "Caradoc is known for its hospitality."

Ulric looked up and down the tables as his fellow Englishmen awaited his example to begin the meal. He exhaled heavily, as if forcing out an inner frustration. "What of those who don't like cheese soup? There's naught else for them. . . ."

"There is hot bread, butter, and jellies put out."

"Gogsdeath, woman! These men have been riding for the last six hours without sustenance and you'd feed them *bread?*"

Good Cymry could go all day without food, if need be, and still fight with the most stouthearted of men! Branwen's cheeks were singed, not only by his comment, but also by the struggle to withhold her own. She motioned for Griffin to approach. "Master Griffin, have the servitors inquire if our guests would prefer the sweet almond and cabbage soup being served at the opposite end of the hall."

"You'd feed them the *servant's* fare?" Ulric hissed under his breath.

"Milord 'tis but an alternative to sustain them until the next dish arrives. Pray be patient, for Griffin and I have conferred long over my first meal, and Master Maitlen has done you proud."

Ulric replied with an unconvinced grunt and turned to accept the hanap placed before him. When he removed the lid, which was identical to the cup holding his beverage, his bristled jaw clenched so fiercely that Branwen heard the clashing of his teeth. *"Milk!"*

It might have been poison from the way he carried on. " 'Tis warmed and sweetened with honey, milord, to take away the chill."

"Harold!"

Branwen flinched as Ulric shouted for his appointed steward. Harold appeared instantly, looking like a tall, gangly elf eager to avenge his wounded pride. Even his ears were slightly pointed, she vowed, mimicking his angular chin, and the plain brown color of his raiment was painfully indicative of his personality.

"Milord?"

"Get this milk out of my sight and bring on our best ale!"

"Yes, milord," the servant said, slipping a smug look sideways to Branwen.

"And bring on the rest of our meal. Faith, we're half starved and our appetites are but teased."

Branwen meant to place a gentle hand on Ulric's arm, the real bite of her fingers pinching his flesh escaping her. "Milord, I might remind you that the house and kitchen are my domain. If you would but—"

Hazel eyes snapping, Ulric unclenched her hand and put it on the table. "Milady, my patience is sorely tested as it is, without this affront to my guests," he warned, his voice thankfully muted by the girls who began to play the harp on the gallery above the entrance from the new kitchen. "I would have them fed and fed now, not bit by bit."

As if he had been the only one who had been tested! After finding out about the horse liniment in her husband's sack, doing battle with Master Harold, and studying the menu to see what could be omitted on short notice, Branwen had stalked about the growing "city" within Caradoc's walls in the brisk January air to clear her head of the bitter turmoil. There, to her utter irritation, she had gotten lost! Lost in her own keep! Looking over to where Griffin stood stalwartly blocking Master Harold's exit, Branwen gave a reluctant nod.

"As you wish, milord."

It would serve the man and his pride-puffed knights right if the food grew cold before them! In London, Branwen had been so inundated with dishes of every nature and design that she was hard put to appreciate anything but the variety. Now all Master Maitlen's creations were to be unveiled at once, each distracting from the other, she fretted in annoyance.

In one continuous line under the brittle snapping of Master Harold's fingers, the kitchen was emptied of its preparations. A salmon pie, resplendent with the duplication of the fish raised on its crust and glazed with egg white, was brought in on a charger, one for each section of table, while a roast of beef in pepper sauce arrived laid out on a large round trencher of flat green parsley bread. Smaller trenchers of the same, painted with saffron flowers around the edges to resemble the fanciest of dishes, were placed before the nobler guests and unpainted ones handed out to those seated at the side tables.

Too pretty to eat, Branwen thought, observing the carver as he assumed the duty of serving his lord's meat on the common trencher placed between lord and lady. The scullions and varlets in the kitchen had done wonderfully under Master Maitlen's direction! If it tasted half as good as it smelled, it would surely put a smile on the surly face of her husband. She broke off a piece of hard crust and tossed it in the alms dish, which would be emptied for distribution to the poor later.

After sprinkling seasoning from the ornate boat-shaped saltcellar on the more substantial meat, Ulric helped himself to a portion with his dining dagger. The silver handle, inlaid with an ebony raven, had belonged to Branwen's great-grandfather, who had built the original keep now surrounded by new walls and buildings. She hadn't meant to stare in anticipation of Ulric's reaction, but was rewarded nonetheless by a nod of approval. With a tentative smile, she attended her soup, which was finished by the time the last of the evening's dishes was brought in—spiced pear tarts, laced with raisins and dates.

Unaccustomed to even as much as she had ordered prepared, Branwen gave no more than a taste to the salmon pie and meat, before going straight for the dessert. It was delicious, enhanced by a warm vanilla sauce that was tempting enough on its own. Accompanying it were flagons of hippocras—red wine spiced with cinnamon, ginger, salt, and pepper—just the thing to end a cold winter's feast.

The general conversation and the plucking of the harps by the girls on the balcony above had a settling effect on Branwen's initial anxiety over the meal. She sipped the heady drink and tried to listen to the multiple accounts of the day's findings. But for the vial at her waist, she might have been lured into enjoying playing the part of lady of the manor, for compliments rose from all quarters on her efforts. Dreading the end of what looked to be the first tolerable evening in a long while, she settled back against her chair, engrossed in Ulric's assessment of their findings.

"If we would map out the pattern of these raids, we'd find they are making their way toward Caradoc itself. The men always come in from the highlands at night and leave by the sea, where their retreat is nearly impossible to follow."

"Because of the morning tide?"

Ulric nodded in answer to Branwen's query. "And there are any number of places they might have emerged, all covered with shallows . . . water enough to hide their tracks."

"Our men are too few in number to spread out through the cantref in anticipation of their next attack," the provost pointed out practically. "The village men are able enough fighters, but this talk of halegrins and spirits has made them cower behind their doors."

"More of this superstitious nonsense! If we could catch just one, we could show the people these villains are as much flesh and blood as the next man." Ulric motioned for Harold and pushed his trencher aside with the scraps of his meal. "Bring on the next course, sir."

The steward looked at Branwen accusingly. "There *is* no other course, milord."

"What?" Ulric switched his demanding gaze to Branwen. "Is this more of *your* Welsh nonsense, milady?"

Stung out of her contentment, Branwen regarded her husband stonily, while her insides knotted and quivered, threatening to tear away the shield of composure she had erected. This was not her home anymore, she thought indignantly, it was Ulric's. He had changed not only the exterior of Caradoc, but had also taken over the imposition of its customs as well. Next he would be shoving English law down their throats!

"Aye, milord. 'Twas my *half* of the meal. If you would have more, then . . ." Her voice broke off. Damnation, not now, she warned the sob that rose in her throat like a battering ram driven by tears. "Then see to it you . . . yourself!"

Throwing her napkin at the princely countenance challenging her, Branwen left the table in an angry flutter of skirts. As she stepped off the dais, however, she swung around again, so abruptly that the headdress she wore slid cockeyed on her equally troublesome wimple.

"Your English not only *eat* like pigs, they *snore* like them as well!"

It was a short stomp to her "private" chamber, the other side of the dressing screen between the hearth and the staircase to the upper chambers, hardly sufficient to stamp out her hurt and anger. They didn't know the meaning of frugality, she fumed, only wanton waste. She had had a meal fit for the Prince of Wales himself put before them! Given what they considered a good meal, day in and day out, she would grow fat as a cow!

Branwen stiffened at the sound of booted footsteps preceding the giant shadow cast on the curtain by the firelight. "Get out of my chamber!" she ordered with an imperious sniff as Ulric stepped around it.

Ulric held up his hand in warning, "Madam, I have had a trying day. . . ."

"*You* have had a trying day? Milord, you at least have some say in your own home, which is more than I do! By the gods, I even got lost today in this menagerie of a fortress . . . in my own home!" Branwen shook her head in angry confusion. "I do not know my home. I do not know what you expect of me, and I do not know my husband!"

"Milady, sit down. This hall is full of ears." While his

283

voice was quiet, it was no less taut than Branwen's shrill one.

"Ears!" Branwen repeated, stepping up onto the mattress as Ulric moved toward her. "You think nothing of your companions hearing your disdain for me and my people. Fair is fair, milord. I would have them hear mine for you, *you wife-poisoning cur!*" she shouted, hands cupped about her mouth like a herald.

The harpists, who had until now kept constant with their music, ceased to play, compounding the silence of the dinner guests, so that the echo of Branwen's accusation in the high arches of the ceiling could be heard without strain. Branwen braced herself against the high headboard, ready to spring away should the crimson-faced lord, seemingly growing with fury before her very eyes, move toward her.

"Come down from there, milady, lest you fall." Ulric stretched out his hand to help her, but Branwen would not fall for more of his trickery.

"As if you'd care!" she sneered skeptically. "*I* have the poison, Ulric of Caradoc. Taken from your traveling sack!" The dogs, distracted from the table by the outraged shouts, began to bark at her and race about the bed. "Out, and take your brethren with you!"

At the sight of a sleek boarhound venturing up on the foot of her bed, Branwen tore off her wimple and headdress and slung them at it, at the same time rushing forward with an angry rebuff. The dog leapt backward with a yelp as her coronet struck its nose and crashed against her dressing screen. Her fingers grazed the oak wood of the frame in a frantic attempt to catch it before her little haven was exposed to all when Ulric snatched her up in midair.

The screen struck the stone floor with loud crack that sounded as if lightning had split a tree in their midst. Ulric's voice provided the accompanying thunder as he addressed his knights, Branwen slung unceremoniously over his shoulder. "Pardon me, good sires, but milady would have an audience with me. My cupboards and cellars are yours," the lord informed them with a flourish of his hand. "Master Harold, bring out yellow and white meats, as well anything else easily prepared by the cooks! *Miriam!*"

The maid who had been taking her meal at the opposite end of the hall with the other chambermaids leapt to her feet. "Yes, milord?"

"Fetch some of Father Gregory's tea. Milady is distraught."

Branwen slammed Ulric furiously on the back with her fist. "Damn you, you can't keep me drugged forever!"

"I . . . I can't, milord," Miriam told him timidly. "Milady Agnéis threw it out the window."

Oblivious to Branwen's squirming struggles, Ulric scanned the tables around the room. "Where *is* the old witch?" he bellowed, so loud that the chambermaid dropped to her knees.

"Mercy, milord, she's taken her supper in her room," Miriam cried in a tremulous voice.

Branwen could feel Ulric's deep breath expanding his chest as he struggled to keep his calm, not only for the sake of the girl cowering before him, but for that of his guests as well. "Then fetch a flagon of the hippocras and bring it to my chamber to calm milady's distress."

"There's not enough drink in your cellars to put me at ease in your lair!" Branwen exclaimed, striking Ulric's back again as he took to the steps. "Gogsbreath, Dafydd, you are my protector! Will you leave me to this animal?" She smacked at one of the dogs who dared not only to follow them up the steps, but to also lick her bobbing face. "Damn your black soul to hell, Ulric of Caradoc. I will fight you with my last breath ere I spend the night in your room! If you would not temper your bullish ways for me, then at least do so for my condition."

The door slammed behind them, punctuating their arrival in the master bedchamber. As she was brought around, Branwen recognized the passing loden damask of the cloth that hung over the windows and the crown of the plump bed upon which she'd awakened the day of her arrival. Ulric went to dump her on the mattress, but Branwen dug in, clinging to his belt with all her might, sooner than be tossed before him at his mercy.

"I hate you, Ulric! I hate you and all your English vassals! Would that your poison had worked, for death, at least, is not miserable once achieved. Then my spirit could come back and bedevil you for the rest of your . . . *days!*"

The belt gave way in her hands, startling Branwen. Letting it fall, she clutched the material of his loosened shirt. This time, however, she was peeled off his shoulder along with his clothing, so that when she threw the vacant garments away from her, Ulric stood like a lion-maned demon, naked from the waist up.

Unaware of the blue fire that flashed in a gaze that could not resist taking in the battle scars marring his perfectly developed torso, Branwen raised up on her elbows in a dazed attempt to escape backward in a crablike scramble. Ulric, however, grasped her ankles and yanked her down. Her head bounced on the mattress, dark hair spreading wildly around her face as he pinned her down with his own body.

"This is what I would have of you, milady," he rumbled lowly in the deep purr of the beast he resembled.

Branwen tore her lips from the ones that grazed them, only to have her ear pecked at tenderly. Cold as she had been earlier, the manly flesh pressed against her infected her with a giddy warmth. In a childlike reaction, she closed her eyes, as if to make it go away, but instead his assault, isolated to touch alone, became more devilish. A small groan of frustration vibrated her throat against his kiss and he drew away gently.

"Tell me of this poison you have."

Yes, the poison, part of her demanded in outrage! Branwen swallowed, reacting hot and cold to the two personalities of the man atop her. " 'Tis in my purse."

Ulric raised up enough to untie the knot of the purse from her belt. The vial fell out near Branwen's head as he resumed his hold and spread his legs to brace them, one knee between her skirted ones. His rugged features, now haggard from fatigue, relaxed as he recognized it.

" 'Tis naught but liniment for Pendragon. You'd find a like vial in every knight's sack, including your dauntless Dafydd."

How easily he explained away things. It must be another gift of a seventh son, Branwen mused, gradually acknowledging the disarming effect of her husband's body on her own. "Aunt Agnéis said when taken internally it induced the same symptoms I suffered that horrible night."

"The woman is unbalanced! Gogsblood, Branwen, why would I put you through such a thing, when you carry my child? Where is that sharp wit of yours? You are not the hysterical female."

It was hard to speak with one's heart lodged against one's throat, which was exactly where Branwen's had lurched at the mention of her deceit. "Perhaps that is the c . . . cause, milord," she stammered.

A single tear somehow slipped out of the corner of one eye and detoured over her cheek to trickle next to her ear. To her astonishment, Ulric caught it with his tongue and kissed the spot where he'd taken it. His breath sent warm shivers down her spine and his gaze took on an earnestness that needed no reinforcement of words. He brushed her raven locks away from her face and tucked them behind her ears.

"Someone is trying to keep us apart, wife. They feed your mind with suspicion, when all I am guilty of is falling in love with you. Join me as a wife should. Sleep here tonight. Ours is a new life, not that of your parents nor mine. Let us make it together."

Was there ever such thing as a male siren? Branwen wondered, her resolve now pitted against the compelling urge to believe Ulric's huskily whispered words, nay, to melt beneath him and take him in her arms. She touched his cheek, now rough and in need of a razor, before moving on to his lips—those searing, sensual masters of seduction.

"I . . ."

A sharp knock on the door, followed by Miriam's "Your hippocras, milord!" prevented her from sinking further into the inviting depths of Ulric's gaze. As he rose from the bed and walked to the door, the air rushed in to cool where he'd laid upon her. Gogsbreath, how close she'd come to believing him! How much she *wanted* to believe him. How little she dared believe him.

"Thank you, Miriam." Ulric turned as Branwen propped herself upright. "Shall I have the maid bring up your things, fair raven?"

Branwen wavered, her fingers burying into the inviting softness of the bed while her mind entertained the sheer ecstasy that awaited her with just the nod of her head. She was committed to being the lady of Caradoc, to doing her best to fill her mother's shoes, but was she ready to make that commitment to the man whose name had not yet been cleared of guilt, except by his own confession? A man who had deceived her into thinking him an ally, rather than the one she had sworn to see dead? The man who had snatched the food from

Mam Wales's breasts to starve her children? Her mother would have plunged a dagger into her heart before betraying her people and family.

"Nay, milord, I would leave this chamber at once, lest my mind be poisoned as well as my body."

Ulric stiffened, his bloodless knuckles clenched about the neck of the bottle Miriam had brought. Were looks daggers, Branwen would have been saved the trial of self-destruction she pondered. The gaze that had been tender and golden as sunshine now lashed out with the force of a northwest gale. Ah, the serpent can only act the angel so long, she mused in bitter disappointment.

"Then be gone, woman! I would have peace . . . at least within these walls," her husband amended with a flourish of his arm. "You, Miriam!" he called out as the chambermaid started to shrink away from the doorway. "I would also have the comfort of those talented hands on my neck, for it feels as though a vile chain seeks to draw it into my body, head and all."

Branwen coolly arranged her dress as she walked in silence past her husband.

"If you would be so kind, milady, tell my good fellows we ride at first light in the morning, but tonight this knight would seek the bed early."

She nodded sooner than risk her voice breaking, but at the closing of the door behind Miriam, instead of taking the steps to the lower chamber, Branwen climbed those rising beyond the gallery.

The steps were as narrow and steep as they had always been, but the worn stones had been replaced with fresh ones. Beyond the gallery, no torches burned, but Branwen knew the way by heart. Her parents had found her, escaped from her nurse, in the open tower room of the keep not long after she'd taken her first steps. It was where she came to marvel at the stars and listen to the fisted waves of the sea smash into the rocky wall of the keep, which protected it from human assault.

From there she could see the battlements of the inner bailey, glowing with torchlight from within, like ragged flat teeth against the night sky. Upon reaching the far-thermost part of the room, however, she perched in the thick opening. The princess in her tower, she reflected laconically, recalling one of her childhood fancies, for the idea of a princess was often supplanted by her desire to be a soldier. It was hard to tell how many play arrows she'd shot into the sea, defending her keep to the death.

She'd been surrounded by love and protected by stone and Tâd's well-trained men. No one threatened her contented little kingdom, much less the prince she dreamed of. He was supposed to rescue her and win her heart, not steal it under false pretenses. She tried to swallow the despair in her throat. Her parents had pre-pared her for her station in life, but they had never an-ticipated Lord Ulric of Caradoc. If the serpent in Eden had wielded half his charm, it was no wonder Eve had given in to temptation.

Chapter Eighteen

"No one will disturb your sleep tonight, dear."

Aunt Agnéis's promise, made after the girl had sought the warmth of her aunt's small room to ward off the chill of the tower air, floated in the netherworld to which the tea she had made for Branwen had taken her. Oddly enough, there were other voices as well—voices that sounded as though they were there in the bed with her. They didn't wake her. Aunt Agnéis had been right about that. They were just . . . there.

Of them all, Dafydd's was the most discernible. He seemed closer than the others, as if he were carrying her. Even the air temperature changed as he stepped into a narrow passage—narrow because Branwen could feel the cold, rough stone scraping at her bared feet, which grazed it. With each step, she felt as though they were descending deeper and deeper into darkness. She mumbled his name once uncertainly, but he hastily reassured her with a kiss on her forehead.

" 'Tis all right, milady. I am here. There's nothing to fear."

Dafydd was her royally appointed protector, yet Branwen was not comforted as when she was in Ulric's arms. Damn the contradiction of it all! she swore, burrowing closer to the young knight's chest, strained taut, like his arms, with the burden of her weight. What the devil did he think he was doing? Ulric would surely kill him for this. Besides, her toes, peeking out from under the hem of her nightdress, were frozen. Nay, wet, she realized groggily.

Sleep claimed her again, so that when she stirred upon being placed on a bed hard as stone, the same irritated humor occupied her dazed collection. She would have risen up on her elbows and told Elwaid just what she thought, except that she seemed to have no control of her limbs. It was as if they belonged to someone else and were unable to hear her mental commands. Not even her eyelids would respond beyond allowing the haziest peek out from under them.

Where the devil was she? Branwen wondered, straining to keep her eyes open in the strange surroundings. It was a large room, oddly warm in contrast to the tunnel through which she and Dafydd had descended. Fires burned in cressets along walls that were not clearly marked as to where they stopped and the ceiling began. Indeed, it all seemed out of focus, ragged and broken darkness and shadows pierced by flickering light.

And singing. There were people singing . . . chanting actually. Had she paid more attention to her Latin studies, she might know the nature of the eerie song. As it was, she merely squeezed the hand holding hers, the only thing that was tangible. Thank God Dafydd had come into this strange dream with her, for she would have been terrified to come this far alone.

"Diana . . . Diana . . ."

The name echoing in Branwen's mind was instantly displaced by total silence. To her dismay, Dafydd's hand dropped away and she was suddenly alone in the darkness. Again she forced her eyes open. No, not darkness . . . firelight, she told herself, trying to maintain her calm.

"Great goddess, bless this ceremony this night."

A woman's voice cut boldly through the silence like a vengeful blade. Branwen tried to crane her head backward so that she might see the speaker, but all she could make out was a white robe bedecked with jewels.

"Tonight your son will be born of Caradoc as foretold in the prophesy."

"*Diana . . . Diana . . .*" The whispers echoed in the heat-damp chamber.

"When the estrons shall rule your traeth and morfa, you promised to send him."

"*Diana . . . Diana . . .*"

"From the womb of Caradoc!"

Branwen felt someone pressing on her abdomen lightly, as if in demonstration. It belonged to a long-sleeved arm, richly adorned with gold and silver bands.

"Planted in the midst of the estrons, without their suspecting!"

"*Diana . . . Diana . . .*"

Blending in with the growing chanting came a baby's protest. Hers? Branwen wondered, trying to piece it all together. No, she'd had the green stone. It couldn't be.

"The child!"

Through the crack of her eyelids, Branwen made out on the ceiling the shadow of a kicking baby at the end of extended arms.

"*Diana!*"

"The mother!"

"*Diana!*"

Suddenly, Branwen felt her night shift being tugged. The ribbon at her throat was loosened and her neckline pulled away from her body. The baby was now before her very eyes, squalling in great outrage as it was stuffed down the front of her dress.

"Hear his cries, great goddess! See how he swells the womb of his earthly mother!"

Her dress was smoothed down over the child squirming on her abdomen, naked flesh to naked flesh. Branwen's head swam in confusion. But the stone . . .

"He begs to be free to fulfill the prophesy!" The woman's voice was almost as hysterical as the gathering's as she pulled the material tight, binding the child to Branwen.

"Diana!"

Caught up in the bizarre frenzy, Branwen dug into the rock bed, trying to rise on her elbows. Where was her protector? He couldn't leave her here in this nightmare alone! "Dafydd!"

She heard his voice as their hands joined again and fell back against the hard bed in relief. " 'Tis nothing but an adoption, fair raven of Caradoc."

"Hear the mother cry out in the pangs of birth!"

The soothing reply meant nothing. What were they doing to the child? Branwen fretted, feeling herself drifting away again. *Her child! Ulric's son!* She willed her hands over her abdomen, but they lay unresponsive at her side.

" 'Tis time!"

"Diana . . . Diana . . . Diana . . . Diana . . ."

The chanting began to echo as fast as the blood racing through Branwen's veins. Gogsdeath, she could feel them taking her baby. Their hands were all over her, groping for the child through the folds of her gown. Suddenly, the child began to slide down from her abdomen, its tiny feet and hands beating in protest.

"Dafydd!" Branwen breathed frighteningly. "Don't let them take my baby! *Dafydd!*"

Her scream brought her upright in her own bed, panting and damp beneath the heavy linen of her nightshift. Hand flying to her neckline, chastely tied with a bow, Branwen shivered. So real! It had been so real! She crossed her arms, her hands locking under her elbows.

The resulting sting brought her attention to where skin there had been rubbed raw. No doubt from digging into the stiff sheets in her sleep, she reasoned, beneath the growing weight of reality.

This was her reward for lying to Ulric about the likelihood of her being with child. The guilty assault prompted Branwen to cover her flat abdomen with her hand. Gogsblood, she'd heard so much about her bearing an heir that she'd dreamed of becoming the brood sow! Tugging a blanket about her, she got up and stepped around the screen to warm herself by the smoldering hearthfire, although she knew her chill was not the result of the temperature in the room. Hers was a spiritual one, much harder to assuage.

She scanned the sleeping figures of the knights and spied Dafydd ap Elwaid resting peacefully near her screen. Sadly enough, despite her father's training, Dafydd had not turned out to be much of a protector . . . in dream or in reality. He lacked the courage of his convictions. She actually felt a bit sorry for him. He was decidedly shy of Ulric's imposing person. Considering the English lord's expertise in all aspects of knighthood, from battle to love and chivalry, he was well justified, she supposed.

Thus far, her own battle had not fared so well. Had Miriam not interrupted them, she might have succumbed to his masterful, if rather forceful, seduction. Gogsbreath, Ulric could make her feel so alive . . . even in anger's passion, she mused, which was not so far removed from love's, considering the ease with which he could convert one to the other. *And the bards call women the manipulators!*

Branwen glanced toward the stairwell that rounded upward toward Ulric's chamber. When had Miriam come down? she wondered, still stung by her husband's pointed appropriation of the girl. Naturally, he wanted it to bother her, and damn his soul, it did! Rising to her feet from the bench in the hearth, Branwen tried to make out the girl's form among those of the maids sleeping on rush mattresses brought out for the night's repose.

The general murmur of snores and the crackling of the hearth echoing in the hall was suddenly drowned by the startling bellow of Ulric of Caradoc, who stood struggling into his clothes at the top of the steps.

"To arms, men! The bastards burn Caradoc's village beneath our very noses!"

Branwen caught her breath as Ulric stumbled unsteadily near the top step, thankfully catching himself against the wall with a scowl. The menservants came up from their beds at once and began to scramble about for weapons, while the maids commenced a wail of startled screams, but only one knight struggled up from his bed.

"For the love of God, men, hearken to you lord's command!" she shouted, rushing over to one and shaking him roughly. "You women, help me wake these ale-sodden oafs, lest the halegrins take Caradoc's keep out from under them!"

At the mention of halegrins, the women hurriedly set about awakening their protectors with hysterical cries and fierce shaking. The men stirred but, to Branwen's disdain, were a pitiful showing of knighthood. They stumbled about, bumping into the women and each other in a daze. But for the squires, who had also been roused, they would not have ridden out toward Caradoc before morning broke. As it was, they rode, but not with much enthusiasm. Even Ulric seemed to lack his usual spark for impending battle.

"Miriam!" Branwen shouted, catching sight of her maid amidst the gathering of women at the gate seeing the men off. "Get my shawl!"

Aunt Agnéis, awakened by the noise and confusion,

eased down the steps fully attired as Branwen raced behind her screen to pull on the kirtle she'd worn earlier. "This is the devil's work!" the old woman swore upon reaching the bottom. "If I had not seen it in my sleep, the village would have been ruins by the time we awakened."

Branwen's blood stilled *"You* awakened Ulric?"

Agnéis nodded smugly. "Indeed I did. If they hurry, they can catch the swine!"

Ulric would have her flayed alive if her aunt had sent him off on a wild-goose chase. "Oh, Aunt Agnéis, are you certain?"

"My aching toes, geneth, you can see the fire from the gallery windows! You're getting more bullheaded than that husband of yours."

Branwen didn't know whether to be relieved or worried. "Please have one of the squires saddle McShane!"

"You've no business riding out with the men to meet the likes as they're up against!" Aunt Agnéis protested. "Your father wouldn't—"

"I am lady of this keep now and Tâd isn't here, Aunt Agnéis. Now, will you do as I ask, or shall I have to send Miriam?"

Everyone was moving about in slow motion, she fretted, as her aunt turned stiffly and shuffled off toward the bailey. In truth, she was having trouble functioning herself. She got stuck in the kirtle Miriam tugged over her head and then could not seem to get her gillies on her bare feet. She had leggings and stockings, but too much time had passed already to fool with them and she was anxious to be away. Donning her shawl as she reached the steps leading to the ground and storeroom level of the keep, Branwen called to her aunt below.

"Can you see anything?"

"Not from here. You can from the gallery windows where I showed milord."

Bless her dear absentminded heart, Branwen thought as she rushed down the steps, skirts billowing about her slender form. It was well that her aunt was not given to lying, for she would surely be caught for forgetting what she'd previously stated.

"Milady! I would come with you!" Miriam called out, running to catch up with Branwen as she hurried across the inner bailey and to the outer, where the horses were now being kept. "If you would not listen to your aunt, would you at least take me with you?" she asked, short of breath upon reaching the spot where Branwen waited for McShane to be saddled.

Seeing the real concern on her maid's face, Branwen conceded with a nod. "Though I was going to ride out behind these good men," she told her companion, referring to the footmen who were assembling to march out after the mounted retinue.

As they set out across the rocky grassland, Branwen could see that most of the village was ablaze. Her heart thumped with each strike of McShane's hooves until, unable to honor her commitment to go with the men on foot, she spurred the horse onward and their progress deafened the pounding in her chest. Against the fire-lit blackness, figures ran back and forth. Their screams reached across the morfa through the smoke and mist.

Then there were mounted men, difficult to identify as either Ulric's knights or the halegrins at a distance. They darted in and out of the melee, clashing with one opponent, then seeking another. Had there been time to don their mail? Branwen wondered, trying to sort out the resulting confusion of Ulric's alarm. The squires were there, but the horses had to be saddled. . . .

"Milady, I beg of you, go no closer! Even the simplest of captains would wait for his men!"

At Miriam's sound, if disagreeable, advice, Branwen reluctantly reined in McShane and her compelling urge to know what was happening. Had Ulric put on his mail? Faith, he'd charged through the midst of the knights and run straight through the servants sleeping farthest from the fire, dragging the same with him, like a straggling tail of sleepy ducklings. But then, if he was free of his armor, he would be more equal to the villains in speed and agility.

No amount of reason could still the mounting dread building in her chest. The footmen, who seemed to move in slow motion, finally reached them, led by Harold, who looked like a vengeful monk with his bowl-cut hair and drab brown robes sweeping around him in the night breeze from the coast. At the head steward's command, the group, armed with such as the castle yards and kitchens would afford, swept forward into the thick of the fire and smoke.

"Miriam, if you are frightened, then slide off my steed now," Branwen warned the maid clinging to her waist, "for I am going into it hence and would not have you wailing in my ear."

The maid needed no further urging. Her loyalty established thus far was sufficient to serve her and her mistress, for no woman in her right mind would willingly ride into the fiery melee ahead of them.

"Take care, milady!"

"If the rogues come this way, hide in yon rocks and report their means of escape!"

"Aye, milady!"

Branwen had no weapon, save McShane. Or did she? she thought, testing the ornate pommel of the saddle her father had personally designed. It was stiff at first but loosened as she wriggled it. It was a dagger, his secret, Owen ap Caradoc had confided to her. All she needed was the courage to use it, something she had yet to muster, for if indeed she had, Ulric of Kent would never have become Ulric of Caradoc. Perhaps even this nightmare would not be happening, for surely these were demons stirred by vengeful spirits.

Of her father and his men? Nay, she convinced herself sternly. Tâd would never wreak havoc on his own people to get to Kent. This was demon's work.

Someone is trying to keep us apart, wife. Her husband's words seemed to ring in her ears above that of clashing blades.

And they could be swarming about Ulric at that very moment, while she struggled with her heart! Branwen considered, a cold chill running up her spine.

The smoke stung her eyes as she plunged into the village past the smithy's and the mill at the edge of the town, toward the commons where she had often come to play with the village children while her mother handed out alms and medicines. The thatched roofs of the wattle and daub cottages on both sides of her were ablaze. Women and children ran about crying and as dazed as the frightened cattle and livestock.

Upon recognizing the miller's wife, Branwen pulled McShane up short. "Matilda, gather the women and children. We must get the animals to the keep! There's naught else to be saved here! Our men will keep the brigands at bay."

Much as she wanted to find Ulric, the task that rose before her was her duty. Houses could be rebuilt from the land. The replenishment of livestock already dwindled in numbers from the rebellion was another task altogether.

"I'll ride through the alleys and buildings and drive them out," she shouted over her shoulder.

Tearing off the shawl she'd wrapped about her nightshift and kirtle in her haste to be on her way, Branwen began to twirl it overhead and whoop. She circled the cluster of homes, coming close to the commons where the battle raged. There she doubled back, intending to sweep through any open paths or plots in search of stunned survivors, both human and animal.

McShane balked at the smoky alleys, but Branwen's insistence was assurance enough for the stallion to bend to his mistress's will. Pigs, chickens, cows, and oxen had scattered everywhere, mostly to the edge of the village. There, the wandering villagers, given a purpose, began to round them up and chase them with staffs toward Caradoc's imposing walls.

There were some animals, however, who were as disoriented as their human counterparts and wandered at risk through the village, as if seeking their homes. At the sight and sound of Caradoc's lady charging at them, swinging her scarf overhead, they bolted for the nearest exit in the opposite direction toward the towering keep. In the midst of her fourth and last sweep through, for the fires now made the air impossible to breathe, Branwen heard a pitiful chorus of mewing cries.

McShane stopped abruptly at the slightest tug of the reins and the girl slid off his back to the packed earth, her shawl wrapped over her nose to filter the smoke-filled air. Above the crackling and snapping of the fires, she managed to narrow the location down to an over-turned barrel. Inside, there were four newborn kittens, their eyes open and no more. As to the mother's where-abouts, Branwen could only guess, but she was not about to leave them to roast alive. Hurriedly, she made a sack of her scarf and, after putting the frightened kittens into it, tied it to McShane's saddle.

The stirrups were high, but fighting horse that he was trained to be, McShane responded calmly in the midst of the chaos. At the tap of her foot behind his front fet-locks, he stretched out front and back feet, lowering his back until his mistress could slip her foot in the strap and hoist herself up into place. Ahead, Branwen could see the train of people and animals making their way toward Caradoc's gate, but instead of following them, she turned McShane toward the commons.

A few of the brigands remained in combat with the knights and footmen, but as she approached the majority of them, mounted on horses with ghostly trailing skirts and painted faces, struck out for the traeth. For a moment, Branwen considered giving them chase but, recalling her instructions to Miriam, thought her cause better served to find Ulric. She had put it off for too long now.

Sir Hammond, Ulric's boisterous second-in-command and the man whose revelry with his lord had cost her the most sleep, was dismounted and fought two of the brigands, also without steed, who converged on him at once. The knight's efforts seemed labored to Branwen, as if it took great concentration to perform them. When his assailants realized this, they divided their attack, one slipping around to his right to take him from the rear. Without second thought that this was one of the estrons who had brought Wales to its knees, she gouged McShane's ribs with her gillied heels and charged straight for the attacking rogue.

The knife raised at Hammond's back was knocked into the air as McShane plowed into the man, sending him sprawling even as he turned at the thunder of the stallion's approaching hoofbeats. The noises of battle must have triggered the steed's fighting instincts, for he quickly pivoted before Branwen could give him the signal and reared at the fallen man. Although the fire provided plenty of light, Branwen could not identify the terrified face turned up at her as her prey scrambled backward, for it was painted hideously.

Indeed, it alone was enough to still the blood, much less the sight of those ghostlike horses with eyes the size of trenchers! Her fingers clutched in McShane's golden mane, having lost the reins in the stallion's fierce pawing attack, she held her seat and let the charger do what he'd been trained to do. The bag containing the howling kittens fell against her leg, their tiny claws pricking through the thin material of her shift.

Yet she hardly noticed, for a shout at her back gave warning of an unseen assailant. Suddenly, the hem of her gown was tugged furiously, nearly unseating her. She looked over her shoulder to see one of the painted hoodlums trying to spring onto McShane's back to make off with her and the horse. She lunged for the hanging rein to her right and tugged McShane away from his chase to the more immediate danger. The horse came down on all fours, dragging the ruffian around in a circle as he tried to gain momentum enough to spring upon the prancing steed's back.

Her head dizzied by the constant turning, Branwen hung on, her hand clenched about the hilt of her father's hidden weapon. When the realization of its potential aid finally registered, however, she brought it out. Clinging with one hand to the stallion's mane, she slashed at the hands of her would-be abductor. While McShane's circling maneuver could not deter him, the sting of her blade did. He fell away with an outraged shriek and McShane broke free of its pattern to promptly run down the villain.

"Gogsdeath, milady!"

Still shaken from the narrow escape, Branwen glanced up to see Dafydd ap Elwaid cutting his way toward her, riding bareback on his shadow-grey charger. Upon reaching her he deftly shifted his blade to his left hand and caught her by the waist.

"Have you lost your wits, woman?" he demanded as he hauled her across the back of his mount in front of him.

"I'm fine, but . . ." Branwen broke off, for at the edge of the dwindling battle, she spied a crossbowman aiming his weapon at the broad back of the scarlet- and black-clad Lord of Caradoc. "Dafydd! There!"

"I'm taking you out of here!"

There was no time to argue, much less convince Dafydd to let her go to her husband's aid. Branwen jabbed at Dafydd's ribs with the knife she still wielded in her hand. With a startled yelp, Dafydd loosened his hold and she threw herself away from the horse. She blinked as the first bolt sailed just over her husband's shoulder, but Branwen kept running toward the bowman with one sole intent. Oblivious to her approach, the man coolly put another bolt into the sling and reset the firing mechanism.

Were she Mercury himself, her feet could not move swift enough to prevent the unleashing of the second bolt. The thought registered as the man lifted the cross bow to aim once again. *But the knife could.* Branwen stopped and flipped the blade deftly in her hand. Not a moment to spare for prayer, she simply sent the knife flying as God's holy name slipped through her lips in a fervent whisper. The second bolt flew straight up as the bowman jerked with the startling and deadly shaft of steel that buried in his back. The crossbow clattered to the ground, followed by the thud of the blank-eyed knave's falling body.

She heard a woman's scream and didn't realize it was her own until Ulric spun around. His soot-streaked face glistened in the firelight, stricken by the sight of her standing over the body of her victim. Branwen, however, could only see the hilt of her knife protruding from the dead man's body. It was Owen's and she wanted it back, but could not bring herself to withdraw it.

"Get her to the keep!"

"Aye, milord!"

Dafydd was upon her again, hauling her up by the folds of her gown onto his grey. This time there was no arguing with the bands of muscle that tightened about her waist as she was dragged into place, much less attempting to arrange decent cover for the bare legs exposed by her hiked hem.

"McShane! They'll make off with McShane!" Branwen objected as Dafydd urged his steed into a full gallop around the edge of the village toward the grassland separating it from the keep. To lose the stallion would be even worse than to lose the knife!

"Those brigands left are fighting for their own lives now, milady. That's the only prize they're interested in keeping."

Unconsoled, Branwen glanced back in time to see a small group of stragglers set off toward the traeth. "Dafydd, look! Let's follow them and—"

"If one hair of your head was harmed, your husband would skewer me!" Dafydd averred stubbornly, adding the stipulation, "If I didn't do away with myself first for allowing such a thing."

"But—"

"Hush, milady," the Welsh knight insisted, pulling her closer to him. "You are cold as ice, if you do smell like a fire."

Neither the cold of the night air nor the warmth Dafydd offered her could distract Branwen from her concern over Ulric and her people . . . even his knights. As they reached the gate, she remembered Miriam, hiding near the traeth. "Faith, Dafydd, I've left my maid to watch the path the villains took." She pointed to the cluster of rocks. "She's there . . . in those rocks."

Dafydd let her down gently. "At least she had the good sense to hide, sooner than try to ride down half the hooligans and knife the rest!"

Branwen didn't have the chance to retort before the young knight rode off toward his second rescue of the night. Within the outer bailey, the chamberlain shouted

305

directions from the gate tower to the grounds below, now packed with people and livestock. Eager to gain the advantage of the view the added height would afford, Branwen accepted the offer of a cloak from one of the guards and climbed the narrow winding steps to the open room above.

"Milady, your aunt . . ." the chamberlain began upon seeing Branwen step to the battlement beside him. He broke off at the sooty and filthy state of her dishevelment.

"Yes, milord?" Branwen prompted, somewhat bewildered that he should want to discuss Aunt Agnéis now, in the midst of the chaos.

"She would not listen to reason and took off for the cliff. I would have stopped her, but milord's order was to prepare the defenses for assault and take in the refugees."

"The cliff?" Branwen raced to the other side of the tower in the hopes of getting a good glimpse of the steep seaside embankment. But between the mist and the drifting smoke, it was impossible. "Did you send someone after her?"

"Aye, milady, and then I've had to put the matter aside, though they should be back by now."

Touched by the man's genuine dismay, Branwen placed a reassuring hand on his arm. "We are a tough lot, we Caradoc women. My aunt knows the traeth as well as her own hand."

"But should she take a chill at her age . . ."

"She'd take some mistletoe tea and laugh it off . . . after complaining of her aching joints, that is."

Blanchard actually smiled—with affection, no less! Gogsbreath, the man was taken with Agnéis! To what extent, Branwen could hardly guess, especially with her own concerns weighing upon her. She rushed back to the rail, where the fires lit the passage between the keep and the village. Men and horses were making their way across the grassland, leaving the flames and debris in their wake. It was over.

Leaning through the window, Branwen stared down until she could make out Pendragon. The stallion not only bore Ulric's fair-haired figure, but also had the golden McShane in tow. As the knights passed under the gate, she noted with alarm that other steeds among them carried bodies slung over their backs. Dafydd ap Elwaid, with Miriam riding before him, joined the last of them, ahead of the men-at-arms returning to the keep and leaving the blaze to finish its devilish work.

Branwen scurried down the steps, emerging from the tower as Ulric handed the chargers over to a stableboy. As she rushed toward them, the knight turned and held out the scarf sack containing the mewing kittens. The relief in her heart was not reflected on his face, however. Ulric was angry, yet, as his appearance indicated, too wearied to vent it. His rugged features were streaked with dirt and sweat, giving his face a haggard appearance.

"Were I not exhausted, I would take you over my knee this moment for leaving the keep," he told her grimly. "Instead, I will attend chapel and offer my thanks that only by Divine grace were my brave men and reckless lady spared."

"Milady!" Blanchard restrained Branwen as she started after her husband, who, instead of heading for the chapel, climbed halfway up the steps to the battlements. "I would let milord be. He is sorely tested," the chamberlain advised.

Uncertain as to just what to do, Branwen listened as Ulric shouted above the wails and cries of the people and their livestock. "People of Caradoc!" He snatched a torch from the wall and waved it over his head, bellowing again until the commotion died and he had every-one's attention.

"I would have you know that these halegrins are no more than devils of the flesh, bound to use your own su-perstitions against you. Look you to the bodies my knights have brought back and see for yourselves, 'tis no more than paint and black hearts that have terrorized you."

"But what will we do, milord? Faith, we're within spittin' distance of the keep and our homes are gone!"

"What took ye so long to come to our aid?"

The questions were thrown at the new lord like a fleet of arrows, all well aimed. Branwen cringed in compas-sion. Instead of reacting the same, the lord of Caradoc straightened, taking the criticism head-on.

"There is an evil among us, good people. I will make no excuses, but that my men rallied as quickly as we were informed of your plight. But instead of letting this drive us apart, let it bind us together. *Together*, we will ferret out these villains. *Together*, we will rebuild."

"And will we starve together, milord?" A chorus, echoing agreement with the question, rose from the dis-placed crowd.

Ulric nodded solemnly. "If need be. Caradoc's store-rooms will be open at dawn for rations to those whose stores were destroyed."

Astonishment hardly described the murmur that swept over the crowd. Branwen felt it herself, uncertain her ears were hearing correctly. The lord opening his stores to his villeins? It was unheard of. Not even Owen ap Caradoc, whose generosity was renowned, had ever done such a thing! The poor and needy were subject to alms from the church and from the lord's table after he and his family had had their fill, not before.

"Until then, my men will light fires and set up such tents as we have for your cover. I urge you to rest the

308

remainder of the night. Tomorrow we address this nightmare. The bodies of the slain halegrins will be hung on Caradoc's walls. We must identify them. From there, my provost and I will do everything we can to find their accomplices and bring them to the same justice! Are you with me, Caradoc, or against me?"

The unanimous assent that met Ulric's challenge released Branwen's frozen breath from her chest. She joined in the cheering for Caradoc's new lord, amazed, relieved, and grateful. Why tears trickled down her cheeks, she didn't try to guess. All she was certain she wanted to do was show Ulric that she was with him.

"Miriam," Branwen said to the servant who had come to her side, "take these people in and help Aunt Agnéis see them cared for. I would join my husband at the chapel."

"But she isn't back from the cliff yet. Lord Dafydd and I saw her and offered her a ride, but she refused."

Branwen glanced back at the gate, bewildered by her aunt's presence at the cliff. "There she is now," she told the servant in relief. "Go see if you can help her in. I need to see my husband."

It was impossible to catch up with Ulric before he entered the holy place. No king was ever paid such homage. Men and women clamored to tug at his cloak and mantle, blessing and thanking him for his unsolicited kindness. All about her, Branwen could hear accounts of the way he and his knights had plunged into the midst of the halegrins.

"Like a fury, he was, golden as them others was black-hearted."

"He run right through me 'ouse an' snatched me bedrid'n mam right outta the fire's teeth."

"They was draggin' me wife off by the hair o' the head and two o' them knights come at 'em, slashing and shoutin' enough to spook the devil right outta the black-guards!"

These were the men who had killed her parents? Branwen scanned the beleaguered knights ordering their squires to set up their field tents within the outer bailey, while the steward Harold instructed the villagers to light fires by which to warm themselves. Meanwhile, Blanchard had the women and children gathered into the hall, out of the night air.

Once through the black alley separating the baileys, her way to the chapel was clear. She found Ulric inside, kneeling at the altar where a single lighted candle flickered stalwartly against the drafts. As she made her way to the front, Father Dennis, looking as if he'd pulled on his robes on the run, rushed in, but Branwen waved him aside.

She resisted the urge to throw her arms about him, to hug those wide wearied shoulders and tell him how proud she was of him. Instead, she took a place at the altar beside him and bowed reverently to give her own thanks, as well as to issue a plea that Ulric and his men might put a stop to this horror soon.

"Gogsbreath, woman, are you daft?" At Ulric's indignant interruption, Branwen looked up blankly. "You've naught on but a nightdress and kirtle!"

Branwen broke into a grin. "You sound like my father more and more." Ulric started to continue his chastisement, when she silenced him with a hand on his arm. "Milord . . . I . . . if you would have me warm, I suggest you do it yourself."

It wasn't all what she'd intended to say. She basked in the questioning gaze where the candlelight flickered warmly. Or was it those amber flecks among the combative blue and green hues that could charm her so easily? Whatever, they were hypnotizing. Branwen could not have moved from the spot if she'd wanted to. Suddenly, she was smothered in Ulric's embrace.

"I have never been so frightened as I was tonight, woman," Ulric confessed huskily against the top of her head. His hands moved up and down her back, warming . . . caressing.

"Because of their painted faces?"

"No, damn your stubborn hide, because I looked up and there you were in the midst of the fray! Faith, if anything had happened to you and the child . . ."

The child. Branwen backed away. "Well, it didn't . . . and I would like to think I was able to help."

Ulric hugged her more tightly. "You did, woman! You were brave as you were beautiful, but *think* of the risk!"

"You said we will fight these fiends together, husband. 'Twas what we were doing."

"For all the good it did those wretches in the bailey." Ulric's dour remark drew Branwen's attention to his face. "I don't know what was the matter with us. It was like we were sorely hungover, yet we had little enough to drink and ample rest. If I didn't know better, I would vow the hippocras had been tampered with."

No one will disturb your sleep tonight, dear. Aunt Agnéis's assurance rang worrisome in Branwen's thoughts. God in heaven, had her aunt innocently slipped a sleeping potion in the hippocras to make them sleep? A sick feeling washed over Branwen. If Ulric even suspected . . .

At her involuntary shudder Ulric caught her up in his arms. "I am taking you inside before you and the babe take a chill, though I'm willing to admit, you Welsh are a hardy lot."

"And loyal, once we give out our trust," Branwen informed him. "The people believe in you, Ulric."

Ulric halted at the door of the chapel. "And what of you, wife?"

Branwen felt her words with all her heart. "I want to, milord. As God is my witness, I shall try."

311

Chapter Nineteen

Breakfast was delayed by the clearing of excessive numbers of beds and people from the hall the following morning. Great portions of porridge were cooked and served from the lord's kitchen as well as from the many fires lit in the baileys. Tents of every manner were set up, and canopies stretched over the wooden beams suspended between the outer and curtain walls of the keep, where servants quarters had yet to be completed.

It reminded Branwen of the stories her paternal grandmother had told, when Caradoc's first keep, now long destroyed, had marked the center of the village proper, where the commons were now. Its remaining stones had been reused to build the new keep on the cliff a short distance away, but when it was in its prime, it overlooked the markets and shops that were the life-blood of Caradoc like a giant stone mother hen over its chicks. Some families had already petitioned Ulric for permission to move within the outer bailey permanently as in old times, for safety's sake.

Ulric promised to consider their request at the council, which took place after chapel and breakfast. For the time being, however, he intended to focus on salvaging what was left and rebuilding. To do this, he asked the villeins to choose leaders among themselves, who would

312

work directly with his appointed men and the provost, as well as handle petty disputes that were bound to result from the close quarters.

"We will work on two fronts. One will see to the finishing of Caradoc's new bailey, which will accommodate most of you until the village can be reconstructed. The second will begin to cut timber for the latter project, so that it will be workable when we are ready to start this spring. Until such time, our collective stores will be gathered into the keep and rationed according to need."

When the villagers had been dismissed to begin the salvaging of their belongings at the still-smoking site, Ulric called for the provost and his knights to remain. To each, he assigned specific duties. Some were to work on the procurement of materials, others to see to the dispensing of the quarters being built between the castle walls as they were finished. Determining the need of each family fell to Father Dennis and the chamberlain, with Aunt Agnéis as consultant, since she knew almost every family in the cantref.

Branwen and the master steward Harold were assigned the administration of the keep itself. Guests were expected for the celebration of Ulric and Branwen's wedding, as well as for the memorial service for the late Lord and Lady of Caradoc, and plans had to be made, not only for the food, but for accommodations as well. Although her head ached dully, Branwen began to think of ideas that would enable the keep to entertain all the invited guests within its walls.

"I tell you, we are knights meant to fight wars, not builders and administrators!" one of Ulric's men complained, drawing her attention back to the present. "How are we to know what to do?"

"What was it we did last night, sir?" Ulric demanded just as impudently. "Those vermin hanging on the walls

313

would, if they could, swear it was battle and not council that we were doling out."

A few amused snickers rippled through the assembly, but it was clear that not everyone was at ease with the lord's new plan. Regardless, each man present knew the full assessment of Ulric's gaze as it moved from one to the next. His clean-shaven features and fair hair made him look a youth compared to most of his comrades, yet his size and collected manner left no doubt as to his maturity, much less his ability to see his will done.

"Most of you know those men were identified as having come from Anglesey. I have sent Elwaid and Hammond to the island to find out what they can, who their associates are. When we have information to act upon, we will. Until then, I believe we've proved riding over hill and dale, searching without rhyme or reason, is a fruitless and tiring pursuit. We will put our energies to use for the good of Caradoc, so that when our esteemed guests arrive, they can see that we have at least been doing *something*." The knight leaned over the table on the dais, glowering with a myriad of emotions from anger to compassion. "We must show these people that we are *for* them! That this enemy is a *common* one we are willing to fight *together*, be it by ferreting him out or by replacing what he has destroyed." Ulric pointed to Branwen. "Our wedding symbolizes that we are no longer at war with the Welsh, we are their brothers."

"Is that why your wife takes a separate bed and the marriage not yet beyond its first quarter?"

"How know you *she* is not behind this uprising?"

"Good knight!" Branwen exclaimed, hoping to avoid the eruption of the temper she'd seen lash tight her husband's twitching jaw. "First, I would not take my plight out upon my own people. Second, my husband's and my private affairs are none of your concern . . . but since you have had the ill manners to bring them up, I shall address them for the sake of this good man standing before you."

"You need address nothing, milady, that I cannot with my sword!" Ulric snarled beside her.

Branwen shuddered inwardly. Gogsblood, what had she done? Even his own knights were questioning him because of her private war—a war he was rapidly winning, not by force, but by goodness of example.

"I pray you let me settle this, milord! 'Tis a quagmire of my own creation, not yours. Gogsdeath, do not let this rift turn English against English as well as English against Welsh. 'Twould do naught but satisfy our mutual enemy to have one less knight to deal with. You are all exhausted and, thence, short of temper and good judgment."

A murmur of agreement wafted through the crowd. Branwen smiled tentatively up at Ulric, a plea within the sapphire depths of her gaze and a promise . . . to make amends. With so much tugging them in different directions upon leaving the chapel the prior evening, they had had no further chance to deal with their own problems, which had now exploded in their faces before all.

"There! Your men agree with me! May I speak, milord?"

"I think you will, milady, with or without my consent."

Ulric's eyes were as unfathomable as their true color. Hues and feelings of all sorts were veiled with caution— caution she would allay, if it was at all within her power. Branwen backed away and stepped down from the dais.

"Our cultures are so alike and yet so different, milords, much like Lord Ulric and myself. I would not sleep in his room because of my rebellion against what I considered frivolity on his part. I thought the entire rebuilding of Caradoc wasteful nonsense, the English

315

showing off and grinding our Welsh noses into the dirt . . . *until last night.*" She swung around to face the silent lord upon the dais. "Last night, you did more than offer lip service, milord. You and your men risked your lives for Caradoc's people. You fought for us. Neither I nor they will forget that . . . and had you not expanded the walls and outer bailey, where would they have gone? You have proved not only your loyalty to my people, but your wisdom as well, my lord protector. With your permission, I would have my things moved into the master chamber."

Instead of answering, Ulric stepped down from the dais and approached her. Although she kept her eyes humbly lowered, her heart measured each step until he halted with the booted feet within her view. At the coaxing finger crooked under her chin, she lifted her face to her husband's haggard one to see him smile—a smile that smoothed the lines of worry from his brow and brightened his countenance like the sun streaming through the gallery windows.

"Permission granted most heartily, fair raven."

It didn't mean what he thought, Branwen fretted, having noted the kindling of desire in his victorious gaze as he claimed her lips. But with the sweet tide of assurance and truce conveyed by his kiss, she hardly felt the inclination to correct him. Trust was won one step at a time. She would explain that later, she thought, hardly aware that the knights were taking their leave of the lord and his lady until she heard one of them raise his voice.

"Shall we await you outside, milord?"

Reminded of his duty, Ulric pulled away reluctantly and raised Branwen's hand to his lips in parting. *"Until later, milady."*

The whispered words were hardly a parting as much as a promise, leaving a mingle of disappointment and anticipation for Branwen to endure. She watched as he took his leave, his men falling in behind him, every bit the lord protector of Caradoc.

Yet, even as her admiration and affection warmed her, she knew that her proud and handsome Ulric would need help . . . her help, which was as it should be. With hunters already sent out to provide the lord's idea of a modest feast and the menu from the stores planned accordingly, Branwen was momentarily free to pursue her own investigation. First, she needed to speak to Aunt Agnéis, and then seek retreat from the castle chaos to the sun-warmed traeth and give McShane his long promised exercise.

She found Aunt Agnéis in the solar on the gallery, seeking the morning sun's healing and soothing rays on her arthritic bones. Perched in a windowseat housed in the vaulted opening, the older woman appeared worried. The lines in her face, which were usually relaxed in kindness or crinkled in laughter, were knitted taut beneath the peppered white wisps of hair that always escaped her ever-present wimple and veil.

When Branwen was a child, she used to think that her aunt did not possess ears, for she'd never been privy to see them. How Agnéis and her mother had laughed at Branwen's innocent inquiry. Then and there, Aunt Agnéis had put her niece's mind at ease by stripping the headgear off to expose the objects in question, which, Branwen recalled, were as wrinkled as her face. Her aunt had been old forever, she supposed.

"The Lord has outdone Himself today," Agnéis commented, pointing to the sun-strafed waters rolling up to the traeth and receding rhythmically, "and shown mercy on these winter-stiffened bones. If the good sunshine continues, faith, I might even dance at this coming celebration of your wedding!"

Branwen grinned. "You always threaten to do that, but I've yet to see it."

"I've never met a man who could keep up with me, geneth . . . until now, that is."

"Master Blanchard?"

Her aunt's eyes were actually twinkling! "The same."

"I thought his manner as stiff as your knees."

"Under the right circumstances, they both loosen up."

"Aunt Agnéis!" Branwen chided fondly, joining her aunt's girlish giggle. However, reminding herself of her purpose, she came back to it.

"Aunt Agnéis, did you put something in my drink to make me sleep last night?"

Odd, the girl mused, that she should be the one who was serious for a change. Both Agnéis and Lady Gwendolyn had told her that would happen one day, and then she would know the utter frustration of her incorrigible spirit.

Her aunt answered with guileless candor. "Of course, I did! Poor dear, you so obviously needed it, although I hadn't counted on the village being pillaged."

Branwen cringed inwardly. God bless her, her aunt had meant well, but Ulric would have her flayed alive if he knew of this. Here was something best left alone.

"You did sleep well until the commotion, didn't you, dear?"

"I . . . yes, I did. That is, I *slept*," Branwen amended, "although my dreams were most unsettling."

" 'Tis no wonder, with all the mischief that's about! I can guarantee sleep, but I can't control dreams, I'm afraid."

Branwen dismissed the nightmarish dream before it had a chance to unfold again in her mind. "Well, I think, since Master Harold has supper under way, that I shall take McShane out on the traeth. It's nearly low tide."

"Faith, geneth, take care! 'Tis where the halegrins es-

318

caped!" Agnéis cautioned, hurriedly crossing herself as she afforded a furtive glance toward the rugged coastline to the west.

Some of her incorrigible spirit slipping through the ladylike facade she had maintained, Branwen grinned impishly. "Precisely!"

When the sun bathed the traeth, it robbed the coastal breezes of their bite. Even on cloudy days, however, Branwen's woolen cloak, lined with the warmest fox, would render them harmless to her. She'd been riding the stretch of wet sand since she was old enough to sit upon her first pony at the age of seven. Naturally, one of the stablehands accompanied her and her nurse, content to watch the raven-haired cherub race from one end of the beach, where the morfa joined it, to the high rocky cliff upon which the keep was perched.

Low tide was the only time it was possible to ride completely around the north wall of Caradoc. From the base of the cliff, the towering castle seemed twice its size. The salty tang of the air filling her nostrils, Branwen finally reined in McShane from his reckless racing and started around the point slowly. Throwing back her hood to allow the sun to stroke her jet-black tresses, she studied the rocky wall intently.

It had been on a similar day that she had stumbled upon the cave leading to the hot springs, although as she recalled she had been approaching the morfa from the cliff. It was a good distance from the keep itself. The entrance had certainly been large enough to see, for it had accommodated not only Branwen herself, but her pony as well. Yet, as she scrutinized the grey-black rock with large patches of sea moss and lichens, she saw no sign of any such entrance. If the men had taken to the sea at the point Miriam showed Elwaid, their only escape could have been death in the tide or emergence down the coast to the wetlands.

Where was that cave? Even dismissing the common sense conclusion to the outlaws' escape, there remained the possibility of an ideal bath, heated winter and summer. Perhaps the opening had appeared larger to her because she was a child, Branwen reasoned. If only she had not let Aunt Agnéis's fear over her discovery frighten her from ever trying to find it again. Devils and demons lived in caves, along with bats, snakes, and other fiendish creatures. Faith, for the longest time, it had given her shivers just to ride around the point of the traeth. Then the gaping black hole seemed to disappear with time.

And memory, the girl mused in chagrin, her gaze climbing once again over the rising mass of rock to Caradoc's stone fortress, impenetrable from the seaside. Even at low tide, the cliff was too high and steep to be climbed by an invading army. She sought out the uppermost height of her tower, where she'd fired blunted arrows at the imaginary foes who tried their luck, and caught sight of a woman peering out of the wedge-shaped opening in the stone.

Aunt Agnéis? she wondered, lifting her arm to wave at the person bedecked in the grey-blue color her aunt had worn earlier, along with half the castle staff. No amount of coaxing from Branwen or Lady Gwendolyn could convince the older woman to give up her plain choice of color for those more suited to the gentry of the castle. The dear was probably concerned for her safety, Branwen mused, though she must be getting blind as a bat. The moment Branwen waved, her aunt ducked inside the tower room, out of sight.

Much as she was loath to do so, it appeared Branwen was going to have to ask Aunt Agnéis if she recalled the location. After all, her aunt already knew she was looking for it. It could hardly upset her any more to ask, devils and demons or nay.

Branwen turned McShane back toward the north sea wall, to sweep around the point as far east as the traeth went before dead-ending in a rocky embankment. Once there, she turned the horse, which splashed proudly in the curling froth, ready to give him free rein for one more run before going back to the keep where her duties as mistress of Caradoc awaited her. Infected by the wildness of the scene, Branwen leaned forward over McShane's golden mane, ready to challenge the very wind, when she caught sight of Pendragon rounding the cliff, bearing his master on his back.

"Branwen!" Ulric's bellow blended with the splashing of the surf on the wet sand.

Rising in her stirrups, she waved merrily at her husband, noting with mild humor that his charger was in no way comfortable with the water washing up around its prancing feet. She doubted the steed, accustomed to the dust and mud of a tourney or battlefield, had ever been ridden in the sea before. Nonetheless, the golden warrior, whose jet-lined scarlet cape fluttered in the breeze from a fine brace of shoulders, kept the stallion in control, despite its laid-back ears and sidestepping.

"Isn't this wonderful?" Branwen called out as they met halfway to the point. She waved dreamily at the sea-green tide, glazed mirror-bright with sunlight.

"Gogsdeath, woman, have you taken leave of your wits?"

Branwen met Ulric's demand blankly. "I don't think so, milord."

"I don't want you riding about unaccompanied! God knows what those brigands would do were they to happen upon a lone woman, much less Caradoc's lady. I don't want you to end the same way as your maidservant."

The mention of poor Caryn dented the brief surge of lightheartedness her beloved traeth always offered her.

"As you can see, milord, 'tis no way out, but down the west side of the keep, in plain view of it and its workers. Besides," she added practically, "I thought I'd take a look myself at the cliff side. When I was a child, I found a cave and, in it, a hot spring, just perfect for a bath like . . ." Her cheeks gained color as Ulric raised one questioning brow. "Well, not exactly *like*, but similar to the bath near Coventry. That is, it had a hot spring in it."

"If you would have a bath, milady, I should be most eager to accommodate you later, in the privacy of the master bedchamber."

A beguiling combination of embarrassment and annoyance flashed in Branwen's gaze. He was laughing at her, silently enough, but nonetheless laughing! "I am serious, milord! There is a cave, possibly big enough to hide horsemen, until a search be given up."

Still dubious, Ulric swept his arm at the tall rocky wall. "Then show it to me, milady. Perhaps we might try its warm waters now, before the tide returns to strand us."

"I couldn't find it," she admitted grudgingly. "But if you doubt me, ask Aunt Agnéis about it. She knows of its existence."

"Your aunt is a doting old fool, though she did see fit to tell me you were riding the traeth alone."

And he had let the old woman's panic seep into his own blood at the thought of his bride and mother of his child riding the isolated traeth unprotected—the same traeth frequented by the bloodthirsty outlaws who'd become the bane of his existence. Ulric had saddled Pendragon himself and ridden out, sooner than wait the ministrations of the stablehands. When he'd first set foot on the wet stretch of sand and seen no trace of Branwen, except that of McShane's tracks, his heart had nearly stopped.

He'd followed the tracks and was relieved to see that they rounded the bend upon which Caradoc was built. Upon clearing the rocky point, there she was, raven hair and rosy cheeks haloed by the sunshine. She might have been a sea imp or a cloaked siren, as untamed as her surroundings, as she tossed back her cape and leaned over McShane's neck, riding toward him as though racing the wind itself.

"I'll race you to the keep!"

Ulric shook himself from the reverie. Gogsblood, she'd kill herself and the child with that reckless spirit of hers! "Nay, I'll not have you . . ."

Ulric's objection was lost in the loud whoop Branwen gave as she urged McShane forward. Pendragon, startled by it and thrown off guard by the splash of a more aggressive wave, pitched sideways, nearly throwing the knight into the wet and slippery rock wall. Cursing under his breath, Ulric slammed his heels into Pendragon's ribs. The horse bolted forward, seemingly glad to at least be moving from the whispering waters sloshing around its hooves.

McShane, however, had a good headstart, so that when Pendragon eagerly emerged from the wet sand onto the wild, dry pastureland, the lady of Caradoc awaited her knight with an annoyingly smug expression. If ever there were bluer eyes, Ulric had not seen them. When he'd thought her Edwin, a mistake he'd yet to absolve himself of making, they had been striking. On the woman, his wife, they were utterly bewitching. If there was anything supernatural about Branwen or her precious Caradoc, it was this irresistible attraction they held for him.

If he had wanted to sweep her up into his arms and carry her to the master bedchamber this morning, upon her fervently stated pledge of allegiance to him, Ulric literally ached to do so now. Even when he was so angry

323

with her, that he could choke her, he knew the moment his fingers touched the smooth white skin of her throat, it would be as a caress and nothing more. No woman had ever affected him so conversely.

"Would you care to assist me in gathering lady's trees from the beach, sir, or are your duties as lord too pressing?"

Suspicion clouded Ulric's face instantly. *"Lady's trees?"*

Branwen pointed to the beach strewn with bits of seaweed. "There, milord. I thought with so much ill luck as we've had and the number of people and fires within the bailey, I might dry some and hang them about . . . to avoid fire within the walls."

Ulric snorted disdainfully. He'd thought the uneducated English were a superstitious lot, but there seemed no end to this Welsh nonsense! "Surely, I would think the lady of the keep would have more to do than gather seaweed and strew it about when we have guests coming in less than a week!"

"I seek to protect you and my people, milord, in the best way that I know."

"Branwen, our bad luck is born on flesh, not of spirits. Gogsdeath, look you at those men!"

Branwen followed the direction of his pointed arm to the bodies hung on Caradoc's wall, and she shuddered involuntarily. Still, when she turned back to Ulric, she was insistent. "Lady's trees and such have kept Caradoc well all these years, milord. Your approach to this problem has not yet proven effective at all."

His patience strained by the innocent but nonetheless pride-sticking point, Ulric swore beneath his breath. "Damnation, woman, I am an educated man of God and science!"

"My aunt says many men are education-blind."

"Your aunt is a silly old fool!"

Branwen lifted her chin as if struck by the insult.

324

"Fool, milord?" She chuckled softly. "Well, that same fool awakened you to warn you of the attack on the village. She's healed more people with her herbs and potions than any physician. If there be a fool amongst us, I would look close in the mirror, sir!"

Throwing her leg over the saddle, Branwen dismounted in a sliding motion, which made Ulric cringe when she struck the wet sand with a thud. "Well, I hope she can conjure some way to keep you from losing that child, because it's obvious the mother hasn't a thought for it."

Branwen hoped the guilty color rushing to her face could be passed off as embarrassment. "Pregnancy does not make one an invalid!"

"I shall remember that tonight, milady."

"Half the bed, milord, is all you are entitled to," Branwen stammered awkwardly. She dropped to her knees to pick up a nice branch, perfect for her purpose.

"Then I choose the half you're on."

Branwen flushed, heated by the very wickedness in his tone. Curse a man who could be charming and insulting at the same time and curse a weak woman's body that had such a keen memory! "I would think the lord of the keep has more to do than drive its lady to distraction!"

It was a lame retort, yet the very thought of what her husband was suggesting began to gnaw away at her indignation as hungrily as did his rich peel of laughter. Gogsblood, it was unfair that he could insult her intelligence in one breath and stir her in the next. Despite their differences, Branwen could not deny the common, carnal bond between them that defied logic and all her attempts to dismiss it as inconsequential.

She had meant it when she pledged her loyalty to the noble lord of Caradoc. She hadn't meant to pledge her body, which was what he, as a man, assumed. A wife

325

should support her husband, at least for all appearances; hence, the move of her things into his room. But that didn't mean that all their personal problems were settled! He had won her respect and, although reluctantly extracted, her love. Wasn't it only fair to expect the same in return?

"Gather your seaweed then, milady, if it pleases you, and I shall keep watch until you are done," Ulric patronized, his lips curling in a manner as maddening as his voice. "But place none about our bed tonight. 'Tis one place in *need* of a fire."

Bristling, Branwen rose upright from her kneeling position, a handful of the lady's tree in hand. By all that was holy, she would not permit him to goad her so, much less stand over her with that insufferable tolerance on his face.

" 'Twould serve you right to stuff the blasted mattress with it, you pompous, condescending oaf!" She marched over to where McShane waited patiently, stomping on the hard-packed wet sand with such ferocity that the stallion's ears fell back, wary of his mistress's stormy humor. "You can have the whole of your bed, sir, for I vow, I shall not share it this night—or any night—until I have your apology!"

Ulric's amusement faded as he gingerly dismounted to help her mount the charger. Like everything else she attempted, his wife had an irritating knack for taking on more than she could aptly handle. First, she was ready to single-handedly avenge her parents against him, a seasoned warrior. The very naivete of her ambition had won his heart and plagued his thoughts.

From there, she shifted to a cold war of stubborn rebellion against everything and anything he proposed, which had tested his patience past endurance. And now she expected to spend the night in his room without the natural and rightful consequence he had denied himself longer than any normal man would allow?

"Get away from me!" Branwen snapped as Ulric stepped up to assist her.

The damp gillied foot that struck him, leaving a sandy imprint on his chest, did little to improve his rapidly dwindling beguilement with the confounding creature. It was bad enough she harbored all those ridiculous notions, but her recklessness went beyond the point of common sense!

"Your feet are soaked, you witless ninny!" Ulric protested, stepping out of the way as McShane's hindquarters swung around his way while Branwen obstinately bobbed, one foot caught in the stirrup, in an awkward dance to gather enough momentum to vault up on the animal's back.

Unaware that they'd moved so close to the waterline, Ulric was hardly prepared for the sudden swell that washed up on the beach, catching him full behind the knees. That alone would not have toppled the knight, but Pendragon, thoroughly unnerved by the icy water that slapped his underbelly and hindquarters, sidestepped, knocked his master full tilt into the now-receding wash.

As Branwen finally gained her seating with a merciful and obliging stretch by McShane, she swung the animal about in time to see her husband climbing to his feet with a doused, but no less fiery, fury. While she was in no frame of mind for laughter, she could not help the giggle the sight inspired. The cape that made her husband appear half again his size now clung to him like a second skin, coated in sand, and water seeped over the edge of his fine leather boots.

"What ho, milord! It seems you've gotten more than your feet wet!"

"By God, get you out of my sight, you cold-blooded

327

vixen, before I'm tempted to see how your native constitution can withstand a full dunking in your winter water!"

Keeping well out of Ulric's range, Branwen glanced over to where Pendragon had run up on dry land. "It seems your charger likes the sea as little as you, milord. Shall I fetch him for you?"

Ulric's answer was hardly fit for a lady's ears. Branwen might well have had every right to ride off in indignation. Yet, it was not indignation that prompted her to prod McShane into a full gallop toward the keep. It was laughter. Not that Ulric didn't deserve every bit of the humiliation of entering the keep looking more like a drowned rat than its lord, she thought, trying to force the corners of her lips down for propriety's sake.

It was just . . . his expression! Never had she seen his handsome features battle, twisted and contorted, in such outrageous confusion. It was utterly beguiling—at a distance.

Chapter Twenty

"I saw you on the traeth, geneth. That is no way to treat your husband," Aunt Agnéis chided gently. "I vow, I've never seen you so contrary. You're usually of a single mind, particularly when it comes to men."

"He has got to be the most maddening man God ever created!"

Branwen closed the parchment-shaded window of the solar, which permitted light through but hampered the entrance of cold air. All the women not directly engaged in cooking or cleaning had been called there to put their skills at needlework to the test. Linens needed to be mended if they were to entertain the marcher lord, Giles De Clare of Merionwythe, and his retinue. The Englishman came to congratulate his peer and the new overlord of Caradoc, with whom he'd fought in the rebellion.

"I think he's handsome and considerate for a man of his position," Miriam ventured over her needlework. "I've seen absolute tyrants."

The titters of agreement halted as Branwen addressed her servant. "I do not recall addressing you, Miriam."

"Now don't go getting so high and mighty with your girl just because your husband's ruffled your feathers,"

Aunt Agnéis stepped in. " 'Tis time to swallow that stubborn pride of yours and let him smooth them down."

"I will not submit myself to a man who does not respect me."

Her aunt laughed. "Ho, so you want it all at one time—love, respect . . ."

"He doesn't love me!" Branwen argued. "He lusts after me, perhaps, but—"

Aunt Agnéis shook her head, making a clucking noise that caused the girl's tirade to fade. "He loves you, geneth. If he did not, he'd have dragged you up to his bed by the hair of the head and taken his rights, with or without your consent. I think, perhaps, he loves you too much."

Branwen was take aback by her aunt's stalwart defense of Ulric. "You'd have me bow to the man who possibly was behind the murder of my parents?"

Agnéis rose from her chair and put her needlework aside. "I think we'd best speak in private, dear," she whispered, affording Branwen a wink intended to lighten her mood.

It didn't work. Branwen coolly excused herself from the ladies' company and followed the older woman to the private room that Blanchard, in his lordship's absence, had assigned her. It was cozy, with a shallow beehive-shaped hearth that still offered heat, although its coals had been banked to save the use of wood during the daylight hours when her aunt was about the keep. A single window overlooking the southern exposure permitted ample sunlight through the parchment curtain.

Aunt Agnéis sat down on her bed, a long, narrow affair curtained on three sides to protect her from joint-stiffening drafts, and patted the mattress beside her for Branwen to take a seat. "You are a silly girl, but I suppose love does that to all of us at one time or another."

Branwen stared down at her fingers as she idly wove them into a double fist. "I am not certain if it *is* love, Aunt Agnéis. I have so many conflicting feelings about Ulric, and some of them frighten me."

Her aunt put a hand on Branwen's arm and squeezed it reassuringly. "Those will take care of themselves, dear, 'tis the others that are cause for concern. You know your husband was not responsible for your parents' murder."

The statement brought Branwen's attention from her fingers to her aunt's face in wonder. "Have you seen the one who is?"

"Nay, but I've put hair from each of your brushes to the water, and each time gold and black have met. You would not be so well matched with the murderer of your own flesh and blood."

Branwen digested her aunt's words. Lady Gwendolyn had once told her that Agnéis had accurately predicted scores of successful matches. To question the woman would be absurd. "So . . . so you are saying I am foolish to expect respect for the efforts I've made to save Ulric's arrogant hide?"

Agnéis chuckled softly. "He does what he does because he loves you. You should do what you do for the same reason. Respect will follow if you both do your best." The older woman folded Branwen's hands between her own affectionately. "You two remind me of Gwen and Owen. 'Twas a rocky start until you were conceived. They had so much to learn of one another and expected it to all come at once."

How she wished her mother were there, Branwen mused wistfully. Not that she didn't take Aunt Agnéis seriously! It was just that, despite her sage advice, her aunt had never married, never known what it was like to feel this way about a man.

"Have pity on him, Branwen," Agnéis went on patiently. "He is a seventh son, but he is an estron, too. Not all peoples are as attuned to the unknown as we Welsh, despite their God-given ability. Until he opens his eyes, we must be patient and protect him as best we can."

Branwen shook herself from her nostalgic retreat. "How?"

"The things he's done were well intended, but he has unwittingly offended the wrong spirits. The trees he cut to rebuild Caradoc were sacred to them. The sooner they are appeased, the sooner peace and love will rule Caradoc again."

"Are these spirits those of the cave in the cliff?"

Her aunt stiffened sharply. "You *found* it?"

"Nay, I was going to ask you if you could recall—"

"*Where* it is?" Agnéis finished with an incredulous lilt. "Faith, child, I get lost in this very keep now with *two* baileys. 'Tis all I can do to walk through them both. Do you think I go traipsing up and down the traeth?"

Branwen sighed in resignation. "I suppose not."

" 'Tis best we worry about what to do about these spirits and less about where they are. You've a husband and child to protect, not to mention your people." Agnéis raised her brow to challenge Branwen's denying shake of her head. "Don't think I haven't heard the murmurings."

How quickly lies could spread! "Nay, Aunt Agnéis, there is no child. 'Tis but a ruse I conjured to keep my husband at bay. We . . . we shared the same bed but once . . . intimately." Heat singed Branwen's neck and ears, rising until the crown of her head felt aflame. "But I had the green stone from Anglesey.'"

"Silly girl!" Agnéis chided smugly. "Do you think the green stone would work against a *seventh son?*" She laughed and hugged Branwen in delight. "I've seen your firstborn son, geneth!"

"Gogsbreath, say you are teasing me!" Branwen gasped, her heated flush draining from her face along with the strength seeping from her knees. Were she not already seated, she would surely have collapsed. The weakness spread through her like a plague, leaving her light-headed and nauseous. "But the stone," she murmured as her aunt lowered her back on the pillow in concern over her sudden pallor.

"I told you a seventh son is a special man. There's naught ahead of you but good fortune, once you accept each other, body and soul." Agnéis brushed Branwen's tangled hair out of her face tenderly. "I have but one caution: Until the spirits are appeased, you mustn't tell anyone of your condition."

"But you said . . ."

"People are guessing what the natural result of a marriage should be . . . no more. I believe I am the only one to actually know."

Branwen's hands went to her abdomen, as if they might have some detective ability to confirm her aunt's diagnosis. "Is the child in danger, Aunt Agnéis?" When Branwen looked up, her aunt's loving face had grown drawn.

"You mustn't tell anyone."

The urgency in Aunt Agnéis's voice brought to mind the nightmare of the previous evening, a hazy recollection of someone taking Branwen's baby from her. The spirits? the girl wondered.

"Aunt Agnéis, you *must* tell me! What danger?"

The older woman's countenance crumbled in dismay. "I would if I could, geneth! 'Tis up to the seventh son to see, not I. We can but guide him and protect him until he recognizes his sight. His love for you and the babe will bring it out in him."

For all her aunt's keen intuition, Branwen wondered if the elderly female knew how long that could take.

Ulric was steeped in knowledge that he could measure and grasp, as sure as his sword. A child . . . *Ulric's* child! Gogsblood, what a turnabout of deceit had fate played on her for lying!

Supper, consisting of two delicious courses, modestly ample, was impossible for Branwen to give justice to. She was almost grateful for Ulric's surly humor, for he had yet to recover his dignity from their afternoon ride. At least he was not disposed to remind her of the evening ahead, when the door to the master bedchamber would be closed with her behind it for the first time. Indeed, she wondered if he'd even permit her in. One would think she had conjured that rogue wave, the way he acted. Besides, it was his horse, not her, that had actually knocked him down in the water.

A grin twitched on her lips at the recollection of him struggling to his feet in utter disbelief. Faith, he had been anything but his collected, lordly self at that particular moment!

"To what do I owe this giggling abuse, milady?"

Unaware that she'd actually laughed aloud, Branwen did her utmost to straighten her lips. "To your face when Pendragon knocked you down into the water, milord. 'Twas just as well your son could not see your indignity."

His son. Branwen was startled by the glow that warmed her from within at the very mention of what was now a reality. *Her son. Their son.*

"No doubt your own shaking belly called it to his attention," Ulric quipped wryly. "Solomon had less trial and tribulation with all his wives than I have had with but one!"

Teeth clenched, Branwen humbly lowered her eyes to the table. When she unlocked them, her words were softly spoken in repentance. "I should not have laughed, milord. You might well have drowned, I suppose."

Although she could not see her aunt's approving face, she could sense it turned toward her, for the idle chatter between Agnéis and Master Blanchard had suddenly halted. When Ulric's wary one compounded the attention upon her, however, she could stand it no longer. She looked up somberly into the curious hazel gaze.

"I'm sorry, husband. My humor has not been the best of late ... nor my appetite," Branwen admitted, putting her napkin down beside her hardly touched portion of pork roast and rabbit stew. "If you will excuse me, sir, I would make ready to retire for the evening."

Ulric rose as she did, concern mirrored on his face. "Should your aunt or Miriam go with you?"

"I'll summon Miriam, milord."

Naturally, she didn't expect Ulric to come himself. With all that was under way at the keep, his men would need to report their progress to the lord. Plans would have to be laid out for the morrow. Harold had presented her with the next day's plans after she'd awakened that afternoon from the short nap that had claimed her in her aunt's room, so there was naught to keep her after supper but whimsical entertainment, something she was not disposed toward at the moment.

Perhaps it was the newness of the idea, but Branwen's hands found their way to her abdomen again as she climbed the winding stone steps to the master bedchamber. A boy, she thought, somewhat awestruck by the prospect. The future lord of Caradoc. *And this is your father's room,* she mused, stepping inside timidly. It's as grand and imposing as he is ... and he's not a murderer. He's just a big, belligerent warrior with a gentle heart, like your grandfather Owen.

Branwen tossed open a shutter and peered out over the inner bailey. The lord's kitchen was processing a line of villeins displaced by the renegade raiders. One would have thought their plight would make them despondent, but they were far from it. If anything, they were a bit boisterous, particularly the men who had come in hungry from the southeast forests, where lumber for the new village had started to be cut.

Beyond Caradoc's walls, the first trees had been stacked, stripped of their brush and dragged by oxen from the woods.

"Planting a village," one of the jovial comments drifted up to her. She smiled and strained to hear more.

"A good man, his lordship."

"Cymry in spirit, if not in blood."

"Ain't many Cymry lord what will open his stores to his villeins."

"And 'ansome as he is smart!"

" 'E'll do Lord Owen proud, rest his soul."

"A seventh son, so I hear."

Seventh son. Like as not, charm was one of her husband's greatest powers. He'd certainly worked his way with the villagers, as well as with the castle staff. And with her, Branwen admitted, closing the shutter tightly in the dimming light of the setting sun in the west.

As she left the windowseat, Miriam came in to help her prepare for bed. Caught in the oddest of moods, Branwen listened to the girl chatter about how beautiful milady's hair would be when it grew to her waist. That it had managed to reach her shoulders was an accomplishment Lady Gwen would have delighted over. Branwen waited patiently while the maid worked its length into a short braid and adorned it with a white bow.

"Of course, you'll want to braid it every night. My grandmother swore hair grew faster if a lady slept with it in a braid. When not, she said it would break and tangle, begging to be cut."

Instead of arguing, as she used to with her mother, Branwen admired the maid's handiwork. She did look more like a girl . . . a mother, she amended. Had she been asked before if she wanted a child, she'd have denied it vehemently, but now that the make-believe baby was real, Branwen felt almost giddy with satisfaction.

God bless Aunt Agnéis for helping her sort out her muddled thoughts and easing her conscience concerning Ulric! Absentminded as the woman was, Branwen believed in her predictions and proclamations. The people of the cantref called her a natural-born healer. She'd certainly healed Branwen's troubled and broken heart with her reassuring words of wisdom.

Now all that stood between her and Ulric was a sudden case of jitters, spawned the moment Miriam left the room. Faith, she'd been tired at the supper table! Yet she knew no sleep would come to her wide open eyes until her husband had joined her.

The thoughts had no sooner registered than the door swung open to admit the subject of her concern. He must have been waiting for Miriam to leave, Branwen mused, holding her seat on the bench at the end of the bed with clenched fingers as he approached her.

"I . . ." Ulric paused, as if gathering his courage before he spoke again. "You said at the table, if my *son* could see me. Does that mean, milady, that the child is now a certainty?"

Such an endearing expression, she thought, affirming the hopeful look in his gaze with a nod. Ulric let his breath out heavily, his lips curling into a bone-melting grin. Pivoting, he strode a few steps away and then returned, slapping his chest with his fist. "Well, it appears we are well matched, milady! At first, I thought this might be one of those female wiles you tormented me with to keep me at a distance." He laughed nervously. "One night, one child . . . gogsbreath! I shall have to add on another tower for the nursery!"

"Milord!" Branwen exclaimed, not even her guilt able

337

to smother her delight over Ulric's reaction. "I would have one at a time, please! A son first . . . for you."

Ulric rushed to her so quickly, Branwen gasped as she was drawn up into his arms and swung around. "Son, daughter . . . it matters not! If a girl, she'll take after her plucky and beautiful mother and see her castle and lands well provided for, should a brother not follow to do so for her." He bussed her on the forehead as he paced about the room, carrying her back and forth in his excitement. "We'll announce it tonight!"

"No, milord!"

Ulric halted in mid-step. "And why not, pray tell? If this is not enough to make a man shout with pride, I—"

"We mustn't let anyone know yet." Branwen felt her heart sinking. How the devil was she going to explain to her logical husband the risk involved? "Because I fear there are those who would do me harm if they knew I bore Caradoc's heir."

Keeping her within his grasp, Ulric eased down on the side of the bed. "And you think they might be here among us? Who?"

Branwen shrugged. "I do not think it is worth the risk. I beg you, hold our news back until these halegrins are caught and peace and order is restored. Aunt . . . that is," the girl said, reconsidering using her aunt as the source of her suspicion, "there could be a connection with the contamination of my food on the journey and the raids. Someone, whoever brutally did away with Caryn, wants me dead." She shuddered against him, evoking a reassuring tightening of Ulric's embrace. "I know it doesn't make sense, milord, but will you indulge my whims about this?"

Ulric leaned down and grazed her lips. "Milady, I will indulge you anything within my power to indulge."

Whether it was relief that robbed her of her breath or her body's disconcerting response, she didn't know. Col-

338

lected thought was impossible when Ulric was with her, much less kissing her and stroking her with that seductive rumble in his voice—deep, like the purr of the lion he reminded her of. Despite her knowledge of the blissful heights to which the man before her could take her, both physically and emotionally, her own words were far bolder than she felt.

"Then, sir, I would have you join me in your bed and hold me, to keep away the troublesome dreams that have plagued me."

"Gladly, milady, but . . . is that *all?*"

Branwen inadvertently clenched her thighs together to check the gnawing feeling that seemed to increase with each velvet syllable Ulric spoke. Gogsblood, were he to keep on, he could talk her into the wild convulsion she had known but once, when joined with him as intimately as woman could be to a man! Her gaze dropped to the juncture of his leather-clad thighs and then moved quickly onto his feet, before she died of complete humiliation and embarrassment, for her thoughts were far from ladylike at the moment.

She cleared her throat. "Well . . . you could remove your boots, milord."

The burst of Ulric's rich laughter gave Branwen a start. "Woman, I'll remove more than that."

Which was exactly what he proceeded to do. His surcoat and shirt posed no problem, but the leggings, with their multiple buckles among the full length of Ulric's long legs, took what seemed like forever to Branwen. Propping up on one elbow, her bare feet tucked under the turned-back covers, she ran her fingers over the battle-scarred ridges of his back.

"You're *still* Wolf," she mused aloud, trying to merge the two men who were her husband into one in her mind.

Ulric tensed. "Nay, milady, I am Ulric. Wolf is only a namesake, like the raven is yours."

"But there's something ... *wolfish* about you."

Her candor was so earnest, the knight couldn't help but grin as he assaulted the length of buckled leather. "Aye, and *you* put me to mind of the wild bird. Just when I thought you were within my reach, you'd fly away ... not far enough that I would lose sight of you, but just out of reach."

He stripped the last of the leggings off and peeled off his hose and trousers simultaneously. "Why don't you do the same now, milady?"

Ulric's questioning gaze caught Branwen's heart, for here was a part of him that had never shown ... in Caradoc's lord or in the mercenary. It was vulnerability, as if with his clothes he'd stripped away all but that which was really him. Suddenly, Branwen knew the full extent of her lord's suffering—suffering at the hands of unknown enemies, his new people's mistrust, and worst of all, her own.

She blinked to clear her eyes, for she did not want this good, noble man to go just yet, as the lord of Caradoc and the mercenary were both masters at hiding him. "Because ..." Her voice trembled with all that she wanted to say, to confess. "Because, milord, I am weary of flying. I long to be held and protected by the father of my child, be he Wolf or Ulric, for they have both found a place in my heart."

"And what of your trust, milady?"

"For all his might, Wolf could not restore it, milord." Branwen fell back against the pillows and held out her arms to the scarred warrior standing before her, seeing for the first time all of his wounds, both physical and emotional. " 'Twas Ulric's example of wisdom and kindness that prevailed."

His hunger as naked as he, Ulric covered her with his

body as his lips did her own. The pulsing arousal that she had been hard pressed to ignore as they spoke demanded that ready acknowledgment of her body, as if there were two levels of communication, each soul-wresting in its own way. Branwen had been about to give Aunt Agnéis her due for setting her mind at ease as well, but the time for talking had past. She had wasted too much effort on words that never truly rang from her heart, but from a grief-stricken and beleaguered mind.

At the impatient tugging of her gown, Branwen struggled out of ecstasy's tide to help her companion divest her of the garment, before it was rendered in shreds by the urgency with which his manner infected her. It was hiked above her waist, and then it was gone with a flourish that would have put the court's best magician to shame. As she saw it fly off to some unknown destination, as if possessed of its own will, a perfectly wicked giggle escaped her lips, only to change into a gasp of delight at the wild rampage of Ulric's exploring fingers and lips.

A master on the battlefield, he was no less so in bed. Her body convulsed with the onslaught of too many fronts, making anything less than total surrender and shameful desertion out of the question. She wanted to join him, to dole back some measure of the heady delight he stirred into frenzy, yet her caresses became pleas, tugging him closer than flesh would allow, and her intended terms of endearment, little gasps of pleasure, interspersed with a guttural semblance of his name.

When he would be gentle in the ultimate taking of her quivering and eager body, Branwen arched her hips to meet his victorious thrust, clinging to his passion-taut body as if life itself were at risk. No reckless ride on the windblown traeth had ever offered such complete abandon. No beating of galloping hooves could match that of the thundering hearts racing toward fulfillment.

"Gogsblood, husband!" she rasped to the wolfish growl of the man shuddering over her as well as within. Her body was a riot of sensations, burning, exploding, until she lay in the quivering aftermath of it all.

With a loud groan, Ulric rolled to Branwen's side and stared at the ceiling. "I'm bewitched, woman. What manner of passion is it you spin that can make a man feel as though he's been turned inside out and wrung dry?"

With a lazy smile, Branwen curled into the cradle he made about her with his arm and splayed her fingers on the love-damp fur of his chest. " 'Tis not me, milord. 'Tis your own magic."

Ulric chuckled lowly. "Magic is it?"

"You're a seventh son. Aunt Agnéis says that makes you a very special man." Branwen kissed the taut dark circle crowning the flat muscled breast that served as her pillow. "If you were not, I would not be with child."

"You've a protection that doesn't work against me, then?"

She could tell by Ulric's tone that he was toying with her, but Branwen didn't mind. As her aunt had said, it would take time for him to learn such things, being an estron. "Aye, 'tis a stone that sweats if a couple so much as hold hands. A girl cannot get with child in its presence."

"A *magic* stone?"

She smacked him playfully. "If you will make fun of me, I'll not say another word! It's worked for years in our family."

"Until *I* came?"

"Because you are a seventh son, you rogue!" Branwen rose up on her elbow. "I had the stone in our room at Westminster, but—"

"Have you seen it of late?"

Taken aback by her husband's sudden turn of sobriety, Branwen shook her head. "Nay, I assume it's in the pouch. . . ."

"Then like as not, 'twas melted away that first time!"

She slapped his stomach, bringing the recalcitrant knight upright with a yelp. "Damn you, milord, I am serious."

To her astonishment, Ulric grabbed her and wrestled her down against the pillows, his face a picture of sheer devilment. "So am I, fair raven . . . and right now, this seventh son would have his wife"—he caressed her lips—"in his bed"—each of her breasts tingled with the playful nip he afforded them—"making love to him."

"Again?" Branwen exclaimed, her pitch rising at the press of his renewed passion against the yielding juncture of her thighs.

"You said yourself, milady, this is no ordinary man you've taken to husband," Ulric chided. He poised above her, tensed, and then drove his point home, both physically and verbally. *"This* is a seventh son."

Chapter Twenty-one

Giles De Clare was an older man than Ulric and, self-ishly, Branwen was afraid the new guest chamber would not be finished before he and his wife arrived, and she and Ulric would have to give up their dream chamber, for if ever there was a place where dreams came true, it was there. Branwen adapted readily to the privacy she had disdained as frivolous and was loath to give it up so soon. As it was, by the time the Lord of Merionwythe arrived, the women were just putting the finishing touches on the room, hanging tapestries and curtains over the bed and shuttered windows, since it was opposite the master chamber and overlooked the north wall of the cliff.

Like so many of the English lords and ladies, the couple at first acted as if their blood was blue to the bone. Their narrow aristocratic noses seemed to lift as they walked toward the keep, hawkish eyes missing nothing of their surroundings. There was a gathering of villeins watching the procession, but it did not break into cheers of welcome until Caradoc's lord emerged from the keep to meet them. With his lady on his arm, he was followed by those of his knights who were not engaged in the construction and procurement projects.

The uproar sent the chickens pecking in the inner

bailey yard darting for cover, adding their clucking to the general noise of welcome. Branwen was nervous and perspired, despite the chilly air that made her rich gown of burgundy and fuchsia flutter about her slender form. She had entertained before, but not as lady of the keep. Or *fortress*, she amended, following De Clare's curious gaze along the new curtain walls lining Caradoc's original ones.

Gogsblood, she'd given her all and prayed this guest of her husband's would be pleased, for that would please her beloved lord. Not that Ulric hadn't worked day and night himself. She'd watched from their chamber window as he, his knights, and the craftsmen from all over the cantref worked by torchlight to finish the walls and roof the cells between them. Gradually, family by family moved into their new dwellings, some permanently. Bad as the plunder of the halegrins had been, there was a sense of security present, perhaps spawned of the very measures they were taking.

Although her opinion was admittedly biased by that lighthearted, head-spinning, and body-warming feeling she got each time her husband entered her presence, Branwen could not help but think the new lord's example was at the root of all the enthusiasm. He'd worked side by side with the lowest of villeins, despite their astonished protests, and set the pace and the mood.

The result was the miraculous progress that he'd prayed for each morning at chapel, where even there, much to Father Dennis's delight, more and more men joined their lord in his daily devotions. There, under the priest's lead, spiritual warfare was launched, lest this enemy, who had been proven flesh and blood, was possessed by demons. Their work was blessed and each man anointed.

Now the walls were done. The fortress, which had been intended to convey English sovereignty but had come to symbolize the union of Cymry and English countrymen, was secure from outside penetration and the concentration was placed on finishing the inside work. As one approached from the forested hills beyond the morfa, Caradoc looked like a gleaming pearl with its freshly limed walls mounted on a majestic grey-black setting. Its colorful jet and scarlet banners flew from the battlements, brilliant against an azure winter sky.

Resplendently attired in gold studded velvet rather than the work clothes that had been his costume of recent days, Ulric looked every ounce the lord of the manor as he greeted Giles De Clare and his lady. His manner appeared to be inborn, as if he'd been an heir of landed gentry all his life instead of the seventh son of a lord, entitled to nothing but good wishes.

"Welcome Lord Giles! Lady Maria," he said, bowing gallantly to kiss the older woman's extended hand.

"We had hoped that you would have stopped with your new wife at Merionwythe on your way to claim Caradoc, Lord Ulric," Lady Maria chided stiffly.

"My wife took ill on the journey, milady, and we hastened home as quickly as we could."

The woman lifted a thin brown brow at Branwen. "Then home must have agreed with her, for she looks in the peak of health now. Good day to you, Lady Branwen. We have heard much about you."

Uncertain from Lady De Clare's tone as to the nature of her information, Branwen dipped politely. "Good day to you both, milord, milady. Welcome to our home."

Our home. It was the first time Branwen had referred to Caradoc that way. She glanced over at Ulric and basked in the approving warmth of his smile, until he was distracted by his English guest.

"I have heard you enlisted the help of your villeins to finish Caradoc and must readily admit, milord, that I scarce expected to have a roof over my head, much less enter a well-fortified keep."

"My wife and her women have prepared a comfortable room for you and your lady, milord. It's our privilege to have you as our first guests."

Lady Maria and her servant were turned over to Branwen to settle in their room, while Harold saw to refreshments for the men. Branwen literally glowed at the compliments Lady Maria handed out, for she and her women had been as busy as the men preparing for the English couple's arrival and making the most of what was available. Since entertainment at Caradoc had previously been more conservative than what was now expected, there was no time to purchase, much less weave, linens and cloths for the new additions.

While the drapes and linens were not new, they were freshly laundered and updated with new embroidery to make them appear so. The bottom-most sheets were no more than the heavy coarse cloth used to encase rush mattresses, but the colorful stitchings were attractive and gave them a rich look, heretofore lost. The bed Branwen had occupied in the great hall, gracefully bedecked with drapes and curtains, brought an instant smile to Lady Maria's face. She confided her fear that she would end up sleeping on a bench next to some snoring oaf. Once aside from her husband, she'd added mischievously, thawing Branwen's initial reserve.

The lady took a light repast in her room so that she might nap while the men took to the fields for hunting. Still determined that not a thing should go awry to spoil what had begun as an enjoyable visit, Branwen nearly wore out her new slippers walking back and forth from the kitchen to the keep to look over Master Harold's shoulder at the preparations for the evening meal. Two meats, venison and pork provided by Caradoc's able hunters, along with fowl and fish, would grace his lordship's table.

The fowl, delicious chicken potted in a wine sauce that would make one's mouth water, had been an ingenious plan on Aunt Agnéis's part to conquer the proverbial two birds with one stone. Not only did they supply Caradoc's table, but each one had been carefully slaughtered on the stump of every oak tree in the grove Ulric's men had cleared. The bloodstained stumps would surely appease the outraged tree spirits, which would not harm Caradoc, and certainly would help allay some of the misfortune of late.

In addition, dried sprigs of lady's tree hung from iron nails over every door, adorned with a ribbon. Not only were the lord and his guests protected from the outbreak of fire, but the iron was known to combat evil powers. It also guaranteed protection of an expectant mother and her unborn child, keeping the infant from becoming possessed of a demonic spirit before it received its own. This accounted for the nail driven into the footboard of the bed she shared with Ulric, although in keeping with her husband's teasing, she had left the lady's tree off. It was a fire of a passionate nature that burned between them, but Branwen would take no chances of *putting it out*.

The hall looked fit to entertain a king when the men returned at dusk with a large boar carried on a pole by servants. Baths were ordered for each private chamber and Miriam sent to attend Giles De Clare. Branwen would see to Ulric's scrubbing herself, although the highest honor she could pay Lord Giles would be to help Miriam. Perhaps when she was older and less prone to embarrassment, she might consider the custom, but as a new bride, she had yet to look at her husband's body without flushing profusely, much less that of a stranger!

She sent word to her husband that his bath was ready and waited anxiously for him to come to their room. The hearthfire danced brightly, filling the room with a cheery glow, and his clothes, as well as towels that Branwen had embroidered "She" and "He," had been laid out on the bed by her own hand. As she sat next to the fire in Ulric's chair, she wondered if it was the lively flames that scorched her cheeks or her anticipation of washing her husband's scarred and muscle-ridged flesh with admittedly mischievous fingers. After all, there would be another hour before supper would be ready to serve, ample time for a bath and anything else his lordship might desire.

Branwen heard Ulric's booted approach on the winding steps and sat up alert, hands folded primly in her lap to await his entry into the room. Lady Maria's compliments crowded her brain as she lined them up to share with him, for Branwen had come to love sharing everything with her husband, from work to play.

"Your bath, milord," she announced as he stepped into the room and closed the door purposefully behind him. When Ulric turned, a scowl darkened the features that had earlier mirrored approval. A shiver of foreboding invaded her excitement. "I sent Miriam to attend to Lord Giles, sir," Branwen offered, wondering if she had done wrong not to see to the guest personally.

Surely Ulric would not want *that*. He didn't even like the attention his knights had been giving her of late, although his protests were made in a good-natured manner, sufficient to let it be known that he had noticed.

"Good. That shows there is some semblance of reason to that addled brain of yours."

"What?" Branwen came to her feet, confused by the unexpected assault.

"Damn you and that silly aunt of yours. If you have

done nothing else, you've made me the fool before my guest!"

"Milord, no fool could have designed and built such a fortress and—"

"And let his wife strew it with seaweed! When the devil did you do your mischief?" Ulric demanded. Fists clenched, he teetered before her as if struggling to keep from actually choking her. The mottled red of his face further told of his trying restraint.

Not the least intimated, Branwen held her ground. "Yesterday, milord. You must have been too tired to notice."

"And the chicken sacrifices? When did that bloody nonsense take place? Gogsdeath, it looked as if a massacre had occurred when we rode past! Can you imagine my telling Lord Giles that my wife thinks I've enraged the tree spirits and has sacrificed every damned hen in the cantref to appease them?"

He doesn't understand. Branwen kept repeating Aunt Agnéis's advice to her, but it would not slow the rapid rise of her own temper. He doesn't understand. She inhaled deeply for fortification.

"Milord, the hens are about to be put on your table in the numbers you yourself specified as appropriate. I hardly thought it mattered where they were slaughtered, so long as they weren't clucking and pecking the peppercorns off your venison roast before your very eyes."

Choking, Ulric turned and walked to the hearth, but upon reaching it, he was vexed by the lady's tree spread on the mantle. Branwen started as he cleared it away with one angry sweep of his hand and glowered at her.

"How can you believe this?" he ground out in frustration as he seized up a handful of the dried seaweed and contemptuously tossed it into the fire. "I know you have more sense! Will I have to rid Caradoc of your aunt? Will *that* restore your God-given wit, woman?"

Throw her aunt out? The idea was as preposterous as his anger! Branwen's lips thinned in stubborn indignation. "This keep has been my aunt's home since my parents were wed and she will remain here as long as I do! If you throw her out, then I and the child will go as well! She was trying to help you, you ungrateful, *ignorant* ass! She even takes up for you, and yet you would throw her out of her home! How . . ." Damn a chin that trembled on its own! "How could you?"

Ulric inhaled and rolled his eyes to the ceiling. "Gogsblood, I cannot argue with a crying woman!"

With her sleeve, Branwen resolutely wiped away the water that had sprung in her eyes, so that he could witness the full extent of her glare. "Crying? By God, I am *not* crying! 'Tis a sign of weakness and surrender, and *this* is neither," she declared, striking him full in the chest with both her fists. "*This* is anger, milord!" she threw her body with her punch this time, slamming into the man and forcing him to budge on his firmly planted feet. "*This* is fighting!"

Exasperated by the hands that, undaunted by her attack, caught her by the waist and lifted her from the floor, she kicked furiously. Branwen had meant to make him put her down, and she was not prepared when he threw her completely dressed into the wooden tub of water she'd had drawn for him. With an outraged shriek that was smothered as she slipped under the sloshing water, she scrambled for a hold and came up sputtering curses, fit to singe the ears of Satan himself, in her native Welsh.

"How dare you!" she finished, when the man bent over in strickened silence did not rally.

"Gogsblood, woman, consider yourself lucky I did not drown you!" Ulric's voice sounded as if it had been squeezed through a pain-constricted throat. He backed toward the bed in retreat from the dripping figure regaining her footing in the tub. "If you ever kick me there again, I'll—"

"Ulric, watch—"

Branwen's warning was silenced by the simultaneous tearing of her husband's sleeve and the resulting oath that assaulted her ears. Bolting upright, one pain forgotten momentarily for another, he examined the bleeding flesh of his arm and sought out the guilty nail that had inflicted the wound. Uncertain as to whether to jump out of the tub and leave a wet trail over the freshly scrubbed floors and steps or to simply sink back into the water and drown herself, Branwen stared as Ulric grasped the offending iron with his bare hand and yanked it out of the footboard, where she and Aunt Agnéis had agreed it was the least conspicuous.

"What is *this* for, milady?" he snarled, thrusting the nail toward her. "Spearing a demon through the heart?"

Despite the hot water in the tub, Branwen shivered. " 'Tis protection from evil spirits . . . for our baby. Everyone knows iron has—"

"So it's only in *our* bed?" he asked warily.

Branwen glanced away, a guilty scarlet creeping to her face.

"Not in Merionwythe's bed," Ulric prompted hopefully. At her continued silence, he flung the nail across the room, bouncing it off the tapestried wall. It rang as it hit the floor and rolled a short distance. "Where *else*, milady?"

"All the lady's tree is hung with an iron nail, sir . . . and the guest bed is the only other that has a nail."

"That is the only other bed in the keep, woman!"

" 'Tis just a precaution, Ulric! What harm can it do?" she protested. "And if, just *if* by chance it does keep our baby from harm, isn't it worth a little embarrassment on your part?" She lifted her skirts and wrung them out, when she heard Ulric marching toward the door. "Where are you going?"

"To remove the nail from Merionwythe's bed before someone gets hurt!" Ulric stopped in the opening. "Lord Giles is a scientific man who has had occasion to work with Sir Francis Bacon. Do you know who that is?"

Branwen shook her head.

"A man who could revolutionize warfare with his experiments. I have asked Lord Giles to show me some of the miraculous results of their work to advance Caradoc's might, and you make me look the fool with your silly potions and charms!" His nostrils flared with his outraged breath. "I want all the seaweed cleared from the keep, and from this moment on, all slaughtering of fowl or meat will take place at the butchers, if every oak in the cantref is cut down for building, is that understood?"

"Tyrant!"

"Is that understood, milady?"

Branwen nodded reluctantly. Damn the man! It was just as well he didn't get in the tub. She'd drown him! "And the nail, milord?"

Ulric did not miss the protective way Branwen covered her abdomen with her hands. A resigned sigh escaped with his answer. "Put it under the mattress, where it can't hurt anyone."

Poor Miriam shrieked at the sight of her mistress wringing out the clothing she was wearing while standing in the midst of the bath drawn for the angry lord who passed her on the stairwell. Aunt Agnéis, spirited from her room by the maid's outcry, took one look at Branwen and walked off chuckling and talking to herself, despite her niece's furious, " 'Tis painfully hard to deal with *ignorance*, milady aunt!" Realizing Miriam's obligation to attend to Lord Giles, Branwen ignored the

353

girl's questions and sent her straight away to the guest chamber.

When she emerged later to find Ulric entertaining her guests on the dais with the tun of Gascony wine they'd brought with them, Branwen had dressed herself in a pale blue surcoat over a shift trimmed with gold banding. Blue and gold ribbons had been woven into her short braid and trailed down over her shoulder, giving her hair a look of additional length as she'd seen on other young women. A single golden circlet glistened about the crown of her head, a halo in the light of the tallow dips spaced along the length of the lord's table against the loose raven tresses that could not be tamed and fringed her face with wispy curls.

Still clad in his hunting coat of green cloth, Ulric possessed a ruddy hue that told of his day in the sun and wind . . . or perhaps of the amount of liquor that he had consumed after he'd left her to enjoy the bath alone. She'd been so angry, relaxation in the increasing cooling water had become impossible. Hence, she'd done a quick once-over with the scented soap made by the women under Lady Gwendolyn's sharp supervision and abandoned the tub to dress before she took a chill.

"Milady, you look refreshed."

The lady's tree she'd strung along the mantle over the hearth near them was gone. Most likely burned at the lord's orders, Branwen guessed. A quick perusal showed, however, that the nails remained intact, except that they had been driven in completely so as not to draw attention. She avoided the openly admiring and disconcerting gaze fixed on her to address her guests.

"As do our guests. I hope everything is satisfactory with your room."

"Child, I am flattered to have a private room, much less the offer of a bath to wash away the filth of our journey!" Lady Maria assured her. "Such hospitality is rare, even in *English* castles, but to find it in wild Wales ..."

"Is still the result of English ingenuity," Ulric injected callously.

"And Welsh sweat and skill, milord," Branwen reminded him sweetly. "Why, I heard Blanchard remark only this morning that more progress had been made in the last week than in any *four* weeks with the laborers brought in from England by the king."

Giles De Clare lifted his cups. "To the union of England and Wales. May it prosper as well as the marriage of these two young people."

"You know that, short of Edward's most recent projects at Caernarvon and Rhuddlan, there is nothing to compare to this," their lady guest complimented. "Giles will be sure to pass on your success to His Majesty, for I am sure it will please him."

"Humph! Everything this towheaded rooster does pleases Edward ... me as well!" Lord Giles snorted in agreement. "If you would have more of my men to help you flush out these vagabonds that have been troubling you, just say the word."

Ulric expelled the prideful breath that had swollen his chest and nodded. "My thanks, milord. It is good to know the marcher lords are brethren eager to support one another. But enough of this business. 'Twill be time enough for that on the morrow. Nights are made for pleasure and entertainment, isn't that right, milady?"

Branwen colored at the attention her husband called to her. "Indeed, milord. *Guests* certainly increase the prospect of a diverting evening at Caradoc." She glanced up to the balcony on the gallery where their ensemble of harpists, flutists, and singers were assembling. "I do believe our music is about to begin. A touching ballad will warm my heart quicker than a flagon of the best ale or wine," she confessed to Lady Maria, "and Damaris knows more lyrics by heart than I can name."

Spared acknowledging Ulric's assessing look by the outbreak of a lively tune, Branwen fixed her attention on the balcony until Lady Maria moved from her husband's left to Branwen's right, so that they might talk of things more interesting than the afternoon hunt from which Ulric still reeked. 'Twas like supping in a stable, she mused later, reluctantly sharing a charger topped with the roasted meat with him. He smelled of sweaty horseflesh and damp leather.

Having come with the line of servitors led by Master Harold, the dogs forcing their way in and about their feet under the table did little to improve her regard for the man. That, and the fact that Ulric encouraged them by dropping chunks of meat and fat on the floor, caused her to consider her dining dagger with malicious regard, but that she would not spill, nor see spilled, one drop of her husband's blood. She could, however, were it not for their guests, slap that ruddy color right off his shadow-roughened face! Gogsdeath, love was the most confounding state she'd ever found herself in!

Because of the guests and the bounty of Caradoc's forests, three courses were served, each containing one meat, one fowl, and one fish dish. Maitlen's masterpieces drew more than one compliment on looks as well as on taste. Nuts, olives, jellies, finger breads, and other assorted side dishes rounded out the feast nicely. Branwen was full after the first course but nibbled daintily out of politeness, until her guests had eaten their way to the conclusion of steaming fruit tarts and other various pastries.

Despite the presence of noble guests, the hall was full of tables as usual, occupied not only by the castle staff and servants, but also by some of the villeins who had not yet found shelter. They filled themselves with the less choice cut of meats, as well as with the pies and stews remaining from the lord's table. Yet, even they considered those less fortunate than themselves and contributed to the alms dishes set out on each table, instead of stuffing their pockets for later.

"I can see why you are so well thought of, Lord Ulric. It does you great credit to see these homeless cared for until their village can be rebuilt."

"My obligation was to protect them. When I failed at that, it was only right to help them as best I could." The anguished reflection in Ulric's voice caused Branwen's irritation with him to waver.

"But there might have been more carnage and destruction had you and your knights not arrived when you did, milord," Giles objected. "I know defeat is something that does not come easy to a man like yourself, sir, but it happens to the best of us at one time or other. I have no doubt in my mind that you will get to the bottom of this trouble and stamp it out."

"Lord Giles is right, milord," Aunt Agnéis chimed in. "Take the advice of an old woman and put your thoughts toward what *can* be done, rather than what *should* have been done."

"Well said, milady!" Lady Maria cheered. "Lord Ulric, you mentioned we might play games after the meal. Might I suggest blindman's bluff?"

Giles De Clare chuckled. " 'Tis her favorite game, though I will warn you, the man . . . or lady," he said to Branwen, "who is caught is obliged to forfeit a kiss to the blindman, or in the case of two men, a handshake will suffice."

"Then blindman's bluff it is!" Ulric announced, motioning for Harold to fetch the necessary accoutrements. " 'Tis been a while since I've indulged in such a game, but the kiss is certainly incentive."

Branwen could not miss the unsteady sway of the

357

man who offered his arm to her. She found herself supporting him instead. She had seen her husband loud and boisterous but not drunk, which was surely his state. He must have been drinking since he'd left her earlier!

"Perhaps milord would care for a breath of fresh air?" she suggested. "You could take the hounds with you and have them penned, lest they become excited and interfere with our game."

Which would take care of two nuisances at the same time, she thought in annoyance. Branwen was going to have to speak to Ulric about the dogs. If he insisted they come into the house, then they would have to be taught manners. Laying their heads on the laps of the diners and trying to steal food from the edge of the table was as repugnant as their indiscriminate use of the hall floor for their refuse. The women of Caradoc had always prided themselves on clean floors, fresh with the smell of spices, dried flowers, and rush.

"I need no air but the sweet scent of your soap, milady," Ulric replied, sweeping low in an exaggerated bow that nearly toppled him. As it was, two of the greyhounds took it upon themselves to show their affection by licking his face. "And as for my dogs," he went on, seizing them around the neck playfully and chuckling in satisfaction, "they have the right to be with their master."

Branwen bit back her thought that perhaps, then, it was best she have them all put out, and she gave her guests an apologetic smile. Gogsdeath, it was going to be a long night.

Chapter Twenty-two

The games lasted well into the night, even if Caradoc's lord did not. While he slept peacefully, slouched in his chair, Branwen and her guests, as well as Ulric's knights and company, spent a pleasant evening. Even Aunt Agnéis participated in ragman's roll, although the considerably coarser verses she drew made her stammer in embarrassment as well as in humor. Then she sat back for someone else to make an utter fool of himself, which was easily done. The verses were designed to do just that.

When sufficient time had passed, Lady Maria retired to her room, leaving Lord Giles to make merry with the men, which gave Branwen the excuse she needed to see Ulric moved to their chamber. The moment the lord was stretched out on the bed, she and Blanchard set about undressing him for a bath, for she would not have him in her bed reeking of horses, ale, and dogs. Upon dismissing the chamberlain to return to their guests, Branwen set about washing the naked man.

As Ulric was her first and only lover, he was also the first and only man she had ever bathed. The fact that he was sleeping soundly from too much ale and not enough food made her curious observation far easier, for in the heat of their lovemaking, it was difficult to give her husband's magnificent body the attention it deserved. At least he would not be distracting her with those talented hands and lips that seemed to touch her everywhere at one time.

He was actually beautiful, she thought, warming in spite of her intentions to remain impartial to the ridges of muscle and sinew. It was not a flawless beauty like the statues of young gods in Roman loincloth, but one that bespoke perfect proportions and strength. His scars were worn like medals, each demanding respect and, from Branwen, a tender kiss. Yet it was his loins that fascinated her most, for she had no idea that simply washing them would produce the growing result she was compelled to examine with untold curiosity.

"Gogsbreath, it does have its own mind!" she murmured, hurriedly tossing the coverlet over her husband as if the independent member might assault her.

Not that she would have minded. The touch of her husband's manly flesh and her gentle exploration of his body left her own with a gnawing emptiness that grew intense at the unspoken call of a primitive nature far beyond her comprehension. Besides, Ulric would surely think her the wanton tart if he were to awaken to find her taking her own pleasure with him, which from what she had just witnessed, seemed entirely possible to her. While she'd never heard of such a thing, she supposed by his being a seventh son that perhaps anything was possible.

Shamed at the very baseness of her thoughts, Branwen hurriedly cleaned up from the bath and changed into her night shift. Since Miriam had built up the fire earlier, she climbed into the bed, keeping stiffly to her side in self-imposed punishment. After all, she *was* angry at Ulric, Branwen reminded herself. He'd behaved deplorably that evening, not to mention his earlier stormy rebuff of her and Aunt Agnéis's genuine attempts to help him.

The late hour, combined with the regular lullaby of the wind whistling around the outside of the keep, soon had Branwen asleep. In the world of dreams, she had no reason to keep the distance between her and the softly snoring man at her side. The space between them closed. Each welcomed the other into their arms until, legs entwined, they slept contentedly.

While the eastern horizon glowed with the prospect of the new day, the sun had not yet risen when Branwen stirred to Ulric's furtive mumblings and convulsive jerks. Struggling out of her dreamless sleep, she opened her eyes just as the man pulled away from her and bolted upright. Her start was invaded by the realization that she was damp. Almost as damp as his skin, she thought, placing a comforting hand on his back.

"Ulric? Are you ill?"

At the sound of her voice, Ulric turned toward her. "Gogsblood, woman, come here!" His voice broke with emotion, and suddenly Branwen was engulfed in a desperate embrace.

Alarm tripped up her spine. He was trembling, actually shaking, as he held her. "What is it, Ulric?" Had he seen something? Aunt Agnéis had said he would.

"You're all right . . . you and the baby?"

"Of course we are . . . that is, until you gave us a start, jumping up like that." She hesitated, wary of his reaction. "Did you see something, sir?"

Ulric shook his head as he buried his face into the soft flesh of her neck and kissed her there, as if reassuring himself that she was indeed no figment of his imagination. " 'Twas only a bad dream, but it seemed as though it were real." He swore under his breath. "All this talk of spirits and demons has given me nightmares, and I don't even believe such nonsense!"

"Tâd didn't, either, but he didn't take chances."

"Christ's toes, my mouth feels like it was packed with lint!"

Branwen sat up. "I'll fetch you some water, milord. Shall I brew some oak bark tea for your head as well?"

Ulric scowled. "How do you know my head aches?"

"I've seen drunks before, milord! 'Tis the usual penance."

"And what is *this?*" Ulric picked at the sleeve of her shift.

"This," Branwen grumbled sleepily, "is a night shift."

"I can well see that, but why, pray tell, are you wearing it in our bed, when I thought I'd made it clear last night that anything more than nothing is too much?"

"Are you always so talkative at this wee hour of the morning?"

Ulric chuckled at her cross retort. " 'Tis not *talk* I'm thinking of, woman."

Cutting a suspicious look at her husband, Branwen eased a timid hand under the covers to discover a hard eagerness that instantly dispelled the last of her sleepiness. "Gogsblood, it's *still* alive!"

"Still?"

Realizing her admission too late, fire surged from her neck to scorch her cheeks, even in the dim light of the room. "In case you hadn't noticed, milord, you are bathed and smelling sweet as lavender. I wasn't about to have you in my bed stinking like a barn animal." She withdrew her hand to her lap primly. "It came to life when I washed it."

Ulric leaned forward, curling over her back to whisper in her ear most disconcertingly. "And what, pray tell, did you do then to the mangy beast, milady?"

"What any decent woman would do! I covered it up and put it to bed with the rest of its hairy master, who was as dead as it was alive, I might add!" Branwen snapped, suddenly hot in the thin linen clinging to her body. Ulric's belly laugh did not improve her humor. She pulled up the covers and, with an angry twist, turned over on her side.

"You will note now, milady, that I and *it,*" he mimicked, "are of one accord."

There was no ignoring the lean and hungry male body that pressed at her back, nor the hot breath against her neck. Indeed, she struggled with the will-weakening twinges of her own desire, which but a few moments ago, she *thought,* had been soundly at rest. It was as if her senses had waited with bated breath until Ulric could unite in intent with his overzealous body. If the man could do not naught else, he could stir her most maddeningly . . .

And dizzily, she thought, a wave of anticipation rippling through her as she felt the material of her nightshift being eased up with purposeful caress. How naturally it was to turn at its gentle guidance to permit easier access to the erotic grounds where deviously playful fingers might drive her wild with want. How inviting was the kiss that somehow lifted her up, unveiling her gowned body and disposing of the garment with but a breath of a break.

Neither the passion pressed against her inner thighs, nor the man himself, could be put to bed now, she thought with a wry twitch of lips that found their way to the furred span of Ulric's chest. The same arms that had facilitated the removal of her clothing slipped beneath her again, taking her with him as he rolled on his back to permit her instinctive seduction its freedom. Recalling the shrill bombardment of sensations evoked by his lashing tongue, Branwen sought out the circles hiding in the golden bristle to find them as taut as her own, which brushed his coarsely downed abdomen.

Her blood surging at the ragged intake of Ulric's breath, she rested against him, flesh to flesh. She could feel his heart beating as if to burst as she began to work her way downward, leaving a trail of kisses that were diverted to this scar and that until she was startled to acknowledge the throbbing member nestled between her breasts. Branwen raised her thunderstruck gaze to Ulric's as he pressed her shoulders down with a anguished groan, as if to smother his passion, but his eyes were closed and his chiseled features contorted.

Slivers of alarm fought against the hot tide that would not set her free but to whisper, "Milord, have I hurt you?"

Ulric forced his eyes open with a rakish chuckle. "Milady, you are killing me with a pleasure, I fear, I may not withstand much longer. The beast needs be trapped within your womanly confines before I lose control."

Even as he spoke, urgent hands drew her up toward him, guiding her hips until his meaning was made clear by the poised, yearning flesh slipping unerringly between her legs. Fingers splayed against his damp chest, Branwen rose up and accepted its delirious thrust. Skilled as she was with horses, no steed had ever challenged her with such a fierce and jolting ride. It was like being fastened to the saddle with a most compelling bond that made unseating an impossibility, despite the slick film of perspiration between them.

Had she seen Ulric's face or heard his groaning, she might have known the moment of his shuddering surrender to her stubborn possession, but Branwen was too busy riding out the tempest that raged within, deafened by the pounding of her pulse and blinded by pure pleasure. As her senses gradually recovered from the heady bombardment, she collapsed against Ulric, still bound in the most intimate of embraces. Her breath slowed, even as the beating of his heart, until her limbs felt lifeless and leaden.

Still, she smiled dreamily as Ulric brushed her hair back from her face and wriggled, as if to remind her of their union. Branwen tightened her thighs about his hips in response and made a purring sound of contentment.

"I love you, fair raven of Caradoc. Of all my blessings and conquests, 'tis you I treasure most."

Ulric's voice rumbled in his chest as he began to sing, not in the clear booming voice with which he rendered his drinking songs, but in a husky, melodic way. It was a familiar tune, one that could bring romantic tears to the eyes of the coldest of humans and melt the heart of any maid. Branwen was no different as she listened to her lover sing of her sweetness, her beauty, her warmth, and heard the lilting pledge of his heart and soul to her.

She toyed idly with a scar on his shoulder, wondering at the tenderness of the battle-hardened soldier and wondering, too, of her incredible good fortune to have been made his. There was no denying the tears of joy that spilled over her cheeks and onto his rumbling chest any more than that she was irrevocably and hopelessly in love with the man.

Branwen must have fallen asleep, for the next thing she knew, the sun was literally blazing through the seams around the shuttered windows, slicing through the room with blades of light. No longer was she sprawled upon the virile body of her lover, but upon a pillow not nearly so inviting. A quick glance around the room told her Ulric had risen and dressed, thoughtfully leaving her to sleep as long as she could instead of rousing her for morning chapel. She stretched lazily, smiling at the warm memories and lingering sensations of their earlier awakening and loath to give them *or* the cozy bed up.

Duty called, however. She was Ulric's wife and, as

such, had guests to entertain ... at least Lady Maria, who over the course of the evening had become quite friendly and likeable. With that in mind, she threw her legs over the side of the bed and vaulted onto the cold floor before she was tempted to change her mind. Cold-footing it over to the warm hearth where she'd put the wash water the night before, she donned the robe that had been tossed across the chest at the foot of the bed and tied it at her waist.

Miriam appeared a little later with fresh water for her morning bath. After dumping out the window the old water that Branwen had scrubbed Ulric with the night before, the maid filled the washbowl with the scented brew of dried flower petals. Whether it was Miriam's thoughtfulness for taking the time to scent the water or the coldness in the room, the hurriedly taken bath was invigorating. Branwen was fully awake when she emerged a while later to join her husband and guests for breakfast.

Ulric broke off in mid-sentence at the sight of his wife coming down the corner steps into the hall, and he rose to his feet. He had heard that women possessed a certain glow about them when they were with child but until that moment had thought the idea sentimental nonsense. Gogsdeath, if anything happened to her ...

It was just a dream, he told himself as he held out his lovely lady's chair for her and then resumed his own seat. He returned her smile with a mischievous wink, which heightened the pink of her cheeks to a deep rose. With a saucy dip of shadow-black lashes, she turned to address her lady guest, leaving him to continue entertaining Lord Giles. Yet, even as he renewed their conversation about the experimental gunpowder the English lord had brought to Caradoc, he found his mind wandering back to the horrible dream that had awakened him, wet with sweat and trembling.

He'd felt so helpless. Faceless people in white and dark robes had Branwen bound to a table. Even as he entered the torch-lit chamber, with its stubby fingers of rock protruding from its floor and ceiling, he was ready to defend his wife with his last life's blood. Yet his veins froze at the sight of a raised dagger flashing over the rapid rise and fall of breasts he'd so tenderly worshipped. He ran as fast as his legs would carry him, but there was no reaching her in time. His own cries of rage and frustration had awakened him to find the girl, not dead, but sitting next to him in their bed. Then . . .

"For the love of God, man, are you daft? I see nothing to smile about . . . blowing a man's limbs off with an explosion! It was just a dreadful accident."

Ulric felt the heat of uncharacteristic embarrassment flush his neck to the point of burning. "My apologies, milord. 'Tis the curse of a newlywed and addlepated knight. I would have a look at this concoction after our meal, while Blanchard finishes the preparations for the memorial ceremony for my wife's late parents in the vaults below."

A good hot bowl of honey-sweetened porridge accompanied by fresh cakes and pan breads served to sustain Ulric against the cold air that struck him when, after eating, he and Lord Giles descended to the lower level of the keep where the supply of salt-peter, charcoal, and sulfur had been carefully stored. Ulric watched the man curiously as he took great care to mix the three ingredients according to the parchment given to him by his friend Bacon.

Blowing on his hands to keep them warm, Ulric wondered if it were wise for Branwen to come down to the level of the burial vaults cut into the rock upon which Caradoc was built. Father Dennis was known to be excessive with words when sufficiently moved, and there was no doubt that his attachment to the former Lord and Lady of Caradoc would insure a good hour's worth of testimony, if not more. All Ulric wanted was for Branwen to see that her parents had been properly buried, complete with the stone effigies he had commissioned for their tombs. Yet, even that was not worth her taking a chill in the dark and damp enclosure.

"All right, sir, stand back!"

Using a torch from the wall, Lord Giles lit a waxen fuse half the length of his arm and rushed to push Ulric to what he considered a safe distance. At the same time, a shout deep inside the recesses of the keep rose, raising alarm from where Blanchard was seeing to the opening of the family vaults. As Ulric looked back toward the door of the crypt, which was flanked on either side by carved arches with stone reliefs of the Holy Virgin in one and the angel Gabriel on the other, a stampede of panicked footfalls ensued. Lord Giles rushed over to the charge he had set and stamped out the fuse before it ignited. Wide-eyed workers met Ulric's demanding inquiry as to what was wrong with a mimic of Latin and hurriedly made a cross over their chests before running out of the keep.

"Guards!" Ulric barked, reaching automatically for the sword he was accustomed to wearing and grasping at air.

Swearing that marriage was making a cripple of him, he seized the weapon from the first guardsman who responded to his call and led the way back into the inner keep, past the dungeon and storerooms. Although his sword was ready, Ulric could not help the prick of uneasiness at his spine as he charged toward the unknown. The knight swore once again, this time condemning the fact that all the silly talk of spirits and omens was eating away at his patience, as well as at his nerves.

* * *

Aunt Agnéis was at her favorite spot in the solar repairing a doll, no doubt for one of the servant's children, when she noticed the commotion in the inner bailey and called Branwen and Lady Maria from their own needlework over to the window. "It isn't good," she fretted. "They're swearing to the cross like they've just seen the devil!"

As the crowd began to move its cautious way toward the entrance to the keep below, Branwen saw the fervor to which her aunt referred. Men were crossing themselves, women were shrieking. . . .

"Something terrible's happened. I feel it in my bones."

Without the least bit of doubt, Branwen took her leave and rushed down the steps, skirts hoisted in her hands. Lady Maria remained behind to help Aunt Agnéis down the winding stairwell, so that Branwen was on her way back into the recesses of the lower floor of the keep when they reached that level.

A sick feeling knotted in her stomach, deafening her to the expressions of horror and sympathy that echoed on either side of her as she forced her way through the crowd. The closeness and smoke-filled air from the pitch lighting did not help, nor did the faint odor of burning sulfur. Ulric, she thought desperately. Where was Ulric? If she could only find him, she'd be all right. She could face whatever terror had stricken the faces flying past her.

Finally, she was able to see the arches of Mary and the angel, which had been carved when her great-grandfather was placed into the family vault years ago. As a child, she'd thought they were as ghostly and unnerving as the inhabitants of the crypt, with hallowed eyes that seemed to follow her, just as they did at the moment. She spied Ulric's golden locks above the heads still separating them and called out to him.

"Branwen, no!" the young man shouted, upon finding her in the crowd. "Get her back!"

The closest bystanders reacted, but not soon enough. Her husband filled the opening to the vault with his large frame, yet Branwen could still see the destruction she'd glimpsed behind him. In a single flash, the scene was etched in her mind. Gogsblood, was there no end to this nightmare? Hadn't her parents suffered enough degradation upon their brutal murder without plaguing them in their own tombs? Who would have dismembered their bodies like that? Who, but . . .

"Branwen, beloved, go back upstairs. There's naught you can do here."

Ulric wrapped his cloak about his stone-still wife, not only to keep her from seeing the ransacked tomb, but because she had left the warmer hall without her own wrap. He felt her hands clawing at his back in her fierce attempt to seek refuge in his embrace and shook with the sob that tore from her throat.

"Why!"

"Oh, my stars!" Aunt Agnéis gasped behind her. "I knew it! I was afraid something like this was going to happen. 'Tis the work of halegrins!"

The very mention of the fiendish outlaws who were known to eat the flesh of the dead shot through the gathering like a bolt of lightning, instilling even more panic.

"Silence, old woman! 'Tis the work of vile men, but not demons. Worse yet, the villains are among us!"

Ulric gathered Branwen up in his arms. He could only deal with one panic at a time, and at the moment, he was worried about his wife and the child she carried. He'd heard too many tales of such shocks causing miscarriages, and ofttimes, the mother's death followed.

Branwen didn't protest when her husband carried her

through the crowd and up the steps to their room. She had seen all she could bear.

" 'Twas h ... hard enough, mi ... milord, to see them mutilated by their murderers, but to be dismembered in their own tombs ..." she cried as Ulric placed her gently on the bed.

"Dismembered?" He stared at her tear-swollen face for a moment until he realized her mistake. "Faith, love, that was not your parents on the floor, but the remains of the effigies I had carved of them. I vow, their graves were not disturbed. Whoever did this was of a vandal's bent and not ... not a graverobber or halegrin," he finished in contempt.

"But they're here in the castle!"

For the second time that day Ulric knew a gut-wrenching helplessness, except that this was no dream. He wanted to take her in his arms and swear that she had no reason to fear, but he was not certain he could be as convincing as he would like. Instead, he held her and rocked her back and forth like a shattered child, until her sobs subsided and her breath was ragged against his chest.

"I'll have the tomb restored and Father Dennis bless it. As for your safety, milove, I will have you in someone's company when I am not with you. You mustn't ride the traeth. ..."

"But if they're here in the—"

"I'll find them," Ulric averred strongly. "As God is my witness, I will find them and hang their bodies on the castle walls for the carrion."

"Excuse me, milord. I ... milady's aunt thought she should have some tea to calm her nerves."

Ulric resisted the urge to say what he thought of Branwen's troublemaking relative. Instead, he released the priceless treasure in his arms. "You rest, milove. Miriam will remain here with you." He held up his hand to silence the distraught girl who rose up on the bed in protest. "Remember," he whispered in caution, "the babe."

Branwen eased back against the pillows in resignation. She didn't feel like lying down, but kind as the woman was, she hardly felt like entertaining Lady Maria, either. Gogsdeath, who in the castle would do such a terrible thing? It had to be someone inside to get past the guards in the bailey and at the entrance. But it couldn't be anyone who knew her parents. Everyone loved Lord Owen and Lady Gwendolyn.

"Drink this, milady. Lady Agnéis says it will soothe your nerves."

Branwen rose up on one elbow thoughtfully. "Miriam, fetch me a board!"

"A board, milady?"

"A board, Miriam," Branwen confirmed, swinging her legs over the side of the bed. "I'll drink the tea, but for now, just get me the board . . . about so long and wide." She held open her arms to demonstrate.

The maid put the tea on the table by the hearth and followed Branwen to the trunk at the foot of the bed. "Milady, I don't mean to be overly curious, but . . . why do you want a board?"

Branwen sorted through Ulric's belongings. She knew she'd seen it there, the knife he'd taught her to throw and then taken from her in Westminster. Her hand struck the smooth bone handle and she drew the weapon out. "There!" she said in satisfaction. "*This* is why I need the board, Miriam. With all sorts of villains about, I am not about to fall the helpless victim!"

When Ulric left his chamberlain to oversee the restoration of the crypt and climbed the steps to the great hall, he was covered in dust and filled with a helpless rage. Lord Giles and his knights joined him at the table for the noneday meal. Masters Harold and Griffin worked side by side to see it served as her ladyship would have it, but the alliance between the new and old head stewards went unnoticed by the preoccupied lord.

"I would say your man fell asleep at his post," Lord Giles declared gruffly. "I'd have him whipped to remind him to be more alert."

"Or mayhaps, he is the one who—"

"Nay, sirs, I'll not do it," Ulric averred stubbornly. "You saw the poor oaf. He was as frightened as the rest."

"And well he might be, sir," Giles pointed out, "especially if he were guilty of neglect."

"The poor soul was overcome with remorse. He didn't do piddlely!"

Aunt Agnéis marched into the room, as grubby as the rest who tried to help gather up the pieces of her sister's effigy. She'd insisted on personally wiping off the vaults and left a pouch of garlic and herbs to ward off evil spirits.

"What makes you so sure, milady?" Giles challenged.

Agnéis helped herself to a noggin of ale and eased down in the chair next to Ulric. "Because I do, milord. I know it here." The woman placed her hand over her heart. "I've nursed that boy through fevers, set his broken arm, and taught him how to write his name. He didn't do it . . . did he, son?"

Ulric nearly choked upon realizing his wife's aunt addressed him. With a sniff, he cleared the tickling residue that had somehow gotten up his nose and stung his eyes.

"Well, *you* know, don't you?"

Gogsdeath, this was all he needed, the knight thought in chagrin. "I believe the man is sincere in his remorse."

"I would look to my Welsh servants. They've reason to—"

"No Cymry would commit such a crime against my sister and her husband!" Agnéis informed Lord Giles indignantly.

"Milady," Lord Giles began with a patronizing smile, "you women aren't given to understanding politics. Why don't you go see how your niece is doing and—"

"And you *estrons* don't understand the spirits, but I do," the older woman replied in an equally condescending manner. "You've angered the tree spirits, cutting timber without proper sacrifice."

"What is she, a *witch?*"

"Lady Agnéis . . ." Ulric began, trying to diffuse the mounting argument.

"I don't know enough to be a witch! If I did, I'd turn you into a toad, you English backside of a mule!" Puffing up her ample bosom, Agnéis turned away from Lord Giles with a sniff of disdain. "You, seventh son, you listen to your instincts, not him." She seized Ulric's hand between her gnarled arthritic ones. "Your gift will tell you more than all the eyes and ears of a normal man, much less an estron."

Ulric rose from the table to help the woman out of her chair and out of the room, if necessary, before she witlessly stirred up any more trouble for him or herself. "I will, milady, but for now, I would have you check on my wife. She was dreadfully pale when I left her, and I think if anyone can convince her to take some food, it might be you."

Agnéis's smile for Ulric melted the irritation on her face. "She'll be all right, son. You and I will see to it, won't we?"

"Of course."

"*Milord!*"

Ulric turned abruptly at the excited hail from the knight coming up the steps from the storeroom level. At that moment, he was beginning to wish someone else were Lord of Caradoc, someone more capable of making decisions than he. He could fight any enemy he could see, but this spirit nonsense was beginning to drive him insane.

"Aye, Gaylord. What is it, man?" he asked, noting the breathlessness of his companion.

" 'Tis what we've been waiting for, milord!" the man told him excitedly. *"From Hammond and Elwaid in Anglesey!"*

Chapter Twenty-three

Branwen knelt by the hearth in the master bedchamber and discreetly dumped the tea Aunt Agnéis had sent up with Miriam, while the servant prepared her dress for the day. She knew her aunt and maid meant well, but if ever there was a time for a clear head, it was now, when danger lurked *within* the walls of Caradoc. The consequence was she had had precious little sleep until the wee hours of the morning and had not awakened until after noon.

Ulric had issued orders that she was not to be disturbed or left alone after the night they'd spent in each other's arms. His presence and strength offered reassurance to her shattered nerves and soothed the reopened wounds of her parents' demise. His gentleness bespoke the noble man that he was, for he made no demands to satisfy the carnal appetite that revealed itself, in spite of his efforts to keep a blanket between them. Indeed, it was Branwen who became the aggressor, declaring her own need to be momentarily lifted from her troubles and transported to a world of physical and emotional rapture.

She had never dreamed love had so many facets, each precious in its own way. There was a lifetime ahead to discover them all. That's what Ulric had whispered to her. And then he had made her laugh until, curled in his arms, she fell asleep to a tender love ballad as only his deep, rumbling voice could deliver it. The notes were not pure, but the message came straight from the heart, leaving her more contented and soothed than any potion her dear aunt could concoct.

The women of the keep had retired to the solar after the noneday meal Branwen had missed. When she entered the room with Miriam, staunch at her side, Lady Maria greeted her with a heartfelt hug.

"Good day to you, milady. We have all been so worried!"

"Did you sleep well, dear?" Aunt Agnéis inquired from the trunk she was rummaging through.

"She's lost a doll or something she was working on yesterday," Lady Maria whispered at Branwen's curious face.

"I slept too well, it seems, Aunt Agnéis. The day is more than half gone." Yet Branwen would not have traded last night for any amount of sleep. She and Ulric had transcended the union of their bodies as man and wife to the melding of their souls. "Where are our good husbands, milady?"

Lady Maria exchanged a guilty look with Miriam, which lifted the hair at the nape of Branwen's neck in alarm.

"Is something wrong?" she whispered, wondering how anything worse than yesterday could happen.

"Yes," Aunt Agnéis piped up, slamming the lid of the trunk down in annoyance. "I can't find my doll! I had it yesterday and then was distracted by that vile business in my sister's tomb. . . ."

Ignoring her aunt's outburst, Branwen addressed her guest. "Milady?"

Lady Maria put a reassuring arm over Branwen's shoulder and guided her to the windowseat. "I would

377

say there is something *right*. Our husbands are off to catch the villains. Sir Hammond and Elwaid sent word that they were planning to pillage Beacon Abbey tonight and have left with men to await them."

"Milord said that we were not to worry you with this, milady," Miriam apologized. "He is afraid for your health."

" 'Tis *milord's* health that worries me," Agnéis injected crustily. "I don't like this . . . not one bit! My bones are aching most fierce and—"

"Milady," Miriam interrupted, " 'Tis because you spent so much time in the tower this morning! The sea air must surely make your stiffness worse."

Lady Maria turned to Branwen. "I tried to get her to take a blanket, but she wouldn't have it."

"There were six ravens on the tower wall."

Branwen felt the blood slipping from her face. *Six ravens*. She could still see the flock that had perched in the barren trees above her as she'd forged her way around the lake. Aunt Agnéis's bones had ached that day, too. Owen ap Caradoc had chastised her into silence for her uneasy feeling.

"Gogsblood!"

But for the windowseat, Branwen's knees would have collapsed, for they were the consistency of water. One death? Six? *All* of them? she wondered frantically, the toll on her father's ill-fated party all too fresh in her mind. And how could she explain to Ulric her reason for riding out to warn him? Close as they had become, her aunt's premonitions and superstitions were a sore subject, not well received.

"Miriam!"

"Milady?"

"Have McShane saddled at once and summon Master Blanchard. I would have a word with him." If it were a trap, there would be no need for explanation. If

378

not, what harm could be done by bringing additional men? Reinforced as her plan began to take shape, Branwen rose and waved her aunt toward her. "I would have a word with you, Aunt Agnéis, in the meanwhile. Lady Maria, I pray you will excuse us. Our servants know our keep is yours. Do not hesitate to ask for anything."

Concerned, the lady placed a restraining hand on Branwen's shoulder. "Our husbands are seasoned warriors, milady. Why do you not heed Lord Ulric's wishes to remain within the safety of the castle?"

"Because, milady, I fear this may be a trap. *Aunt Agnéis!*" Branwen summoned authoritatively, before turning and following in Miriam's wake.

"Your husband, I think, will be safe, geneth," the older woman assured her niece as they stepped into the master bedchamber, so that Branwen could put on additional clothing for the journey. "I insisted he wear an iron broach on his mantle."

"Tâd's raven?"

Agnéis nodded. "The same."

Her father had refused to take his sister-in-law's gift on the journey to London. Only gold and silver were to adorn Caradoc's retinue. He had humored Agnéis by wearing it during the rebellion but was not going to wear such a mean piece of jewelry before the king. It surprised her that Ulric would even consider such a request from her aunt, considering his disdain for her ways.

"Are you saying that I do not need to warn Ulric?" She wished her aunt were more coherent, but then that would not be Aunt Agnéis. From her aunt's expression, the woman wished the same.

"I don't know, geneth. Up there in the tower . . ."

Branwen slipped another dress over her current one. "Yes, tell me about the tower."

379

"Well, one of those blasted wolfhounds found its way up the steps from the hall and sent them flying off, barking like a hound from hell! My aching toes, I thought the echo alone would burst my ears, and I don't think my heart has yet to resume a normal beat."

Refastening the belt bearing the sheathed knife she'd been practicing with when Ulric entered the room the night before, Branwen glanced up. "I don't think I could be assured by one of those damned dogs!"

"They have more run of the keep than I," Agnéis agreed grudgingly. "Gwendolyn would never approve. Have you seen my doll? I seem to have misplaced it."

Hesitating momentarily upon her aunt's regression, Branwen fastened her heavy cloak at the shoulder. "I'm sure you will find it, milady. Perhaps one of the children picked it up."

Agnéis's face brightened. "I would wager that is *exactly* what happened!"

Branwen followed her aunt out of the room and down the steps into the great hall, where tables were already being set up for the evening meal. The dais would seem empty without Ulric and his knights, she mused, but Lady Maria would have Aunt Agnéis to entertain her, as well as the chamberlain, which absolved a portion of Branwen's guilt for abandoning her guest. Doughty as she was, her aunt was quite entertaining. At least Master Blanchard and Branwen were of that one common mind. Ulric and his knights were another story.

Her husband was going to be furious at her, firstly for leaving the keep and secondly for heeding Aunt Agnéis's concern. Perhaps that was why he wore the broach . . . to assuage them both. There was so much about her husband's mind she did not understand! Branwen despaired. However, she was taking no chances of being denied the lifetime together to get to know everything about him.

380

While decidedly against Branwen's leading a group of men across the cantref to Beacon Abbey, Master Blanchard agreed to assemble as many as he could, just on the off chance that Lord Ulric might be subject to a trap. The word that the overlord could be in danger spread through the keep and baileys with such speed and effect that Branwen was touched by the overwhelming show of support. Ulric had won the hearts of her people as well as her own.

Although Blanchard pleaded with her to remain behind and let him lead the assembly of farmers and craftsmen, when the foot army left, McShane and Branwen were at the lead with the chamberlain. Most were armed with whatever weapons were left by Ulric's company and the rest with pitchforks, staffs, and scythes—the tools of their labor.

She had never seen a more motley-looking group, nor more noble, Branwen thought as she looked over her shoulder at them. Behind them, Caradoc's new walls glistened in the afternoon sun, although its older tower stood grey against a winter-blue sky. There in the covered parapet was the blue-grey garbed figure of a woman watching their departure. Although Branwen waved, her aunt did not return the gesture. Poor dear's eyesight more than likely could not make her out in the group.

Standing still and solemn, the woman reminded Branwen of the stone relief of Mary in the crypt as the girl turned her sights ahead with a purpose. The figure remained that way until the entourage faded into the forest beyond the morfa. Only then did she turn to the east and raise her arms, as though reaching for the dimming horizon. Her voice was smooth and melodic with the youth guaranteed by the goddess she served as high priestess.

"Now, great goddess," she called out reverently, "they are *all* yours."

It was normally cloudy on the coastal reach where Beacon Abbey had been constructed some two hundred years before. However, that night the moon seemed to have swept away the misty shrouds with golden fingers, making visibility excellent. And making it difficult to surprise anyone, Ulric mused as he scanned the level, rock-strafed land to the east, lying fallow and eager for the fulfillment of summer's promise when it might burst with the fruits of the monks' hard labors. Most of the plunder the abbey had suffered came from the seagoing Danes of times past. Until now, there had not been an occasion to need protection on the southern forested boundary, where the compound's crumbling walls made it an easy target for pillage.

Despite Ulric's warning, the bishop was hard to convince. It was outrageous for even the lowliest of mankind to attack a church. The stores of grain and food put up for the monks and alms were hardly worthy of such dastardly conquest. However, when Ulric revealed news of the vandalism in Caradoc's crypt and the senseless burning of the nearby village, the man was shaken into granting him permission to hide the troops within the walls.

Now they waited, Ulric thought impatiently, something he was loath to do. At least half of them did. The others, under Lord Giles's direction, were taking places in the cover of the forest, from which they could spring after the outlaws made the initial assault to entrap them. The division was most likely an unnecessary precaution, but he had good reason, aside from instinct, to expect the unexpected.

Before Sir Hammond had left with Dafydd ap

Elwaid, Ulric had given his friend and fellow knight his seal. It was to be applied with the tail of the wolf straight up at the twelfth hour. In actuality, this would cant the seal counter clockwise several degrees and tell the receiver exactly whom the missive was from. The wax Ulric had picked off the parchment from Anglesey had been stamped neatly upright, as it was designed to be, but the tail of the wolf pointed instead at the third hour.

Ulric slammed his fist into his other hand in frustration. His friend was dead. He'd warned Hammond to watch Elwaid, for the lord had never been comfortable with the Welshman. Until now, he'd accounted most of his discomfiture as jealousy. Elwaid made little effort to hide his lust for Branwen and her land. He even admitted it to Ulric's face and, in the same breath, swore allegiance to his new lord, acting the noble loser.

He should have sent others with them, Ulric chided himself in remorse. Yet, Elwaid's point was valid that the more Englishmen accompanying him, the more suspicious and less likely the islanders would be to talk. Then there was the alternative, the knight considered thoughtfully. Perhaps Elwaid was dead as well. If not, he would wish he were before Ulric was finished with him, the lord vowed silently.

Spirits or Satan himself, Ulric would fight till his last breath to spare Branwen further distress. How helpless he'd been made to feel, an uncharacteristic symptom that had become worse when he walked into his bedchamber, fully expecting to find his bride sleeping peacefully, and instead found her practicing with a knife! Yes, she had welcomed his arms and attentions, but still felt the need to protect herself, since her husband had been so inept.

Tonight, however, God give him the power, he would right things once and for all. Not a man was to escape, if it meant death to them all. That was his order. There was too much at stake to even think otherwise. What those poor villagers had been through, not to mention Branwen, was enough to demand a penance worse than death, but that he would have to turn over to a greater power than he.

Neither iron nor spirit, he thought scornfully, fingering the heavy broach that fastened his cloak at his shoulder. One corner of his mouth twitched. A strange creature, his wife's aunt, as loyal and devoted as she was crazy and superstitious. He'd overheard her praying for his protection and success at chapel, which to his chagrin, she'd insisted on attending with him. How could he refuse her gift, which he had no doubt, came from the heart. Love did have its way with a man's thinking, he supposed, for he was actually starting to like the old soul.

"Milord," one of the watches called out, interrupting his thoughts. "There are riders coming across the fields bearing torches."

Ulric snapped to attention. "How many?"

"No more than a dozen, sir!"

A dozen? The answer echoed in Ulric's mind with a shallow ring. There were ten more than a score that night at the village, and that was after some had ridden off.

"Open the gates," he shouted, bounding up on Pendragon's back. "We'll meet them and invite their brethren!"

Pendragon charged to the lead at his master's beckoning kick, the others falling in behind, two by two. Upon clearing the narrow gate, however, the knights fanned out, lances ready, and formed a line. At the command of "Archers!" foot soldiers rushed out of the monastery to push through their ranks. The trained men quickly formed a line before the knights, three deep.

384

"Shoot!"

The rain of arrows sent by the first line fell just short of the charging halegrins, who reined in their horses abruptly to turn them.

"Archers to the rear! After them, good knights!" Ulric shouted reluctantly.

Something was wrong. Their number was too small. True, he admitted, resting his lance against the leather sling at his thigh, the villains were not trained fighters and did well to turn and run, but . . .

Upon reaching the end of the large span of fields, the fleeing outlaws turned their steeds once more, facing the foreboding charge of the armed knights. Ulric instinctively held up his lance, signaling the group to slow their charge. Something was definitely wrong. Cowards don't turn to fight unless cornered, and there was a forest waiting to offer them retreat.

"Milord, the abbey!"

Ulric twisted in his saddle in time to see a tide of mounted bandits, in numbers more in keeping with his expectations, spill from the very woods where Lord Giles had taken his position. So that *was* it, he thought. It was an ambush, set up, no doubt, by Elwaid.

The horsemen rushed between the archers and the knights, making it difficult for the longbowmen to fire without endangering Ulric and his outnumbered men. "Turn your steeds!" he ordered, setting the example with Pendragon and charging back toward the greater number. Mounted men with swords were hardly a match for his seasoned lancers, but the numbers would even up the difference in skill.

Where the devil was Giles? Ulric wondered as the distance closed between the two factions. The clash seemed to ring the bells of the church, initiating the beginning of the midnight hour. Metal flashed and shouts rose above the night as the armies merged. Having unseated two riders before losing his lance, Ulric drew his sword for horse-to-horse and horse-to-man combat. Their adversaries fought like demons, shrieking and howling in victory and defeat. Upon cutting his way through their eerily painted horses, Ulric brought Pendragon around.

It was only then that the mystery of Lord Giles's men was solved. Hot on the heels of the baiting halegrins, the Englishman's calvary of knights bore down on them with a vengeance. Now, not only was skill on their side, Ulric realized, but numbers as well. With a fiendish howl of his own and adrenaline pumping through his veins, Ulric kicked Pendragon's side and launched back into the fray.

The knights were practically invincible on horseback, which was why the outlaws fought hardest to unseat them. Once on the ground, they were clumsy in their armor and less mobile, making it easy for a nimble and unprotected enemy to slip up behind them and drive a dagger or spear through the joints of metal, where they were most vulnerable.

Upon seeing a fellow knight he recognized as Sir Gaylord of Rhysdale struggling to his feet, thrown from his wounded charger, Ulric urged Pendragon to his side, slashing furiously at the human wolves closing in on the man. The pack scattered, some felled by his fierce blows, giving Gaylord a chance to gain his footing and draw his own sword.

"Mi' thanks, milord!" the man acknowledged, before turning to engage swords with one of the bolder knaves, who had ventured back again.

"Caradoc, behind you!"

Pendragon kicked at Ulric's signal, but the man who sprang up behind the lord of Caradoc was too quick. Ulric fell forward at the impact striking his back, only to jerk backward as his assailant used his cloak to strangle him. Fully expecting to feel the sting of a deadly blade at any moment, he reacted with the training and experience of years on the battlefield. His sword useless at such close range, with one hand Ulric secured it beneath his leg and wrestled the material sufficiently loose to seize a shallow breath while seeking the hilt of the dagger sheathed in his saddle.

Then, twisting violently, he thrust it upward, burying it beneath the ribs of his opponent. The man screamed in agony, letting off the breath-robbing pressure of Ulric's cloak, and fell from Pendragon's hindquarters to the winter-hard ground, clutching his side. Without wiping away the blood, Ulric re-sheathed the weapon and recovered his sword.

A quick survey of the field told him the engagement was all but won. The ground, partially lit by burning brush from the dropped torches intended to set the abbey afire, was littered with bodies. Horses wandered about without riders. Some of their knights had even stopped fighting to help comrades, while the others brought the few remaining outlaws to their knees.

"Lord Caradoc!"

Ulric shifted in his saddle and looked over his shoulder in time to see a single bowman standing in the shadow of his horse, his long bow drawn and aimed squarely at the overlord. Instinctively, Ulric snatched Pendragon about to present a smaller target from the side, but the arrow was already in flight. He was jolted forward with its impact, and an eternity seemed to pass as he waited to feel it pierce his armor and burrow into his flesh.

Nothing happened. Stunned, he slowly straightened, trying to peer over his shoulder to see the nature of his wound, for he was certain he had been struck. Gogsblood, it felt as if the arrow had had a head on it the size of a fist, strong enough to knock the wind from him but not sharp enough to pierce his armor.

387

"Tonight you die, Caradoc!"

A keenly developed sense of survival was all that saved Ulric from the death-dealing sword of the now-mounted bowman who charged at him. Ulric raised his arm to block the blow, causing it to glance off his weapon with such force that he lost his hold on the hilt and dropped it in his wake. Back still aching, he rode toward a lance that was buried upright on the battlefield and snatched it up.

His adversary was upon him even as he brought Pendragon around for the charge, but Ulric was able to lift his lance to meet him. A single slash of the knave's blade broke off the tip of the lance, but there was sufficient length left for Ulric to slam his adversary, horse to horse, lance to his mail-protected chest. The lance cracked, splintering against the metal as it grazed it and rolling the man backward off his horse as Ulric bypassed him.

By the time Pendragon was in position to charge the downed opponent again, Ulric had regained his seating and waited, sword ready.

"Milord!"

Ulric caught the sword tossed to him by one of his comrades and kicked Pendragon's sides. Snorting, the horse lunged forward, prepared to ride the armed man down as it was trained to do. His master, however, had other plans. Just as they reached their adversary, Ulric leaned sideways, swinging to deflect the sting of the blade awaiting him. Sparks flew as the two blades clashed, grinding metal against metal until the hilts locked.

Left with little alternative but to let his weapon go or be unseated, Ulric loosened his hold, when Pendragon stumbled. Suddenly, he was atop his assailant, bearing him to the ground with his excessive weight. This time there was acute pain, sharp and piercing. Forcing himself to roll away, he discovered the source instantly. A sword had found entry at the juncture of his arm and shoulder.

Gritting his teeth, he withdrew the debilitating blade and lifted it as his lighter, less-winded opponent attacked him. Again he was able to parry the blade and roll away. Getting to his feet, however, proved too slow. His dizzying vision cleared in time to see Gaylord intercept the vicious charge intended for him.

Using his sword, Ulric pushed himself up to his feet unsteadily. "I would have this one, good knight!"

Cold as the night was, sweat seeped from his brow and trickled down to sting his eyes as he squared off with the hideous warrior. The man's painted face, with large white circles around his eyes on blackened skin streaked with blood-red bolts of lightning, was enough to make Ulric blink in doubt of what he saw. Within the circles, the villain's gaze took on the glow of the burning brush surrounding them.

"What keeps you, villain? Will you fight like a man or run off like a whipped pup? You say I die tonight, yet I can promise you, I will not oblige you on your say-so. You must make your word good, if you've the courage."

The man was clearly unnerved by the sight of the golden-haired warrior towering upright, sword poised. He continued to circle Ulric but made no attempt to answer or charge.

"Didn't they have yellow paint to match the jaundiced streak down your spine?"

Ulric turned deftly, keeping his face to his adversary. Beneath his armor, he could feel the warm, sticky pluck of his hauberk's underpadding over the bleeding wound with each step he took. He willed away the light-headedness that swept over him and stiffened sooner than sway.

"Gogsbreath, is this a fight or a dance?"

He would have to get on with it soon, or the burning of his torn and bleeding flesh would overtake him. Breaking the monotony, he moved forward toward his opponent, carefully measuring the remaining distance between them. To misjudge and be caught in mid-stride with his feet and sword at awkward angles could be fatal. Yet, his calculation proved needless, for the man, upon seeing him take the role of aggressor, turned and tried to break out of the circle of men who surrounded them.

"I would know who this coward is," Ulric shouted to those who wrestled the man to the ground and disarmed him, "for he is no ordinary outlaw. He wears a shirt of mail and carries himself like a man of training who is afraid to use it."

Ulric's mouth was dry, so dry that even his words seemed to stick to his tongue, slurring in their effort to get out. Despite the sweat on his brow and the sickening burning of his shoulder, a shiver ran through him like a blade of ice. He staggered forward and caught himself on his sword.

"Milord!"

Sir Gaylord and Giles were at his side, gripping his elbows in support. Ulric hadn't the strength nor the will to push them away, yet he would not give in to the blackness that darted in and out of his vision.

"Who is he?" he demanded stubbornly.

" 'Tis Elwaid!"

Elwaid. There was no surprise in Ulric's acknowledging "Ah." He'd suspected the Welshman all along. But if Elwaid was behind all this, who was the accomplice still at large in Caradoc? the overlord wondered in pained confusion. *Who?* The question echoed in the canyons of darkness that opened beneath him to swallow his consciousness.

Chapter Twenty-four

Branwen sat by Ulric's bedside and watched her sleeping husband through a haze of tears. She knew he was going to be fine. Aunt Agnéis had sworn to that on her aching toes after washing out the sword wound with boiled herb water and cauterizing it with a hot iron. Dazed from the loss of blood but conscious, Ulric never uttered one complaint when the sizzling metal welded his flesh. Branwen, on the other hand, nearly swooned from the burning hiss and stench, but kept up a brave front. Jaws knotted and teeth clenched, her husband suffered in silence and expelled his pain with the perspiration that beaded on his forehead. When it was over, he fell asleep, drained by the trauma and fatigue.

She had thought the time it took to intercept her husband's returning forces an eternity, but it was just a passing moment compared to the long night she'd spent at his side. There was naught she could do but fret, which she did well enough for a score of women. When had she come to lean on her husband so? When had he become so much a part of her that she could feel his pain? Gogsblood, but love was as hurtful as it was pleasurable!

The women of the keep treated the wounds of the other men in the great hall, although Ulric's forces had fared better than the outlaws imprisoned in the dungeon or those left for the carrion to feed upon. Hanging was undoubtedly in store for the first and would no doubt be welcome after Lord Giles and the provost were through with their interrogations. Branwen hated the idea of using force to find out their purpose and numbers. For that very reason, she had not gone down to the lower levels, even for the excommunication ceremony performed by the bishop, who accompanied the forces from Beacon Abbey to see justice done to the souls of those who would insult the church by their heresy.

That Dafydd ap Elwaid was one of their leaders had run her through as surely as his blade had stabbed Ulric. What could have happened to him? He had been like a big brother to her, someone she could argue with incessantly but for whom she had always held a degree of sisterly fondness.

Her father had been his idol, yet Lord Owen never stooped so low as to associate with the likes in the dungeon. It would take days after they were hanged to rid the lower level of their stench. As for their memory, she wondered if she'd ever forget their hideous painted faces and unwashed bodies. Wolfsheads, Lord Giles had called them.

She might have felt sorry for Elwaid, had he not tried to murder Ulric. Not only would he suffer the indignity of hanging rather than the beheading due a man of his noble station, but his body would not be given a decent burial. Like the dead halegrins, he and his excommunicated counterparts would be left for the carrion to pick to the bone.

Dafydd was disappointed not to become her husband and the lord of Caradoc, she knew, but was his disappointment so bitter that he'd see her and her family massacred? Branwen closed her eyes sleepily. There was no proof, of course, that Dafydd was connected with the royal- and orange-clad murderers, but somehow, after last night, she would not be surprised to see evidence turn up.

Worst of all, it was *she* who had asked this poisonous apple into their castle, where he might work his contemptuous way with those of lesser intellect and turn them against their new lord. She prayed they were all locked up, never to plague her loved ones or Caradoc again. She prayed it was all over now and that she and Ulric could live happily ever after, just like in the stories told to her as a child. She, Ulric, and their *son*, she mused, the fog of exhaustion eventually overriding her troubled mind.

It was after noon when the creak of the bed awakened Branwen from her overdue sleep. She bolted upright from the curled position in which she had eventually settled, to see Ulric sitting up on the bed. The dressings on his wound showed no sign of fresh blood and shifted as he experimentally rotated his arm. His resulting wince told that it was as sore as Aunt Agnéis had predicted.

"What are you trying to do, sir?" Branwen exclaimed, jumping up to wrestle his arm back to his side before he broke open the knitting flesh. "You'll start the bleeding again!" She tugged the covers up over his bared torso. "And you'll take a chill, uncovering yourself like this."

"Then help me dress, wife. I've prisoners to—"

Branwen silenced Ulric with a loud kiss. "I'll hear nothing of the sort. Lord Giles, the bishop, and your provost have that situation under control. Besides," she added with a mischievous twinkle in her gaze, "I have you right where I want you and am not about to let you ride off again to God knows what danger!"

The protest building in Ulric's expression gave way to a lopsided grin. "If that is so, woman, why are you fully dressed and sleeping in a chair?"

"I didn't wish to hurt you, milord."

Ulric's responding "Humph!" was seasoned with a growing suspicion, which he eventually voiced after a long study of her face. "Speaking of riding off to *God knows what danger*, I had the strangest dream last night. I thought I spied you coming across the lowland on that charger of your father's at the lead of a mass of villains armed with such as a farm or village might afford."

Blood crept guiltily to Branwen's cheeks.

"So you *were* there!" Ulric scowled darkly. "Damnation, woman, must I keep you in a dungeon to avoid your witless shenanigans? Do you know the danger you put our child in, not to mention yourself!" The angry knight threw off the covers Branwen had just tucked around him and swung his bare legs over the side of the bed.

"Ulric, I'm sorry and I won't do it again. Now *please* stay in bed! You're not well!" Branwen planted herself firmly before the towering figure of her husband to keep him from going any farther from the bed, lest he fall.

Pleading was her only choice. There wasn't any way she could bring herself to explain how her aunt had seen the ravens, much less the fear Branwen had felt upon associating them with her family's death. It would only make him more furious.

"You are weak, sir, and need your rest! See!" Her voice rose as Ulric swayed unsteadily and then caught himself on her shoulders. "Both of us being muleheaded won't make things right."

Although she could see that it annoyed him to admit her words had substance, Ulric sighed in resignation. "Aye, there's a ring of truth to that . . . but *you* look as though you haven't slept in a fortnight yourself." He dropped back to the mattress and tugged her to him by her waist. Upon placing a tender kiss on her abdomen,

394

he raised his earnest gaze to her. "Why don't you and the little one join me?"

Somewhere between basking in the glow of hazel-warm eyes and shivering at the velvet caress of his words, Branwen conceded. After all, she was exhausted, and if this is what it took to keep her husband abed, it was her duty to do so.

"Though I will say," she protested half heartedly as he helped her off with her dress, " 'tis shameful to be abed in the middle of the day. What will our guests think?"

"They will think . . ." Ulric broke off and winced.

"Here, let me do this! *You* can watch!" Branwen stopped her ministrations long enough to ease her husband back against the pillows. "I'd not have Aunt Agnéis sear your shoulder again!"

" 'Tis not so much my shoulder as it is my back. Damnation, it feels as though I've been kicked by a horse!"

There was no fighting the grateful twinkle that settled in Branwen's gaze as she backed away. She had seen the terrible bruise brought on by the arrow that had wedged in the iron broach Aunt Agnéis had given Ulric for protection. Whether by mystic power or by the prayer that went with it, it had kept the deadly missile from penetrating his armor and mail, as well as his flesh.

It was too much, however, for Branwen to keep to herself, particularly in view of Ulric's blatant disregard toward her aunt. "You were struck with an arrow from a longbow, milord." As disbelief streaked across her husband's face, she went on. "And were saved by the broach my aunt presented to you. We found the point of the arrow wedged in it, its shaft broken off by your fall."

Ulric's expression became veiled at the mention of her aunt, which was an improvement over his characteristic verbal irritation. Leaving him to reconcile his evident ponderings, Branwen bolted the door and most willingly finished stripping to the specifications her husband had set down for her. While she had no intention of kindling fires of passion, there were those of companionship and a deeper, more settled love to be enjoyed.

She carefully curled up against him to keep from jarring his injury, savoring all the dimensions of their new closeness. There was the transfer of heat from his flesh to hers, which relaxed muscles tightened from the quick trip across the cold floor from the door to the bed. Too, there was gratitude for all the blessings this man had brought to her. Lastly, but far from least, there was a wonderful sense of security, which made it easy for her fatigue to seduce her once more.

Masters Harold and Griffin once again did Caradoc proud with the evening meal. The artistry of the cooks, combined with the prompt and courteous presentation of the assorted dishes and courses streaming from the kitchen, was fit for a king. Lord Giles, his wife, and the bishop literally raved to Branwen, ofttimes with packed jaws that reminded her of her mother's table rules: Do not stuff your jaws with bread, as it makes you look like an ape; do not slurp your soup; and, last and above all, do not spit in the laver while washing your hands, especially if a priest is present.

While she had seen no spitting, there had been enough slurping apes at the table to send her mother into a swoon. And the English considered the Welsh an uncouth people! Branwen mused behind a smug grin. Then, there was the waste! It was just as well they had the village to feed, for the alms dishes were brimming over with barely tasted foods. But this was her English husband's way, she sternly reminded her more frugal self. For Ulric, she would compromise her Spartan upbringing. For the man resting in the master bedchamber, she would . . .

The smile teasing Branwen's lips froze as Lord Giles wiped the front of his shirt with his napkin, drawing attention to stains she had not noticed before.

"Damned wolfsheads," he grumbled to the bishop. "They even spit their blood at me!"

Gogsdeath, what manner of torture had these men been about? Branwen wondered, her stomach clenching queasily. "You drew *blood*, milord?" She could not remember a case when her father had ever mentioned having to do such a thing, especially at the supper table.

"The sight of their life's blood running ofttimes loosens their tongues, milady," the marcher lord explained patiently.

"Giles, this is hardly stuff for mealtime discussion," Lady Maria reminded him.

Although she heartily agreed, Branwen paid little notice to the lady's gentle chiding. "But these men are in chains, are they not, and helpless to defend themselves?"

" 'Tis the only way to keep such outlaws, milady. 'Tis best that you leave this business to men and tend to your sewing and household duties."

Dafydd! Angry and hurt as Branwen was, she and Dafydd had grown up together. There was some unspoken bond that declared itself even as she rebelled, astonishing herself as much as her guests.

"The man of this castle is my husband, milord, and as he is mending from his wounds, 'tis my duty as his wife to attend to Caradoc's business, not that of a visiting stranger. Please enjoy the rest of your meal." She should have seen to the prisoners herself instead of selfishly spending the better part of the day cradled in her sleeping husband's arms. She should have . . .

Branwen took to the steps leading down to the lower

level of the keep, denying further self-incrimination. If the blood on Lord Giles's tunic was any indication, she needed to fortify herself. She had never been one of those women who swooned at the sight of blood, but since witnessing the carnage of her parents' murder scene, she had become less predictable. Perhaps it was the baby.

She almost stopped. Dared she carry her child in the midst of demon-possessed villains? She ran her fingers down the length of chain around her neck to where the iron broach, which had saved Ulric's life, hung. Pressing it reassuringly against her flat abdomen, she addressed the guards on the lower level.

"I would see Dafydd ap Elwaid."

Being fellow Cymry, neither of the men questioned Branwen. Not only was it her right as lady of the keep, but they weren't about to cross that stubborn streak of determination etched on her face.

One of them took up a torch. "This way, milady . . . though I warn ye," he cautioned, " 'e's not a pretty sight."

But for his clothing, Branwen would not have recognized the young man her father had trained from page to knight. One eye was swollen completely shut, and his face was a collage of bulging bruises and dried blood. For a moment, she forgot this was the man who had driven his blade into Ulric.

"Gogsblood, Dafydd! What have they done?"

The man lifted his head, just barely enough to see her with his one good eye. " 'Tis your Englishman's justice, milady." His words were slurred through thick, split lips. He ran his tongue over them to catch the fresh blood spilled from his effort.

His reminder of Ulric stiffened Branwen's melting compassion. "Nay, Dafydd! 'Tis not so! *My* Englishman lies abed, wounded by *your* hand! Oh, Dafydd, how

398

could you? What possessed you to join with these ...
halegrins!"

Dafydd made a semblance of a smile, so hideous it
was all Branwen could do to keep her gaze fixed on his
face. "The prophesy, Branwen. 'Tis coming true."

Gogsdeath, he *was* possessed. The very fire of the
torch seemed to dance in the one shadow-dark eye
cracked open at her. "What prophesy, Dafydd?"
Branwen heard herself say. Gooseflesh crawled up her
spine to lift the hairs at the base of her neck. Suddenly,
she wished she'd brought along Aunt Agnéis.

"Merlin's prophesy, woman! A Briton will be born
here who will rule over all of England and Wales ...
just like Arthur of Pendragon. 'Twill be Arthur incar-
nate."

There wasn't a Cymry alive who hadn't heard of
Merlin's prophesy that a Prince of Wales would rule
over all of Britain again as Arthur once had. After
Llewelyn's humiliating defeat, however, it seemed a lot
of superstitious nonsense. There would be no future
Prince of Wales ... at least of Llewelyn's line.
Gogsbreath, Edward still held Llewelyn's bride!

"Ask him why he killed your family, milady."

Branwen turned abruptly at the sound of her husband's voice. "Ulric!" Without heed to the bishop and
the guest who accompanied him, she flew to Ulric and
wrapped him in her embrace. "You should not be up
and about, much less down here in this dampness. . . ."

"Without cloak or mantle, like yourself, wife?"

Wincing inwardly at the sharpness of Ulric's re-
proach, Branwen stepped away. He was pale, but anger
had given his cheeks a painted appearance and sim-
mered in his gaze. "If you will not ask, then I will,"
Ulric went on tersely. "Why, Elwaid? What had Lord
Owen done to you, much less his family?"

Dafydd's voice broke in reply. "He turned the coward! All his talk about courage and he was ready to sell his daughter for peace!"

"Dafydd!" Branwen stared at the man as if for the first time. She'd sworn not to be surprised to find Dafydd's hand in her father's death, yet this final betrayal was incomprehensible. *"You would have that fate for me?"*

"Better than have what you've got with *him!*" Elwaid spat. "But when you would not die, we found a better use for you."

"We, Elwaid?" Ulric queried. "Who is your accomplice?"

"A goddess. You've angered her, milord."

The bishop crossed himself. "This man is lost!"

"But she promised me Lady Branwen, in life or in death."

Instinctively, Branwen shrunk beneath the protection of Ulric's free arm. *Life or death?* The man was obviously insane.

Her thoughts were interrupted by the bishop's grim, ominous voice. "Let him be cursed in the city and field; and in his granary, his harvest, and his children. Let him be swallowed up by the gaping earth like Dathan and Abiram. So may hell swallow him." Seizing a torch from one of the guards, the bishop leveled his gravely pious gaze upon Dafyyd ap Elwaid. "Even as I quench this torch in my hand, may the light of your life be quenched for all eternity, unless thou dost repent! Deny this goddess, son of man, or face eternal damnation."

Instead of answering, Dafydd summoned spittle and sent it hissing into the flames thrust before him. At this, the bishop thrust the torch down and trampled it out in the eerie silence.

"So goes the light of the English and all their spawn, milords!" Dafydd split the hush with a raised voice, his words stirring similar responses in the other prisoners, who rattled their chains and chanted along with him.

"Diana . . . Diana . . . Diana . . ."

"Nooo . . . !" Branwen glanced furtively at the faces that turned to her. How could she explain to them? One hand clutching the amulet and the other her abdomen, she backed away. It was too real. The dream was going to come true. They were going to take her baby, to pull it out of her body, crying and screaming!

"Branwen!" Ulric grabbed her arm, but she easily pulled free from his single-handed grip.

"Listen to him!" she pleaded, backing toward the steps. "I must see Aunt Agnéis!"

"I'll have you, Branwen! Our son will rule Britain!"

"Treachery!"

"Heresy!"

Lord Giles and the bishop sentenced Elwaid simultaneously, but Ulric shoved past them, all the while swearing at the folly of it all, and followed the girl who took flight up the winding steps. Her fears were silly and unjustified, but might as well be as real and dangerous as she perceived them for all the effect it had on her. If Elwaid caused Branwen any harm with his rantings, Ulric vowed, he would personally cut the Welshman's tongue out and make him swallow it!

He found his wife in her aunt' arms, having rushed past those who remained at the tables and up to the woman's room. Agnéis acknowledged him with a cautioning wave of her hand, indicating he remain in silence, and then continued to pat her distraught niece on the back. The room was scant of space even with its small bed and trunk, and Ulric waited in the doorway, his large frame filling it as he leaned on the jamb with his uninjured shoulder.

"There, there, dear, that boy is babbling nonsense! He can't hurt your child!"

"I won't allow it!" Ulric injected, at a loss as to exactly what to do and yet feeling compelled to do *some-*

401

thing. Gogsblood, the woman he loved was trembling and he wanted to put all her fears to rest. Yet, how did a man deal with this hysterical sort of drivel? He might boil Elwaid's tongue and feed it to him yet.

"Wh . . . why me? Why Caradoc?" Branwen sobbed brokenly. "What have we to d . . . do with the prophesy?"

"Not a thing!" Agnéis averred indignantly. "That boy could never get his facts right. 'Tis Caernarvon, not Caradoc, that promises a king of all England and Wales."

"But my dreams. I saw them in a cave and they were taking my baby! They p . . . pulled it through my clothes. When I awoke, my elbows were scraped from trying to get away from them, it was so real."

Agnéis looked up at Ulric, as though there were something of significance in her niece's words. "*Through* your clothes, did you say?"

"Through clothes or flesh, 'tis just a dream!" the man declared impatiently. He was tempted to take his wife to their chamber, yet reason was not always successful in dealing with Branwen . . . especially in this state. Women with child were known to be flighty.

"As a seventh son, you know better, milord," the woman snapped.

Her warning was not gracefully received. Ulric's features were twisted in exasperation. "Damn a seventh son!"

He clenched his jaw too late, but Agnéis went on, undaunted by his explosion. "These pagans cannot hurt your child. Neither the death plot nor the poison worked. Doesn't that tell you both how special this baby is?"

"It tells me *Providence* is on our side!"

Aunt Agnéis smiled. "Of course! There is no greater power in flesh or spirit! We can but do what is in our means to help ourselves and leave the rest to the Almighty. He helps those who help themselves, you know."

"Woman, I do not need a Bible lesson from a superstitious old cow!"

"Ulric!" Branwen chastised raggedly, as if to say, "How could you speak to my aunt so?"

" 'Tis all right, dear. Seventh sons may have a gift, but they've also got a stubborn streak we must overlook. They mean well." Agnéis sighed heavily. "I only wish my memory was what it used to be. Then I could open his eyes."

"Gogsdeath, my ears have sorely punished me enough with this nonsense without adding my eyes to their ranks!" Ulric denounced irately. "I will be conferring with my men, should milady wish to find me."

"But your arm—"

"Is no more painful than this galling travesty!"

Pulling the door to behind him, Ulric started for the winding stone steps. He could wring Lord Giles's neck for permitting Branwen down to the dungeons and blaspheme the church by a like assault on the bishop for his stirring performance of disavowal. Politics he could deal with, but this spiritual garbage of goddesses and prophesies was enough to drive a devout, scientific mind insane.

Chapter Twenty-five

The decision was made to hang the prisoners at noon the following day. None of Giles's nor Ulric's men had seen a soul escape the night of the assault on Beacon Abbey. They were either dead or in the dungeon. Furthermore, whenever interrogation was pressed, all the rogues would babble about was Diana and the prophesy. The more they ranted on, the more ill at ease Ulric's newly-won Welsh loyalists became. The sooner the lot was hanged, the sooner all this demonic hysteria would all end.

Then, perhaps, Branwen would wear the smile a mother-to-be was supposed to and devote her energies to her duties as mistress of Caradoc and preparing the household for its new heir. As it was, her sleep had been troubled with nightmares that awakened her several times during the night, until she sat up in the bed next to him with her knife at her side, determined to remain awake sooner than suffer further. He could not coax her into his arms again, nor would she take the tea Miriam brought up for her, for fear it would trap her in the realistic dream world for the remainder of the night and cloud her ability to think.

And now *this*, Ulric despaired angrily, peering over the battlement at the troops gathered on the morfa beyond. The news that the antagonistic force from Anglesey had landed on Caradoc's shores interrupted his time at chapel that morning. Leading the soldiers was Dafydd ap Elwaid's father, Lord Gundulf. In the distance a messenger approached, waving a white flag and signaling the wish of his prospective attackers for a meeting.

"I think we should take out our knights and trample them into the dirt," Lord Giles declared at Ulric's side. "They're clearly no match!"

Ulric nodded in agreement that the Anglesey troops were outranked all around, but he denied the request. "Nay, milord, which is why a simple talk may solve this dilemma without loss of blood. At least I would know why these good men are bent on attacking Caradoc."

"Because you have their kin in your dungeon," Giles exclaimed, following Ulric down the steps along the curtain wall to the outer bailey, where initial defenses had been put into place.

Archers lined the battlements, some in black and scarlet, others in blue and orange. Interspersed with them were some of the villagers who had pledged their allegiance to Ulric, wearing the rags they had escaped with on their backs but just as determined as their richer garbed counterparts. A select few of Lord Giles's men were working in the inner bailey to pour the right mix of the experimental gunpowder into small kegs, with waxed fuses protruding. Although Ulric didn't think its use would be necessary, this was an ideal chance to test it. He doubted any of the islanders even knew of the powder's existence, much less what it could do.

There was a constant informal reporting from those on the battlements to the interested women and villagers below, who had sought asylum within Caradoc's walls. There was no panic there, Ulric thought gratefully. At

405

least he had convinced them that he was a capable warrior against armies, if not spirits.

Ulric was seated in his place as lord of Caradoc when the messenger entered the great hall. Those knights not assigned to a post were present, along with Lord Giles and the bishop, to hear what the aggressors had to say. The young knight, still pale from his loss of blood, did not give a weakened impression. As the messenger came forward, Ulric stood and watched his approach with a tolerant gaze.

Master Blanchard took the missive and passed it on to Caradoc's lord, as ceremony required. After opening it and reading the first few lines, Ulric raised an incredulous brow at the visitor.

"What manner of jest is this? This is no Welsh persecution! I have just cause for holding Dafydd ap Elwaid in my dungeon." The overlord wadded up the parchment and tossed it aside. "You tell Lord Gundulf his son stands tried of murder and pillage, not only of Caradoc's villages, but of the sacred grounds of Beacon Abbey. He has been excommunicated by the Church and sentenced by myself and his peers to hang at noon."

"Shall I take your message down on parchment, milord?" the chamberlain asked.

Ulric brushed the idea aside and repeated his disclaimer in Welsh, much to the astonishment of the messenger. "Now you've heard it in English and your own language. See that Lord Gundulf understands. I have no wish to do battle with him, but I will tolerate no insubordination such as he has inititated!"

The man nodded, eager to get out of the range of the hawk-sharp eyes following him. As he turned to dash from the hall, Ulric called after him. "And tell Gundulf that if he wishes to speak with his son, he is welcome to enter Caradoc's gates *without* escort. A father deserves that right," he added, with a twinge of sympathy for the older man. No matter what a man had done, blood was blood. A son was still a son, Ulric averred to himself with heartfelt conviction. God preserve him from ever having to face such a dilemma.

As soon as the messenger was out of sight and earshot, Ulric turned to Giles, the luxury of his personal reflections ended by his pressing responsibility as the king's overlord. "Milord, follow me. I have an idea which may discourage future whimsical affronts to my keep. I am a reasonable man, but I am not a patient one!"

Behind the door of the master bedchamber, Branwen caught her breath. What was Ulric going to do? she wondered. Peace was too tentative to rest on such a volatile temper. She hurried to the window and threw open the shutters, oblivious to the wintry air that rushed in. In a few moments, Ulric emerged from the keep with Lord Giles and their company, walking to the center of the outer bailey where Giles's men had been making up small kegs of the stinking powder, which had assaulted her nostrils the day they discovered the pillage in her parents' crypt.

Lord Gundulf was known for his temper as well. She had never, however, had reason to suspect the Anglesey lord of association with wolfsheads and halegrins. He paid handsome tithes to the church and made certain all on the island knew of it. The man was upright to the point of sinfulness, she'd heard Tâd observe wryly.

"Excuse me, milady, I have a message for you."

Branwen turned at the sound of her maid's voice, her hand against her chest, where her heart had lurched. Gogsblood, she was a knot of nerves! "A message . . . from whom?"

"One of the guards said that Dafydd ap Elwaid is asking for you."

"A shiver skipped along Branwen's back. "Elwaid?"

"Aye," Miriam affirmed, a frown crossing her face.

"Though I don't think his lordship will like it . . . even if there *is* talk of treachery."

"Treachery?" Branwen pulled the shutters closed and fastened them. "Does Elwaid know his father is threatening siege to Caradoc?"

Miriam shrugged. "I don't know, milady. If so, it seems he ought to warn the man how strong milord and his men are. I've never seen so many soldiers. The battlements look ablaze with their colors and Lord Giles's men are talkin' . . . I mean, talking like they're going to blow the Welsh to kingdom come!"

The fact that she had just seen Ulric approach the men from Merionwythe, who were working with the powder, did little to slow Branwen's impulsive race for steps. Miriam followed on her heels, her voice rising in alarm.

"Milady, take his lordship down with you, I beg you! He'll not like this at all!"

"Won't like what? What's happening?" Aunt Agnéis demanded behind them, bewildered by the commotion that drew her from her favorite vaulted windowseat and her stitchery.

"You speak to her, milady!"

Branwen heard Miriam's plea to her aunt as she hurried through the hall to the winding stairwell beyond, which led to the lower level of the keep. She'd have Elwaid taken out in chains to speak to his father. The least Dafydd could do was tell the truth, now that it was out. Such an act could mean his very salvation, considering the lives it would save. At least, this was his chance to do *something* honorable before his sentence was carried out and avoid the eternal damnation the bishop had foretold.

If Ulric had warned the guards not to let her into the dungeons of the castle, they, as well as the dungeon master who had been making nooses for the execution, were too distracted by the proceedings outside to notice her. Her footfall light, she rounded the last of the stone steps and pressed on past the heavy oak doors of the storerooms in the dim, smoky glow of the torches. Her hand rested over the iron amulet she wore hidden beneath her clothing so as not to irritate her husband further.

She spied Dafydd, still hanging listlessly from the chains mounted over his head on the dungeon wall. With an urgency in step and voice, she approached the excommunicated knight. "Dafydd, your father's here. . . ."

Before Branwen knew what was happening, a hand came out of the darkness and pressed over her mouth. Then, to her astonishment, Dafydd straightened and uncoupled the chains about his bloodied wrists with no effort. He grinned at her, wincing as the gesture cracked his broken, swollen lips.

"Of course he's here, milady. 'Tis only fitting for our wedding day!"

Wedding day! Branwen struggled against the hands that dragged her further into the recesses of the keep. Gogsbreath, what was he speaking of? How did he and his companions get loose? She fought the dizziness caused by the hand pressing against her mouth and nose and twisted her head for air. The sniff of the damp, moldy smell that always permeated the sun-starved chambers did little to help. Her knees nearly went out from under her as her captor pulled her back to allow Dafydd access to the door of the crypt.

Her eyes widened when instead of attacking the locked chain on the wrought iron door, the dark-haired knight assaulted the statue of the Virgin Mary! At least, that was how it appeared at first. At the scraping sound of rock, the stone figure was moved aside, revealing a narrow opening in the rock.

"Bring her along and cover our tracks!"

Although the opening was small, it gaped at Branwen like the foulest monster of her dreams. *This was it!* This was the tunnel through which Dafydd had carried her— the tunnel leading to the cave where they'd taken her baby. At the thought of her child's danger, Branwen thrust aside her fear and came to life. She bit the flesh of the hand clamped over her mouth, causing her captor to momentarily loosen his hold. Her scream for help, however, was cut short as Elwaid leapt at her to stifle it with a piece of his tattered shirt. Desperately, she whipped out the knife at her waist, only to have it knocked ruthlessly from her hand.

Its clatter to the floor was drowned in the scuffle of feet that ensued. Then the hole seemed to swallow her *and* the men forcing themselves through the narrow passage. The darkness ahead closed in on them. That they were going downward, Branwen could make out, for she'd ceased to struggle for fear of them dropping her. Behind her, she heard the scrape of stone against stone again, and the thin thread of faint light from which she'd come was snuffed by a black, heavy breathing, then silence.

Ulric of Caradoc stood on the battlement as Lord Gundulf rode up to the gate accompanied by six armed knights. The island lord's stallion showed the signs of weathering a lean year, for its dull brown coat was stretched over a frame meant to carry more meat. Gogsbreath, destroying the Welsh crops and taking their stores had not left a pleasant taste in Ulric's mouth. Yet, it had to be done to end the rebellion.

Now was a time for peacemaking. He was a warrior and even *he* had had his fill of warfare. Blood battles and adventure had amused him too long. Now it was a warm, willowy wife with haunting blue eyes and a kiss sweet as an angel's own that obsessed him and set his pulses racing. He wanted to spend his life with her and raise their children here on the rugged coast, which spawned her and enchanted him. But to do so, he had to show strength and perseverance or all would be lost. For that reason, Ulric nodded to the men by the catapult.

The rope snapped, releasing the spring. Its lighted fuse hissing, it flew through the air and landed a distance in front of the approaching company. Their horses balked and backed away a few steps before they were brought under control again.

"I said *without* escort. Keep your men back or suffer the consequences!" Ulric warned them.

"How do I know I can trust you, Ulric of Caradoc?"

"You can trust me and stay away from yon keg for the count of ten to a score!"

Beside Ulric, Lord Giles began counting. His voice seemingly grew with the whispered echoes along the battlements, until every man on the wall was marking off the time with him. If the powder didn't go off when it hit, it would surely do so when the fuse burned through the hole in its side and ignited the powder, he thought, waving at his archers to prepare them to keep the entourage back by force, if they should ignore his warning. He wanted no bloodshed, only a show of force.

"Seven and ten, eight and ten, nine and . . ."

On *ten*, the air filled with the thunder of the explosion. The horses and riders staggered backward and turned to run from the shower of splintered wood that rained about them, while the men on the battlement cheered boisterously. Ulric's eyes glowed with appreciation for what he had just witnessed.

He looked to where Lord Gundulf waved at him fran-

411

tically. "I will come alone, milord! Keep you your barrels of thunder!"

Exchanging a wry grin with Lord Giles, Ulric answered. "Come then, sir! You will see I am a man of my word."

To reassure the shaken lord, Ulric walked down to the gates himself to greet him. Lord Gundulf swung down off his steed with the dignity of his station and handed it over to one of Caradoc's grooms, before turning to meet the fair-haired lord he had heard so much about.

"You have my son in your prison, sir. I demand to know why."

"Dafydd ap Elwaid has been sentenced by me and my court for murder and pillage."

"What proof have you, sir? Until just a few days ago, he was on Anglesey doing *your* work."

"And what of the knight I sent with him . . . Sir Hammond?" Ulric queried. Despite his furtive hopes, he was not surprised when Gundulf's expression became confused.

"There was no other knight but my son."

"Our proof against your son, sir," Lord Giles interceded, "is catching him in the act! He attacked Lord Ulric and buried his sword in milord's shoulder, before he was scrubbed free of his pagan paint!"

"Pagan paint?" Lord Gundulf swore and raised his eyes heavenward. " 'Tis the work of that south Wales witch he met while serving with the prince. She enchanted him, that's what happened." The man extended his hand to Ulric. "My humblest apologies, milord. I was told Dafydd was taken without cause and came prepared to fight to my last to save him. Instead, I have been humiliated."

The spiritually wounded man turned to look back at the morfa where his troops awaited him. "Dafydd had a

412

hand in that vile work?" he echoed, staring at the remains of the village between the coast and the forested hills.

"He was only recognized during the attack on Beacon Abbey, milord," Ulric informed him grimly.

"Only God can save his soul!" the bishop added, crossing his chest. "If he would but repent, he would not suffer eternal damnation . . . only that on this earth. Perhaps you, milord, might speak to your son. He only spits in contempt at myself."

The proud carriage with which the Anglesey lord had ridden up to Caradoc fell with his shoulders. He nodded solemnly. "I will try, Your Grace."

There was little said on the walk through the black alley to the inner bailey. Lord Gundulf did not fail to notice the stack of kegs Ulric had had brought forth in preparation for battle, but he made no comment. His silent acknowledgment of it was enough to tell Ulric he recognized the meaning of the powerful explosion as well as did the overlord himself. Ulric also knew there would be no attack on the castle while the island lord was inside, not because of Gundulf's presence, but because the superstitious Welsh were no doubt still murmuring over what they'd seen.

"Milord!" Shaken from his ponderings by a panicked shout, Ulric glanced ahead to where one of his guards bolted out of the keep. "The prisoners have escaped!"

With an oath not fit for the ears of the devil himself, Ulric broke into a loping run, his hand ready on the hilt of his sword. "Which way, man?"

At this the guard stopped, his face contorted, as if his words pained him. "I don't know, milord. They . . . they just *disappeared!*"

A singular gasp rose from the crowd gathering around them as Ulric grabbed the guard by the front of

413

his hauberk and shook him. "Damn you, I said where did they go?"

"S . . . so 'elp me, milord, they're just gone! None of us saw or heard a thing!"

"Impossible!"

Tossing the man aside, the lord of Caradoc drew his sword and charged into the lower level of the keep. His long strides made it necessary for those who followed to hasten their steps to a near run. Ahead of them, the dungeon master fell, frightened, to his knees.

"I swear, milord, 'tis like they melted out of their chains and into the air! They was here when I went to fetch the extra rope for the hangin', and when I come back, they wasn't!"

After examining the chain that had held Dafydd ap Elwaid, Ulric slung it aside. It had not been forced. Somehow, someone had slipped past his guards and let them go. He would not consider the idea that they had simply vanished. *Flesh* did not simply vanish.

"By all that's holy, they must be here somewhere!" He looked over the sea of faces ready to back him, despite the uneasiness in their gazes. "I want every nook and cranny of this keep searched . . . and gather all the women into the hall with an armed guard. If they took weapons . . ."

"The weaponry has not been opened, milord!" a guard reassured him. "I checked that first."

"Then disperse!"

At his own command, Ulric broke through the ranks and started up the steps, but at the sight of Lord Gundulf coming with him, he stopped. "And what are you about, milord?" Had the island lord come to afford a diversion for the escape? Instinct told Ulric the man was as shocked as he, even as Gundulf pledged his sword.

The elder lord met Ulric's gaze steadily. "My son has

414

disgraced me, milord. I ask that you allow me to exonerate the name of Elwaid by my service to you."

Branwen, Ulric thought, distracted by a flash of alarm in the midst of his bewilderment. Aunt Agnéis's advice haunted his mind. *Listen to your instincts.* Taking them to heart, he accepted Gundulf's offer and turned to vault up the stairs two at a time.

Unwittingly, Gundulf had provided a diversion for his son's escape, and if Elwaid and his men were free, Branwen was in danger. By the time Ulric crossed the hall and climbed the steps to the second floor, his wound had begun to ache fiercely. Ignoring the pain, he threw open the master bedroom door.

"Branwen!"

Instead of his wife, the maid Miriam bolted upright from the windowseat and hastily fumbled with the shutters. "Is something the matter, milord?"

"Where is my wife?"

The maid clasped her chest, her brown eyes widening. "As God is my witness, milord, I begged her not to go to Elwaid! Ask her aunt!"

"Milord!"

Ulric pivoted, nearly running over his chamberlain. "What?"

"Lady Agnéis is missing! I found this doll in her windowseat and her dropped stitchery. I fear she has met with misfortune."

Although he didn't move, Ulric felt as if someone had delivered a massive blow to his stomach. Branwen, the old woman, *and* Elwaid missing! The facts ran through his mind again, as if to convince it of that which it refused to accept.

"God preserve us!" Miriam shrieked, darting down the steps as if the devil himself were on her heels.

"Let me see that!" Lord Giles ordered, taking the straw doll from Blanchard's hand. *"This,"* he cried,

415

shoving it into Ulric's face, "is witchcraft! 'Tis *you*, milord, and here is a pin driven into your shoulder!"

Ulric stared at the likeness blankly, his thoughts consumed by his missing wife. One man or woman might have slipped past his guards, but the lot of escaped men could not possibly have done the same, he reasoned, trying to ignore Giles's incriminating evidence against Branwen's doughty aunt. Which meant that there was *some sort* of exit on the lower level.

"Blanchard, assemble the guards on the lower level!"

"But we were just there!" the chamberlain stammered.

"I told you the woman was a witch!" Giles declared, shoving the doll at the bishop, who refused to touch it but crossed himself for protection from whatever evil it might carry.

Ulric seized the doll impatiently and tossed it to the floor. "This is not the work of witches, but of flesh and blood men! Gogsdeath, you are a man of science, Merionwythe! Those men did not vanish, they escaped . . . and I intend to discover how!"

With a train of men behind him, Ulric descended to the hall and stopped only long enough to take a handful of tallow dips from the candelabra on the table. Upon reaching the lower level, he turned to address his following.

"The lives of my wife and possibly her aunt are at stake, and time is of the essence. I want six men of sound wit, who do not soak their trousers at the thought of spirits or like things!"

Hazel eyes burning like the torches on the walls challenged the gaze of each man who stepped forward, before coming to rest upon Lord Gundulf. He handed the first candle to the islander and then the others to each man in succession, until one was left for himself.

"Light your candles, gentlemen, and scan every crack

and crevice with their flames. Search for any sign of a draft which might indicate a hidden passage. My wife said there was a cave with a hot spring accessible from the traeth. It is entirely possible that is how the villains escaped into the sea. Blanchard!"

"Aye, milord!"

"Take half these men and search the seawall beneath the keep for any openings." Gogsbreath, why hadn't he listened to Branwen that day on the traeth? If his shallow manly pride had caused her to suffer any harm . . .

Ulric broke away from his thoughts and marched straight to the back of the keep where the family crypt had been constructed. There was no time for recrimination, only for action. His own lighted candle in hand, he began to run the flame slowly along the damp rock walls, when he noticed the torch that had been hung in the bracket beside the crypt door flickering more brightly than the one on the other side. His heart stilled as he abandoned his methodical search and followed his instincts.

He had never noticed the statue of the Virgin Mary was covered with more soot than that of the angel on the other side. He shoved the candle behind the statue, affording enough light to see what might never have been discovered before. A thin crack outlining an opening filled with stone. As he moved the candle flame around its perimeter, the fire danced hungrily as if seeking the draft that pulled it into the rock.

"Giles!" Ulric shouted, throwing down the candle to move the statue out of the way. As he did, he struck something with his foot. It skittered a short distance away, but the very sight of Branwen's knife numbed the overlord with growing fear. "Giles!"

"Here, man!" the marcher lord assured him, grasping the statue from the other side. Their combined efforts brought the stone figure out with relative ease, revealing a dark opening. "By all that's holy!" Giles swore, crossing himself.

" 'Tis nothing holy nor spiritual about this! The architect and master mason who were assigned to the repairs of the existing keep were murdered because they discovered this, I'll wager!" Ulric averred, giving free rein to his reason. "And this leads to the cave below. 'Tis no doubt some pagan temple."

The scene from his nightmare flashed clearly into his mind as he snatched down the torch to enter the abyss. *Listen to your instincts.* God forbid, he prayed, motioning for the others to follow him. God forbid that he had somehow had a vision. God forbid that Branwen . . .

Ulric refused to acknowledge the sickly fear that turned green in his stomach and rose bilious at the back of his throat. *He knew!* Damn the old woman and her superstitious seventh son nonsense, he knew! But Branwen had not died in his dream. He'd awakened. Would that this too was a dream, but the cold, wet walls and the weight of his body on his booted feet was as ominously real as the sounds of the men moving behind him.

The stone walls seemed to close in on Ulric, crushing his very breath from his chest, yet he forged onward and down the narrow incline. The feeling was not new. He'd known it once before when he'd led a group of soldiers through a tunnel cut out by sappers during the siege of a French castle. It was devilish fighting if ever there was such. Hell itself afforded more breathing space! He'd vowed never to allow himself to get in such quarters again, but he'd made other vows since—vows far more important to him. If he suffocated, it would be trying to save the wife and unborn child to whom he'd pledged his life and his love.

The tunnel seemed endless. They had surely gone below the very level of the sea, Ulric thought at one time, yet they had not heard it. One step in light was like a

418

hundred in darkness. At long last, the incline beneath them leveled off and Ulric handed his torch to the man behind him, so that his vision might not be impaired by its glare. If there was light ahead, he wanted to see it first. He preferred the element of surprise on his side.

"Weapons ready!" he whispered over his shoulder.

The hushed command echoed behind him, dying in the darkness of his wake as he rounded a curve in the passage. As instinct had told him, there was a faint glow of light indicating their destination was at hand. He ordered all torches passed to the rear and gave the men time for their eyes to adjust to the change in light. It wouldn't do to charge blind into the midst of their enemy.

"Diana, Diana!"

Chanting wafted softly into the tunnel from the main chamber of the cave, carrying with it the warm, damp air of the hot springs Branwen had told him about. Even the walls had lost some of their chill, Ulric thought, his free hand splayed on the damp rock. Ahead of him, he saw a singular shadow of a guard, left as a precaution, no doubt, should their escape route be discovered.

"Great goddess, we offer you the daughter of Caradoc and the unborn bastard that seeks to make false Merlin's prophesy."

Without hesitation, Ulric handed his sword to the man at his back and with his dagger slipped up behind the guard. The guard's grunt of fatal surprise blended in with the chanting, which was now increased in volume. Taking back his sword with his good arm, Ulric moved stealthily behind a large protrusion of rock.

Through the steam from the hot springs and smoke from the torches, he was able to make out a circle of robed figures standing about a flat table of stone. Those in white gathered about the table wearing hoods and gold adornment on their arms and round their waist.

419

The torch-lit walls were painted with astrological signs and murals of the sky.

"We praise the mother of your firstborn son, great goddess! Caradoc's one and only lord and heir to the throne of all England and Wales!"

"Diana . . . Diana . . . !"

"But curse the womb that carries an English bastard!"

"Diana . . . Diana . . ."

"Bless this blade which will cut the false lord from her womb and spill the shameless blood of deceit in ultimate sacrifice!"

To Ulric's horror, the group parted to permit view of the woman he knew was to be sacrificed, before he even saw her struggling against the bonds that held her down on the table in the midst of her faceless tormentors. As in the dream, there was no way he could cross the bed of rock broken by the random formation of the hot springs and reach her in time. Her name choked in his throat.

"Hold!" The figure next to that of the priestess grabbed her arm, freezing the deadly blade in midair. "You promised her to me!"

"So you shall have her, Elwaid . . . in the *next* life!"

Seizing upon the moment's reprieve, Ulric found his voice. "Attack!" His feet barely touched the ground as he raced between the startled robed figures, straight for the table where Dafydd ap Elwaid struggled with the priestess. "I will cut your pagan hearts out and feed them to the fish!" he swore, waving his sword and clearing the way for his men like a charging demon from the depths of hell.

The pagans stripped off their cumbersome robes and hoods, revealing less than pious weapons with which to defend themselves against the attacking soldiers. Death flamed in their eyes, for to lose this battle guaranteed its certainty. Iron clashed against iron and sword to wooden staffs, as all nature of combat was engaged.

Just as Ulric reached the foot of the table, Elwaid wrung the knife from the priestess's hand and quickly laid it to Branwen's throat. The girl on the table cried out Ulric's name, but the bloody rag stuffed in her mouth smothered it. Her eyes were almost as wide as her deathly white face, reaching out for him with her heart.

"Hold, milord, or I promise, I will slit the lady's throat."

Much as he strained to unleash his fury upon the bludgeoned-faced knight, Ulric checked his momentum. "Then neither of us will have her, and I promise, I shall take great pleasure in sending you speedily to hell."

"But you heard our priestess! I shall have her in the afterlife. You would but speed our reunion!"

"Son, for the love of God!" Gundulf shouted from the opposite end of the cave, his feet littered with the bodies of the two pagans who had tried to stop him.

"Nay, Father! For the love of our goddess, who has delivered Branwen to me, despite *your* God and honor!" Dafydd nodded to Ulric. "Cut her bonds with your sword, as I would prefer to take her with me now and enjoy her in this life."

Sweat beaded on Ulric's brow as he complied with the order. Although there were no flames save those of the torches, he felt as if he had walked straight into the devil's own chamber. "I will hunt you down, Elwaid. Surely you know that."

"But where, milord?" Dafydd taunted, keeping the knife cold against Branwen's flesh as he helped her to her feet. "Look you now! Where is our priestess? Why, she has vanished! *Vanished!*"

Ulric scanned the mottled wall of the cave quickly, confirming the man's statement. The woman had gone, but with so many places to hide, it was not likely very far. "I have men on the traeth. She'll not get far."

Dafydd's confidence wavered momentarily as he thought. "But she doesn't have the escort I do," he recovered quickly. "Lord Ulric of Caradoc will precede me and procure a horse for me and his lady."

"Where?" Ulric inquired. If he could catch Elwaid unawares in the darkness of another tunnel . . .

"Put down your sword and dagger, milord, and I shall show you."

Unaware that the fray had ceased behind him and that his victorious men watched, helpless to come to his aid, Ulric stepped into the tunnel Elwaid indicated with a motion of his head. Like the other, it was long and narrow, but at the opposite end, there were specks of light, as if pricked through the surface of some sort of crude blanket over the opening.

"Damn you, Elwaid!" he heard a familiar voice behind him swear. "You've a turkey's wit if you think you can escape!" Although he could not see her, Branwen had evidently spat the gag from her mouth. What she proceeded to say in her native tongue would have put a smile on his lips, were her situation not so tenuous.

"Gogsbreath, you've a sharp tongue, geneth! I shall enjoy curbing it!"

Undaunted by Dafydd's threat, Branwen ranted on. "And I can't see a damned thing! I . . . ouch!"

Ulric swung about at his wife's startled scream, barely able to make out her slight figure pitching forward. Taking advantage of the distraction, he charged at the upright Elwaid. Their bodies crashed with a thud as Ulric's superior weight carried Elwaid to the ground. He could feel Branwen scrambling away from their flailing feet and experienced a flash of relief before concentrating on overpowering his adversary.

Somewhere between them no doubt was the ceremonial knife, but as he did not yet feel its sting, Ulric assumed it had been knocked from Dafydd's hand by the fall. Rising up, he drove his fist downward and was rewarded by the crunch of bone against flesh and a pained outcry. Suddenly, the side of his head exploded with a balled fist, splintering the darkness with shards of agonizing light, which threatened his consciousness. Dazed, Ulric touched his temple and felt the sticky warmth of his blood, just as the rock-hard object struck him again. A stone, he realized, breaking the contact with the back of his hand and focusing on trying to wrest the impromptu weapon from his opponent.

"Ulric, I've got the knife!" Branwen shouted, her voice ringing like thunder in his ears above the pounding of his pulse.

"Get back . . . Ugh!"

"Ulric?"

Ulric reeled against the stone wall, kicked full in the stomach. His head struck the hard rock behind him, so that darkness swirled dizzily in front of his eyes.

"Ulric, where are you?"

"Lost, you she-devil!"

Branwen's sudden scream cleared the blackness away. Ulric forced himself from the wall toward the struggling figures. His legs felt leaden, slowing his progress as he crawled after them. His wife's name echoed in his mind with each clawing drag of his increasing weight, until he registered nothing except that and his sheer will to go after her.

He never noticed the bulky figure that swiftly crept past him until it completely blocked his vision. At first he thought consciousness had finally slipped away, except that he could still hear the sounds of a struggle and felt the weak sweat trickling down his face.

"For the love of God, Father! You've killed me!" Dafydd ap Elwaid screeched in the canyons of Ulric's mind, conjuring a picture that eventually came to light with the men charging into the tunnel with torches behind them.

Lord Gundulf stood at his son's back, his hand on the hilt of a dagger buried there. In disbelief, Elwaid pulled his gaze away from the man's stern face to look at Ulric. It was then that Ulric saw it, the knife Elwaid had wrested from Branwen. With a vengeful gleam in his eyes, Dafydd turned the blade toward the woman he still held against him.

"I take you to be my . . . wife!" He thrust the knife inward and fell forward, forcing the girl on the blade with his dying weight.

"Branwen!" Although he was lifted to his feet by his men, Ulric made his way to the pile of figures Lord Gundulf attempted to separate on his own. His heart went out with her name. "Branwen!"

"Husband?" she gasped weakly, straightening from her crouched position as the dead man was hauled off her.

"Gogsblood!" Ulric helped her uncurl, his voice strangled at the sight of the knife protruding from her abdomen, where blood stained her dress. "God in heaven!" he anguished, grasping the hilt to remove it. He swore at the glaze that stung his eyes and tugged at the knife, only to have her garments pull away with it. It was stuck in something . . .

"My amulet!" Branwen cried out excitedly, as if hardly believing what had happened herself. "It struck my amulet! I . . . I'm not hurt! *Ulric?*"

Ulric dropped to his knees, weak with relief, and renewed his effort to dislodge the blade from the iron broach that had once saved his own life. He didn't believe in its power, but he thanked Providence for the silly notion that caused his wife to wear it. "You're bleeding!" he whispered hoarsely, trying to find the source of the spreading scarlet stain on her garments.

424

"I . . . I must have cut my finger." Branwen held up her hand to the light to display the culprit. "I tried to grab the blade and then all I knew was that I was falling."

Tossing the freed knife aside, Ulric pulled his wife to him tightly, oblivious to the tears that streaked his face. "Gogsbreath, woman, you will be the death of me yet!"

Branwen thought her legs would melt from the earnest proclamation. She slipped down in his embrace until her face met Ulric's and felt a burst of love within at the contact of their eyes. How she loved this fierce and tender man with all her soul! She embraced him in return, savoring the security and love of the world he'd introduced her to.

"How did you find me, milord? Did you at last follow your instincts?"

Ulric drew back his head to see the impish expression on her face. Gogsbreath, what a fetching creature. "I used my God-given wit."

"The wit of a seventh son?" she asked smugly.

"The same as our first son will have, I pray."

"But he is the son of a seventh son," Branwen pointed out as a burst of sunlight entered the tunnel, where Lord Giles and his men tore down what appeared to be a moss-covered curtain. "And *there* is the traeth, milord. I told you there was a cave containing a hot springs with an access from it. Now I know why Aunt Agnéis didn't want me to come near it when I was little! 'Twas some sort of pagan temple I'd stumbled upon."

Branwen's remark settled uncomfortably in Ulric's mind. After all, the old woman was still missing and . . .

"Lord Ulric! *We've found the witch!*"

Chapter Twenty-six

"*My aunt is not a witch!*"

Branwen stomped back and forth before the dais where Ulric, Lord Giles, the bishop of Beacon Abbey, and the other knights and lords sat. Despite Ulric's request that she rest and let him handle this new development, she had changed into fresh clothing and emerged remarkably renewed, her cheeks ablaze with indignation at Lord Giles's charge. Her raven hair, free of the confines of a woman's traditional headgear, bounced about her white furred collar as she swung about.

"If she said she was trying to find the entrance to the cave to rescue me, when she slipped and hit her head, then I believe her!"

"And how, milady," Lord Giles inquired in a patronizing tone, "do you explain the doll, made in your husband's likeness?"

"And the white robe discarded a short distance from where she escaped from the cave?" the bishop supplemented.

"The priestess escaped and left it there to incriminate an absentminded old woman," Branwen replied with less conviction than she cared to present. She turned to Ulric in desperation, her gaze seizing his very soul with its plea. "Milord, if she wished us harm, how do you explain the amulet saving our lives?"

" 'Twas her tea that left you disoriented, according to your handservant, milady."

"But Aunt Agnéis was not with us when I was poisoned!"

"Her accomplice was Elwaid," Ulric pointed out reluctantly. "However, milords, I contend this woman was no witch, but a superstitious old fool. Her deeds were no more than those of a mere woman of flesh and blood with a knowledge of herbs and potions capable of accomplishing her means."

"Which *were*, milord?" Giles prompted dubiously.

"At first, when my mason and architect were murdered, to stop the discovery of the cave beneath Caradoc and further building."

" 'Tis heresy, nonetheless!" the bishop declared.

Ulric ignored the comment. "As for the poisoning of my wife, I think it can be safely assumed that was by Elwaid's hand. His ineptness, whether intentional or nay, served to our benefit, in that she lives."

"Why the murder of Lord Owen's company, then?"

"To make it all appear spawned by a political cause rather than a religious one. Had Branwen been there during the attack, I believe she would have been abducted rather than murdered like the rest. After all, from what we overheard, she was needed to birth the babe of this prophesy. When the deed failed to thwart our marriage, their means became more desperate. The poisoning itself, I think, was meant to throw suspicion on myself and divide us further."

Branwen stepped up to the dais and leaned forward. "If you think to make it easier on my aunt, sir, you are not! You merely switch her fate from burning at the stake to hanging!" Her voice caught with emotion. "I know my aunt! She would not harm a single soul, much less involve herself in these vile deeds. She is innocent!"

"She is guilty and should be burned at the stake!" Lord Giles insisted, slamming his fist on the table in such a way as to give Branwen a start.

"That decision has yet to be reached, milord! My wife may speak on her aunt's behalf without interruption!"

Ulric shifted in his chair, as if it bore the thorns of the prickly situation he found himself in, and nodded for Branwen to go on. Gogsblood, there had to be some way to resolve this!

"I can produce witnesses throughout the cantref who would swear to my aunt's piety and goodness. Father Dennis, have you ever known a more godly woman?" Branwen addressed Caradoc's priest, who sat in grim silence next to the bishop. "She's gifted in healing and sometimes foresight, yes, but 'tis a *God*-given gift, as you yourself proclaim your wit to be, sir!" the girl declared, turning back to Ulric.

It was like a woman to take a man's words and use them against him, the overlord mused, not without a degree of humor and admiration for his wife's resourcefulness. If she could convince no one of her aunt's innocence, Branwen ap Caradoc stood a better than fair chance with him. Hence, he must guard himself against letting his heart gain the vantage over his head. He did not believe in witchcraft, yet he could not believe Agnéis, the absentminded, guilty of conspiracy, either.

"That doll was planted among my aunt's things by the real culprit, who has yet to be revealed," his wife went on with her logic. "Yes, she was running on about a lost doll, but I saw her mending one of the servant's toys just a few days prior. 'Tis *that* doll she spoke of losing! She worked no sorcery, but kindness toward a child." Branwen crossed her arms in derision. "For *that*, you have her in a dungeon like a criminal. She is not allowed to speak for herself, but to a prelate who has already made up his mind. If she were a witch, do you think bars could hold her? 'Tis likely she'd turn the lot of you into toads, for all the wit you are showing!"

The rising pitch of his wife's voice deepened the frown on Ulric's brow. This distress could do neither Branwen nor her child good. "Milady, I beg you, be seated at my right, as is your place, and let's discuss this matter in a less emotional way."

"Might I speak, milord?" Lady Maria, who watched the proceedings from the opposite end of the hall, rose from her chair in deference to Ulric.

"Please do, milady. We would have as much light shed on this subject as can be."

"I have known Lady Agnéis but these last few days, yet I would vow on my life that she is naught but a kindly old woman, filled with superstition but nonetheless devout in her faith."

"Gogsblood, Maria, has she bewitched you, too?"

Lifting her chin with a defiant tilt, the woman rebelled against her husband. "Only by kindness and a good heart, milord."

"And the *voice!*" Branwen leapt from the chair she had just been coaxed into taking, the renewal of her aunt's defense sparked by a sudden recollection. "The priestess had a higher, purer voice! 'Twas not that of my aunt, which breaks and fluctuates with age!"

"Milady," Lord Giles derided, "you were frightened witless!"

"Unlike present company, which claims to be scientific, I have never been frightened witless by superstition!" Upon glimpsing Ulric's arched brow, Branwen quickly amended, "I have been frightened into caution, but not out of my wits! Admit it, gentlemen, there is someone among us who has outwitted you all *and* your exploding science! You would have us dim-witted, backwards Cymry intimidated by combining your powders into an explosive one, when it is nothing any Welshman with like knowledge could not do!"

"This is outrageous, milord!" Giles decried to Ulric. " 'Tis not I that am on trial here, but the woman Agnéis."

"*Lady* Agnéis!" Branwen corrected heatedly.

"*Gentlemen, gentlewomen!*" As the bishop rose to speak, Branwen gave into the strong but gentle arm pressing her back to her seat. "In matters of heresy, it is customary for the Church to make judgment. I propose the matter be settled by stones."

"No!" She tore out of Ulric's grasp. "She's an old woman with fragile bones. 'Twould kill a *saint* the same age to pile stones on her chest! If you would be so callous, sir, then let *me* bear the punishment in her stead!"

"I'll not have it." Although Ulric's words were softly spoken, they seemed to thunder in the great hall, silencing the murmurs of the onlookers.

"There is another alternative, Your Grace." All eyes turned to the heretofore silent Father Dennis. The humble priest cleared his throat nervously. " 'Tis also acceptable to settle the matter by the sword, if there be a man who would champion Lady Agnéis's innocence."

"Well spoken, Father," the bishop complimented. "We would have Lord Ulric as our champion."

As devout as Ulric was, at that moment, he could have struck down both the robed figures, for the woman at his side backed away from him as if he alone had passed the sentence on her aunt. "Branwen . . ." he started.

"This is as evil a conspiracy as was ever conjured in hell!" Branwen accused. Her searing gaze sought each of the men in turn before coming back to her husband. "There is *no* man who will fight you, milord! Even your

430

chamberlain has abandoned my aunt, for whom he professed affection!"

Gogsblood, the chamberlain! Ulric swore silently. "Blanchard has gone on an errand assigned by me."

The lie set no better with him than the puzzle of his chamberlain's disappearance. It wasn't like the man at all. He only prayed Blanchard had not met the same fate as Hammond, whose body had been found by those searching for the outside entrance to the cave, where it had washed up among the rocks below the cliff. But for his noble garb, he might not have been identified so easily.

Yet, Blanchard had left after bringing Lady Agnéis back to the keep. The danger was over then, at least from the halegrins. Love for a woman made men do strange things, he supposed, and the chamberlain had been decidedly upset upon hearing Lord Giles's charges. The missing Blanchard, however, Ulric could deal with later. It was the present quandary that rattled his waning patience, not to mention his peace of mind, at the moment.

"Your Grace, with all due respect, it is unfair to Lord Ulric to place him in the position of deciding his wife's aunt's fate," Giles of Merionwythe spoke up. " 'Tis I that have brought the charges against the woman and 'tis I who would champion them for the Church."

Bless his friend! Ulric's glance at the bishop was hopeful. On occasion the righteous Giles possessed a keen insight, although no one could miss Ulric's ticklish predicament. Branwen stood like an avenging angel, bristling with contempt for him and the entire proceedings. No matter what the outcome, he and peace at Caradoc was damned.

"Father Dennis, I would have your opinion of Lady Agnéis before this goes further. You know the woman better than us all." Ulric not only respected Caradoc's priest but liked him as well. His opinion fared important in the idea that came to the lord out of desperation.

The priest cleared his throat again and took a sip from his goblet, as if to purchase time to formulate his answer. "I have known Lady Agnéis for twenty years. I believe her to be a very wise woman in her knowledge of herbs and their benefits. As Lady Branwen said, 'tis a heaven-sent gift used only for the good of her people. I would wager, were I a gambling man, that she has forgotten more than the lot of us combined will ever know of—"

"The question is not of the lady's knowledge of healing, but her practice of sorcery against Lord Ulric and Caradoc!" the bishop reminded his compatriot.

"The evidence weighs heavily against the lady, Your Grace, but Lady Branwen has presented a plausible alternate explanation for each circumstance."

"Then let the sword and the Almighty decide!" Lord Giles exclaimed impatiently.

Ulric gave the priest a tentative smile of gratitude before motioning for the guards. "Bring Lady Agnéis to the bailey before the court and public to witness her judgment by sword."

With the departing guards went the observers, who had gathered near the entrance of the hall, all eager to find a good place to witness the upcoming challenge. Much as they respected and cared for the Lady Agnéis, the revelations of the trial were unsettling. A holy combat would surely settle the matter. When the dais was vacated by the officials present, Master Harold instructed a dozen servants to lift the platform, which was built in sections, and carry it out to the bailey, so that the council might regroup upon it there.

"Lord Giles, Your Grace!"

Moved by a growing conviction further fed by Father Dennis's testimony, Ulric started toward his guests,

432

when he felt someone tugging at his scabbard. Turning in surprise, he caught Branwen's hand as she attempted to remove his sword and held it fast.

"What the devil are you about, woman?"

"I would champion my aunt, sir, for none have stepped forward in her stead!"

The despair that glazed her eyes refused to spill, but Branwen could not control the ragged break in her voice. It sounded as if her very heart were being torn in two. While she stubbornly clenched her lower lip between her teeth, her chin quivered threateningly, despite its noble tilt.

"You have afforded too little time for such, milady," Ulric replied, bending down to brush her captured fist with his lips. "As I was about to offer my sword on behalf of Agnéis of Caradoc."

"You can't be serious!" Giles declared incredulously to his friend. "Gogsblood, Caradoc, I meant to spare you a life of wifely torment, not fight you!"

Ulric could well understand his comrade's astonishment. It was a fiendish repayment for his consideration to take the battle out of the overlord's hand, only to have the same offer to take the other side. But if Ulric had his way, it would not be a death duel. If he lost, life would surely be more hellish than death and Providence would have overridden this conviction of Agnéis's innocence that would not be ignored. God forbid he subscribe to the old fool's words, but he had to act on his instincts.

He straightened, his hazel gaze locked with the limpid blue of his wife's, even as he answered his friend. "I believe in the woman's innocence, milord. The law states the ordeal of battle be fought between the judge and the accused. As you have relieved me of the Church's appointment so gallantly, I shall relieve my wife's aunt of the necessity of fighting the battle for herself."

"But—"

"You would not wish to fight an old arthritic-bound female, Lord Giles!"

Ulric's tone negated any answer but Giles's forced, "Nay, milord."

Aunt Agnéis was right! Branwen thought, near collapse with joyful relief. She had vowed Ulric would not let her down, but Branwen had had her doubts. The girl knew of her husband's contempt for her aunt's ways. She closed her hand over the two strong ones holding her other captive and stepped closer, so that she had to look up at Ulric's noble countenance.

"Milord . . ." Her voice cracked with the emotion overflowing in her heart. "Milord, I thank you with all my being!" Overcome, she kissed the battle-roughened hands endowed with the gentlest of touches she had ever known . . . almost as gentle and stirring as his reply.

"You asked me to fight for you once, milady, and I could not. I would not fail you again in your hour of distress."

"I love you, milord!"

Branwen went into Ulric's welcoming embrace and clung tightly to him, as if to convey the most profound depths of her feelings toward him. Aunt Agnéis was right, she mused again, basking in the strength and magic of her husband's presence. Oblivious to the onlookers, she found his lips and reaffirmed her vow with an unladylike fervor that was well met, until she reached around his neck and pulled herself closer. With a grunt of pain, Ulric stiffened and jerked away instinctively.

"Faith, fair raven, if you'd have me at my best, spare me your lusty enthusiasm till the duel is done!"

"Your shoulder!" Branwen gasped, chagrined at her carelessness, indeed her forgetfulness. She was getting as bad as Aunt Agnéis! she thought, as the gravity of what she cheered so heartily sunk in. Ulric was a skilled warrior, but so was Lord Giles; and Giles was not wounded and just out of bed. What if . . .

" 'Tis not my sword arm, milady," Ulric assured her, reading her troubled thoughts. "After such an inspiring kiss, I am a new man."

A new man? Branwen took the good arm he offered to escort her out to the bailey. Gogsblood, he looked now as if he'd been dragged off the battlefield. But then, she thought, glancing ahead at Lord Giles, so did his opponent. They were both sooty and streaked with dirt and blood, but the side of Ulric's head, where Elwaid had struck him with the stone, was swollen and grotesquely bruised.

Aunt Agnéis was hobbling out of the keep as they reached the lower level, supported on either side by two guardsmen. Her face was drawn and tired, and her peppered white hair, stripped of its customary wimple, was as disheveled as her stained blue-grey dress. Upon seeing Branwen and Ulric, however, she brightened.

"Wipe that pouty look off your face, geneth! I hear we've the finest knight in both kingdoms to fight our battles. *He* knows I'm no witch," she said, raising an affectionate gaze to Ulric.

In spite of her attempt to maintain a cheerful presence, however, the steps down to the grounds, where castle and village folk alike had gathered, made her wince with the painful stiffness brought on by the dampness of her cell. At the bottom, she would have fallen, but for the guards holding her upright.

"Aunt Agnéis!" Branwen rushed to her side and took her under her arm. "Miriam, help me get her to my chair!"

Although it was highly unorthodox for the prisoner to be seated on the dais with her judges, no one dared raise an objection, either out of respect for the lady or fear of the imposing overlord, who challenged the onlookers with his warning countenance. When the old woman was settled between Branwen and her handservant, Ulric moved before the dais, where he was joined by Lord Giles, now stripped of his cloak, ready for combat.

When the bishop rose to initiate the decreed ordeal of battle, the onlookers quieted. A monotone prayer sought Divine intervention on the side of truth, followed by a blessing of each of the contestants. Plainly disconcerted by the turn of events, Giles of Merionwythe backed away from the dais and moved to the center of the ring formed by the crowd, with Ulric a few steps behind.

Although his face was haggard and bruised, the eyes peering out beneath Ulric's thick golden brow were sharp as the gleaming metal of his sword in the bright afternoon sun. The two men circled each other, each awaiting the other's move, each assessing the slightest twitch of facial muscle that might precede it. It was Giles who finally broke the cautious dance, charging at Ulric with a bellow that sent shards of apprehension skittering along Branwen's spine.

Ulric met and parried both the forward blow and the upswing with a loud clash of steel. There was no doubt whom the sympathies of the crowd were with now. He was favoring his arm, Branwen fretted, noting he did not move the wounded one bearing his dagger any more than was necessary. The overlord skipped backward nimbly on the defensive, until Giles slammed his blade into the ground beside him. Suddenly, the tide turned, driving the golden-maned warrior slashing into his opponent like a vengeful fury.

The onlookers roared as Giles retreated in a series of backward steps. It was all he could do to meet each of the flashing assaults with sword and dagger. However, by the time Ulric launched a fifth blow, its power had diminished, enabling the marcher lord not only to parry it, but to swing about with a return blow that sent Caradoc staggering forward. Branwen's gasp was echoed all around her as Ulric nearly lost his grasp on his weapon. But for the quick maneuvering of his blade to his back, he would have been cleaved in two.

"Heavenly Father!" she whispered aloud, seeking Aunt Agnéis's reassuring hand with her own without daring to draw her eyes away from the contest of life and death.

Her unfinished prayer strangled in her throat when Ulric continued on as if about to go to his knees. Giles rushed the dazed knight from behind, but just as it seemed he was about to bring his blade down on Ulric's neck, the golden warrior came up with such force that the blades rang and scraped, locking at the hilt.

The swords were well matched, but it was the locked daggers that held Branwen transfixed. Although he uttered no complaint, she could feel the agony shooting through her husband's wounded shoulder as he struggled to keep his opponent's dagger from burying into the bulging sinew of his leather-clad thigh. Time froze along with her breath in the strained silence, which was broken only by the sound of beating hooves . . . or was it her heart, Branwen wondered?

"Cease and desist this fight at once!"

The pounding slowed as the horseman drew up, permitting the crowd time to let him through to where the two men were locked like stone statues in grueling combat. Branwen did not see him until he charged straight at the two combatants, forcing them apart and sending them sprawling to the ground. It was then, and only then, that she recognized her husband's chamberlain. In his arms was a baby—a kicking, screaming baby of twelve months or more!

"Master Blanchard, what is the meaning of this?" the bishop stammered, clearly taken aback.

"My baby!"

Turning from the spectacle on the field, Branwen stared at the horrified face of the servant who had leapt to her feet. *"Your* baby?" she echoed in disbelief at Miriam. *"You?"*

Before Branwen could recover from her shock, Miriam shifted her wild, panicked gaze to her and seized the chain about her neck that bore the iron amulet. Instinctively, she tried to pull the metal noose away, but the servant yanked it viciously. The bright sky over Branwen's head fluttered like the flame of a candle in the wind, threatening darkness as her servant pulled her in front of her and slipped her dining dagger from her waist to press it against her ribs.

"Damn you, Master Blanchard!" she shouted, her voice taking on an all-too-familiar chantlike resonance. "Call back your men, milord, or I'll skewer your bride and heir with this knife."

Branwen cried out as the point of the knife penetrated the thick folds of her dress to prick her skin. "Gogsblood, Ulric, listen to her!"

" 'Tis bad luck to cross the raven, mistress," Aunt Agnéis tutted with a smugness that made Branwen's heart sink. God bless her, the girl thought frantically, this was no time to torment the obviously tormented!

"Draw one drop of milady's blood, wench, and I'll slit your babe's throat from ear to ear," Blanchard threatened.

"Will you have a prophesy die, mistress?"

"Shut up, you old hag!" Miriam growled through her teeth at Aunt Agnéis.

"The child must be born by a daughter of northwest Cymru, not of some ambitious South Wales witch," Agnéis went on, undaunted. "Anyone knows the true prophesy."

"Aunt Agnéis!" Branwen pleaded. Her crazed captor

was actually breathing spittle through her teeth and needed no further antagonism. She was like a cornered animal . . . worse, a wounded one!

"But the child *was*, milady hag! We dragged the babe through this one's clothing as though it were being pulled from her womb. 'Twas adoption, right and proper as a natural birth."

So that *had* been real, too, Branwen realized weakly. Miriam's baby was the child they had taken from her. She ventured a look at the squalling baby in Blanchard's arms, whom she'd adopted against her will. And it wasn't her aunt who had drugged her tea, it was Miriam all along.

"You drugged milord and his men's hippocras!" she managed through the taut cinch of the narrow metal noose about her neck.

"Aye!" Miriam laughed, the knife relaxing momentarily against Branwen's ribs. "And a pitiful lot they were against the followers of the goddess."

"And you tried to poison me!"

"Aye, milady. 'Twas not until I was at Caradoc that I knew you carried the babe of a seventh son. We tried well enough to turn you against the father."

"Let the lady go, witch, and we'll spare your child!" Blanchard warned her sternly.

"A child for a child, a child for a wife *and* a child," Miriam mocked in a singsong voice. "Come, milady, let's fly to the top of the parapet and think this through."

"Kill the babe!"

The young woman sobered instantly, brought into tow by Ulric's harsh command. "No! I'll trade! Your wife for my son!"

Branwen bit her lip as the knife pressed against her again. The cold air chilled the damp spot where its tip had drawn blood. Dare she attempt to ease her fingers

439

from under the chain to try to dislodge the weapon from her ribs?

The choice of choking to death or being run through with a dagger was not made easier by the lack of oxygen to her brain, which made clear thought all but impossible. Her vision was so blurred, she could barely make out Ulric's figure as he took the baby from Blanchard, keeping the knife at the crying child's throat. Gogsblood, she thought dizzily, he wouldn't kill a baby!

The back of Branwen's heels struck the first riser of the new steps leading up to the battlements overlooking the sea. "Step up, milady." At the painful prod of the knife, Branwen clumsily obeyed.

"What are you doing?" Ulric demanded. He was close by, but for the life of her, Branwen was at a loss to see him. All she could see was the overbright sky. It was as blindingly bright as the darkness that clouded the edges of her consciousness.

"We'll make the exchange up here, milord . . . where there's no one likely to interfere."

Branwen's right slipper caught on the ledge of one of the steps, falling away as she tried to keep up with the woman tugging her by the neck like a hound on a leash, prodding her with the sharp dining dagger. So tight was Miriam's hold that Branwen was certain were she to suddenly let go, nothing but the empty air she stared at overhead would be there to catch her. Her life and that of her child were in the hands of a mad woman, pushed to the point of recklessness.

The scrape of the rough wall of the battlement finally assured her that they had reached the top. As Miriam backed onto the platform, she dragged Branwen with her. "That's it . . . *easy*, milord. Now put the babe in front of you and back away."

"Toss the knife over the wall into the sea and I'll do the same with mine," Ulric countered.

"Aowww!" Miriam cackled hysterically, her voice sharp enough to pierce the ears of a deaf man. "It seems we are at a stalemate, milord. But *this* will end it, right enough!"

The servant jerked the chain viciously, her effort slackening the sting of the blade in Branwen's ribs. Driven to equal desperation, Branwen pulled in the opposite direction to keep from choking. Hardly designed to withstand such pressure, the chain snapped, flying back in Miriam's face. The woman squealed, startled, and kicked her captive viciously in the back. Branwen rolled forward, and suddenly there was no longer stone beneath her, nor steps, only thin, substanceless air.

"Ulric!" she screamed, digging into the last remnant of steps slipping out from under her. Her fingers caught on the chiseled ledge as her body slammed against the flat side of the inner curtain wall.

"Over with the knife, milord, and then toss the baby, or I'll kick her fingers off!" Miriam screeched above her, the soft sole of her gillies resting lightly on Branwen's bloodless knuckles.

"All right, the knife is gone! Now step away and I'll toss you the child."

A wave of nausea swept over Branwen, making the moment stretch into an eternity before the gritty soles of the leather slippers lifted. A bawling shadow passed overhead, creasing the sunlight briefly, and then there was a scurrying of feet and urgent breathing. Then the orange glaze of the western sky was blocked from her eyes, and as she regained her focus, it was replaced by Ulric's face. Her fingers nearly gave way with relief, but already a strong hand grasped her by the arm.

"Hold on, love. I've got you!"

Gasping in deep breaths of air, Branwen swung helplessly, her feet unable to find a foothold on the rough wall to assist him. She blinked once, and when she opened her eyes again, Lord Giles was reaching for her other arm.

"I've got my baby and *you've* got yours, milord!" she heard Miriam taunt, her voice growing distant. Gogsblood, she couldn't faint now, not after all this.

Branwen circled Ulric's arm with her fingers. As if floating, she flew to the ledge of the battlement and landed unsteadily on her knees, strongly tempted to give in to the dizzy, beckoning escape of it all. It was by sheer determination that Branwen cleared her head of all such invitation to one more real and sustaining . . . into Ulric's arms.

"Get the bitch and her bastard!" he ordered, his bellow the sweetest sound Branwen had ever heard.

"Milord!" she whispered in relief as he helped her to her feet.

" 'Tis over, milove," Ulric answered, holding her to him as his men rushed up the battlement after the maidservant. "You're safe."

Branwen looked up at the next level of the battlements to which the woman had fled, in time to see her leap with the babe in her arms to the top of the wall. Her pale yellow hair blowing wildly about her, she chided the approaching guards in a mocking voice.

"If you would catch me, good men, you must first *follow* me!"

Branwen gasped as the girl crouched over the edge and pointed into the sea that splashed against the rock of Caradoc's northwest wall, telling of the rising tide that already covered the traeth.

"Gogsblood, woman, are you daft?" Ulric shouted, echoing his wife's stricken thought.

"We won't die, milord, but *you* will if you give us chase! Let's fly my little king!"

Branwen buried her face against Ulric's chest as the woman threw herself over the battlement, taking the cherubic babe with her. Her fading scream and the child's cries blended with the pounding crash of the incoming tide until it was only the sea that dared break the ensuing, startled stillness with its lashing hush.

"She's gone, milord!" the captain of the guards called down to them upon rushing to the ledge and peering into the churning waters below. "Swallowed up, like as not. 'Tis over for certain now."

Over? The word echoed again and again in Branwen's mind as she leaned on her husband's arm and made her way down the steps toward the gathering of onlookers. She pressed her free hand against her abdomen, tears stinging her eyes at the thought of the child, so innocently sacrificed in madness by its own mother. Who would have thought Miriam—sweet, thoughtful Miriam—capable of such debauchery and bloodshed?

"How did you know?" she asked Blanchard, upon reaching the bottom of the steps where he stood, a protective arm about Lady Agnéis.

"Your aunt sent me for the child," the chamberlain answered, looking down at Agnéis in something akin to wonder. "Her wisdom is only exceeded by her goodness of heart."

"And how did *you* know of the child, milady *aunt?*" Ulric queried cautiously, lest he provoke further accusations against the woman.

" 'Twas my God-given wit, milord *nephew,*" Agnéis quipped saucily. "Lord Gundulf said Dafydd had taken up with a south Wales witch. There was an old woman from Usk with a new babe when we last distributed alms to the local villages." She shrugged her rounded shoulders. "And there was but one wench in the castle from south Wales . . . the one you brought with you from England."

Branwen's eyes widened with incredulity. *"Aunt Agnéis, why didn't you say something?"*

443

Branwen suffered the same look from her aunt as she had as a child upon asking foolish questions. "I did! I told Blanchard!"

"To *us!*" Branwen reiterated impatiently.

"First, no one but you, geneth, would listen to me, and no one was listening to you at all." Agnéis's eyes took on a girlish twinkle as she looked from Giles to Ulric. "And I've never had men fight over me before, much less a third come so gallantly to my rescue. 'Twas more than an old maid might dream!"

Branwen glanced at Ulric, her face coloring in embarrassment. If there was anything predictable about Aunt Agnéis, it was that she was unpredictable.

"*That* was the other reason, milady?" the overlord queried, more incredulous than irritated.

"No." Her aunt turned to Lord Giles. "I wanted this English estron to get his comeuppance. 'Tis bad luck to cross the raven, Giles of Merionwythe, and a seventh son as well!"

Lord Giles's face was a myriad of emotions as he moved forward at his wife's coaxing push and took Agnéis's gnarled hand to his lips. Nonetheless, gallantry surfaced above his injured pride. "Since I have denied you your satisfaction, Lady Agnéis, perhaps you would accept my humblest apologies for my misled accusations against your character ... and yours as well, milord," he said to Ulric. "Faith, my heart was not in that combat."

Ulric clapped Giles on the shoulder in earnest. "I know it well, good friend. Think of it no more."

"These estrons have much to learn, geneth, but I do believe they've the God-given wit to do so."

"See, Giles, there's hope for us yet!"

Branwen had been brought up not to snicker, especially at the possibility of insult to a guest, but when Ulric laughed out loud, the entire company joined in.

Whether it was her aunt's wit or the need to release the tension that had choked Caradoc for the past months, the girl didn't know. What she did know was that it was good to laugh again.

"Now, I have duties to see to," Aunt Agnéis declared, above the conversation that spread like a wave over the crowd and restored normalcy to the bailey. "I've a salve for that shoulder of yours, milord, that will help ease the stiffness of young muscles, and that nick in your side needs washing out, geneth. Blanchard, will you be a dear and see to the hall while Master Harold proceeds with the supper plans? Everyone else, inside. 'Tis cold enough to break off my aching toes, and two abed is enough worry for one old woman."

Although her step was slow, the exonerated Aunt Agnéis carried herself like a queen leading her retinue up the steps and into the keep. Ulric dropped respectfully behind her, with Branwen under his arm. "You know, the more I see of her, the more I like her," he admitted in a rumbling whisper meant for his wife's ear only. "Do you think she'll put us to bed and entertain in our stead?"

If she lived as long as the ancients, Branwen supposed that leonine purr would always have the effect of a hundred stirring caresses upon her. "I am certain she is capable, milord, but I hardly think it proper for us to abandon our guests. We've shown them hellish hospitality thus far and—"

Branwen broke off as Ulric staggered forward, and she reached for his arm to steady him. *Milord!* Guards!

Ulric's men were at his side instantly, bearing him to his feet. "Take him to the master bedchamber this instant," she ordered, alarm once again flooding her veins.

Gogsblood, she could not take much more, or the guards would have to carry her as well. Ulric was wounded and exhausted beyond any man's endurance.

445

And him suggesting that she and he . . . She would insist he stay abed, but not for the reasons he intimated, Branwen decided, her own fatigue forgotten with her renewed concern for her husband.

Branwen followed the men upstairs and watched as they laid her dazed husband on the bed. Aunt Agnéis came in as they finished taking of his boots, leggings, and belt, and she placed a jar of salve on the table, along with a vial of ointment.

"This is for his shoulder," she told Branwen, pointing to the jar. "And here are some extra dressings. The ointment is for that cut on your side."

"Aren't you going to help me?"

"Why, yes, dear! I'm going to see to supper and the guests."

"But—"

"There's nothing wrong with your lord some tender care and rest will not cure," her aunt assured her as she hobbled over to the door. "You see to your husband, Branwen ap Caradoc, and take care of the hand that tamed you."

Tamed her? Her aunt closed the door before Branwen could follow up on the odd comment. Was she tamed? she mused, turning to where Ulric rested, his eyes closed. The recollection of the day of their arrival, when Ulric had threatened to do just that, came to her as she approached the bed. Nay, he had not tamed her, he had just loved her . . . and she had come to love him in return.

She eased down on the edge of the mattress and brushed a renegade lock of hair from his face. "I do love you, milord, with all my heart."

As she leaned over to kiss him, Ulric opened his eyes . . . those hazel-warm eyes that kindled with the charge that surged between them. Suddenly, his arms were about her, pulling her to him. Their lips met, his hungry ones devouring her tender caresses. She closed her eyes in giddy compliance as he rolled over, taking her with him, until, when she opened them again, it was he who stared down at her, a lopsided grin betraying his ploy, even as the hard passion making itself known through their clothing belied his feigned weakness.

"Milord, such deceit is unseemly in a man of your station," Branwen chided, finding it impossible to find real fault with that which she longed for herself. "We thought you faint!"

"I was, fair raven," Ulric answered, tracing the outline of her lips with the tip of his tongue, as if tasting the first course of a sumptuous feast that only whetted his appetite. "Faint from hunger . . . for this."

Much as she reveled in the sweet tide his searing assault on her lips evoked, Branwen found sufficient resolve to push him away when breath could no longer be denied. "And your shoulder, milord?"

" 'Tis not nearly as sore as that which the very thought of you in my bed inflames."

She was lost, a voice within warned her, and shamefully glad to be so. "So you think you've tamed me, do you, Ulric of Caradoc?" she rallied playfully, all the while shivering with the anticipation of more to come.

"To cater to my every whim, wench, by your own admission, no less."

"My *own* admission?" Branwen raised a skeptical brow.

A wolfish glow lighted in Ulric's eyes. "Aye, milady. Did you not say *'tis bad luck to cross the raven?*"

Branwen idly brushed the tawny bristle on his grinning face with the back of her hand, unaware of the dancing fires in her own gaze. He was the first fair-haired raven of Caradoc, but he was every bit as worthy of the title as she. He'd fought for her and Caradoc, and had won them as much with his love as with his battle skills.

The raven . . . her raven. Branwen heaved a sigh of surrender, for who was she to challenge the motto of her heritage?

"Then let the raven have his way, milord, for his lady readily awaits."